PART ONE VOLUME ONE

BEYOND KUIPER
THE GALACTIC STAR ALLIANCE

CREATED AND WRITTEN BY

MATTHEW MEDNEY & JOHN CONNELLY

CEO HEAVY METAL   AEROSPACE ENGINEER

EXPERIENCE
THE AUDIO ORIGINAL ON AUDIBLE
SCAN THIS QR CODE

Beyond Kuiper: The Galactic Star Alliance
Published by Heavy Metal Entertainment

Copyright © 2020 Matthew Medney & John Connelly

Editor: Stefan Petrucha
Editorial, Layout and Cover Design: Pete "Voodoo Bownz" Russo
Cover & Chapter Illustration: Utku Özden
Audio Original in Partnership with Podium Audio.
Audio Book Performed By: Kyle Perrin
Original Score For Audio Original By Kyle Perrin & Matthew Medney
Special Guest Performances By
Dylan Sprouse As Odian Spek
George C. Romero As Tordok

ISBN: 978-1-9477-8419-2

Manufactured in the United States

"Look again at that dot. That's here. That's home. That's us. On it everyone you love, everyone you know, everyone you ever heard of, every human being who ever was, lived out their lives. The aggregate of our joy and suffering, thousands of confident religions, ideologies, and economic doctrines, every hunter and forager, every hero and coward, every creator and destroyer of civilization, every king and peasant, every young couple in love, every mother and father, hopeful child, inventor and explorer, every teacher of morals, every corrupt politician, every "superstar," every "supreme leader," every saint and sinner in the history of our species lived there--on a mote of dust suspended in a sunbeam."

Carl Sagan, 1994, Pale Blue Dot: A Vision of the Human Future in Space

"These words sparked our curiosity and excitement about the unknown. John and I were writing the lore for Beyond Kuiper for three years, looking for the spark to dive into the pages. That day came, August 1st, 2017. John and I were on a call discussing the Cosmos, The Great Filter, and the Kardashev Scale when he recited the above Carl Sagan quote. Its emotion, it's excitement, and the reminder of how small we are, compelled us to explore the inner workings of our curiosity.

Thank you Carl for your ability to expand one's curiosity even in death."

Matthew & John

LOVED ONES

A journey is never complete without the reflection of one's path. Creating a world, a way of life, an environment for people to imagine in, takes no prisoners. One's ability to identify true love and devotion becomes apparent during these experiments. Whether it be family, loved ones or friends, drawing up economic doctrines, government ideologies and languages comes with its sacrifices. To my great love, Alexis Leon, thank you for your constant support, your never wavering resolve in your compassion and conviction of my creative prowess. Your love is etched into the life-blood of this novel, your beauty dashes across the ethos of these characters and your brilliance is mapped in the perfection of these pages. For pushing me harder and demanding the best at all times, I love you.

Matthew

Tony, this book is for you. For putting up with all of my craziness, mania, loud noises, louder conference calls, dishes piled in the office, and all the missing pens. For the times you read me Ray Bradbury. For all the times you let me write in a room for hours while you cleaned the entire house and cooked. For the literal days of editing FaceTimes when I wasn't around. For stealing your laptop when mine was dead. For accompanying me to Ad Astra. For working late, and extra, so I didn't have to. For your endless love and patience, encouragement, and support. Thank you, from all the depths of my heart. There is so much time that you sacrificed, for us, so I could pursue my passion. You are my loving partner in crime, my P'tit Grobis. I could not have accomplished this monumental endeavor of three years without you. You gave me the space and power to dream. While occasionally perplexed by my strange love for sci-fi, you understood how much creating this story meant, and you never doubted for an instant that I could see it through. Your love gives me the strength to do impossible things, and your fervor for art in all its mediums inspires my creativity. I love you to Kramer de la Ku.

John

THANK YOU

We would be remiss to forgo acknowledging the indispensable guidance along this journey. Like Q to Picard or Yoda to Luke, these mentors pushed our limits and dared us to be better than we were. From Pete "Voodoo Bownz" Russo with your imagination and gall, you never let an idea go unchallenged. We could never imagine a better partner to creative direct this world. To Utku Özden, what can we say? You took our words and brought them to life in ways neither of us could have imagined. You are family, and as long as we are all breathing, no one else will touch the pages of Kuiper's art. Stefan, you pushed our story into a new light. Your analytical and thoughtful editing took this work to a height we only dreamed of; however, the Yellow Challenge questions have scarred us for life, ha! Kyle Perrin, your ingenuity and imagination with regards to musical composition is astounding. Your vision for what an audiobook should be is the new benchmark. Pushing the boundaries and imagining a better experience like no one else could have.

Matthew & John

David Erwin, my partner at Heavy Metal. I revere everything you stand for, everything you do. Every conversation with you makes me a better person, a more creative inspiration to myself. Thank you for pushing me to be more critical and more analytical. You take the last 10% of anything and make it the difference between great and magical. Lastly, Morgan Rosenblum, 5 years ago we met and you ignited a creativity in me that was dormant. I will always love you for unlocking that potential.

To *A Mander on A Mission of Fun* for always showing me that creativity and emotion could tell a story far better than any education could teach. I love you.

Matthew

My dear friend and librarian, Rachel Robinson, thank you for inspiring me every day of the joy and importance of reading, for the necessity of editors, and for reminding me to always ask, "what story am I telling?"

John

FOREWARD

Curiosity is the spark to all exploration. Are we alone in the universe?

Difficult to say.

We acknowledge the vastness of time, the cyclical nature of civilization, and the obscurity of our own history. When we began debating, "Why hasn't sentient life been found in our galaxy?" all those years back, we were among the era of exoplanets. Every week, it seemed NASA would announce a new outpouring of worlds all vastly beyond reach, but each recalculating the likelihood of potential Earths. But to us, the numbers seemed staggering; compelling. Surely there are others.

So if our galaxy is full of sentient life, we thought of a simple, logical reason why no one has said hello: no one wants to.

Stepping back and casting an objective eye on ourselves, it seems painfully obvious that humans lack a fundamental respect for their planet and each other. They possess extremely short memories and long grudges, and the idea of giving them the motivation or tools to hasten their expansion seems downright foolhardy.

That being said, who are these judges?

From that simple notion birthed a million questions. How is faster than light possible? Could you have cohesive interstellar civilizations without it? How could you even govern a coalition of not different countries, but of species? Each question only created another, and each answer built our world piece by piece until it spanned thousands of answers and millions of light-years. As for the title, from where would our judges watch us?

TAOTA

I Beings should strive to live their existence with compassion and empathy towards all living creatures whether they be born or made, in accordance with galactic rationale.

II Fundamental justice supersedes laws and institutions throughout the galaxy and beyond.

III Any sentient being is the sole decision maker regarding their own body and well being.

IV Freedoms are non linear. All acts and actions whether they are endearing or offensive so long that they are not physically harmful, shall be a freedom. To willfully and unjustly infringe on another's galactic rights is to forfeit their own.

V Any contact or interference with a non-informed galactic entity within GSA space shall be met with the utmost severity.

VI Science above all else shall be used to govern one's logic. Proven science is not open to interpretation.

VII All beings are fallible, mistakes are made; one should seek the least harmful, logical resolution for any harm that may have been caused.

VIII System and planetary law shall supersede GSA jurisdiction for any localized, non-galactic, institution, event, or crime.

IX Technology shall be used for the advancement of space travel, exploration, and elevation of the living condition, throughout the GSA and beyond. Creation of technology for the use of limiting freedoms shall be met with extreme prejudice.

X The understanding of the known universe is a right to any and all beings born or made within or beyond the GSA.

XI All beings, born, made, or other, within the GSA or beyond will have an equality of rights spanning all legislative, social, and galactic institutions.

XII All beings born, made, or other are mandated by galactic law to travel off-world for a minimum of 7.7% of their standard existence, or 15 turns whichever is the lesser of the two.

XIII The governing entities of the GSA will consist of the Council of Worlds and the Assembly of Planets, which will govern across the nine sectors of GSA Space with logical, scientific, and diligent purpose.

THE ACCORDS OF THE ALLIANCE

TIME

HUMAN: SECOND | GSA: NOLAPRIKE

1 Duprike = .605 Seconds
1 Second = 1.653 Duprikes
1 Nolaprike = 100 Duprikes
1 Nolaprike = 1.008 Minutes
1 Minute = .992 Nolaprikes
1 Trike = 10 Nolaprikes
1 Trike = 10.08 Minutes
1 Drike = 10 Trikes
1 Drike = 1.68 Hours
1 Prike = 10 Drikes
1 Prike = 16.8 Hours
1 Fike = 10 Prikes
1 Fike = 1 Week

HUMAN: YEAR , GSA: TURN

1 Turn = 1.3304 Years
1 Turn = 692 Prikes
1 Year = .75 Turns

- The Turn is equivalent to the orbital
period of Mijorn.

DISTANCE

HUMAN: METER | GSA: TRADON

1 Tradon = 3 Meters
1 Meter = .333 Tradons
1 Rudon = 1000 Tradons
1 Rudon = 3 Kilometers
1 Kilometer = .333 Rudons
1 Nolaendon = 1000 Rudons
1 Nolaendon = 3000 Kilometers
1 Endon = 1000 Nolaendons
1 Endon = 3000000 Kilometers
1 Sadon = 1000 Endons
1 Sadon = 3.0 X 10^9 Kilometers

DISTANCE FROM THE SUN TO URANUS

1 Kulon = 1000 Sadons
1 Kulon = 3.0 X 10^12 Kilometer or .317 Light Years
1 Light Year = 9.461 X 10^12 Kilometers
1 Light-turn = 12.615 X 10^12 Kilometers
1 Light Year = .75 Light-turns
1 Light-turn = 4.204 Kulons
1 Kulon = .238 Light-turns

- The Endon came from the mean radii of the orbital
distance of Azoeieo, with an eccentricity of only .000007

LIGHT INTENSITY

HUMAN: CANDELA | GSA: BALON

1 Balon = 11.6 Candela
1 Candela = .086 Balon

TEMPERATURE

HUMAN: KELVIN | GSA: ZORN

Conversion: 1 Zorn = .9105 Kelvin
Conversion: 1 Kelvin = 1.098 Zorn
Conversion: 273.15 Kelvin = 300 Zorn (FREEZING POINT OF WATER)

FASTER THAN LIGHT SPEED

PATCH 0 = 300 LIGHT-TURNS/TURN
- Out of repair or antiquated ships, smugglers, pirates,
or those avoiding the law. Ships travelling at this speed
have an undetectable flowspace tracking signal unless
within 1 endon of scanners.

- Older ships, the economically lower classes, and
those travelling between relatively close star systems.

PATCH 2 = 25000 LIGHT-TURNS/TURN
- Standard GSA private and commercial ships.

PATCH 3 = 100000 LIGHT-TURNS/TURN
- Maximum a private citizen or business is allowed to
have for interstellar travel. This is the standard GSA
government ship speed.

PATCH 4 = 175000 LIGHT-TURNS/TURN
- Standard for GSA Military, Policing, Investigation, and
Disaster Relief ships.

PATCH 5 = 300000 LIGHT-TURNS/TURN
- GSA Special Military Operations, Voidwhisperers,
COS, interstellar crime syndicates, and GSA top tier
government officials.

MASS

HUMAN: KILOGRAM | GSA: KLANT

1 Kilogram = .5882 Klants
1 Klant = 1.7 Kilograms

- The klant originated from the mass of 1 Rakillaegg,
which are always the same size, never varying by more
than 1000 silicon atoms in mass.

ELECTRIC CURRENT

HUMAN: AMPERE | GSA: CHAR

The Char is defined as a Naxar per Duprike, where the
charge of an electron = 1 Xar

1 Naxar = 1.0 x 10^19 Xar
1 Char = 2.65 Ampere
1 Ampere = .377 Xar

AMOUNT OF PARTICLES IN SUBSTANCE

HUMAN: MOLE | GSA: ENTZ

Entz = 7.22 X 10^23 particles
1 Entz = 1.2 Moles
1 Mole = .8 Entz

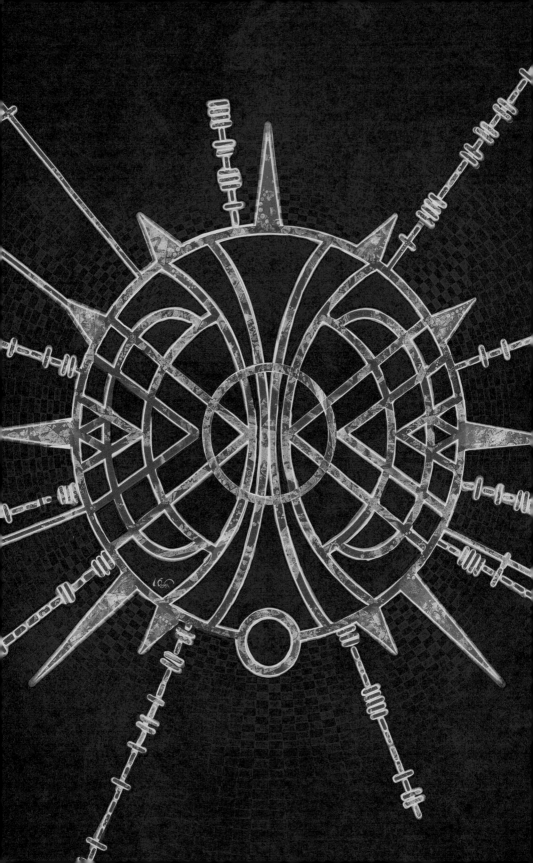

BOOK ONE
THE GALACTIC STAR ALLIANCE

CHAPTER 1

DEAR EDWIN

"As I sit here, realizing the dreams of humanity are within reach, I'm humbly taken aback by just how small we are. Excitement courses through me, for we are like the explorers of old sailing for an unknown horizon, fueled only by the hope of a new world."

June 10, 2091

Bernard Hubert put down his journal and gazed at the Moon. Mining ships with precious cargo zoomed away from the pale lunar aura, sailing across the firmament, back to Earth.

"To think we would settle for this." Bernard sighed while looking over the vast space engulfing his existence. His rocket, soon to be launched, carrying the hopes of humanity and a frontier only just beginning to be explored.

After the war, the main facility had to be moved. Unfortunately, massive land regions had succumbed to depopulation from the rising heat, while the preferred stronghold of Florida had been lost to the rising sea.

Now a volcanic crater cradled his soon-to-be launched rocket. The construction mandates set forth by the World Council being utterly insane, he took immense pleasure in his team for accomplishing the impossible. The pad had been completed in just two months, the concrete still setting.

A neat pile of organized notes and papers sat on his desk. Bernard sifted through, searching for a particular letter, one his great grandfather, Edwin, had received from the legendary astronomer, Carl Sagan. Finding it, he gently lifted the crinkled and yellowed paper.

My Dear Edwin,

Consider again that dot. That's here. That's home. That's us. On it, everyone you love, everyone you know, everyone you ever heard of, every human being who ever was, lived out their lives. The aggregate of our joy and suffering, thousands of confident religions, ideologies, and economic doctrines, every hunter and forager, every hero and coward, every creator and destroyer of civilization, every king and peasant, every young couple in love, every mother and father, hopeful child, inventor and explorer, every teacher of morals, every corrupt politician, every "superstar," every "supreme leader," every saint and sinner in the history of our species lived there — on a mote of dust suspended in a sunbeam.

Never forget, no matter how great we become we will always be small. Yet despite being infinitesimal, we can always find our purpose. I am immensely impressed with your contributions to the fields of astrophysics and cosmology.

Yours truly,
Carl Sagan

Bernard repeated, "The history of our species lived there—on a mote of dust suspended in a sunbeam." Then, with a pen in hand and a smile on his face, he added two words:

Until now.

After a gentle knock, a service woman poked her head in. "It's time, sir."

Bernard gently placed the letter in an empty box, piled the remaining papers atop and then closed the lid. He cracked his knuckles, stood, stretched, and turned off the light.

He considered the strength of his legacy. Henry Hubert, his father, was the most revered MIT professor to ever walk those halls; his great grandfather, Edwin, author of the seminal *Fantastical Stories of Stardust & Rock* was a thought leader in cosmology and friend to Carl Sagan. That lineage led him here, to this mission, all the work done — and yet to come.

Well, that and the fateful events of six years ago...

He delved back in his mind to Switzerland. It was 2085. The final fragments of glacial ice reflected dawn's light, giving the vast mountain ridges an aura. Past that, an enormous range of peaks, each cascading larger than the one before, consumed every inch of viewable space. A winding road cut through the ridges, sharing its secrets with every passing vehicle.

Deep in the range, hidden from view, laid a place unlike any other, CERN. It was home to thousands of gifted scientists, all working to achieve a better, more sustainable life away from this solitary dot.

Bernard remembered it well. It began when he and his scientific comrade, Darren Parsons, were working for Outer Limits, the leading aerospace company. By the early 2050's OL had put a colony in space, mined the ocean floor, and resurrected fifty-seven extinct species. Meanwhile, CERN, attempting to restore an ionosphere irradiated by World War III, implored the World Council to mandate Bernard and Darren's participation.

To avoid the lengthy governmental procedure, Outer Limits CEO Angelika On offered to "loan" her top two employees. The fierce Scandinavian had another reason: OL wanted CERN's resources for a secret project operating from November 2085 to April 2086.

- - -

"Angelika, we've been here five months, FIVE MONTHS. What you're asking us to build, in secret, mind you, it's..." Already exasperated, Bernard fought to keep his composure. "It's just not enough time. Darren's not going to like that... not at all. Leaving sooner when he only has days as it is. You know he's working on PF designs."

At first the voice at the other end was cool and soothing. "While I certainly understand your concerns, I DON'T CARE, BERNARD! Circumstances have changed. Get him back here today. I'll see you Monday."

"Yes, ma'am..." His tone communicated his disgust for a decision he was not— *not*—going to argue with.

The call's abrupt finale left him unbalanced. Abandoning the delicious chocolate pastry, a long standing afternoon treat for the science guru, he departed the cafeteria.

Despite his soured mood, moving through the curved hallways, he couldn't help but admire the canvases lining the walls, each honoring his fellow scientists' journey to Mars, and marking it as their new home.

"We were there once, will be there again, and soon..."

The corridor leading to his office displayed a sleek array of future tech. There were gadgets of all kinds, working and non-working, functional prototypes as well as theoretical models, all of which any good scientist should own, but the public would consider incomprehensible.

A man with unruly silver hair and a colorful plaid button-down tucked neatly into his jeans sat in his chair. Unaware of Bernard's dour state, visible excitement coursed through him.

"Hubert, great. I want to show you my modified calculations for the singularity capture."

"Ah, D, yes, let's have a look. Did you stabilize the quark stream during stage 4?" There was a slight lording to his tone.

"Oh, yes. The new math solves it. I bet William couldn't even do this."

"Much as I find it endearing how academic rivalries never die, I doubt that. William is the better mathematician, you know."

"Right. Just like Iron Man was better than Captain America? Yes, Stark could hold the Gauntlet, but, be honest, that hardly makes him superior to the good ole stars and stripes."

Momentarily enjoying a snarky analogy worthy of their shared love of early 21st century comics, Bernard rolled his eyes. Unfortunately, there were more somber things to discuss.

"D, Angie called. She wants you back, as in today, now—like the Borg Queen calling her ships back to the nest." He finished with a halfhearted wink.

He expected Darren to be displeased, but the man looked ill. He was shaking, as if being slowly consumed by a mix of anger and regret.

"She can't do that, Bernard, not now..."

CERN was where black holes were contained, antimatter researched, the fringes of knowledge pushed everyday. Bernard understood his friend's frustration. No matter how cool or future tech the Outer Limits facility was, it was not, and never could be, CERN.

They talked, and talked more, until Darren was calm enough to agree to a change in plan.

Just before dusk, the low sun's beams cast dramatic shadows down causeways carved by ancient glaciers. Bernard zoomed along in his electric sports car, the crown jewel of ingenuity in 2086, a gleaming, turquoise *Newton 200*.

Having left the main collider facility, he was headed to the airstrip when a burst of light blanketed the world. Before he could react, a shockwave tossed the Newton 200 off the road, slamming it against a rock embankment. His head cracked against the doorframe. The light dissipated, leaving only darkness.

Bernard woke to sirens and a stench of melted stone. It was night. The sky barely illuminated by a smoke-obscured moon, he couldn't see clearly. Trying to remember the warning signs of a concussion, he fumbled for his glasses, but everything he touched was broken glass. Blood dripped down his arm and onto his fingertips.

Newton 200
The 7th iteration of the Newton Fully Automated Sportscar. Electric powered with 2500-3000 km range. By car designer Douglass J. Newton.

The crunch of boots on the radiating dirt felt imaginary. "Over here! Found him!" Following the grinding of metal against asphalt, three men, paramedics, having wrenched the car door free, came into view.

"If he's bleeding internally, we shouldn't move him. We're out of stabilizing packs and there's nowhere to bring him anyway. The hospital's gone. Nearest medical center is Geneva, and we can only assume there's hundreds, if not thousands of wounded."

The dizzying burst of a flashlight beam made him vomit. Somehow, Bernard managed to reach out and grasp a leg. "What... happened...?"

"Sir, not sure. Best guess so far is an antimatter containment failure... a big one." "...damage?" The paramedic choked. "Damage? Sir... CERN's gone. You're lucky... this is about as close to campus as you can get and still..."

His brain splitting, Bernard croaked, "Gone? Where's... Darren? Dr. Parsons? Other... survivors?"

Their dark looks gave him the answer before he heard it. "Sir, there weren't any. The campus was vaporized. All that's left is a hole."

Bernard felt as if his sanity had reached the event horizon of a black hole. His friends, the engineers, the physicists, the geniuses and savants, techies and support staff, all their work, gone. It was a nightmare. It had to be. If he could just fall asleep, maybe he'd wake from it...

"He's losing blood. Screw protocol, we have to get him to Geneva stat. This is Dr. Bernard Hubert. If anyone's worth a medivac, he is. Grab him."

The faces above him morphed and blurred. It *was* a dream; had to be, because he was watching, from somewhere safe and far, his own body lifted onto a stretcher and taken to a nearby helicopter.

After a senseless, unknown duration, a stern man with a cold, analytic look emerged from the blur. Bernard had just about realized it was a medical surgeon before a mask engulfed his sight, and it went dark again.

What was it? Hours? Days? Weeks? No way to measure time without a reference. It was peaceful, though, until warm light and self-awareness dawned together, swiftly followed by excruciating pain. Groaning, he again instinctively reached for his glasses and again couldn't find them. Someone did, though. Firm yet gentle hands stayed his own as he placed them on his face.

Lisa, his wife, came into focus. Before he could make out anything more, she enveloped him in a crushing hug. He could tell through how long and tightly she held on that something was wrong. He could feel her start crying, but any sound was dampened by her long hair and her head buried in his shoulder.

An eternity later, she let go, her figure focusing through the lens in front of Bernard's eyes. By the looks of her, she'd been crying a long, long while.

"Lisa, I had a nightmare. CERN..."

"Bernie, thank god! The doctors weren't sure you'd..."

Her sobs were no longer muffled, but they choked any words. Her tone made one thing clear: It wasn't a nightmare. CERN, everyone, including Darren, was gone. Awareness imploding his mind, his thoughts spiraled darkly.

"It should have been me."

Pulling herself roughly together, Lisa ushered in a skinny, redheaded woman. Bernard thought he should know her. When he realized he did, he thought, "Oh, no."

"Bernard! Thank god!" Lily Parsons flung herself on him, then sobbed along with Lisa. Some automated portion of himself briefly detached from his pain long enough for him to say, "Lily, I'm sorry.... I'm so sorry about your father."

"It's not your fault. You couldn't..."

His eyes filled with sorrow and despair. "No, you're wrong. I could have. He was supposed to go back to OL, but he was so close to a breakthrough on the black hole stabilization, so upset, I convinced him to stay. I said *I* would deal with Angie. He's dead because of me."

Her frown made the tears run down her cheeks. "Outer Limits?" Lily looked from Lisa, to Bernard, and back to Lisa—not knowing what to think. "What do you mean?"

"We were working on a top secret... I can't say, and it doesn't matter, Lily. It should have been me."

She blinked several times, processing the information. She recoiled, glaring at him, her sadness quickly turned to rage. Furiously wiping tears from her eyes, she seemed on the verge of speaking, yet never finding the words.

Lisa put a hand to her shoulder, but Lily shrugged it off. Face full of loathing, she ran out the door. Bernard wanted to do something, but, heart and mind thoroughly drained, all he could manage was to tumble back into a deep sleep.

He awoke again the next day. Lisa still by his side, he'd never appreciated her more. Lily was gone, just as well. He couldn't face her, not yet at least. A knock signaled the entrance of another visitor, a sleek woman with silky hair and crimson lipstick.

"Dr. Hubert, I'm Searcher Jones, from the World Council Scientific Investigation team. Naturally, we have some questions."

She moved swiftly, circling behind the nurses and gesturing for them to leave. As they did, she came ominously close to the bedside, ignoring Lisa's plasma-cutting glare. Searcher waited for the door to click shut before barraging him with questions.

"Sir, what happened in there? What were you working on? Why were you the only one departing CERN at precisely the time of the incident?"

Instantly Lisa was standing, one hand on Bernard's arm, as she partially shielded his body from Searcher Jones. Exhausted as Lisa was, she rallied, her defenses were up. This line of questioning was dangerous nonsense.

"Is my husband being accused of something?"

In a moment of disbelief Bernard looked up to Mrs. Jones, then clutched Lisa's hand, looked to her, and simply said, "I was going home."

As he lay unconscious, Searcher Jones and Lisa Hubert each tried, unsuccessfully, to have the other removed.

"BERNARD!"

A reverberating shout from the hallway proclaimed the arrival of his frantic mother, Minerva. Before the echo faded, she burst in, pushed past Searcher and Lisa and sat beside her son. Surprisingly, he remained asleep, hours passing before he roused and met her eyes. "Mim, they're all..." Bernard couldn't get himself to say anyone else's name. "Darren is gone."

Then he said something entirely unexpected.

"Aliens. Had to be. Sentient extraterrestrials. Nothing else makes sense. The containment had safety redundancies; magnetic field generators, an independent chemical battery system, all tested against any possible threat. Something had to make the antimatter stop behaving like antimatter. The only way to do that would be a quantum event so specific it had to be designed by an intelligence. Humans don't have that kind of quantum disrupting technology. If we did, I'd have designed it."

Mim and Lisa had no idea what to say. Searcher Jones did:

"Is this a joke?"

"No, let me rephrase. Do you expect me to *believe* the incident, which you just so happened to avoid, was caused by aliens? Even if that absurdity were true, why attack CERN? Why not hit weapons stockpiles and military bases?"

Not used to being doubted, Bernard crossed his arms. "If you were competent, you'd realize CERN was the most valuable place on the planet. No one else was working on antimatter fields, propulsion drives and black hole research, not even Outer Limits. Their work was of such importance, they had to buy, beg, borrow, or steal the Earth's best and brightest to make any of it happen."

Searcher Jones didn't seem to hear, or, for that matter, want to hear. "You take us for fools? Four-thousand experts dead and you have the gall to blame aliens? We *will* do a full investigation, and I'll be reporting your disrespect and utter lack of cooperation." Swiftly as she came, she left, her angry whispers of "aliens" following her down the hall. He knew where this was going, and it wasn't going to end well. Bernard wished he'd been more diplomatic, but he could barely think. Looking to his wife and mother for reassurance, he said, "Ignorance in the face of unwanted truth is truth within itself."

Unnerved, Lisa and Minerva gripped his hand, tears engulfing their faces. As he, once again, fell asleep, he realized they thought he'd lost his mind.

- - -

The service woman peered out the control room door to see what was taking so long. "Sir... are you coming?"

"Yes, Amy. Sorry to keep everyone waiting. I'll be there in a moment—promise."

Bernard gazed at the vast scenery around him. Distant as the last six years seemed, the heartache of Darren's death was as real as ever, driving him through the work.

He patted a small cube-like device in his pocket. As he moved towards the hundreds awaiting him in the cathedral-sized space only doors away, he murmured—

"This is for you, Darren."

CHAPTER 2

THE VOIDWHISPERERS

Outside the lounge windows, asteroids floated in a miraculous dance, backdropped by the starry void of space.

Kruktusken, a blue skinned Dragsan, narrowed his eyes. "I hate this job."

Marukjoy, a Drotean, from the **9th Sector's Kramer de la Ku** replied, "Oh, stop complaining. You can't beat the view. We could be overseeing that mining operation in the **Agrippa Trench**. Now, that would suck **barkle** tentacles."

Kruk trilled his vague agreement. "True, but two **turns** and this still feels more like glorified babysitting than protecting the Alliance from barbaric would-be space conquerors. I mean, I've been alive longer than Earth has had fusion."

Maruk, as he preferred to be called, leaned back to evaluate his position on the gobbletek holo-game. "Don't forget, they kill for fun. Even used nuclear weapons on themselves."

"Well, it's not like they've annihilated the species."

"Exactly. We're here, because they still are."

The bored Kruk balked. "Please. Even by GSA standards, Earth's progress is slow. My father's a Prime and even he says so. I mean, they've remained Class-T

9th Sector's, Kramer de la Ku
Sectors are regions of the 9 founding planets of the GSA. This jungle planet is the Capital of Sector 9 and homeworld of the Droteans since before the GSA.

Turn
GSA unit of time: One turn equals approximately 1.33 Earth years.

Agrippa Trench
A massive trench that spans halfway across the planet Agrippa, located in Sector 3. One of the most profitable mining sites of Zurillium in the galaxy.

Barkle
Native to the planet of Teczas, The "Water Menace" has been commonly discovered in packs. This species thrives in polluted waters and has extremely high resistance to toxins and radiation.

for three reviews now."

Those on primitive worlds believing in sky-judges were close to the truth. The *Galactic Star Alliance* searched for, protected, and evaluated them. A Class-T, or Diminishing Lifespan Planet, required three conditions: galactically detectable tech, planetary scale conflicts, and a failing ecosystem. It was a perfect storm, indicating the high likelihood of violent expansion to other planets.

Pushed to the brink, Class-T's inevitably become convinced that, to quote the guide, *the only path to survival is to populate and terraform as many planets as possible, regardless of indigenous species.*

Too dangerous to engage, they'd be reassessed every 55 turns. Improved resource balance, interplanetary travel potential, and a strong preference for diplomacy, could earn an upgrade to Class-S: Safe for Future Expansion. Further improvement, evaluated every 10 turns, might grant first contact.

"If your dad feels that way, why station you as a babysitter?" Maruk was always happy to poke Kruk's privileged streak.

The Dragsan's blue skin flushed purple. "Because... well... it was this or the outer rim of the Alpha Centauri... I mean *Quadlox*. Damn! We've been here so long I'm using their primitive mapping terms. Plus, a quarantine rotation will look good for my move to higher government on *Mijorn*."

"Not me. I'm going to be the greatest fighter pilot this side of Tatooi..."

"If you reference *Star Wars* one more time..." Kruk smacked the table. "It's like every other phrase with you. I swear, human entertainment will rot both your brains! Mine, too, if I keep hearing about it!"

Thankfully, Kruk had rotated out of linguistics, but Maruk was tasked with reviewing their media for peaceful or destructive trends, particularly anything involving space travel and species interaction. So far, they hadn't been selling themselves particularly well.

Maruk chuckled. "But their interpretation of galactic life is so hilarious. Besides,

---

The Galactic Star Alliance
An 11 million turn old galactic government which oversees 600,000 planets and millions of species. The Council of Worlds and Assembly of Planets enact the will of the governing document of the GSA: The Accords Of The Alliance (TAOTA).

Quadlox System
Known to humans as the Alpha Centauri System, this GSA outpost was established 6 million turns ago.

Mijorn
Planet inhabited since the Builders (90 million turns ago), Galactic hub and homeworld of the Metra since the Classical Galactic Era, founding location of the GSA, and Capital of Sector 1.

if they really are so slow, I'll need something other than playing gobbletek to pass the time."

Gesturing surrender with seven fingers, Kruk grunted. "I know. They've got me monitoring extrasolar probes that make ***woofha slugs*** seem fast. 34,000 turns to reach the nearest star, useless bricks within another 50."

In a ***Drotean*** expression of displeasure, yellow feathery tufts emerged from Maruk's neck. His eyes turned orange while the skin beneath them and around his ears went dark and hardened into scales. "Now you're complaining that your job is easy?"

Kruk deflected, "My point, before we went off on this magnificent tangent, is that the Nova system's status isn't changing anytime soon. I just don't understand why so many resources are being wasted on a whole lot of nothing."

Maruk's annoyance receded. "Hey, I don't make the rules. By the way..." He eye-motioned a blue orb to a different game slot where it formed an array of fourteen that surrounded Kruk's eleven pieces in a web. "...***COPEK***!"

"Rooka!!" Kruk buried his face. "What's that, my 17th loss? Never should have taught you how to play. Guess those two brains count for something."

"They do. You owe me a drink."

"Yeah, yeah. Want..."

KU-WAAAKA! KU-WAAAKA! KU-WAAAKA!

In training the alarm sounded like a ***Wavoon*** roar, a cry that could paralyze some species. Now, in their first real emergency, it sounded as if the creature's beak had engulfed the entire station.

The lounge light shifted from warm orange to strobing green. An urgent, but less piercing voice came through the speakers: "Proximity breach. Emergency quarantine protocol now in effect. All Guardians report to stations."

A momentary pause, and everyone leapt to their feet, claws, paws, and tentacles. Running, slithering, sliding, gliding, the crewmembers raced for their posts on

---

Woofha Slugs
Native to Kramer de la Ku, these non-sentient lifeforms defend against predators by secreting super adhesive slime as they move, instantly trapping a predator to the ground.

Drotean
A shapeshifter, the Drotean species has been crucial to the espionage construct of galactic dealings for 10's of millions of turns.

Wavoon
6 legged, neon turquoise, blue, and purple. A Wavoon, is a nocturnal and twilight hunter. Its hunting call temporarily paralyzes prey, so it may catch and eat it. The "Death Roar" is native to the planet Kin'jetanga and can be found in deserts and tropical grasslands.

the bridge, in the fighter bays, or the artillery room.

Speed being essential, Maruk gave himself an extra set of limbs. His uniform's field generators hummed to life, optimizing his unique physiology. "Bored, huh? Rooka you!"

Making do with the body he had, Kruk sprinted in the direction of the bridge *sliptube* a few corridors away. "What could it be? Ship veered off a transit lane? Pirates?"

The hangar sliptube close at hand, Maruk dove in. "No idea. See you soon."

Maruk fell a bit before the powerful, magnetic stream grabbed and propelled him. Accelerating rapidly, he twisted and curved through the monitoring station's infrastructure. Carved into an asteroid, dark, rocky caves of nothingness gave way to an array of glistening lights illuminating walkways, cranes, and equipment. Passing above Outpost Hangar B, Maruk could see *suppressor fighters* launching amid a flurry of activity.

He zipped past a node, two more Guardians falling in behind him. All three were shortly ejected into Hangar A.

Using the momentum to leap into his fighter cockpit, Maruk smirked. "Let's go ARTOO!"

With an elegance suited for a being destined to fly, he launched into the asteroid field.

"Kruk, you make it to the bridge yet?" Maruk barked into his comm.

"Almost there. Stay sharp. I'm here when you need me."

"Copy that, Blue Leader."

"SHUT UP!"

"Luke... out."

Kruk had just reached the last corridor. The blast doors slid open, revealing a hexagonal space of beautiful translucent blues and purples.

Sliptube
Created by the Yallaweh'n Yannisk Indibidus Val, the magnetic field transportation system for lifeforms and machinery was first used by the Baleen to aid moving their water supported bodies around GSA ships and facilities. Sliptubes are the standard means of transportation within structures throughout the GSA.

Suppressor Fighters
The Epikan 9th Generation Suppressor Fighter features a dual pilot configuration (1 biological, 1 sentient A.I.) with a fusion drive. Primarily used by the GSA for short range combat, the supressor fighters have been in use for a million turns.

Copek (occurs on page 15 paragraph 5)
Valkon in dialect, the word can be translated to mean "Victory."

"That show Maruk made me watch, Star Trek, got it *so* wrong."

Quarantine Monitoring Station 17's command center was filled with morphic crystal panes, all flowing with real-time readouts, energy levels, sensor data, comms, and more. Several dozen crew were already in place coordinating defenses, communicating with other stations, monitoring Earth, or tracking the proximity breach.

Kruk knew their stoic *Duma* captain from his father's work in the Echo Quadrant. Paradon, in full form, stood at his central dais scanning pertinent data on his holographic array, barking orders in two directions.

"...Third, we all know there's a breach. Turn that infernal alarm off! My synapses are firing like a *gagaric snow buffalo* from Sentron."

With still-arriving crew only adding to the chaos, Kruk ran to his station, monitoring the extrasolar probes. Sensing him, the holo-emitter and interface spools generated a small system map curated specifically for Kruk's use, marking major GSA installations in the Sea of Rocks, or, as the humans called it, the Kuiper Belt.

"Plot current coordinates of the 5 ESPs beyond the jamming field."

At Kruk's command, in a spectacular display of engineering; codes and calculations streamed across the crystal-encased screens. Each Earth probe having launched long ago, the holomap had to zoom beyond the system perimeter to encompass the five flashing beacons.

Paradon barked, "Mapping, update."

Mapping *Paraguardian* Lutraal answered. "Done, sir. Readouts now updated to include three possible intruders. I must caution that degraded signals from intruders, designated One and Two, decreases position accuracy by 0.0017%."

The captain frowned. "They're beyond our systematic scanning range. How did we spot them?"

Defense Paraguardian Aroxia turned an eye from her station. "We got lucky, sir. They tripped a flowspace buoy. Current telemetry puts them at 1,800 endons with an inclination of 32° relative to system center. If that course doesn't deviate, they'll

---

Duma
Members of the GSA from Rapsidian, of Sector 3, the Duma are from a rocky high steppe far from any ocean. They evolved communities around massive sinkholes. They possess a quad-core respiratory system, each capable of breathing independently and in continuous cycle. Their hands, made from locking cubic fingers that can form into hard hooves, deliver a brutal impact that can easily dent armor plating.

Gagaric Snow Buffalo
The "Cold Thunder" are native to Rapsidian of the 3rd Sector. Living in large herds, they roam polar plains and migrate along a mountain ridge from pole to pole. In recent millennia, they migrated to Sentron, within the 3rd Sector.

Paraguardian
PG is a high ranking officer of the Department of First Contact. There are 100,000+ Paraguardians throughout the GSA, each serving 4 turns.

pass within 17 endons of the jamming field in under 6 nolaprikes."

The room quieted. With a sweep of Paradon's hand, the space above his dais dimmed into a discrete pocket of darkness. Additional morphic panes grew down from the ceiling, generating a larger version of Kruk's system holomap. This shared tactical projection depicted not only the GSA's 19 quarantine monitoring stations, but the 3,278 jamming field generators distributed among Nova System's 15 planets, 197 moons, and 2.6 million Class-V or larger asteroids.

"Not good. Whether they realize or not, those ships are dangerously close to interfering with a massive, secret GSA operation. Any comm transmissions?"

Communications PG Aaroolu responded. "Not a whisper, sir."

"Identify them dammit!"

Propulsion PG Du'olook spoke next. "Three intruders now confirmed, possibly stealth class." Three wiry tentacles adjusted controls, while a gesture from his fourth replaced the tactical map with the faint, fragmented image of a hull. "More specifically, *Dillinger-haist*, probably modded. The drive signatures are weak, well shielded, especially for *flowspace*. That would exclude any legal cargo vessels."

"Why not head straight for system center,? This scenic route is precarious," Paradon mused. "Deploy full countermeasures and netting..."

Aroxia interrupted. "Sir, that would risk alerting the humans to our presence. Unless the intruders drop out of flowspace, we can't stop them anyway, so it might be worth waiting."

Paradon glared. "I'm well aware why we're here. Deploy full countermeasures and netting protocol."

"Yes, sir."

Kruk was happy to hear Maruk's check-in come over the speakers. "Captain, Oga leader. Team is nearing position. Four nolaprikes until intercept."

"Copy that, Oga Team."

Dillinger-haist
Created by Thumatra Industries for GSA military departments. A Dillinger-haist fusion propulsion system is known for its exceptionally low signal output. They are well suited for stealth capability as well as commonly used by smugglers, pirates, police, and high end security.

Flowspace
A parallel dimension, discovered by the Dramurian Scientific Cooperative, through which GSA starships travel faster than the speed of light relative to our universe. There is no changing direction once in flowspace, but gravity alters the jump trajectory. Jumping may be capable through a sufficiently low massed object as a small ship, but an asteroid, moon, or planet would be lethal. Therefore, using flowspace may require multiple jumps to get around a dense area of space.

The GSA spent enormous resources on the jamming shields that kept quarantined systems hidden, but they also knew, sooner or later, someone would happen upon one. It was a scenario they drilled to death, but after a hundred turns of nothing throughout the Nova Station, this was the first time it actually occurred.

The reality, as exhilarating as it was frightening, Kruk felt alive. Tactical map ever-shifting, the scant **nolaprikes** seemed to stretch toward eternity. But then, three neon pink and blue holoflashes indicated that the intruders had dipped from flowspace, then immediately dropped back in with a new course vector.

"Intruders now curving for system entry near QMS 6 and generator 0512." Aroxia's tone grew dour. "It seems they knew we were here."

How? An accident Kruk understood, but this didn't add up. Only signals to and from the Earth probes were unblocked. Protocol prohibited interference in the quarantined species' development.

GSA transmissions were easily shielded from primitive Earth-tech, but... what about the other way around? Picking up the faint ESP signals from settled space would be impossible. Wouldn't it? If not, then who? One answer came to mind, but they were history, dead, gone.

Kruk wanted the stray thought to pass, but it seized him—and it never hurt to check.

"Plot intruders' previous trajectory. Project 2 nolaprikes."

A green line on his holomap angled toward the system edge, passed it, then nearly intersected with ESP 4 at an estimated perigee distance of just 115 **rudons**.

His nagging worry turned to fear; Kruk rushed to the captain's dais. "Sir, I don't think they knew *we* were here. They were tracking a human probe."

Paradon glowered, but didn't dismiss the idea. "From deep space? How? Those signals are so weak, *we* can barely monitor them."

"I don't know Sir, but on their way in, they came so close to ESP 4, it couldn't be a coincidence."

Nolaprike
GSA standard unit of time. The nolaprike is 10^2 duprikes and equivalent to 60.48 seconds.

Rudon
GSA standard unit of distance. The rudon is 10^3 tradons and equivalent to 3 kilometers.

Duprike (occurs on next page)
GSA standard unit of time. The duprike is equivalent to .605 seconds.

Maruk chimed over the comm. "40 *duprikes* to intercept."

PG Aroxia nearly spoke over him. "Sir, Intruder 1 has opened a patch and dipped out of flowspace. It's now dropping toward the system plane."

"Warn QMS 6 they'll be in attack range soon."

"Aye... Sir, they're deploying weapons. I count 4 *rainstar* signatures."

Paradon kept cool. "Whoever it is has some impressive firepower. The target?"

"Generator 0512."

"Return fire—with prejudice. We can lose a generator. Our priority is capturing that ship."

Updates flew in from all stations:

"Missiles fired."

"Hit! Took out two rainstars."

"Generator 0512 destroyed!"

"QMS 6 firing all weapons. Intruder 1 taking evasive action. Miss—miss—miss—I've never seen anything maneuver so... wait! Confirmed hit. Intruder 1's flowspace drive is disabled."

"Team Or'en moving in to apply netting field." Aroxia's other eyes monitoring live feeds from the fighters, she turned one to the captain. "They'll have a flowspace netting field locked in around the disabled ship in a nolaprike, sir."

"One down. What are the other two up to?"

The highly proficient Aroxia was downright puzzled. "Sir, Intruder 2 and 3 have been using an overlapping flight pattern. Now they've converged, as if on top of each other."

Maruk, far from the tense noise of the bridge, enjoyed leading his team through several close-pass maneuvers around the many asteroids. Time short, they had to hard-burn through the belt. Passing team Or'en, he glimpsed them knitting their streams around Intruder 1.

Rainstar
A superior space combat missile designed to fragment near target into hundreds of molten plasma balls that drain shields, and stick and burn into any physical surface. This weapon was constructed by Arealta Armor and is now used by both the GSA and the Creators of Space.

Quad-core (occurs on page 21)
A type of respiratory system that has 4 "lungs." Each is capable of breathing independently and in a continuous cycle. The lung passages are directly through their chest. Duma possesses a quad-core respiratory system.

It would be his turn, soon enough. "Mapping, confirm we're approaching field-collision."

Lutraal sounded uncharacteristically stressed. "Confirm you are 2 rudons from field, Oga leader, and target will impact in 3...2...1....."

A crackling covered the final syllable. The stars shimmered against the flowing space near the patch event. Like a whale rising from ocean depths, a ship emerged. No sooner did it appear than a dazzling pulse of light blinded him. When it dissipated, all that remained of the ship were tiny, glittering motes reflecting a pale, distant sun.

"Oga Leader confirming Intruder 2 destroyed on exit from flowspace."

Back on the bridge, the remaining blip, designated Intruder 3, blinked upon reaching the field... then, impossibly, moved through it. Heart sinking, Kruk was increasingly convinced he knew what was coming but couldn't bring himself to say so.

The captain's *quad-core* vocal cords bellowed. "How the Rooka?! All right, Du Nola Ree, initiate *Darkness protocol*. Deploy *Voidwhisperers.*"

Everyone stunned by the name, Paradon pounded his fist, cracking a crystal frame. "Do I have to repeat myself? Initiate order, Du Nola Ree!"

A chill, colder than the Titan's Ridge, swept the bridge. All those with eyelids blinked, but then all obeyed.

The shocking presence of Voidwhisperers was something else that didn't make sense to Kruk. Nova system couldn't violate the Sea of Rocks protocol if it wanted. Why would the galaxy's deadliest troops be anywhere near here?

Not only that, the disgraced program was officially dismantled in the aftermath of the Saaryki War. The rumors that the GSA still used them in the deepest parts of space were apparently true. It certainly explained why Kruk had to go through so many background checks.

They were almost mythical. Sometimes called the *Whisper of Death*,

---

Voidwhisperers
Sometimes called the Whisper of Death, Voidwhisperers utilized high-level stealth-tech with no transponders or drive-signature. One of the GSA founding species, the Valkon, helmed the majority of the Voidwhisperers. Rumors were they never spoke and only communicated via quantum entangled neural interfaces. They are an elite black ops division of the GSA, the galaxy's deadliest troops. The program was "officially" dismantled in the aftermath of the Saaryki War.

Darkness Protocol
A GSA quarantine battle tactic that powers down or hides activity that could be seen by alien sensors, while deploying and reassigning troops to close a perimeter net around a system in the unlikely event a ship gets through.

Voidwhisperers utilized high-level stealth-tech with no transponders or drive-signature at all—or so Kruk's father claimed. One of the GSA founding species, named the Valkon, supposedly helmed the majority of the Voidwhisperers. Kruk didn't even know there were any in this quarantine program. The lore varied wildly; rumors had it they never spoke, and only communicated via quantum entangled neural interfaces.

In any case, Vdubs had one purpose, to make things disappear. Whether Intruder 3 reached Earth or not, its crew was thoroughly, as the humans said, screwed.

"How did that ship get through? I need answers!" Captain Paradon's voice ripped Kruk out of his tangenting thoughts and back to reality.

An obvious question, but it left the crew flummoxed. The silence stretched dangerously until the usually withdrawn **Duraguardian,** Entok, spoke. "Sir, if I may, Intruder 2 opened a ***patch*** directly *on* the field, yet debris analysis suggests it wasn't destroyed by a reactor containment failure."

"We've verified that the field was fully functional?"

"Affirmative."

"Then, what *did* destroy it, Entok? Give me a best guess."

The DG became hesitant, questioning his conclusions as he voiced them. "*Perhaps,* an unknown device allowed the patch to punch a hole in the field at the exact moment Intruder 3 passed through in flowspace. The energy produced could have triggered the destruction of Intruder 2. Obviously, a suicide maneuver like that would require an extensive understanding of field-dampening tech, antimatter manipulation, and some absurdly good flying."

Paradon's spikes twitched. "Let's not admire our enemy too much, Entok."

"Of course, Sir. Sorry, sir."

Aroxia interjected. "Netted ship fully disabled. Flowspace and sublight engines all offline."

"Some good news, at least. Let's bring it in. Vdub status?"

Duraguardian
A mid-level officer in the Department of First Contact. They operate and manage technical, strategic, and personnel teams, actions and upkeep. They are elevated to or demoted from their position by the government computers based on their success in their work. There are 10,000,000+ Duraguardians throughout the GSA, each serving 3 turns.

Patch
Created by the Dramurian Scientific Cooperative, The Builder, Daro Lutican ni Dramur, is its architect. The Patch is a doorway to flowspace created by vibrating spacetime to match the flowspace frequency. Patches are needed to safely enter and exit flowspace. Draumurians understood a way of vibrating a section of spacetime until it matched the resonance of flowspace. At this time, a properly shielded and vibrating ship can pass through the "patch" into flowspace. A Patch uses antimatter as its power source.

"Passing Jupiter. Closing—but they'll be unable to engage until the remaining Intruder 3 drops from flowspace."

At least Kruk knew some major help was on its way. Any crew outside the command loop would be bracing for an imminent attack but Aroxia's next outburst made him think ignorance might be better.

"SIR!!!! 22 additional flowspace signatures have appeared in grid 87, a third of the way across the system. They're using an overlapping flight pattern, making it likely they'll punch through the field the same way. Given sacrifice involved, that would leave 11 intruders active."

"Redirect 94% of the Vdubs to our new arrivals."

Percentages enabled Paradon to avoid revealing exactly how many Voidwhisperers were in play, but the math told Kruk it was at least 47.

"I want every suppressor fighter in range of the field line to plot a direct intercept with the incoming enemies."

Paling, Kruk opened a private channel. "Maruk, you hear that?"

His friend was shaken. "I did. Suicide run is a desperate move. He just sent those **greels** on QMS4 to their deaths. How important *is* this ***quarantine***?"

Shortly, the tactical map displayed fifteen fighters hurtling toward the new intruders, then patching into flowspace. When they met just beyond the field, ten fighters and ten intruder icons turned yellow, indicating their demise. An additional six intruders self-destructed when they dipped out at the field, allowing the remaining six to enter without leaving flowspace.

"We've lost five ships, sir."

Taken off-guard, Paradon snapped, "I can count!" With the crew looking to him, he pivoted to a more dignified tone. "Their sacrifice will be honored. *Glory to the protectors of infant worlds.* Now, get me updates!"

"Vdub Group 1 in strike distance, awaiting Intruder 3 flowspace dropout. If vectors hold, the remaining six will be in Vdub Group 2 firing range in 5 nolaprikes."

Greel
Originating from the language Rakillak of Rakilla, the word refers to a fledgling who jumped before they were able to fly. It is widely used throughout the GSA as a slang term for a military pilot.

Quarantine of Dimur 7
2.3 million turns ago, the GSA almost released a godlike race when they granted the Venu Class-S status. They were normal, peaceful, lifeforms until they had travelled in the first starships away from their sun. The absence of their homeworld's particular radiation signature slowly destabilized their genetic code, eventually killing them over the course of turns. But during that time, the Venu slowly became more radioactive, able to absorb and dispel energy, melt through steel with their bare hands, and kill all around them from exposure. If left unchecked, they would become planet killing entities with their deaths. The GSA asked the Venu to return to their homeworld. Those who did not and those who tried to leave were killed. An indefinite quarantine is placed around Venu until a cure can be found. None has.

After an agonizing five nolaprikes, Aroxia announced, "The 6 second wave intruders have dipped out. Vdubs commencing attack."

A moment later, she added, "All targets destroyed."

"Scans indicate no biological life present. Computer simulated reconstructions confirm machine pilots on all intruder ships, verified with Vdubs encounter as well."

Machine...? The answer hit Kruk as if he'd been smacked in the face by the tail of ***Dragsan eel***. "It's a diversion."

Confident as he was, he'd need proof to convince the Captain. "Give me real time images of ESP4, highest resolution, priority alphe."

"Crewmember not authorized for alphe processing."

Panicking, Kruk nearly screamed out his father's private code. "Emergency override Zucco 27 Alphe Oga Bema!"

"Override approved. Use of override will result in mandatory conduct review."

If he was wrong, there'd be major consequences. If he wasn't and did nothing, it could be much worse. His holo-emitters lit like stars as a quintillion bytes of image data flowed in from every station, generator, sensor, buoy, relay, and scope.

The image built slowly, not yet clear enough for the Captain but more than enough for him. Under other circumstances, he might have been pleased his wild hunch was right.

As it was, he sputtered nervously, then shouted, "I know who it is! THE CREATORS OF SPACE!"

For a second time, the bridge went dead silent. An air of fear swept from left to right, engulfing the life around it. Paradon looked over and spoke gently, as if to a madman or a frightened child. "Son, the Creators have been gone hundreds of turns. There hasn't been so much as the rumor of a resurgence cell in, what...30 turns? It can't be..."

"Sir, all due respect, the Vdub didn't know about the machine pilots, right? That

---

Dragsan
Arguably the "fathers" of the GSA, these blue skinned humanoids posses three sensory tentacles that protrude from the back of their head. Dragsans are prolific for their trained use of "Recall," where one can exist in memories.

Dragsan Eel
Originating on Dragsa, the Dragsan Eel now lives in several Sector 6 planets with oceans. An invertebrate, formed from interlocking armored exoskeletal segments. Has tail fins along its length for propulsion. They can generate lethal electrical shocks to defend and hunt. As lone hunters, they prefer offshore reefs.

makes this the only time they've been outplayed since the Loronzon Incident, the day..."

Captain Paradon's withering look killed anything else Kruk might say. "I know the mission."

Seeing the crew was rapt by the exchange, he addressed them all. "Just in case, let's initiate countermeasures."

Kruk's hi-res scan was nearly complete, but the final stages dragged mercilessly. When it chimed completion, an additional signature appeared so far beyond the Nova System it would, otherwise, have gone unnoticed. With a blink and a hand gesture, he moved the image to the tactical projection. Overlaying the existing map, it showed a bogey closing rapidly on ESP4.

"Duraguardian Kruktusken, what am I looking at?"

"Captain, Sir, I've no idea why, but they don't want Earth, they want their probe. This attack is a decoy."

"Aroxia, options?"

"No time for the fighters to intercept or to power the ***Dark Energy Array.*** At this range, conventional weaponry can't destroy ESP4. Given a more immediate issue with a potential result of mission failure, we have to let it go. I recommend Vdub Group 2 join the pursuit of Intruder 3."

She was right. If Intruder 3 reached Earth, that would be it for the quarantine. Perhaps worse. Millennia of experience had proven that extraterrestrial tech on a Class-T accelerated self-destruction, or worse, led to interstellar war—as in the incident involving COS founder, General Odian Spek. Though few knew, the information being zeta classified—Spek was a former GSA operative.

8.2 million turns ago, 9 worlds established the Alliance. Maintaining galactic order through force proved unstable, so they iterated more covert strategies, finally finding harmony in creating an elite, invisible army to deal with insurrection, defectors, warlords, and pirates quietly, or better yet, preemptively. They were called

---

Dark Energy Array
Instantaneous destruction of matter or an FTL blind jump. Two intersecting beams created by two different dark energy arrays will discreetly destroy matter at their intersection. This is unblockable. All GSA ships are equipped with a miniaturized Dark Energy Array for a one time use. Once it is activated, it cannot be stopped. It can't be weaponized; it is a tool of last resort. 50% of the time it vaporizes the ship; the other 50% of the time the ship will instantaneously jump either forwards or backwards along that vector to an unknown and potentially limitless distance. From an outside observer, the ship will always appear to jump away, so you never know if anyone made it unless they came back. There is a ⅛ success rate with using a DEA for travel. Origin of the DEA, Valkon.

Voidwhisperers.

The Valkon, a GSA founding species, were particularly powerful, flight-capable, and most important, receptive to cerebral quantum-entangled implants. They were the first approached for recruits, while the fiercest, Odian Spek, became the Vdubs most decorated General.

Meanwhile, the Saakyri had earned reclassification, first contact, and trade. Unfortunately, their peaceful aspect was a front that helped them spread an engineered plague to weaken other worlds. Five planets were devastated before they were discovered and their efforts stopped.

It was then the GSA created a more deadly, more enduring foe. Rather than eliminate the Saakyri, they stripped them of GSA tech, burned their starships, EMP'd their cities, corrupted their data cores, collapsed their infrastructure, and irradiated their ionosphere making it dangerous to punch through for over a century. Spek, on a mission far from home when Valkürin became one of their victims, was enraged at the decision. Taking it upon himself to correct the Saakryi's survival, he used the Voidwhisperers to spread his own plague.

His revenge complete, Spek's public surrender forced the GSA to acknowledge the Voidwhisperers. At trial, he argued his actions were not only justified, but necessary. The court disagreed, but the Vdub easily escaped custody.

600,000 worlds outraged and fearful, the GSA officially shut down the program. Unofficially, they made VWs more obedient by adding explosives to their implants. Rather than accept, many existing Vdubs fled, becoming mercs, pirates, criminals or, worse, joining Odian's new army; the Creators of Space.

*For two hundred turns, they attacked **Class-T** worlds, including a few the GSA had yet to discover. At times, they'd pretend to be the GSA. After each assault, they let enough time pass to convince the galaxy they were gone. The biggest legacy of their last appearance was the elaborate, expensive precautions the GSA now used to protect pre-contact worlds.*

Class-T
A classification in the GSA Dept. of First Contact Planetary Index. Considered a Diminishing Lifespan Planet, they have interstellar detectable tech, planetary scale conflicts, and a failing ecosystem. These conditions together, indicate the native species' high likelihood of violent expansion to other planets. Too dangerous to engage, they are reassessed every 55 turns by the DOFC. Improved resource balance, interplanetary travel potential, and a strong preference for diplomacy could earn an upgrade to Class-S - Safe for Future Expansion. Further improvement, evaluated every 10 turns, might grant First Contact.

Most of this Kruk heard from his father, **Prime** *Councilmember KruktuskenBor. He also said Spek died in the* **Loronzon incident***. The rest was scattered, baseless rumor. Only the innermost government and the Creators themselves knew the truth.*

"Duraguardian Kruktusken, are you part of this crew or not?!"

Paradon's snarl reminded him history wasn't one of his duties. "Yes, sir! Sorry, sir. Initiate planetary failsafe?"

"Only as a last resort. Stand at the ready. We let the Voidwhisperers do their work for now."

The choice puzzled Kruk. *What if they appeared over a city? Did Voidwhisperers have a cloaking field? Was that even possible? How big were their ships?* Kruk didn't even know what species VW used now.

An auto countdown began. "Intruder arriving in Earth's atmosphere in 10...9...8..."

"Sir, the planetary failsafe. We should activate."

"And detonate whatever antimatter is planetside? In flowspace, passing that close to Earth's gravity well would tear our fighters apart."

"Sir," Aroxia said, "if the intruder was capable of dropping out of flowspace precisely atop the field, what's to say they can't do the same near the planet's surface?"

"5...4..." The last of the fighters joined the Voidwhisperers in hot pursuit, but the countdown, chirping with increased urgency, told them they wouldn't be fast enough.

"3...2..." Heart heavy, defeat imminent, Paradon's order was soft, but clear, "Deploy Failsafe."

The auto count completed. The icon designating Intruder 3 reached the atmosphere—the flowspace drive presumably destabilized and blinked out of existence, leaving no sign of its alien presence.

Aroxia reported, "Intruder 3 destroyed. Flowspace antimatter reactor breach confirmed."

The Loronzon Incident
The most notable, recent, First Contact failure in GSA history, occurring 30 turns ago. Publically considered a misidentification of a hostile species, in truth, the Alliance granted the Loronz Class S status, but a faction of the COS attacked the first contact proceedings making it look like the GSA attacked. The Loronz retaliated and swiftly destroyed 6 Mayad cruisers with weapons the GSA had underestimated in strength. With heavy losses on both sides and the chance of peace shattered, the GSA withdrew.

Prime
A top ranking member of the GSA that formulate and designs laws. There are 171 Primes throughout the GSA. A 7 turn endeavor, whereas if a Prime is appointed to three consecutive terms, they become a Prime for their life and are retired to Havlangar after their service, never to return. Each Prime leads one of the 19 Departments in each Sector. Primes comprise the Council of Worlds and are elevated to or demoted from a Prime by the government computer algorithm created by the Kaleans. This function uses an amalgamation of data including but not limited to their successes within the role.

Kruk closed his eyes and braced for the bad news.

"Sensors detecting an antimatter detonation on the surface. It's bad sir, blast radius is several rudons. There must have been a research facility stockpiling antimatter."

Paradon was visibly shaken. "Those... maniacs... Get me Prime Abbotkrine," Paradon barked. "The last mapping of this planet showed no warning zones of antimatter production of this magnitude."

"The remaining bogey at ESP 4 has dropped out of flowspace."

All 19 quarantine stations watched helplessly as the probe vanished and the bogey jumped back into flowspace. The Voidwhisperers and fighters too far away, the bogey disappeared from their scopes without interference.

Kruk felt a darkness descend. The humans couldn't help but notice that the devastating antimatter blast and loss of their probe, thousands of *endons* apart, occurred at the same time. This was it...the quarantine was finished.

An *Anduuzian Cricket* could have been heard as everyone awaited the captain's next orders. Finally, he confirmed the failure.

"We're done. Recall the Voidwhisperers. Retrieve damaged and destroyed vessels, get repair teams to generator 0512, and give me a direct line to SAC."

Species Assessment Command, on Mijorn, hadn't been contacted in 50 turns. The mood dour, the future uncertain, everyone tore their eyes from the main tactical hologram and moved with haste.

Kruk continued to wonder why. *If it was the COS, they already knew there was a sentient species here. So, why take the probe? Better yet, why attack to do so? Depopulation could have been accomplished with a bioweapon. If they wanted mayhem, they could've publicized Earth's coordinates through any Alliance relay.*

Paradon gestured to the blast door. "DG Kruktusken, with me. I'll need you to explain the override, but that's hardly the main concern. Clearly, you did the right thing. If high command agrees the Creators may be back, you'll accompany me to Mijorn. It's the SAC debrief I expect will be received poorly."

Endon (first occurs on pages 17 and 18)
GSA standard unit of distance. The endon is 10^9 tradons, and equivalent to 3 million kilometers. The endon was originally derived from the mean radii of the orbital distance of Azoeleo, with an eccentricity of only .000007. The endon, like all GSA units of measure, is defined by fundamental constants of nature.

Anduuzian Cricket
Originating on Anduuz, the 6 legged, bright purple exoskeleton insect moves in swarms, usually herbivores, but likes the taste of Droteans, Baleen, Dragsan, and Osanii. Docile and situationally predatorial.

Species Assessment Command
A powerful division within the Department of First Contact that is in charge of evaluating Class-T planets.

It was an understatement. Under normal circumstances, a return to civilization would thrill Kruk; now all he could do was gulp.

As they passed through the blast doors, Pardon lowered his voice. "The Loronzon Incident is classified. A midlevel *Guardian* having knowledge of it is... noteworthy. That's the biggest issue you'll have to explain. As well as how you acquired a high level override command code. "

Dread filled him. He wished with all his heart he could go back to complaining about the boredom. But after two turns, so many *gobbletek* games, everything—his life, the future of the GSA, had changed in the blink of an eye.

The Creators had returned.

Guardian
A ranking within the GSA for members of the Department Of First Contact. Guardians are a mid-tier rank.

Gobbletek
Created By the Rakila's Felixa sud Rutanus, it was first developed to teach space war strategy. The objective of this 3-D strategy game is to conquer and control the larger amount of space than your opponent. Space is controlled by expanding to and connecting adjacent star systems.

CHAPTER 3

PROJECT PEGASUS

Moon and stars glinted beyond a clear dome ceiling. As if ready for battle, Control Room A greeted Bernard with its beautiful array of radar consoles and lit computer screens. A vibrant collection of people were here, his people. Engineers, cosmologists, astronomers, scientists, creators, young, old, and of course, all dreamers—they were united by a common goal, to prove humanity was not alone. The world's disdain didn't matter. In this moment, they shared a rare energy, the precious feeling of being on the threshold of monumental change.

"He's here!"

All turned to Bernard. A hush fell; the silence summoned words he'd waited so long to speak.

"Four years ago, CERN was destroyed, many of our greatest minds lost. I was damaged beyond repair... or so I thought. Lisa Hubert, my wife and the world's foremost leader in nanotechnology, knowing the stakes, not only helped seed the very ethos of what *CORE* is today, she helped me out of the darkness—helped us all find and lift each other, and something equally magical happened; you believed me. You believed IN me. You've left your blood and sweat on these keyboards,

---

CORE
The Center of Radiometry & Elements, a R&D company and technological thinktank established by Bernard Hubert after he was fired from Outer Limits during the CERN incident. The facilities are located in NA Zone 3, formerly New Mexico.

put in seventy-hour weeks, ran thousands of tests, sacrificed careers, credibility, relationships, marriages, because while the world called us fools, you knew the answers were there. I'd pick the people in this room over any other, any damn day. I am proud to call you my colleagues, prouder still to call you friends."

The crowd erupted in a dragon-roar. A sweeping grin consumed Bernard's bearded face. Absorbing their passion, he returned it, shouting over the cheers.

"And we're not fools, are we? We're the tip of the spear, not the crude spear our ancestors used for meat and murder; a spear of discovery, a belief that cannot abide the arrogant assumption that among forty billion worlds, only one can harbor a single intelligent species. We are not alone."

Echoing him, they chanted. "WE ARE NOT ALONE!"

Bernard smiled.

"And tonight we stand ready to send our pride and joy, our Mayflower, to the edge of the solar system with a new hope, a new expectation of what lies beyond. No governmental organization, nor private company has flown this far or built this fast since the tragedy at CERN. This is our time to discover. She will show our world we are ready to step beyond the comfort of this rock to the next. She will carry the evidence of our intelligence to our neighboring species, the ones who must have caused the containment failure. The ones who must have done so by mistake, or we would have been overtaken by now. The ones who are waiting for us to rise above our differences and ineptitudes to meet them in the stars."

On the launchpad, visible from the control room's cliffside perch, spotlights bathed their pillar of destiny. Every rivet gleamed, the subtle angles of the booster tips more than pleasing to the eye. Atop the Atlas X, nestled in its fairing, lay humanity's two most advanced creations, the *Mayflower* probe and the first fusion drive, which would propel her to the Kuiper Belt faster than could previously be imagined, let alone engineered.

"Intelligence...most think they have it, few do." Titters were quickly hushed. "My mother, Minerva Mary Hubert, once told me, 'Without understanding why, you'll never be able to understand how.' We understand why. We feel it in our bones that something is out there. If all that stood in the way of becoming better humans, better stewards of this earth, was our failure to try hard enough, then what does it mean to be human?

Rest assured, if ever asked what you did for Earth, you can say, "I sailed past the horizon, because I understood why." And at journey's end, our brother or sister will stand on some distant rock orbiting a nameless star, gaze back upon Earth with a smile and say, "You're welcome."

The CORE team chanted again, louder than before, "WE ARE NOT ALONE!"

Bernard's arms rose. "Initiate the countdown sequence!"

All moved with great purpose; commands given, codes punched, forty-seven subsystems monitored for the slightest anomaly. The countdown clock, set at 00:05:00 began ticking down. The team enrapt by their crucial work, Bernard quietly exited.

Ducking into a side office, he lifted the phone, pausing before dialing. How long had it been? Five, six years? Not that he'd ever forget the number. After one ring, a machine picked up.

"We need to meet. Call me back."

Michael, his lead engineer called. "Bert! It's happening!"

A sucker for history, especially when he was part of it, he hurried back. At T-Minus 2:00, flight controllers called out their status upon command:

"Booster"—"GO" "Payload"—"GO" "Telemetry"—"GO" "Control"—"GO" "Guidance"—"GO" "Network"—"GO" "Navigation"—"GO" "Flight"—"GO"

At 00:30, all systems switched to onboard computer control as the loudspeaker was consumed by the automated voice command. "5...4...3...2...1... Ignition..."

The boosters flared, brightening the landscape, darkening the sky. Opaque exhaust plumes mixed with a cloud of steam from the sound-suppressing water system, briefly engulfing the rocket. The Atlas burst through, rising, accelerating to the heavens.

There were more cheers as the rocket passed max q without incident. Once it was out of visible range, they focused on the scopes to track it as it leveled towards orbital trajectory.

"First stage engine shutdown in 3...2...1..."

The fact that Bernard alone knew the full truth brought a moment of deep shame. But it passed, replaced with a sense of duty. He'd hoped to be completely honest with his team, but compartmentalizing was the only way to ensure success.

Another cheer went up, following a successful first stage separation. He used the excitement to slip out again, this time into the far quieter Control Room B. It was vacant save for a laptop and lone man, Simon McDonald, Senior—and highly trusted—flight operator.

Bernard spoke in a low, cool tone. "Ready to initiate Project Pegasus?"

"Yes, sir. Mayflower is now out of ground-tracking range. Trajectory is nominal and we're thirty seconds out from fairing separation. Blindspot package ready to initialize."

Bernard weighed giving the order carefully. Of course, his species had the capacity to create great things. But how often were they used responsibly?

"Do it."

He heard the countdown to fairing release over the intercom: "3...2...1..." As the explosive bolts flashed, the video feed froze a moment, stuttered, then showed the fairings as they flipped back towards Earth.

During that brief blackout, a tiny spacecraft had separated, the momentary signal interruption giving it enough distance from the Mayflower to hide should anyone be looking. Its radar-defeating design was covered in spectrum shifting tiles capable of matching any background. With the flying engines dead, it was, for now, untraceable, save through a transponder aimed at a relay in western Peru.

It, too, carried a fusion drive. More important, it was the real probe.

He called it the *Sagan*.

Fudging the fairings' mass numbers and sensor feedback to mask its presence before and during launch, was, if Bernard did say so himself, a work of considerable genius.

"Mayflower Payload separation in one minute."

Shouts came from next door. "Bernard, you're missing it!" "Where is he?"

He sighed. "Back to keeping up appearances. Simon, let me know when we're one minute from Lunar blackout."

With a nod from the senior operator, Bernard stepped back into the happy cacophony of Control Room A. "Payload separation in 10...9...

Launch Director Peralo jogged up to him. "There you are! Can you believe it?"

"Hardly."

"Payload separation complete." Yet another roar erupted.

Peralo tried to temper his jubilation with the gravity of the moment. "This is it, sir. Do we have a go to activate the ***Hubert Drive?***"

It may have been ostentatious to name it after himself, but having successfully kept the Sagan hidden, he really didn't care. "You do. Initiate Mayflower fusion drive."

"Yes, sir!"

Peralo shook as he returned to his station. Holding the activation key twixt thumb and forefinger, he turned it. A hologram, center focused, showed a scaled model of the Hubert Drive spinning up. No one breathed. Bernard waited. Following his mother's footsteps at Cambridge, his father's at MIT, all his education, all his work, had led here. Was he as brilliant as they? As ingenious as everyone once believed? As he continued to believe? Would it work?

Artfully rendered representations of the reaction projected colorful looping

---

Hubert Drive
A magnetized target fusion (MTS) propulsion drive designed by Bernard Hubert and built by CORE. The first ship to use the Hubert Drive is the Mayflower.

magnetic fields that grew and solidified. The plasma temperatures rose steadily, readouts showing the containment remained stable. A hot, compressed ball of star birth blazed to life.

Peralo punctured the silence: "Fusion Drive activation complete, reaction is sustaining. Ready to divert power to propulsion." He looked expectantly at Bernard. "Sir? Go, no-go?"

"Go." Bernard spoke as the room palpitated with excitement. *This is where most would say the story began.* On the video feed, the Mayflower's thrusters flared; the Earth noticeably shrank.

"Bernard... sir!" Peralo was ecstatic. "We're holding strong at 15gs! The drive works! This is the dawn of a new era!"

If only you knew how true that is.

The roars made the reaction to Bernard's speech sound like a wake. The mayhem was glorious: papers tossed, people screaming... until it all screeched to a halt.

"Instability manifesting in cusps 6 through 34."

Bernard snapped, "Analysis!"

They flew back to their posts, double checking data, sweating bullets.

"Instability increasing. Dial back?"

Everyone looked anxiously to the drive's creator. "No. Continue the propulsion test; we have to know its full capabilities."

"Containment failing, sir. If it continues, we'll have a reactor breach."

Bernard shrugged it off. "So be it. Make sure we're recording everything."

After a few agonizing seconds, the video feed died. The point of light representing the Mayflower vanished.

"Signal lost. Time: 17:39 ENAT."

A depressing chill descended, but Bernard found it difficult to appear somber. *How delighted they'd be to know that they succeeded after all. ...In due time they will.*

His loud, emphatic claps echoed off the domed ceiling. "Everyone! Don't you understand? We've just done what billions thought impossible, completed the first successful fusion propulsion test in space. Yes, there are issues, but we're going to solve them, yes?"

The question provoked a collective. "Yes!"

"Then, be proud! We held fire in our hands... all we need are better gloves." Smiles formed. He heard chuckles.

"Core analysis, wind back the clock. I'm ordering the rest of you to take the next four days off. Relax, recuperate, reset, and we'll all dive back in."

Four days? The workaholics were stunned. They'd been at it one-hundred forty-two days straight. Rest was inconceivable. What would they do with the time? Luckily, a telemetry expert quickly figured out the answer and let loose a joyous howl. The mood more than broken, the room laughed.

As Bernard hugged and shook hands with those nearest, he spotted Simon peeking in from a sliver of open door. "Excuse me. I have to call a few news agencies, give them their pound of flesh."

Returning to Control Room B, he looked at the laptop screen. The *Sagan* was moving towards an elliptical lunar orbit. Its Hubert Drive wouldn't kick in until it reached the Moon's dark side, hiding its powerful energy signature from Earth detection. Unlike the Mayflower, it didn't have a built-in flaw. *Sagan* was to be the true test.

Bernard leaned over Simon and pushed a key to begin the countdown. As the *Sagan* passed behind the Moon, they lost the signal. Once the fusion drive discreetly powered-up, it came back. Raw data flowed as the blip of the *Sagan* moved beyond Earth vicinity.

Simon's eyes darted along the screen. "Containment fields stable, not a whisper, as expected."

"Do you see that redshifting."

"By Galileo's beard," Simon replied. Pencil in hand, he scribbled numbers frantically. Bernard admired Simon's quick processing and admiration for numbers, a key reason for his recruitment of the man. "According to my calculations of this successful trial, the Hubert drive will take the probe to the outer limits of our system in less than 2.5 years. Voyager took 35."

Bernard alone knew the truth: humanity had changed forever. He also understood the irony; the very moment that could have exonerated his legacy had to remain secret, at least for now. But it didn't matter. Control of the breakthrough had to be maintained as long as possible.

"I wish you could see this, Darren."

Bernard took the written calculations. With a lighter from his pocket, he lit the leaf then dropped its flaming mass into a metal waste bin. Simon shut down the laptop, pulled the drives, and snapped them in pieces.

They shook hands. Simon departed through a different door. Wanting to linger in the moment forever, Bernard took his time, watching the flames until the last paper ember faded into pale ash.

On his return, he realized he needn't have worried about being conspicuous. The Core Analysis team, hyper-focused, barely noticed him. Deep in thought, Bernard strode gallantly to his office. It was an unusual space for a CEO, no flashy furniture, no gaudy flaunting power or wealth, just history. The chair was a worn-down cockpit seat, but it was Neil Armstrong's, from Apollo 11. The wooden desk was Albert Einstein's. All the books in the study belonged to Stephen Hawking.

They were geniuses the world once believed Bernard Hubert belonged with—until he was accused of sabotage. But it wasn't him, and it wasn't an accident; it was an attack. With the help of the *Sagan,* he'd prove it.

There was a knock. Amy put her head in. "***Kepler Institute*** is calling. A William Hunt is insisting on speaking directly to you."

He expected his friend to call about the failure, but not so quickly. "Put him

---

Kepler Institute
The first of the SETI School; The Scientific Education Technological Institutes founded in 2043. Located in World Council NA Zone 3 (Western Colorado), it is a center for advanced learning from ages 11 to 19 over 8 cycles. Kepler is not applied to; it invites students who display gifted or genius behavior. It was founded by Grayson Freedman (MIT undergrad), Candice Oliver (Harvard grad), and Aiden Alexander (CalTech postdoc), who together, founded RNA Industries, the father of A.I. Kepler. Along with its brother and sister institutes, Hubble & Jefferson have a focus on advanced robotics, nanotechnology, nuclear physics, aeronautics, and cyber tech.

through."

Lifting the phone, he waited for the transfer click and managed one word before being cut-off. "William..."

"No time to catch-up. Can you make it here this week? We have to speak in person."

His parental instincts kicked in. "Is Isaac okay? Did you try my parents or Lisa?"

Isaac Tyco Hubert, was a gifted mind whose proud father publicly boasted he was smarter than the fictive Tony Stark, even if he never managed to express that properly to Isaac.

"He's fine, better than ever. It's not about him, it's... Bernie, we need to talk."

William hadn't called him Bernie in ages. "I'll make my way there as soon as possible."

The trip wouldn't be easy. Kepler wasn't particularly accessible for someone in Benard's standing, but before he could say anything else, the line went dead. Strange. What didn't he want to say on the phone?

A second interruption from Amy didn't give him time to ponder further. "I'm sorry, sir... I don't really... I think you should pick up line 3."

The CID showed a secure number used only by a handful. Dreading who it might be, Bernard froze. If he was right, he expected this call, too, but anticipation didn't diminish its intensity or importance.

Pulling himself together, he answered in a cool voice. "Hello?"

And there it was, that sultry voice, oozing calm power. "Bernard William Hubert, it's been a long time."

Only one person could say so little and mean so much.

"What I need to say to you has to be face to face. One week after the summit, Thursday, 1700 hours. Your place." Bernard hung up the phone without waiting for a response.

As the moon dipped below the horizon, Bernard opened a bottle of Scotch and lit a cigar. There was a lot to be done, but for now on this clear summer eve, he stared into an ocean of stars captained by moonlight. With a gentle smile and a puff of smoke, Bernard sipped his scotch and dreamt of the day he longed for, the day he'd set sail on that ocean himself.

CHAPTER 4

SUITE 11021

Councillor Godric Adams addressed the Council Hall. "Our mistake has always been failing to reach our potential. If humanity had focused on the stars, our new, little dark age could have been avoided."

The walls and ceiling were smooth, cut from pale grey and green granite that reflected light on the diverse crowd of people from every corner of the globe. His tailored paisley suit of iridescent blue matched the iceberg of his eyes. Known to be persuasive, he was pleased but not surprised by the murmurs of agreement, but one portly fellow at the edge of the room, shot to his feet and screamed.

"No! Absolutely not! You want to waste what few resources we have left on a pipe-dream of conquering space. We need to regrow the population we've lost, not try to live in some bad science-fiction novel!"

Godric waited for the echo of his peers, as well as the multiple translations, to subside before answering.

"Yes, we've conquered. YES, we've pillaged. There was a time it was necessary, but we've evolved. We've unified." He gestured at the insignia on each long tapestry, a dove encircling the world with its wings. "At the same time, we can't allow peace to diminish the drive toward new horizons. When we explore, when we invent, when we immerse ourselves in the new and unique—we flourish."

His booming voice resonated across the sea of businessmen and women, politicians, diplomats and dignitaries, leaders, scientists, artists and explorers.

"Having been at our worst and come through, we now run the risk of losing the impulse to seize the future. Blessed with this second chance, let's not waste it. Let us touch the stars—not to abandon Earth, but because every child must leave home to become an adult."

His challenger wasn't pleased but conceded with a polite bow. The applause grew to a crescendo. Godric basked in the power granted by the occasion. The other *Councillors* excitedly slammed their ceremonial gavels, signifying the start of the 19th World Council Summit.

As the crowd dispersed, a jovial Bernard walked over to congratulate his old friend. "You never fail to mesmerize, Ric. No wonder you were chosen for the opening address."

"Thanks Bernie. I'm happy the Council finally accepted my plea to restore your seat on the Cosmology Board. I've always said CERN wasn't your fault, and your absence in the debate and decision about our future in space would've been blasphemy."

"I am forever indebted, Ric." Bernard gave him a look that decades of friendship interpreted instantly.

"Yes, yes, you wanted to talk." His expression grew boyish. "I'm more than curious. On the message, you sounded like you did when we used that small telescope on your roof to look at the sky and wonder if we'd ever get back up there."

Bernard smirked. "This is a bit more... tangible."

Godric raised an eyebrow, but Bernard shook his head. "Tonight, after the summit. I'll be in the *Spear*, Suite 11021. There'll be a key for you with the concierge."

Councillor
A high ranking elected official of the World Council. Each Councillor leads a different geographical region of the world. Councillors are the primary legislative power. They are responsible for writing and voting on laws, matters of money, treaties, managing branches of the government, and being a voice for the people. There are 50 Councillors in the World Council each serving a 5 Years, with a maximum of 4 Terms. Candidates have a fortnight to campaign.

Spear
An elegant glass enclosed hotel adhered to a minimalist aesthetic but was no less magnificent. Built in 2081 and located in Manhattan's upper west side, it's preferred for it's discretion to high-end clientele.

The politician tingled at the thought of big accomplishments in the shadows. But then he noticed the disapproving glances cast at his familiarity with Bernard. Both understanding, with swift, stoic nods, the friends parted company.

Accompanied by his personal assistant, Paige Spark, Godric headed for his office hoping to rest. Near the last turn, he heard a familiar voice apparently sharing his biography.

"He's the son of Quincy Adams, 53rd and last U.S. President and the man who ceded American sovereignty to the World Council. After the Third World War, many felt a global government was necessary to restore stability. America, one of a few nations still capable of sustaining itself, found Adams' decision highly divisive. Without him, the World Council wouldn't exist, and it's through Godric's leadership that..."

It was Madeline Good, his NA Zone 3 counterpart, addressing a small group of teen students. "Thank you, Madeline, for the family history lesson.

"And wouldn't you know it—Godric Adams, Councillor of North America Zone 1, advocate for the dissolution of nations, and now in charge of our new space program. What convenient timing! If I didn't know better, I'd think you have me under surveillance."

Her sarcasm was hidden just enough to be civil. Ignoring the jab, he turned to the students. "Madeline and I have what you might call professional disagreements. She believes my views are too... robust. Let me ask you, do you want to search the stars?"

After a resounding, "YES!" Godric couldn't help but give Madeline a snide grin.

She motioned the group to move along. "Of course; we'd all *like* that, wouldn't we? But we enjoy eating, too, don't we?"

Once alone, she turned to Godric, their respective guards and assistants moving back to provide privacy. "Well, well, the mighty Godric Adams, whose boyish dreams are going to cause our next great war."

"Ah, Mrs. Good, whose naive views deeply stunt her growth as a person. At least arguments such as ours are the cornerstone of what makes the World Council great."

She batted away the compliment. "Stop. I have nothing but loathing for everything you and your father cost this great nation."

The fiery glare obliged Godric to drop any pleasantries. "That nostalgic, narrow-minded hubris makes it clear that you, or anyone you cared for, weren't living in coastal cities when the lights went out. Safe and sound in the heartland, with your crops and your guns, far from starving masses, yes? How long do you think we would have lasted?"

"Longer than a global empire can hold, versus one strong nation."

"If we fall, we fall together."

"Then we might as well fall. What would your ancestors think of your father throwing away the greatest democracy on earth?" Her slight, disapproving head shake conveyed her contempt; *poor thing, you're not even capable of understanding this argument.*

It didn't work. "Threw away?! Please, the three-hundred year history of the United States is a momentary speck in an indifferent universe."

"Which makes it okay to abandon our national security without a thought about what the *next* three-hundred years of cosmic indifference might bring?"

Godric appreciated her ability to use his own words against him. He took a breath and tried to continue in a cooler tone.

"Next time a global crisis kills a quarter of the population and leaves the remaining 9+ billion lives on the line, I'll be sure to consult you first." Knowing Madeline could go on berating him for hours, he strolled into his office and closed the door.

Inside, he stared at the portrait of his distant ancestor, John Adams, one of America's founding fathers, and reflected on the World Council. Nineteen years, nineteen summits, and in some corners of the earth, they still struggled to maintain order.

For him, a born pioneer, the exploration and exploitation of space was the obvious solution. With Earth depleted, mining the moon and the asteroids was a win-win. It gave this planet's ecosystems a reprieve and provided resources to develop interstellar travel tech.

He did have one reservation; a fear, really, which he could never express—that the man who heckled his speech might be right, that the conqueror in humanity could win out over the explorer.

He sifted through the papers on his desk. A true technologist, Godric was untrusting of digital files after the third war. Skimming through the pages until he found what most heavily burdened his mind: the *Space Exploration Act.* It was exactly the legislation needed to properly return humanity to the last frontier.

Once the ionosphere was no longer lethal, after the devastation of the third world war, they began salvaging remaining satellites. Almost two decades had passed with no passage into space; fear of the unknown consumed the surface. Finally, proposals were drawn for journeys to Mars, the Belt, Callisto, Ganymede, and Titan. Lunar mining had resumed, asteroid mining was in the near future, and interstellar exploration around the corner.

Godric believed what he said, that the spirit of exploration had to be rekindled, but he was also painfully aware of history. The moons and planets beyond Earth would become a wild west, every corporation and private interest rushing to stake a claim.

If they stumbled on life, *would they act accordingly? Heed humanity's better angels? What if they were attacked, or worse, started a war, wiped out another species?*

This bill was the answer. If it passed, entities planning to explore areas hypothetically capable of supporting life would have to submit a proposal defending their ability to properly represent Earth in case of first contact.

It was controversial; its necessity doubted. Some thought it too controlling, the proposed consequences too Draconian. Godric thought it genius. Despite bottlenecking the very pioneering he hoped to foster, it would protect humanity from its own evils.

Space Exploration Act
Allows much wider latitude for companies and private interests to freely explore space. However, all persons travelling to space must pass rigorous Government testing and standards for competency, purpose, psychological fitness, and diplomacy.

It was the bill's providence that made him uneasy. It was submitted by an anonymous think-tank, no one taking official credit. Anyone choosing anonymity over potential political capital must have ulterior motives. He'd checked the usual suspects, but all came up clean.

Godric's speech being more than enough work for the first day, he stayed far from the summit. He'd return tomorrow, when he'd be in prime shape for the mandatory mingling.

A breeze beneath the jamb, so slight he'd forgotten about it, gusted. At once, the French doors opened revealing the blonde, razor-haired CEO of Outer Limits, Angelika On.

"Got a second, Ric?" Without waiting for an answer, she walked in.

Once, he might have been surprised by her forwardness. Not anymore. "What brings you here?"

Smiling serenely, she ran a hand along the globe bar in the center of the room. "As you know, we're working on an 8th gen rocket that could reach the outer planets in fifteen years. It would be much easier to build with more resources, so, long story short, I want your support on the Lunar Resource Allocation Bill."

"Right. Because as the council's space geek, my vote would go a long way. And here I'd hoped to get through the summit before this conversation. See, I also know you've built an empire on the heels of decisions I've made when I believed we were both working for the greater good of mankind."

Angelika circled like a wolf sizing up its prey, but spoke gently. "Godric, old friend, didn't the 'Great Explorer' bill of 2081 help elect you? Didn't the thousands of lunar mining jobs I created amply demonstrate the benefits of your beloved exploration? Yes, it helped position Outer Limits for the future, but does that preclude good intent? You must admit I've not only never gone back on my word, I've helped achieve our mutual goals quite a bit."

Leaning, she made herself seem vulnerable.

"Fair enough. So tell me, what benefits does passing *LRAB* bring us both?"

"Well, it allows companies..."

Godric snorted. "*A* company. Yours."

Angelika broadened her smile. "Today, but who knows what companies will benefit from in the future?"

Godric counted the worst possible offenders on his fingers. "Weyland, Yutani, Tyrell, Wallace..."

"Alright, Ridley Scott. As I was saying, it allows companies to mine, research, and explore without cumbersome W.C. oversight and fees, coupled with a prioritized use of the resulting resources by the only company capable of expanding the endeavor. That not only benefits free enterprise, but humanity as well. Besides, when else will you have a defining hand in establishing the basics for extraplanetary enterprise legislation?"

Godric smiled and leaned back. "As a matter of fact, there are several current opportunities which provide that option."

Let her chew on that for a moment.

So far, the conversation was a formality. She knew he was already in favor of the Lunar Bill. The CEO of the world's biggest engineering company didn't just stop-in to chat, even if they were friends for twenty-five years. There had to be something else.

"You're referring to the new 'space exploration' bill?" Her sarcasm was minimal, but apparent. "Or should I say the 'make space elitist bill?'"

"Which you're also behind, no?" He feigned confidence in the assertion but knew the tactic would prove ineffective against her.

"What makes you think that bill had anything to do with me?"

As expected, her poker face, endearing as it was, gave away nothing. She was good. Really good. Getting better with age, like a fine whisky.

LRAB - Lunar Resource Allocation Bill
Function is to permit a much broader scope of companies and private interests to freely mine the moon utilizing the W.C. as an arbiter.

"For starters, O.L. has an **IRAD** for prospecting on Titan. It's already pretty fleshed out: manifest, refinement capsules, chemical conversion pods..."

"Well, well, look who has access to classified documents."

"Makes sense," Godric continued. "The hydrocarbons alone would provide all the polymers Earth would ever need. Plus, someday soon Titan will be the most strategic spot in the outer system. The exploration bill has exactly your sort of long game written all over it."

Smiling innocently, she smoothly paced around the chair, fingertips stroking the smooth, blue leather. "I'm planning to run a business in the most inhospitable environment possible. Keeping the riff-raff at bay is sound risk reduction. I am, of course, fully confident that Outer Limits will exceed any expectations put forth by W.C. I don't hear you *complaining* exactly. The bill aligns perfectly with that idealism you desperately want to bring to the stars."

"That it does, but when something sounds too good to be true, I like knowing who's agenda I'm supporting."

She leaned over the chair back, closer to his face, and whispered, "I prefer to revel in one of the rare moments we both get what we want."

The Space Exploration Bill *was* hers. Sure of it, Godric bounded to his feet and extended a hand. "You always know how to get to me, Angie. You have my vote for the Lunar Resource Allocation Bill, but I'll be watching every step along the way, to keep you honest, of course."

She met his hand with a strong clasp. "Wouldn't have it any other way."

Sphinx-like, she exited, not a hint of pleasure. If her visit here was a success, or a failure, there was not a trace of joy or disappointment on her fleeting face. It was only after the doors gently closed behind her that she dared wonder: *Who really did submit that bill?*

Convinced she'd left with exactly what she came for, Godric thought, *O.L. really is the best company for the job. She hasn't lost my trust, not yet, anyway.*

IRAD - Internal Research and Development
A common engineering acronym that refers to a company's self funding for the purpose of mission or program risk-reduction, advanced concept development, and long-range, high-impact activities.

He sat in his four-legged armchair. The window overlooked a sprawling metropolis, but he dreamt of the emptiness faced by the old explorers as they wandered in the vast, pure, trackless ocean, peering about for anything new.

Hours passed before Godric headed to the duplex unit adjacent to the Council complex. It was elegantly simple, with a magnificent view of the East River and its seawalls. The pieces hung throughout by artists from Van Gogh to Escher to DaVinci, still providing inspiration and awe. It was the smallest dwelling any Adams ever occupied, but it was home, a haven from political posturing and positioning.

Changing into less formal attire, he jumped into his classic Tesla Roadster. Like most of his possessions, it was exceptional, having belonged to Elon Musk. It drove silently beneath a dense network of raised monorail tracks that made the skyscrapers almost impossible to see. Despite the walls, the subways had long been abandoned to flooding, leaving every remaining form of public transportation eternally packed.

Making it across town on the dark, crowded streets, he pulled into the Spear's entrance. The glass enclosed hotel adhered to a minimalist aesthetic but was no less magnificent.

A product of the 80's, Godric thought.

The concierge, a stout, prim man in a three-piece suit, greeted him. "Good evening, Councillor Adams. How may I help you today?"

Godric was always taking in his surroundings, especially name tags. "Good evening to you as well, Richard. I believe there's a key waiting for me. 11021?"

"Ah, yes, from Mr. Hubert."

Godric entered a lift tube that brought him to the door. Full of expectation, he inserted the key, but it didn't work. A fail-safe lock had been engaged.

Curious.

Nothing else to do, he knocked out a pattern he and Bernard created ages back: three times, once, then three times more. A murmur came from the other side.

"Greatest 24th century explorer?"

It being the 21st century, it might seem a peculiar question, but Godric knew the answer. With a sigh and fleeting grin, he supplied it.

"Jean-Luc Picard, USS Enterprise."

Bernard opened the door, chuckling. "Dear Ric, I *did* hope you'd remember."

"Must be three decades since we used *that* password."

Both laughed as they entered the comfort of the living room. Bernard poured two glasses of nineteen-year-old Harlem Gold and they sat, whereupon Bernard peered at him as if hoping he was ready to run off for an adventure.

"We go back, what—forty years? Our bond has always been rooted by a mutual love for exploration, a primal human need that, as you said in your speech, many no longer understand, let alone embrace."

"And most of them work on the other side of the aisle. With the new space program barely on its feet, a lot of the W.C. still sides with Mrs. Good, angling for the short-term gains. That said, there's a rumor you're going to meet with Angelika. Is it true? After she left you to the wolves?"

"She had her reasons, and there are bigger fish to fry. Back to your speech, though, with ecosystems continuing to collapse, we need to be thinking less about *global stabilization*, and look toward the next technological revolution, one that will allow us to evolve. Don't you agree, Councillor?"

The set-up, the ritual, the friendly pretense of formality, all conspired to make Godric feel as if he were playing chess and trying to look three moves ahead.

"Bernard, much as I love a full meal, it's been a long day. Can we get to dessert? Now that it's nearly possible, I'm guessing you want me to go explore the stars with you. I'd like nothing more, but I have to stay here to make sure we do it right, creating interplanetary law, ensuring we don't annihilate ourselves, or anyone we run into. Angelika thinks she can get us to the edge of the solar system in fifteen years. That's a monumental achievement, but there's no way I can commit to a thirty-year round trip."

Godric's passion was precisely why Bernard knew there was no one else for the job. Understanding his needs, he moved his final piece into position.

"What if you could do both? What if we could make the trip in five years?"

Eyes glazing over, Godric said one word. "How?"

Checkmate, Bernard thought.

- - -

By sunrise Godric was enthralled, yet unable to shake the feeling that the chess master was leaving something out. Bernard kept urging him to fight for the Interview section of the SEB. It read like a glorified interrogation, but Bernard insisted it would filter out reckless profiteers. Bold of him to fight for it, but odd considering what might lay ahead if they were ever interviewed themselves.

Space adventures aside, Day Two of the conference had arrived. There were major bills, including the SEB, that needed politicking.

Arriving at the great hall, he took in the words stretching across the plaster ceiling's gleaming mural:

"Those who follow lead not, while those who lead must follow."

Quite clever. Not long ago, a few brave nations chose to lead by creating the World Council, making themselves followers as well. Following the wishes of the people, they had created this omni-ruling government to exist within. As Godric contemplated this, a jovial man of tall stature and robust spirit trod toward him.

"Godric! My dear, come here this instant!"

Breaking his gaze, Godric smiled broadly. "Marcus, my dear friend, how are you?"

His warm embrace, matching Marcus' zeal, turned a few heads.

"Wonderful, my old friend. Splendid. You know the lunar mining bill? We should have a chat on it."

"Oh? When were you thinking?"

"Today. Lunch."

Unsure what to make of the request, Godric obliged. Marcus Medneon was a childhood friend and as CEO of Space Oasis, perfectly suited to balance the coming race.

Entering the private sector after the war, he ascended like a rocket literally buying one to helm a lunar salvage crew and bring mining back to the moon. He and Angelika were peas in a pod but different in style and strategy. Mining was his end goal, while Angelika saw it as a means to further expansion.

"Excellent! *Frequency* at 1:00pm. I'll have the table in back just for us."

The amiable encounter left Godric conveniently cheery for the coming hours of handshakes and small talk. There were hundreds of people at the Summit, all with a cause or an idea for a solution to the overarching problem the world was facing: resource depletion.

He called to redheaded Councillor passing by. "Janine, do I have your support on SEB?"

"Dunno, Ric. Do I have your support on the *Border Reduction Bill?*"

The easy answer produced an easy smile. "Of course. It's long overdue."

"I don't know how Ann Marie puts up with that boyish charm of yours," she joked. "Coffee Thursday?"

"Yep—you, me, Anne and Robert."

He continued the waltz—negotiating, trading, teaching, learning. His enthusiasm... contagious. Some likened him to JFK, the charismatic U.S. president, who mandated the first manned moon mission. Like Kennedy, he'd lost an older brother to war. It was the day Fred died in the nuclear fire that devoured Pyongyang that Godric abandoned engineering and devoted himself to preserving the ideals his brother died to protect.

After dozens of chats, he lost track of time. Paige, fortunately, was always a step ahead.

Frequency
A restaurant with nanoboard walls that depicts the current night sky. Owned and operated by Neil Brooks.

Border Reduction Bill
A piece of legislation designed to eliminate border control of remaining 27 former sovereign nations that were slow to recognize the new NA zone designations.

"12:30, Godric. Should I call the car?"

"Yes, Paige, thank you. Can we schedule some time next week with Richard Rockwell? I want to see him before the Regional Council convenes."

"The usual breakfast meeting?"

"Perfect."

In the pickup zone, Godric entered his day car, a rare Aston Martin DB9. Multiple modifications were needed to make it street legal. For one, the use of fossil fuels as barbaric as spears, it was now fully electric.

Turning at Washington and Fairfax, he sped to reach Frequency in time for lunch with Marcus. Upon his arrival, Neil Brooks, the owner and designer, stepped out from a tumultuous black hole simulation to greet him. Frequency was always a treat.

"Our champion! How are you? Marcus is waiting in the Pleiades."

"You're too kind." Godric pointed at the ceiling, actually a *Nanoboard* that projected a crisp real-time image of the cosmos. "I love those stars… business good?"

"Fantastic, especially since Space Oasis approved our new satellite feed. Now the place is everything I ever wanted."

"Excellent. Love to hear more, but Marcus awaits."

Godric remembered enough celestial navigation from his Kepler days to follow the galaxy-covered halls to a quiet back room. There, the Pleiades' seven sisters shimmered above a silver table set for two, scotch poured and waiting.

Marcus, in an impeccably tailored suit, faced the entrance, as usual so to survey his surroundings. Grinning, he gestured for Godric to join him.

He did. "You know I don't need much convincing to lunch at Freq., but what's so urgent it couldn't wait until after the summit when we both have more time?"

"There are projects at the lunar station requiring personal oversight. I launch in two days and may not be back for months. I wanted us to talk before I left."

Godric returned the smile. "About?"

Nanoboard O2L
A visual and tactile display medium, it is a screen comprised of tiny shifting magnetic LED cubes that can stack to generate augmented reality images and with textures. The Nanoboard was created by Lily Parsons of Outer Limits. It began an early prototype for the Nanofloor.

The powerfully built man shrugged. "The Lunar Allocation Bill. It will expand mining operations three sectors northwest of the South Pole-Aitken Basin Crater. I think it should be put on hold."

That was a surprise. The ask made no sense. It would cost Space Oasis millions. He was throwing back a clear win. Godric leaned for the obvious question. "Why?"

"Because we can't utilize the new sectors as quickly as Angelika claims OL can." Marcus said with an indifferent tone, and continued. "If I thought they could actually do what they're promising, frankly, I wouldn't mind, but the estimates aren't believable. They might have the largest presence in space, but they can't build six new mines, five refineries, and sixteen orbital platforms in four years. If I'm right and they botch it, it'll cost billions to undo the damage, not to mention a loss of political capital we can ill afford. Her greed could derail the space program for decades." He wasn't angry, but his intense dislike for OL's questionable plan was painfully clear.

"Angelika plays close to the chest. You believe she's actually lying?"

He gestured uncertainty. "She's certainly exaggerating... and wildly. Strategically, it makes sense. She's worried Space Oasis is building too fast, that we'll catch up. Boosting OL operations now would limit our ability to compete. I love Angelika. I love everything Outer Limits does, but for everyone's sake, for the sake of common sense, the expansion should be slowed."

Godric could see Angelika's thinking in it, but what Marcus asked was no small task. It would also be a step backwards for Godric's vision. Was there anything else to it?

"Marcus, do you support SEB?"

The question left little room for an ambiguous answer, an anathema in politics and business, but Marcus replied casually. "Absolutely. It's brilliantly written. To use 19th century terms, it will open the frontier, remove the burden of exploration from a centralized bureaucracy, and hand it to the people. Anyone would be able to go to space. Well, not everyone. There's an elitism baked in by the cost of the technology, not to mention that clever interview to prove intent. Without it, though, the expansion will be perilously reckless. My only concern is the bill's origin. Any light to shed on that?"

Rather than mention his theory about Angelika, he said, "No, and I'd really like to know." No further information forthcoming, he raised his glass. "Well, Marcus, I do trust you when it comes to risk assessment, so cheers."

It would be another hour before Godric insisted he had to get back to the summit. But it was only after enjoying a glorious chocolate-covered banana almond fudge bar, that Marcus finally relented.

"Enjoy the summit; give Angelika my best. She won't be happy with me, but I'm sure it won't be a surprise. She has to know it can't work—not yet, at least."

"Be safe up there."

They parted ways, far from a childhood of staring longingly at a few winking stars, yet much closer than they realized.

CHAPTER 5
COUNTERPARTS

The cascading Icelandic waterfalls silenced by the mansion's giant windows were hypnotic. The pass of a raven security drone did nothing to distract from their beauty.

Bernard stared at the undulating ribbons of mist as he spoke. "...I need a fusion drive ship capable of extended duration without resupply... and the ten best people in these fields."

He took a folded slip from his pocket and put it on the table. After a moment's trepidation, he slid it across the smooth bristlecone pine to the woman across from him. Angelika read it, raised her eyebrow briefly, then tossed it into a magnificent obsidian and quartz fireplace where it crackled into nothing.

"Quite the list, Bernard William Hubert. And very interesting choices for a space-crew. And where, exactly, will your mighty band of *Avengers* travel to again?"

All they'd been through and she still poked fun. Still, he appreciated her ability to reference the comics he loved in these intense moments of pressure and purpose.

As he debated how to deliver it, what cadence to use, and what the revelation would mean, his response bounced between tongue and teeth. Angelika was seated, but seemed somehow taller. Was it her posture? Her pale blonde hair, cut with razor precision around her head, as perfect as a planet's orbit?

Finally, he peered over his spectacles and met the piercing green eyes. "Beyond the Kuiper Belt, to the last known position of Voyager 2."

"Jesus, Bernard! Wasn't being blackballed by the world science community enough for you the first time?"

Poked the wrong way, he roared, "I was a scapegoat! If our project had been revealed, support for any scientific research would have vanished."

Angelika tsked. "Scapegoat or not, you barely survived that trial."

"But I did, no thanks to you, because I was innocent. Not a shred of evidence against me, but *someone* was guilty. The CERN antimatter stockpile was never intended to be more than a microgram, but there was enough to create a blast explosion magnitudes larger than our worst projections."

She took on a calmer tone. "Let the dead rest. There are plenty who'd still love to see you hang, literally."

"My life's work was destroyed. And Darren, we lost Darren that day. How could you think for a moment I was a part of that?"

Her face twitched, as if she were actually holding back tears. "I didn't!"

"No? Then why on Earth didn't you cover for me? Give Searcher what she needed to exonerate me instead of supplying gasoline for the pyre. Do you even know the truth, or were you too busy protecting your reputation to bother looking for it?"

Collecting herself, she peered about as if someone might be watching, even in her private estate. "I know Darren was supposed to return to OL, but you took his place. Why did you do that, Bernard? Are the rumors true? Was there some other experiment that could have destroyed the antimatter containment?"

Knowing this moment would come didn't prepare him as well as he'd hoped. There was a lot he'd have to face, not only here with Angelika, but with Lily and others.

"Darren was working on a mini-black hole, but it couldn't have caused the incident. His prototype had been stable over 2 weeks. It's why he was so excited. He came to me, upset he'd have to abandon it, so I told him to stay, that I'd deal with your wrath. The explosion happened as I was leaving the facility."

The revelation was the only thing Bernard had ever seen throw Angelika's game. She didn't know her next move, what to think, or feel. She couldn't even adjust her expression properly.

"Why didn't you tell me sooner?"

"Why?" Bernard scoffed. "Because when Jones cornered me in the hospital, you chose to protect yourself by telling her you'd no idea why I was leaving. On the basis of that alone, I was fired, removed from my advisory positions, tried as a traitor and terrorist. You can't imagine the pain that caused. Lisa had to move her work to another city. Isaac changed schools because of the bullying. And you fueled Lily's cause to despise me.

"And where were you when I was made out a madman for claiming an unknown intelligence was involved? The issue was never my sanity, just people's ability to see only a square when presented with a cube. The same sort who thought a fusion drive was a fantasy, but you know we were *this* close six years ago. Why didn't I tell you sooner? Because I haven't been inclined to share. But, here, right now, I'm giving you a chance to make up for some of that, to help ensure all that work wasn't for nothing."

Having regained most of her composure, Angelika shook her head. "If you're trying to appeal to some sense of ethical obligation, forget it. Last time you convinced me to risk everything to further your research, it literally blew up in our faces."

"I'm not some penny ante scientist peddling nonsense for grant money; I am, supposedly, your lifelong friend! You owe me!"

"My confidence in your work is irrelevant. You know there are powers that-be, then and now, that won't allow your papers, let alone proof, to go public. Let it lie. You have Isaac to worry about. He's sixteen; he needs you."

Bernard used the expected parental lecture to clean his glasses. He knew Angelika would never accept his proposal carte blanche. Her shrewdness was one of the qualities that once captivated him completely. What happened to them was eons ago... long before he married Lisa... even before Angelika took Outer Limits from being an unknown bankruptcy in the making to a preeminent scientific conglomerate.

Still, Angelika's curiosity seemed piqued, if only as a thought experiment. "The operation would be far too large to keep quiet. We'd need to hide in plain sight. Which means the board, the World Council and the scientific community will need a damn good reason to return you to the fold. AND before we even got to those barriers, I'd need a lot more than cosmic coincidence to convince me an intelligence was involved."

Bernard spoke softly. "Voyager 2 went offline fifteen seconds after CERN's containment failure. That's less time than it took light to travel that distance. But if they had something traveling faster than..."

She threw up her hands. "Enough! You try floating *FTL* on top of aliens, you'll be crucified."

He peered over his newly-shined glasses. "Sounds like you still care about me."

"Don't you dare go there. OF COURSE I care. You don't know the half of what I've done for you, Hue, or how far I'd be willing to go."

FTL - Faster Than Light
Being capable of moving at velocities greater than the speed of light. "We need ships with FTL capability to make the interstellar journey."

"I won't stop, Angelika. I can't live not knowing what happened to CERN. I can't face Isaac with half-answers; I need to..." An idea hit him. "Those barriers you mentioned. What if I could get the mission crew to convince the world for us?"

Raising an eyebrow, she headed for an ornate corner bar. Taking her time, pretending to admire the landscape, she uncorked a bottle of Riesling.

Her tone became subtly patronizing. "How do you propose doing that, Hue?"

"William," he said, matter-of-factly. "They'd listen to William Hunt. Everyone does. He's the modern-day Carl Sagan."

Field Medalist, part-time professor, full-time genius, his old schoolmate sat on more boards than a chess piece. His work was bleeding edge, whether in quantum programming or revolutionary advances in nanotech. Even more impossibly, it made math *cool*.

Angelika returned to her chair. "You want to risk dragging him down too?"

"Please. He'll drag us up. He's smart. He must know CERN wasn't my doing."

"Then why has he remained quiet?"

"Probably for the same reasons as you—to protect himself. But he'd know how unifying it would be for the people in those fields to reach the edge of known space. Humanity hasn't done anything like it since the first moon landing."

"Public appeal does more for me than ethical obligations."

"I don't give a queefing quark about the masses. I'm talking about restoring a sense of purpose to the species."

"...and to you." Angelika added wryly.

He smirked. "You underestimate two things: pride and human ambition."

Rather than dissuade him, Angelika's eye-roll only gave Bernard a second wind. The roaring fire crackled in sync with his rising cadence. "Space has always had a polarizing effect: love at seeing the curve of the earth, panic at the realization we're suspended in a cold, dark void. Either way, it's always been beautifully revealing.

Who wants to be that person who, when asked, said no and then spent forever wondering why?"

Her face remained blank. "There's no financial incentive."

"There is. Alien tech."

Her eyes narrowed. "Are you actually trying to turn me into a stereotypical, sci-fi greedy CEO? Besides, you don't know for certain that there is any."

"True, but I wouldn't be going unless I was convinced there was."

She subtly shifted the subject. "Do you honestly think your crew will be so equally convinced, that they'd sacrificed thirty years of their lives to get there and back again?"

"Five."

Surprised again, Angelika frowned. He could see her gears turning, practically hear her think: *He couldn't possibly, unless...*

"Yes, Angelika. We resurrected Phoenix Fires under a new name, Project Pegasus, and kept it secret, even from you."

"Don't play with me, Bernard. You mean you and Simon crunched some numbers. Don't think for a second I'm going to open O.L.'s propulsion program to you because you passed a paternity test."

Bernard balked. "I don't need O.L.'s proprietary research. The design is complete. We've even run a successful field test. The ship *can* be built. I just need the resources."

She pushed her chair, stood and strode to the massive, curved windows. Her back was to him, her arms folded across her breasts. Beyond the silent, silver ribbons of the glacial-melt waterfall, snow-capped peaks ringed the horizon.

She was back in control, nigh impossible to read. Even as a wild teenager, it wasn't possible to tell when she was powerfully emotional or deadly serene. He had no idea what she would say.

"I want the fusion drive, Bernard."

When she faced him, they exchanged cold stares.

"Even for what I ask, handing you the future of spaceflight seems a steep price, Ang."

He wondered if using her nickname went too far. He was the only one who ever called her *Ang* and lived to tell the tale. In a single, fluid motion, she glided back into her chair. Her silence bade him to continue.

"Add to that, the hard work of everyone at CORE would be taken without giving them any recognition. Trillions for Outer Limits and an undying legacy for you."

"First, Bernard, my legacy doesn't need your inventions to be immortal. Second, who do you think funded CORE to begin with? NASA?"

He waited until she smirked before delivering his last surprise. "Are you referring to the forty-seven Swiss Bank and Kingdom of Deseret accounts? The ones that distributed funds through 267 proxy servers with 256 bit encryption, then masked them as randomized private charitable donations for the past five years?"

To her credit, this time, Angelika relegated her shock to the sort of facial expression one gets when a trapdoor opens beneath their feet.

Bernard put on his own smirk and wore it well. "Think I didn't know? Having lost your two best scientists, you needed an ace in the hole—even if it meant funding another company."

She forced herself back to detachment, though now it was clearly feigned. "How?"

Everything on the table, Bernard felt a wellspring of repressed emotions.

"The best astrophysicist and engineer in the world doesn't simply vanish because illiterate plebeians wish it. You should've watched my island of misfit toys more closely. It was easy to find disgruntled hackers who sympathized with my plight. You threw me under the bus to distance yourself from the accident. A professional decision I respect. Pointless to have us both fall, but admit it—you miss me, Ang— you miss my mind, my intelligence, my vision, and yes, my ego."

She countered with her own unfiltered truth. "Bernie, until a minute ago, I didn't know why you changed flights with Darren. It was strange not knowing, especially after we'd been close, but 4,000 people died. It was under surveillance, my phones were tapped. All of OL was under a microscope. Even with my resources, there was no safe way to contact you. And you'd been sloppy with your secrets. If there'd been no explosion, sure, it would have gone unnoticed, but Searcher Jones found traces of the duplicate data packages you and Darren created. My choice was either burning you or pinning it all on Darren. That, I would never do. So, yes, I let you burn. With all the investigations and audits, Phoenix Fires was going to die anyway. But you're quite correct, I knew I had to keep you and your research close, that I would somehow fund any facility you started, in secret. I'm sorry it came to this, but think about it. It was the only way to get us where we are today."

Where we are today. Bernard's anger was blunted by the reminder of destiny. It did not, however, keep him from getting in the last word.

"To be clear, then, you used CORE as your under-the-radar pet and six years later, after your betrayal, here I am, a good dog delivering as expected. Fine. I'll give you the future. We'll finish what we started with Darren. The dollar signs should blind your stakeholders enough to let me focus on finding out what really happened."

He realized he was standing, arms outstretched, sweat glistening on his forehead.

Angelika slowly clapped her hands. "There's the man I know: unbowed, unbent, unbroken. Good to see him again. I'm convinced, Bernard, not because I believe in the mission, because I believe in you. You'll get your ship and crew. I already have a few in mind."

She raised her wine glass. Still flush with feeling, he did likewise.

Angelika boomed; Bernard echoed, "For Darren."

CHAPTER 6

THE KEPLER INSTITUTE

The sun was a cool, bright orb, barely noticeable over the eastern horizon. The chilly dawn was a fitting end to a hot, energetic summer that was already a distant memory to the students at the Kepler Institute for Enhanced Learning. Classes had been back in swing long before the high-sloped trees could turn yellow. Brisk winds accompanied the *hurling* and discblade meets, annual design project proposals past due.

The singular learning haven had the architecture to match. Lofted spires of rock and glass were woven seamlessly into the mountainside. Impossible structures were hewn from the ridges: tall ponderosa pines covered in moss rose between a marvelous design matching the technological wonders it contained.

Along a forest path between the library and Nanobot lab, a great grey owl perched motionlessly on a dead branch. It remained impassive as the gleam and blur of two tiny drones zipped by. One fired a practice laser, the second evaded the blast by changing into a metallic tree-swallow. Students walked beneath the owl, ran, hover-boarded, but it remained stock-still. Even leaves landing on its eyes yielded no response.

Hurling
An outdoor team game of ancient Gaelic Irish origin. Known as the fastest field sport on earth, Hurling combines the skills of baseball, hockey, and lacrosse. The game has prehistoric origins and has been played for 4,000 years. One of Ireland's native Gaelic games, it shares a number of features with Gaelic football, such as the field and goals, the number of players, and much terminology. Two teams of 15 players compete to score the most points by hitting the ball, called a sliotar, between the opposing team's goalposts in one high speed, high scoring, high octane sport.

Hours later, a teenage boy strolled into view awaking its attention. Isaac Hubert seemed typical for his age: lanky, untidy, lost in thought as Stravinsky's Firebird Suite flowed from his tiny nano-earbuds. The final overture beginning, he stopped about ten meters from the owl to gaze at the trees. His first astrophysics exam was coming up as well as discblade practice, office hours with Professor Hunt, the secret weekend camping trip, and his impulse engine core was currently 3D printing in engineering. Oh—and had to submit his proposal for the ***Explorers' Cup.***

A green-eyed, dark-haired girl approaching, he paused the music with a seemingly magical finger-flex. At Kepler, science was often indistinguishable from magic. In this case, it was a palmer: a partially nanotech controller that hid by quickly orbiting his wrist. Voice commands were so 2049, not to mention impractical to use in class.

They exchanged a secret handshake. "Hey, Chels. Why the covert meeting?"

A monarch butterfly fluttering around her, Chelsea gave him an imploring look. "You know why. You'd think five years would bring closure, but every fall they re-up their hatred for you."

He retorted indignantly. "Reacting irrationally is why we nearly blew up the planet in the mid-twentieth century. My father's purported actions should not—and do not—have any bearing on my work or sense of self. If some find it invigorating to focus their anger on a tangible target, so be it. They're only holding themselves back."

"Right..." Chelsea said. It was the fifth time in five years he'd said exactly the same thing. "You should know Andy Dufranes tinkered with his ***lightsaber*** safeties. If he hits you at the next duel, instead of a 150 volt shock, you'll get a nasty plasma burn. He'll make it look like a core instability feedback loop built up the charge."

Unperturbed, Isaac watched the palmer shimmer around his wrist. "If he tries it, I'll make him look like Anakin fighting Count Dooku for the first time."

Chelsea ignored the reference. "We're still a go for Saturday. Matthew imbedded a thirty second window in the northeast proximity LIDAR. With the all-day hurling

---

Explorers' Cup
Kepler Institute students compete in an annual innovation challenge. The winner must provide a thesis on their best and boldest innovation, a feasibility plan, and why their project deserves to be funded. The winning student gets an internship at Outer Limits, a grant for project funding/research, and a lifetime networking opportunity.

LIDAR: Light Detection and Ranging
A surveying method that was created by Malcolm Stitch of the Hughes Aircraft Company for the National Center for Atmospheric Research. It measures distance to a target by illuminating the target with laser light and measuring the reflected light with a sensor. Differences in laser return times and wavelengths can then be used to make digital 3D representation of the target. LIDAR was developed as an evolution of radar, but with the power and accuracy of lasers, to map distance and features with tremendous accuracy.

tournament and the W.C. guest dinner at 19:00, no one should notice us gone."

Isaac adored tinkering; the lab was home, but camping, escaping to the wild far from the judgmental, was equally sublime. "They'd better not. It took four months to build the nanofiber tents. They're under 2 lbs, Chels: waterproof yet breathable, they can withstand temperatures below freezing, winds to 120 km/h, and they support 40 cm of snowfall."

"Impressive, Tycho"

He ignored the compliment. "Transportation set?"

"Lydia's *borrowing* two jetpacks from the field house. Their transponders were damaged and haven't been repaired yet. I'll have my hoverboard. You?"

Isaac found the question mildly offensive. "My new body drone config, of course. The engine's printing now."

Chelsea had seen him do wonders but still worried about the expectations he set for himself. "You're actually planning to use that crazy attempt to recreate ancient comic book tech?" She gave him a playfully hard punch in the arm. "It'd better work, Tycho. Remember last time?

Isaac rubbed his bicep. "It will."

Most likely. He was fully confident in his math, reasonably confident in the 3D printer's accuracy, but only mildly confident he wouldn't have to fight potential saboteurs, like Dufrane.

"I'm infinitely more worried about Matthew getting his homework done. Did you see Dr. Robinson's last assignment? Orgo might be as difficult for him as the 6th *Cycles* complain about."

"That's some harsh academic judgement from the guy about to try for the Explorers' Cup. Matthew will be fine. Have fun doing your thesis over midterms."

"Please. I've got this juggling act down to a..."

The butterfly fluttering around Chelsea glowed blue. She put her hand out and

---

Cycle
An annual education term for a student under the W.C. academic restructuring. Most schools run in 4 or 8 cycle terms for a completed degree.

it glided to her palm. "What is it, Nothra?"

The butterfly opened its wings and projected a tiny holograph of their surroundings. A blinking red dot was about forty feet away.

"Damn it, something's broadcasting." Chelsea hissed. "Take it out."

Its orange and black morphed into matted metal scales and it zipped away, wings locked. As if rocket-propelled, it swooped in growing, concentric circles, then split the air between two trees as it made for its target. The great grey owl lit from its perch, soaring across the glen. In hot pursuit, Nothra barrel-rolled through the owl's wing like a molten razor severing it.

With an unearthly screech, the owl dropped like a stone. A sharp, crunch accompanied its impact on the forest floor. Nothra morphed back to its natural hues and went back to fluttering, restoring the peace and silence.

Isaac and Chelsea headed to the owl. Mute, it lay shattered, its former glory reduced to metal shards, synth feathers, and scattered tech. Fine carbon fiber bones and wiring protruding what remained of the body. It wasn't completely silent; a slow, mechanical clicking came from within. The cracked glassy eyes had a subtle orange glow.

Any technologically proficient student body would be rife with surveillance, hacking, and the appropriate countermeasures. Nearly as much R&D came out of Kepler dorms as O.L. 35% of 8th cycles already had job offers from them. If Isaac's life had played as expected, he'd been one of them, like his father. Alas, that door was closed.

"Nice job snuffing it," Isaac said, "but why didn't Nothra pick it up sooner?"

"It wasn't transmitting, just recording. Someone got impatient. Lucky us."

"That kills our camping plans," Isaac said angrily. "You should broaden Nothra's frequency range. It's crucial we know when we're being watched."

"I know! I'll look into it!" Unwilling to take all the blame, she eyed him. "And where's Albus? He would have detected that recording signal."

"Which is why he's in the lab guarding the 3D printer." He put a hand on her shoulder. "You should go. They'll be coming for this."

She recognized the fiery look. "Dammit, Tycho, not again. You're going to play right into their hands."

"Maybe, but I'll enjoy it."

"Fine. Come find us after," she said, walking backward. Northra following, she turned and jogged away.

Her footsteps fading, Isaac put down his backpack and unzipped the main pouch. Pretending to look for something, he reached inside and listened carefully. Other than a woodpecker's thrum, there was nothing audible to the human ear. Fortunately, his earpods had a nifty mod for such occasions. Another finger motion and a microphone array brought the forest alive with sound.

Now he heard something—a whining accompanied by a low hum. Sonar interpolation told him an object was blistering right at him from a hundred meters. In a fraction of a second, he calculated the approach vector: *5 o'clock!*

In a single motion, he drew his **discblade** from the backpack, jumped and rotated so that his arms swung down and around in time to deflect the projectile.

With a sharp ping and thud, the rogue discblade buried itself in a tree trunk.

Adrenaline pumping, he shouted at the woods. "If you want to play, all you have to do is ask!"

Chuckling menacingly, three boys and two girls stepped into the glen and surrounded him. Naomi, a tall girl with copper skin and green eyes spoke first.

"You really *do* think you're better than the rest of us, don't you?"

Isaac smirked. "No, just smarter."

One boy spat. "Pretentious prick."

"Hey, Howard, at least I didn't shift the bell curve eighteen points left in vibrations class."

Discblade
A fast paced team sport where each player is equipped with an hollow disc encoded to them that is thrown, guided, hovered, and boomeranged. One member of each team carries a disc, through which a ball must be thrown by another teammate to score, but only in specific locations. Two team members temporarily neutralize other players by hitting them with discs. Discs may be blocked by discs or very rarely caught, which eliminates the thrower from the game. There are 9 to a side; the field is a hexagon or circle. Discblade began when a group of Kepler Institute students tried to replicate the TRON combat disc wars inside their dorm. The plans for a disc were stolen by a Jefferson Hall student who was dating a Kepler student. Soon after, Jefferson Hall's first Discblade Club was founded by Christopher Dryson. In time it became a SETI varsity level sport and went global after WWIII.

He nodded proudly at the broken owl. "Yeah? At least I'm not stupid enough to talk in front of a drone."

"That feathered toy? Haven't you ever heard of a buzzer? Or don't they teach 1st cycles Spying 101 anymore?"

Isaac's taunts did nothing to diminish the victorious look on Howard's pimply face. "We heard you *buzzing* about the Explorers' Cup."

"Damn right. I'm going to use the grant to prototype a space elevator."

The five howled with laughter. One actually fell to the ground. Naomi wiped tears from her cheeks. "Oh, that's rich. What's next? A warp drive? A transporter? Last I looked it was 2091, not 2391. But don't let that stop you. Clearly, you can't distinguish science from science-fiction anyway."

The dour Brian stopped laughing to sneer. "Jesus, like father, like son. Always needing to be needed. You should step aside; this contest isn't for people like you."

"But it is for someone like you?" Isaac scoffed. "So, you can be like *your* father and blow up your lab trying to build antimatter containment without a proper protocol, costing Iron Corp. billions? If you want to talk realistically, what would *any* of you do with the grant? Pioneer earth-shattering breakthroughs in the field of gossip? It's the only thing you're good at. None of you would even be here if your parents weren't filthy rich."

Brian leered. "More hypocritical bullshit from the son of the man who destroyed CERN and killed 4,000 people."

Isaac's discblade hand twitched. He gave Brian such a disturbing look; the bully backed up a step.

"We don't care who gets it," Howard said, "as long as it's not you. Nobody wants a mass murderer's name on a published paper."

Isaac turned to him coldly. "Continuing to misplace blame on my father for your mother's death at CERN won't make it true."

Howard hissed. "But the part about aliens being responsible *is* true?"

Many at Kepler lost parents or siblings at CERN or knew someone who had. His arrival had been met with hostility, bullying, and ostracization. By the end of his 1st cycle, he'd set a record for being involved in fights, but he'd learned to fight back.

Isaac brought his foot down crushing what was left of the avian drone. "So, did you like that owl, Howard? How long did it take to build?"

Abandoning all pretense, Howard dove at him. Isaac sidestepped, but before a victorious smirk could form, Brian took out his right leg with a kick to his knee. He fell face first, a pine cone slashing his cheek. Bleeding, he dropped his discblade and tried to roll away.

A kick slammed Isaac's abdomen. He coughed up blood. As more blows found their mark, Isaac flexed his fingers in a complicated sequence. After crunch of pine and a pained yelp, the beating stopped. He got to his knees, gasping before standing and spitting more blood. His ribs were throbbing, but he smiled through his bloodstained teeth at the loathing and bewilderment on the faces of his attackers.

The discblade that tried to hit him hovered protectively nearby. The five rubbed and held the bleeding spots on their arms, legs, and backs where it had cut them.

With calm finality, he announced, "That's quite enough."

Howard was bug-eyed. "How? That's MY disc!"

"Second rule of hacking—never let anyone touch your stuff. When I deflected it, I also transferred a *controller virus*. As you've seen, it not only let me take over, it disabled some of the safeties.

One of the girls, Elisha, shouted. "You'll regret this!"

"I will? How about we all walk up to Professor Hyderion's office and tell him how five students stalked and beat one lanky boy in the woods?"

The five shuffled uneasily.

Having no choice about the hatred for his father and himself, he relished this fleeting moment of control. But real control meant knowing the smart choice. He never reported incidents like this. Snitching was a sign of weakness from those

---

Controller Virus

A computer virus that gives complete control of a discrete tech item. Developed by Chinese hackers, controller viruses came to popularity in the mid 21st century alongside the rise of robotics. While controlling entire security systems or defense grids took tremendous effort, a controller virus could be locally uploaded directly to a target, overwhelming networking protocol, and giving full control. They were widely employed when the Chinese were fighting US robot troops in dense Asian cities.

who lacked the imagination to create options.

"Now get out of here." He nodded up at the disc. "Once you're far enough, it'll find its way back to you."

Naomi snarled. "The world will never forgive your father, and it will never accept you!"

The hovering disc wobbled threateningly. Isaac's response was icy. "My humanity wears thin."

Quickly, they slunk into the trees leaving the wrecked owl behind.

Isaac eyed it. "Hm. Keep what you kill."

With a gentle upward thrust of thumb, he restored the music in his nano-earbuds and, for the next twenty minutes, salvaged what he could of the drone. Much of that time was spent cursing at the pain in his knee. When he finished, almost as an afterthought, he smacked the air sending Howard's disc back to its defeated owner.

Reaching the trail to campus center, a light wind patted his shoulder reminding him... *Oh no, Hunt's office hours. I have to see him today.*

Limping aggressively, he knew that even without the bloody cheek, his wounds would be tough to hide. Thankfully, he emerged on a campus green full of things more interesting to look at than him. Students were everywhere; tossing holo-Frisbees, playing music, watching pre-recorded holograms, testing body shields (always amusing to watch), and training morphic drone pets, not unlike Nothra and Albus.

Two girls in matching Kraftwerk t-shirts live-programmed their golden eagle and diamondback rattler for an adaptive strategy battle. When the eagle tried grabbing the snake in its talons, the rattler's scales shifted into protective spines driving it off.

Surreal to outsiders, the flat oval green stretched hundreds of meters periodically interrupted by massive granite slabs. At their center, a natural spring bubbled into a serpentine waterway that spiraled along before disappearing into a cave.

To Isaac's left was the nanotech lab: indistinguishable from the mountains save a few windows and one door hewn into the rock. And to his right, the large triangular stones of the planetarium dome.

Keeping to the shade of a forty-meter ponderosa pine grove, Isaac ducked three racing drones. Evolution moved faster at Kepler. Even so, his father had taught him to be a history junky. Most students found the past too barbaric to contemplate: a reflection of the World Council's efforts to move away from painful memories for the sake of unification. But his father found many truths about the future in the past—patterns that repeated—the same flawed governments repeating the same inventions rediscovered after each civilization fell. Now humanity was at the edge of space travel, yet it still had its internal conflicts. Memory made wisdom, not just technology.

Wondering what his great-great-grandfather, Edwin S. Hubert, would think of it all, he limped past edgy gals doing hoverboard tricks on the slabs, while the jocks played **Hunterball**, a 21st Century game based on wit as much as physical prowess. Isaac occasionally played, a mild surprise to friends, as he was seldom seen outside his lab. But it explained how he managed to deflect Howard's disc.

Watching students cheered as the floating hunter angrily buzzed among the 3rd cycle players. When it accelerated at one, the boy used a holo-mace to deflect it. There were whoops and howls as the purple ball ricocheted, forcing an opponent to eat dirt in order to avoid being hit.

Meanwhile, Isaac stoically limped to an unoccupied tree at the edge of the clearing overlooking the glorious ridge. Exhausted and aching, he slid to the ground.

"Saac, whatcha doing there all alone?"

Chloe Peppercorn, a goofy, awkward, yet somehow still incredibly cool looking girl walked up. She was the daughter of world-renowned cosmologist Hannah Peppercorn, who not only worked with his father, but was one of the few who believed in his innocence.

Isaac smiled. "Hi Chloe"

Her blue hair, blue eyes, and ever-present **Hoverhoop** always attracted attention.

Hunterball
An individual elimination combat sport. First played by SETI students, it was concepted as an attempt to replicate the "snitch" from Harry Potter. The rules are to hit the the other players with the "Hunter," a small, flying, limited AI ball that tries to attack each of the players, choosing targets based on likelihood of success. The hunter can be hit with physical tools but is also programmed to be deflected by holograms. There can be anywhere from 2-7 players, for >7 another "hunter" is added. Usually played outdoors, even higher intensity versions are played in courts similar to racquetball.

Hoverhoop
A levitating hula hoop. If imparted with enough initial velocity, miniaturized airfoils and microjets will keep the hoop afloat. Created by Rumiko Miyazaki of Japan, hoverhoops were first used by ravers seeking to evolve the LED flowarts by looking for new ways to push performance boundaries. While giving a hoop the ability to fly defeated the purpose of hooping, it was beautiful and became very popular post WW3.

Unfortunately, she also drew some glares his way. "Don't mind them. I've been experimenting with my *nano-cream,* and I'm pretty sure I've got it perfect. You look like a perfect test subject."

Without asking, she pulled him behind a tree away from prying eyes, and Chloe rubbed a clear gel across his face. The bleeding stopped. With a gasp of amused excitement, he looked at Luna, rolled up his pants leg, and pointed at his knee. She applied the goo with similar results.

"The pain's gone!"

Minutes later, his bruises were soothed, his cuts scabbing over. "Luna, *that's* an invention, right there!"

"Don't mention it, and don't tell anyone. My patents on the thirty-seven different genetic pathways that make it work haven't gone through yet." She plopped down next to him. "I can stay awhile if you like; they've got a good match going."

She gestured to the students still battling the tiny ball of chaos.

"That's okay. I told Chelsea I'd catch up with her at the dorm. Thanks for patching me up." They exchanged a secret handshake, and she skipped toward the Hunterball madness.

He felt lucky for a change. There weren't a ton of people like Chloe or Chelsea here. Smart didn't necessarily mean enlightened or compassionate. When he was twelve, his parents asked if he wanted to transfer. Loving Kepler, not wanting to give his tormentors satisfaction, he refused. Now, he was top of his class, discblade proficient, and savvy enough to avoid the wrong sort of attention from the faculty.

The attacks even diminished as he grew more formidable, but some, like Naomi and Howard, wouldn't let things go. Truth be told, they provided a stimulating challenge that helped temper his expectations of people. It also helped him imagine how his father felt.

Shifting his leg, he winced. *Chloe still has work to do.*

Isaac thought his faith in his father's innocence would bring them closer, but

---

Nano-cream
An experimental transdermal rapid healing gel created by Luna Peppercorn at the Kepler Institute. When the gel is applied to the skin, it begins repairing light to moderate tissue damage. Nano-cream is more versatile than a healing pack and runs off of human metabolic energy.

Bernard Hubert had withdrawn from everyone, including his son. His favorite time of the year, a three-week marathon spent locked together in a private lab, had been cancelled two years running. Something came up with dad's schedule, then school started. It was okay, he needed some time with everything happening, but Isaac missed him.

"Newton?" Lydia, a petite Japanese girl, was using his nickname. "Chelsea told me about the owl. What happened? Naomi's posse?"

"As usual."

"Why do you even let them get close?"

"And give up the fun? How could I? Especially when they make it so easy." A chuckle caused a weird little spasm in his ribs.

Huh. Chloe may have a lot of work to do.

She tsked. "Look, *Euclid's* sweeping the green. I've got a quilting pack in my room."

"Where's Chels?"

"Telling Matthew Saturday night is off. She didn't trust our secure channel."

"I don't blame her."

"He will. He spent all Tuesday on that window program instead of his genetic grafting homework."

"Don't hyperbolize. He spent two hours at most. It's not like he was reprogramming a ballistic missile with a flip phone."

Lydia chortled, then put her hands on her hips and shook her head. At the signal, a blue and bronze falcon dipped from the sky and lit on her shoulder.

After a glance at the hologram it provided, she said, "All clear, let's go."

Isaac grabbed her, offered a hand, and hauled himself up. "I have great friends."

"Can't let you die before you contribute something meaningful to the world, now can we?" She eyed the rolled pants leg curiously. "Hey, from the look of that

---

Euclid
A morphic drone pet; a protector, security, spy tool, and limited AI platform. Euclid, and other drone pets like it, are the merger of drone technology with AI advancement, aka, the "robot dog." They are specifically modelled AI after nonhuman cognition to eliminate "skynet" possibilities. Commonly used recreationally, SETI students build their own, but morphic drone pets are used by the military and for protecting high level assets.

Crawler (occurs on page 80 paragraph 5)
A small insectoid looking spy drone, perfect for fitting into small spaces and being unnoticed, the crawler is an inevitable result of technological improvement and miniaturization. Crawlers originate from drone bees used to replace decimated real populations before WW3. They were banned after because of the ethical danger of drone swarms; however, individual ones are still used.

knee, you're not limping nearly as much as you should."

"Wish I could tell you, Lyd. It was an experimental med-gel I won in a game of Cubes"

"Cooool."

Together, they slowly cut a path across the green, past the library, to the student village. Isaac nodded at the Mobius shaped dorm complexes for 1st-3rd cycles, vast pythons on either side of a narrow rock ridge. "Aren't you glad we aren't in those anymore?"

"Remember having to leave a *jammer* on in your room every time you went to take a piss?" Her nostalgia was tinged with sarcasm. "And *magtape* around your door to fry *crawlers*?"

They reached the Towers, a collection of twenty beehive structures, prototypes of 3D printed lodging for future Mars colonies that housed upperclassmen. They were also a live experiment in micro ecosystems and social organization in small populations.

"Think they'll ever actually use these off-planet?" Lydia mused.

"They have to. Even if exploration has been replaced with mining—god, I hate saying that out loud—the war proved our species needs a backup plan."

At Tower #11, unseen retinal detectors granted them access retracting the curved door like a reptilian eyelid. Leaving Isaac to collapse on the common room couch, Lydia sprinted up the central circular staircase, taking the steps two at a time. Euclid flapped after her. Above, balconied walkways had entrances to their private quarters: two on the second floor and two on the third.

Her voice echoed. "Want a thermal pack, too?"

Feeling his cuts reopening, his knee swelling again, he shouted, "Yes, please!"

Rather than returning footfalls, there was a light humming and buzzing as a four foot floor ring glowed to life. Lydia gently descended through the air touching down on the ring's center. Isaac, Lydia, Chelsea, and Matthew were thrilled when

---

Jammer

An electromagnetic and sonic signal blocker first built by the Russian military. It is a surveillance countermeasure developed as a prototype to electromagnetic cloaking. It is capable of blocking out any radio transmissions within its range. Later versions created a type of "static" that interferes with remote listening technology. Jammers were popular in the espionage battles between Russia and the United States in the 2060s

Magtape

Electronic device barrier used to create closed "circuits" that if tripped, zap the target with a small dose of electricity. Magtape is popular as a surveillance countermeasure against small drones. It collects power from static electricity and is commonly placed around doorways, window frames, air ducts, and utility lines. Once the tape has been activated, it needs to be replaced. Magtapes are perfect for disabling Crawlers, small insectoid looking spy drones. They were banned after WWIII because of the ethical danger of drone swarms; however, individual ones are still used.

they won the housing lottery. The former occupants, who went on to design the *Hyperion Loop,* really knew what they were doing when they installed the glide rings.

Many of the Towers had similarly unique leftovers. One had a ferrofluid 3D-suspended manipulator that could create morphing statues (great for parties) and hold gamers aloft while in VR. Another had moss growing on the inner walls, providing natural air and natural water filtration. One hive even had a laser infusion forge that used the sun and mirrors to create a concentrated beam furnace (great for customizing *lightsaber* designs.)

Lydia applied the quilt pack patches to the cuts on Isaac's face and head. Bioengineered fibers stitched the wounds and applied a balm to accelerate healing.

Isaac wrapped the thermal pack around his leg. "Ahh, that's the ticket."

After giving him a minute to enjoy the thermal pack, she said, "You sure you want to use the space elevator as your submission? You really have to blow them away, Newton. Start talking theoretical application, you'll be dead in the water."

He gave her a hard stare, which she returned with equal vigor.

"I am aware, and yes, I'm sticking to it. I'm sick of people treating big ideas as if they're science fiction. I already have solutions for printing it from the surface up, trans-atmospheric tethering... shit, I even have an asteroid picked out that can be easily redirected to a geostationary orbit once it passes near the moon."

Lydia's eyebrows went sky high. "Riiight. You also have a space tug with a fusion drive I don't know about?"

Isaac went quiet.

"Noted. Do me a favor and grab the cryptocube from my room? I can't do stairs yet. Door's open."

"Sure, where you headed?"

"Office hours with The Hunter."

Hyperion Loop
Underground high speed maglev train route in evacuated tubes, max speed is 6500 km/hr. It travels from Minneapolis to Quebec City, operated by the North American Migration Effort (NAME). As the population of North America drastically shifted northward by the late 2050s to escape rising temperatures, the US and Canada created NAME to build a new mass transit system to support the growing northern metropolis. Work began in 2064 and completed in 2077.

Lightsaber
Kepler device that was developed by nerds to emulate the "lightsabers'' from Star Wars. They are handheld sparring weapons that generate a mild electrical charge and are comprised of photovoltaics over a telescoping metallic "blade." Initially used in lightsaber dueling clubs at SETI schools, later, lethal, more powerful versions were developed and quickly banned except for the military. These can slice through a human with ease or cut through an 8 cm thick steel wall. Deadly but inefficient: at full cutting power, the battery can drain in 30 seconds. Though the lightsaber can be devastating in close quarters combat, they are useless against enemies with firearms at any distance, thus remaining predominantly a sporting instrument.

"Calc 5?"

"No, I want to go over the tensile matrix numbers for the elevator."

"Cool." Lydia ran back up and a moment later, glided down and placed a jade cube in Isaac's hands. Gingerly, he stood.

Lydia eyed the leg. "Need help getting there?"

"Nah, the pack's working. Catch you at dinner."

CHAPTER 7

K.I.N.G.

Professor Hunt's office was the structure atop a high ridge on the campus upslope looking down on the southwest foothills. Reaching it required climbing a seemingly infinite number of stairs, creating, for Isaac, a personal purgatory.

As he trudged along, the late afternoon light illuminated dust particles in the air. Finally nearing the entrance, he stopped to rest his leg. Below, panes of glass in stone buildings glimmered like gold. The campus green had quieted. The forest was a verdant sea. In a moment of self-awareness, he realized the mountain palace made for an optimal life.

He took the *cryptocube* and pressed a sequence of glyphs on its six sides. With a click, it opened revealing an air-gapped computer, its drive, with tesseract compression, an imbedded holoprojector and a lithium-ion power core. Isaac built it himself, even the native programming language was his.

It provided the security necessary at Kepler. Each iteration of the password was created by an independent numerical linkage to a progressive rotating code, which, in turn was based on an algorithm only the owner knew. More than two incorrect attempts, or for that matter, any sort of tampering fused the box and

---

Cryptocube
A personal, secure digital storage container. A 5 x 5 x 5 cm box machined from a single piece of titanium tungsten alloy, it is capable of withstanding an Abrams tank being dropped on it. It houses a quantum processor with tesseract compression, un-networked drive, em shielding, physical data dock for hardline data transfer only, imbedded holoprojector, battery, and a mechanical keypad interface. The passcode combination is an independent numerical linkage with a progressive rotating code. Each iteration is based on an algorithm only the owner creates and knows. More than two incorrect passcode attempts or any tampering will melt the battery and contents along with it.

instantly melted the contents.

With a few taps, a hologram of his space elevator appeared. He reviewed the vibrational math to make sure he'd ask the right questions. If a 36,000-kilometer-long harp string could hit resonance, there wasn't really a point, was there?

Completing his calculations, he continued toward a building that was half-window, half in the rock. At the final landing he heard Professor Hunt speaking with someone else. He paused outside the closed office to listen.

"I did the math; I know none of it was your fault, and I agree with all you're saying, but have you considered the risk, not just to yourself, but to future attempts at expansion?"

"If there are any. Why does everyone think that because we survived three world wars, we've become so enlightened that we're somehow above annihilating the planet? Exploration is one of the few human characteristics we can take pride in, and it needs to start now."

It was his father. Here. Isaac could hear the blood pounding in his ears.

"How was Angelika's?"

"Snowy."

"Seriously?"

"We talked it through. We're good."

"Just like that?"

"Just like that. Well, and she's providing the money for the ship you're going to build, and she admitted she was funding CORE, which I already knew."

"Wait. She was doing what?! Why didn't you tell me?"

"Didn't seem relevant until now."

"I'll give you a moment to think about how illogical that sounds."

After a clink of glasses, his father continued. "Will, if you're so certain expansion will *have* a future, why does Kepler still maintain a bomb shelter?"

Rather than answer, Professor Hunt asked his own question. "Why does it have to be you? I get that you want to be out there, but it's dangerously narcissistic. Did the Victoria's shipwright hop aboard with Magellan?"

"I don't know, but whose name do you remember? All I am asking is that the three of us sit down and discuss it. When was the last time you saw Angelika, anyway?"

"Last year. Stockholm. And don't change the subject. You have to stay here for your family, for Isaac. How are you planning to tell him?"

"About this or the other thing?"

"Both. Either."

"I... I'm not sure yet."

"Well, you'd better figure it out. More than likely he's been right outside listening for the last two, three minutes."

The game up, Isaac came in. Going from lamenting his father's absence to having him standing there as if teleported was jarring, to say the least.

Warm sunlight streaming in from a semi-circle of windows framed both men. The inside wall was one enormous curved chalkboard. Befitting the mind it housed, every aspect of the room, every edge, curve, line conformed to a mathematical equation. Each cycle, Hunt issued the same challenge. "If you can solve the over-arching equation for my office, you can add a desk for yourself."

So far, his was the only desk.

Capitalizing on the shock in both father and son, Professor Hunt coyly said "Well, Hue?"

Bernard put down his scotch. "Isaac. How are you?"

"What... what are you doing here?"

"I'm discussing a proposal with the esteemed Professor Hunt."

"Why didn't you tell me you were coming?"

"You know better than I how people here think of me. I didn't want to complicate things for you. For that matter, though..." He turned to Hunt. "...why didn't *you* tell me Isaac had an appointment?"

The professor gave them a warm smile. "Must have slipped my mind. Since we're here, let's all sit, shall we?" He gestured to the two chairs in front of his desk.

As he complied, Bernard spoke to his son. "Professor Hunt tells me you're working on a seamless carbon fiber print method."

"Pivot!" Hunt called as if he were a moderator.

Bernard shot him a sour look, but, Isaac, not ready to engage the far heavier topic, answered. "Yeah dad. It's for the Explorers' Cup."

"Fantastic. I'm only sorry that sharing my name will make it more difficult for you. Isaac... what the devil happened to your face?"

Isaac turned a bit red. "Discblade."

Professor Hunt raised an eyebrow.

Stuck between discussing a rock or a hard place, Isaac said, "Dad, you were talking about space exploration and a crew. Are you going somewhere?"

Bernard gave Hunt another steely glance. His answering look said, "You're on your own."

Cornered, he faced his son. "Isaac, I'm gathering a crew of 12, including Professor Hunt and myself, to reach Voyager 2's last known location beyond Kuiper. It'll be 2.3 years each way, roughly 5 years total."

After what seemed an eternity of silence, Isaac tilted his head thoughtfully. "But the fusion drive test failed. Was it on purpose? You built another in secret?"

The speed of the deduction startled Bernard as much as the fact of it. His son's acumen made him proud and to be completely honest, a little afraid. "Yes. Well... now you know why I haven't been around much."

Isaac sank into his chair. "Whoooooooooah."

Interplanetary travel was not only feasible, it was easy. This was...everything.

Bernard leaned in. "You know I didn't cause the explosion at CERN, yes?"

Offended, Isaac grimaced. "Of course."

"Then you understand what that means, that there's something out there."

Isaac's brow crunched warily. "I do."

"The only way I can free our family is by finding it. I have to go, for that, and to be part of what comes next." Fire gleamed in his father's eyes. "Even if I can't clear my name, OUR name, I can still lay down an olive branch to my enemies and say I did my part to further our species."

Numbed by the neutron-star weight of the subject, Isaac felt detached and resentful. "If this is the part where you tell me you'll stay if I ask...you know I won't. Besides, what I think won't change a thing. You've already decided just like you did at our first family dinner-and-a-movie when you asked my opinion, then showed *Interstellar* anyway."

Hunt drew a sharp breath. "Your father has already sacrificed a lot, and he's planning to sacrifice even more. You should show..."

"It's fine." Bernard waved him off. "Isaac, I deserve that, because you're right. I *am* going, no matter what. I feel..." He hesitated, afraid to be vulnerable, afraid to use a highly unscientific term. "I feel destiny calling."

Destiny? No idea how to respond, Isaac turned away and found himself facing his teacher. "So, are you going, too?"

Hunt didn't answer immediately. "Let me show you something. Computer... darken windows and open the most recent Voyager calculations."

Polarizing filters made it seem like nightfall. Projectors hummed filling the office with a giant hologram of equations and proofs superimposed on the solar system. "It's a set of probability calculations comparing Voyager's signal loss with CERN's destruction. I've been working on it for your father. Coupled with several anomalous readings we picked up from the old *SETI* array, I deduced this."

The conclusion of a wildly lengthy equation grew: **Omega = .99999**

SETI - Search for ExtraTerrestrial Intelligence
For over 100 years scientists have dedicated their lives to the SETI effort. It is a collective term for scientific searches for intelligent extraterrestrial life, for example, monitoring electromagnetic radiation for signs of transmissions from civilizations on other planets.

Isaac glanced at the number, then back to his teacher.

"It means the chance of those events being coincidental is so astronomically low, it makes getting a perfect bracket seem downright probable. Sure, I believe in your father, but I believe in math even more. Honestly, I don't know if I'll go, but someone has to convince the other recruits. Social grace has never been his strong suit."

"Yep," Isaac agreed.

Bernard managed an eye-roll.

"Dad... when do you leave?"

"There'll be a window in just under two years that will allow for maximal planetary alignment. It means I'll miss graduation..."

Seeing his genuine disappointment, Isaac stood and hugged his father. "You'll have plenty of time to send a message back telling the world we're not alone before I walk across the stage. I can't imagine a better graduation gift."

Unable to remember how long it had been since he embraced his son, Bernard let tears flow. "I love you. I'll make you proud."

"I know, dad. You already do."

Pulling out of the hug, Isaac found himself distracted by a cube-shaped object in his father's pocket. Did it have something to do with the *other thing* his father mentioned.

Wiping his eyes, Bernard turned to Hunt. "Dinner?"

"Fine," he grunted. "For old-time's sake."

His father polished off his scotch, shook William Hunt's hand, and made for the door. He was at the threshold when Isaac asked, "Dad, how did you sneak onto campus? There's bugs and drones everywhere."

Bernard smiled. "Son, you're looking at the only man ever voted *K.I.N.G.* (Kepler's Innovative Nanotech Genius) for eight cycles straight. No one, not even dear William or Angelika, can say that. It's a title that comes with its fair share of

---

K.I.N.G. - Kepler Institute Nanotech Genius
This award is given annually to a single exemplary student at Kepler who has furthest progressed in the realm of science.

secrets."

With that, he was gone, ending a reunion so brief it seemed surreal.

"Well," Hunt said, "that was a bit more interesting than our usual meeting, eh?"

Isaac blinked. "Do we still have time to go over my numbers?"

"Seeing as how I freed some extra time, certainly. What have you got?"

Isaac opened his cryptocube and placed the drive on the professor's interface pad. The voyager equations vanished, replaced by a pink lattice woven from flowing, organic strands. With a hand wave, Hunt zoomed out to a planetary view. What first appeared large and natural, receded to a narrow structure. Its length grew rapidly, simulating the space elevator's rise from Earth's equator to an asteroid in geostationary orbit.

Hunt's eyes darted about, taking in all the display data. In less than a minute, he pulled the drive and handed it back to Isaac. "I have good news and bad news."

Isaac gulped.

"The good news is, all your math checks out. Procuring the resources could be tricky, but not impossible, or even particularly outlandish."

Isaac breathed.

"The bad news is that the project has to be put on hold."

What? Big day for emotional shifts. In less than half a minute, he'd been afraid, relieved, and crestfallen. "But why?"

Hunt smiled. "Because I need your help to design your father's ship."

That did it. Isaac felt his mind leave his body, lost in a sea of dreams. Even when able to speak again, all he could say was, "What?"

"Yeah, your dad forgot to mention that." Hunt laughed.

His father wasn't just here to recruit his friend; Isaac was being recruited, too.

"Uh... when do we start, sir?"

"We already have." He opened a large desk drawer and took out... what? Not a cryptocube, but—*could it be?* Isaac howled in wild jubilation.

"Is that a-a-a, Nano-matrix vortex holocube?! **NanoCubes** are barely theoretical. No one can crack the math... supposedly."

Hunt grew somber. "Isaac, whatever you see here, whatever we do, whatever we create cannot leave this office. It's not only that our work isn't school-sanctioned, but it will be extremely dangerous—to our species—if the wrong people find out about it."

Isaac nodded, but he was still staring at the NanoCube.

Hunt sighed. "Okay, I know you have lots of questions, but for now, I'll just say that when we were students, your father and I did crack the math, but we also realized the danger of mass-producing. Only ten exist, and I keep a very close eye on all of them."

With a wave, the cube projected blueprints for a manned interplanetary vessel. "This is my design, dubbed *The Dreamcatcher,* actually based on something *you* wrote."

"Me?"

Hunt seemed surprise by Isaac's reaction. "Yes. Hasn't your father ever told you? The equations you wrote when you were ten, on weaving magnetic field lines, formed the basis for his fusion drive."

Isaac knew he was smart; it ran in the family, but he was momentarily at a loss for words. "This is why you've given me so much attention? Because of what I did six years ago?"

"Isaac, listen carefully. I can solve any mathematical problem on the planet. Heh, *this planet* being key, given our goals. That said, I've never seen anything close to your ability to translate theoretical math into practical design. I mean, look at your space elevator. Even incomplete, it's astounding. When you were younger, we worried how that might affect you, how it might affect the world. But if we're

---

NanoCube

A quantum storage device with near limitless capacity, unhackability, and the ability to bilaterally transfer ideas from a user to code for problem solving. The user inputs a problem into their cube and it can solve it using the users knowledge and logic, thus allowing for exponentially higher work productivity and creative capability. It houses a quantum learning processor with tesseract compression, em shielding, neural uplink, imbedded holoprojector, wireless signal, and power source. The first 2 NanoCubes were secretly built by Bernard Hubert and William Hunt over the final three years at the Kepler Institute. Realizing they had effectively duplicated their minds with the cube, the danger of their existence became apparent. The two only ever made 8 additional NanoCubes for key personnel unknown.

to reach beyond Kuiper, we have to tap your full potential and accept any risks that come with it."

What *potential* was he talking about? What did he mean by *risks?*

William's words, were presented cheerily, but indicated the subject was closed. "Let's move onto the fun stuff, shall we? Let me show you how to use the NanoCube to work on *The Dreamcatcher's* latest schematics."

Hungry as he was for more, Isaac wasn't about to do anything to risk his new, amazing role. Besides, the NanoCube was fascinating all on its own.

Hunt took out a palmer. "This is coded directly to my DNA; any other would melt the cube and leave the would-be thief, umm, one-handed. You'll learn about a lot of fail-safes that aren't meant for students. We are, after all, handling data that could, if another war broke out, end the world. Do you understand that?"

"I do."

William used it to unlock the NanoCube revealing a holo matrix unlike any other, a layered four dimensional cube. "It not only interacts visually; it can convey a user's internal visualizations in real-time allowing you to see new ideas as they occur. Look, here's the latest kerfuffle. I'm having trouble stably siphoning power for the ship's grid."

They worked five hours straight; the sky turned an inky black before Hunt admitted it was time for some rest. He concluded the visit with a warm, admiring grin and a handshake.

"See you in three days. Remember, no matter what your father says, don't forget who the real K.I.N.G is."

Isaac left tired and inspired, barely remembering the "other thing" his father mentioned.

William inhaled deeply. He and Bernard planned the conversation before Isaac's arrival. The boy's abilities were growing. His self-made cryptocube provided ample proof that with them came the lure of A.I. He wasn't a danger yet, but he needed guidance.

Given the journey ahead, Hunt felt a need to return to some familiar surroundings even if they might be uncomfortable. He thought of tall bookshelves, city rooftops, a gleaming tower, and a lovely little restaurant.

It was time to reunite a very special trio for the first time in many, many years.

CHAPTER 7 K.I.N.G.

CHAPTER 8
EXTRA BACON

A snowy winter had descended on the quiet town of Hastings in the New Amsterdam Region (formerly New York). A lightly chiming wind gently shook the windows of a lovely little restaurant. Inside, a single oil lamp illuminated a polished oak table where three old friends discussed humanity's future.

William Hunt pounded the table. "I won't go, Bernard. Be reasonable. Who wants to spend five years with no sun, rain, snow, or decent wine?"

Bernard brough his face closer. "I need you! To be honest, I need you much more than you need me."

Sipping her wine, Angelika leaned back to watch. To her, the outcome didn't matter. Whoever went, she still got the fusion drive. Across history, such opportunities were rare and fleeting, but it wasn't the only reason the titan of industry joined her former classmates in this quaint, old dive. Truth be told, she'd never known smarter people. Certainly, no one could defy her the way Bernard did.

It made her wonder; if he'd stayed at CERN and Darren lived instead... would they have come this far? The dark thought stuck with her, raising darker questions.

"Gentlemen?"

Bernard remained fixated on Mr. Good Will Hunting, as he called William—G.W. for short, but William disengaged. "Angelika! Oh, there you are."

She returned his smile with a wry glare. "Bernie, I hadn't thought about this before, but Pegasus accomplished what Phoenix Fires couldn't with significantly fewer resources *and* without Darren. If Will really wasn't involved, what changed?"

As she waited, the answer dawned on her. "Ah. Isaac."

So, the small boy Bernard once brought to work to see daddy's rockets was the key. The very thought took her aback.

Bernard seemed to be searching for a reason not to speak. He couldn't find one.

"Yes, Ang, it was Isaac. I knew you'd figure it out eventually. When he was ten, his abilities exploded. I tried teaching him, but there was no need. He was a natural, he got everything I threw at him. So, I tried him on some of the calculations from Phoenix Fires. By the end of the day, he'd written an equation that accurately predicted plasma field currents during fusion. That formed the basis for the drive. He's a scientific virtuoso, but at that age, innocent to the possible repercussions. Without proper guidance, I was afraid he'd make some advances in A.I. that would create self-aware machines, resulting in a *Skynet* apocalypse. So, I brought him to William."

Eyes narrowing, Angelika sat up. "William knew?"

"Of course." William shrugged. "I'm his teacher. But I wasn't going to broadcast it. If you really think I'd put a student's best interests second, even to you... well..."

Bernard sighed. "I should have been more candid. I've lied to you and many others to get here. But, no more. I have something to show you both, something no one else has seen."

Once the waiter took their drink orders, he took out a portable DVD player and pressed play. By the time the waiter returned, the video was over.

"Who had the martini?"

Though stunned, Angelika managed to say, "Me."

"Oban 22 on the rocks?"

"Mine, thanks," Bernard answered.

"And the Mojito must be yours."

William nodded numbly. "Correct, much appreciated."

They sipped slowly, quietly, until William, searching the depths of his drink, found his voice. "We can't show that to anyone else, not even Isaac. Not yet."

"I agree." Bernard removed the DVD and cracked it into pieces. "The only other copy is on a **VHS** tape locked in my safe, and I've worked hard to be sure I'm the only one in the northern hemisphere who still has a machine to play it."

Angelika frowned. "William, you have to go with Bernie. I need you both on that ship, and you'll need each other. This mission *has* to succeed."

William was agreeing before she finished. "I know, Angie. I'm in. Bernard, tell me what you need and who. We will do this."

Things getting too dramatic for Bernard, he tried diffusing the mood in his usual, pop-culture way. "I'm Danny, you're Rusty. It'll be like *Oceans 11*."

William blinked. "Don't ever change, Bernie. So... who do we need?"

"You two are our astrophysicist and mathematician," Angelika said. "That leaves an engineer, chemist, botanist, and biologist. Past that, to be truly representative, we have to look beyond STEM. We'll need a politician, historian, a former or current military mind, a linguist, and a doctor."

William counted. "That's eleven."

"Twelve. I'm not funding this without a say." Angelika interjected.

Bernard shook his head. "Wouldn't work in an emergency, not with sketchy communications across billions of miles and hours of time delay."

She smiled sweetly. "In that event, I'll give a crewmember my proxy."

"Hm. I know someone, but Bernie won't like it," William said.

They knew instantly who he meant. Bernard's harsh response rattled their drinks.

VHS
An obsolete, late 20th century audiovisual storage method.

"ABSOLUTELY NOT! I will not have her on my ship."

Angelika patted him. "*My* ship."

He glared indignantly.

An undeterred Will made his case. "An objective, balanced crew should be a team of rivals. She'll give us legitimacy, a bridge to CERN, and provide a sense of reparation. If he were here, it would've been Darren. We owe it to him."

Bernard grimaced. "You can't have reparations for a crime that didn't occur. Besides, it doesn't matter; Lily Parson does not want to see me."

"Is that entirely her fault?"

William's question stung. Bernard had known Darren's daughter from birth, watched her mature into a talented nano-physicist, but her vehement belief that he was responsible for her father's death opened a rift that neither attempted to bridge. The resentment festered into a misguided conviction that he'd actually asked Darren to stay on purpose.

"She's brilliant, clever, loathes you—and I can keep her under control," William said.

"Control Lily?" Angelika wasn't convinced. "You can do that?"

With a massive sigh, Bernard put the mission first. "He can. She was his student."

Angelika was satisfied. "Okay. That's one down, nine to go. More names?"

Bernard looked to Will. "Have you kept up with Aubree?"

"Gates?"

"Yes, your brother's wife. Which other Aubree could I possibly be talking about? Your past may be painful, but she's the best historian I know of."

It was William's turn to be somber. "A fantastic choice," he admitted. "I'll reach out. As long as we're going where angels fear to tread, Angelika, have you kept up with...um, Godric?"

The table went silent until William broke in with a rare ardor. "Look, this *has* to be done correctly. Given our preeminent careers, we're going to have history with some, if not all, of the experts we need. But think—any past friction will be nothing compared to our combined power."

Angelika half-smiled. "Bernard's wearing off on you. I haven't heard that sort of passion from you since you worked for me at O.L. Yes, I keep up with Godric. I wouldn't be doing my job if I didn't stay connected to the head of the W.C. space initiative. He's married, and I couldn't be happier for him. I'll set up dinner."

"I guess we all have social sacrifices to make. Who else?" Bernard tensed as a name flit by in his mind. After a moment, all three said, "Ilya O'Connell."

Ilya was an incredible post-war mechanical engineer whose designs were ubiquitous. He wasn't as famous as the others, but only because few who saw his work understood what they were looking at.

"He's also a liability," Bernard said. "Maybe more than Lily, but I'll talk to him."

Staring off into some invisible abyss, Angelika spoke almost to herself. "If we really are going to reach deep beyond any comfort zone, fine. I haven't seen him in a few years; we were never 'objectively' good together, and I kinda broke it off last time, but we need an eminent botanist, and he makes Mark Watney look like a weekend gardener."

William rolled his eyes at the archaic movie reference, but Bernard was shocked. "You don't mean...?"

I do," Angelika snapped, "and I will not speak further on the subject."

Moved, Bernard raised his glass and regarded them with an admiration that reminded him of the look Luke gave Han and Leia at the end of *Star Wars*. "A lot of jokes, barbs, and quips come to mind, as you'd expect, but right now, I very much want to say, thank you. Thank you for dealing with my faults, for seeing the good, and for understanding what needs to be done for the sake of our species."

Angelika and William raised their glasses. "Hear, hear!"

"Evolution took us from stardust to creatures that can walk, talk, think, and create things like the fine Oban 22 I hold out to you." The candlelight glistened in the amber waves as he gently swished the scotch. "But the human goal is to escape evolution, to understand the miracle of our existence, rather than remain a cog in its cosmic wheel."

The drink kicking in, he indulged in a good-sized swig and smacked his lips. "Where was I? Oh, yes. Anyone know a good biologist?" After their amused faces failed to produce a name, he said, "Is it possible we have no clear winner this time?"

Will chuckled. "How could we? You'd want Max or Ava, Ang... want Kelsey or Martin... and I like Herman."

"I'm surprised we agreed on the first three." Angelika snapped her fingers at the waiter. "I'm going to need another."

The three burst out laughing. For a fleeting moment, they were students again enjoying the night before finals. In two hours, they settled on Ava Auburn as the biologist and Galena Hunter for their physician.

Sensing the right time had come for his final revelation of the evening, Bernard shifted nervously until he couldn't delay any further. At his nod and wink, a man in derby and trench coat rose from the shadows of the bar and started towards them.

"I, uh... put something in motion earlier, some*one* actually. Angie, I hope you understand, but it's only right we include him at this stage."

His friends eyed him. Angelika whispered, "Godric."

"Dear god, what have you done?" William snapped across the table.

Godric Adams removed his hat and coat and surreptitiously glided into a chair magicked in place by the wait staff. "Hello, Angie. Sorry for the surprise, but Bernard came to me the same night you and I talked about Space Exploration Act—and you know how persuasive he is. By the time he finished talking, I knew I had to be here. I'm also sorry I haven't returned your call. Between Heather, the kids—and this—it's been a lot to deal with."

Angelika hadn't been this blindsided since CERN and didn't care who knew.

"*This* being what, Ric...?"

Godric grinned. "Going to Kuiper. I'm your politician, ready and willing to navigate the geopolitical waters needed to get the ship built and then represent our diplomatic side to... whatever we find."

Angelika rounded on Bernard. "Always ten moves ahead, aren't you?"

He shrugged. "Ric was the one who persuaded the W.C. to restore my advisory seats. I know how much he needs to be involved in this. I certainly wasn't going to keep him away."

"You know that I'm here and can hear you talking about me, don't you?" Godric gestured for the waiter. "Gordon, Old Fashioned, extra bacon. Thanks."

"And, um, five more bottles of the cab, Gordon," William added. "The 2049 from Missoula, please."

Everyone giggled, but then William's eyes narrowed at the newcomer. "Aren't you the one who said seven years and one-hundred fifty-one days ago leaving the World Council unattended was tantamount to child abandonment? Why sacrifice five years of your career?"

Godric answered with practiced calm. "Silly me, I was hoping to have at least one drink before the hard questions. You think being a Councillor means I haven't dreamt, since childhood, of being an astronaut? In light of S.E.A., if the committees throw hypothetical first encounter scenarios at you, it'll help to have me there."

"I didn't have to do much convincing," Bernard said. "Godric was already one foot in."

Noticing Angelika and William staring at him with great concern, he realized that Gordon had cleaned the table, along with the DVD shards. In hot pursuit of the waiter, Bernard hurried to retrieve them. Both Angelika and William wondered if Godric had seen any of the video from the bar, but said nothing.

By the time Bernard returned, shards stuffed in his pocket, Angelika was cooling down. "Let's move on. How about the name?"

Godric pursed his lips. "We want the public aware of the ideology: the understanding that we're explorers and pioneers proud to wander the edges, experience the depths of existence. Whatever name we pick should encapsulate that ethos."

William smirked. "If you put it that way, why not..."

Bernard cut him off. "The *USS Enterprise*!"

Angelika rolled her eyes. "*Voyager*?"

"Good idea, Angie," Godric said, "but, ironically, also *Star Trek*."

William grunted impatiently. "If you'd let me tell you what it is, maybe you'd like my idea." Comfortable he had their attention, he continued. "Darren's middle name is Damon, which, backwards, is *Nomad*... a wanderer."

Bernard's chuckle reverberated making each of their drinks dance within their respective glasses. "William, that too is a reference from the original *Star Trek*, but alas, its meaning is core to our mission."

There was a collective, fervent nod as the new drinks arrived.

After a last gulp from their third wine bottle, Bernard said, "I'd like to offer a slight adjustment to help Ric sell this thing... the *W.C.O.L. Nomad-A*. That credits the council, Outer Limits, and highlights the fact that it's the first in a series."

"Good," Godric said. "Every little bit helps. With Madeline looking for any reason to shut down the space program, the mission's going to have a lot of opposition."

"I'd like to be clear on what that mission is, exactly." Angelika was all but accusatory. "What are we doing in space? Clearing the name of a washed-up science hack or searching for ET? I know one's the same as the other, but that's a question we'll have to answer once this goes public."

Bernard scoffed. "Once the fusion drive is revealed, I hardly believe mission semantics will be big news."

"Actually," William said, "Angie has a point. We shouldn't gloss over this."

Godric nodded agreement.

Bernard waved off their concerns. "Once Godric's in the Great Council Hall, facing the assembly, I'm sure he'll find the right words. This man knows as well as I that there's a shadow in the sky we cannot ignore—a path to elevated living we must follow. Yes, for me, part of it is clearing my name, for Isaac's sake, but the much larger part is about leaving the cradle of our solar system, not only to ask new questions, but to find answers to our most ancient question ones. Why we look at the night sky with such longing? And why is *that* so tied to what makes us human?"

Godric slapped Bernard on the back. "Could you repeat that? I'd like to take notes because if that doesn't work, I don't know what will."

Angelika, however, remained displeased. "Inspiring words don't eliminate the cold, hard facts. Half the world thinks you're crazy or a liar, the other half thinks you're both, and we're seeking funding and wide-spread public approval to chase after aliens. Bernie, they're going to need—I NEED—to know, what evidence you have. I know you're still protecting whatever made you crawl out of your six year hole to bring us here, but I won't be a pawn in your chess game. Your knight, rook, and queen? Yes. We'll protect you, fight for you, and win for you. But to make our own moves, we need to understand the King's strategy."

Trying to appear as if he'd been cornered, Bernard looked into his wine glass for the longest time, finished it, then opened another bottle before speaking.

"Voyager 2 worked for one-hundred twenty years, then died within minutes of an antimatter containment failure on Earth. It was a cosmic coincidence everyone knows about. With most deep space hardware abandoned, lost, or out of repair, it's supposedly all we know, and it *should* be enough to convince anyone with a basic understanding of probability. But... Angelika's right. What everyone doesn't know, is that there were several *more* coincidences, all detected by the Deep Space Scanner."

Angelika slapped the table. "Stop! The **Deep Space Scanner's** been offline since the war—no logs from 2085 exist."

Bernard raised his hand. "I thought so, too, but Space Oasis' salvage of the **Lunar Dark Station** discovered that one array remained powered. The data core

---

Deep Space Scanner
A massive multipurpose antenna array that was on the dark side of the moon to minimize electromagnetic interference from Earth for astronomical observation.

Lunar Dark Station
A United States moonbase located on the dark side of the moon used primarily for alien listening and a communication relay post to mars and deep space. Contact with it was lost in 2072 after the remaining occupants abandoned it. In 2091 a salvage mission was successful by the World Council.

was intact, but too corrupted to read. Given Pegasus' involvement in the mission, I was able to retrieve a copy of that corrupted data, which I then successfully recovered... with this."

He placed his obsidian NanoCube on the table. Candlelight flickering on its surfaces, to Angelika and Godric it looked completely alien and valuable. Bernard's eyes lingered on William to be sure his expression didn't give away how much he knew.

"The array recorded a variety of eerily similar electromagnetic spikes... all in the minutes preceding Voyager's signal loss. They originated from two locations, on either side of our solar system, both deep in the Kuiper Belt. They were followed by a slight, omnidirectional attenuation in the microwave background. That much might be dismissed as a reading error if the numbers weren't so specific and equidistant from system center. The odds that the synchronicity of the CERN and the Voyager events was a coincidence are astronomical. Add this, it becomes impossible."

Godric's brain spun wildly. "It could be a shield or a cloaking field."

"Or corrupted data misread by wishful sci-fi nerds." Much as Angelika took them bluntly back to earth, but she couldn't take her eyes off the NanoCube.

Bernard picked up on her interest. "These cubes haven't been wrong yet."

As he lifted the cube, he caught a momentary reflection of William's face. Was it simple concern he saw there or anger at what he likely thought a reckless revelation of their secret. Assuming it was the latter, Bernard, to Angelika's disappointment, put the cube away.

"I have suspicions, calculations, probabilities, but no direct signal. No message. There is no proof there are other beings out there. In addition to everything else, this mission is about trust, the same trust any explorer has, that there is something to be found. In any case, we can't allow ourselves to go backwards."

"What if you do find something and it's hostile?" Angelika asked.

Bernard gestured at Godric. "That's why he's coming."

Pouring herself more wine, she conceded with a nod. "Acceptable for now. Next order of business, the implications for our careers; me and my board, Godric and the W.C., Will at Kepler. This will impact all of us, our friends, family, anyone remotely close."

Godric spoke in a low tone. "I think we all know full well how unforgiving business, government, and academia can be. And I know we all suspect there are things Bernard *still* isn't sharing. But we also know that the importance of this mission trumps all that and more."

Bernard already knew where Godric stood on the hard questions. Angelika played skeptic, but was on board. William, a man of pure reason, didn't often embrace this sort of big question, but, surprisingly, it was he who handed Bernard exactly what he needed to get the group past the last major roadblock.

"If Ric believes we must move forward, I say we put aside any doubts and get on with it."

Bernard had his generals, though wished he could be more open. The NanoCube was necessary for Godric, but the DVD he showed Angelika and William, while seeming, was less than the truth. He would need to explain that to Angelika soon, William shortly after, and Godric *couldn't* know. Not until he was on the alien station. He'd need plausible deniability.

"As for *The Nomad*, William and Isaac are already working on it. Angelika, they'll need to head to O.L. to start prototyping. How soon can you get them clearance and a hangar?"

"Three weeks, minimum. It won't be easy, but if S.E.A. passes this week, I think I can convince the board to reallocate some funds for a T.S. hanger and a few technicians. Isaac may be an issue. Teens don't just show up at O.L. I'll have to create some kind of internship/scholarship competition for him to win."

"It'll pass," Godric said. "William, think you can have The Nomad ready in two years?"

"Don't you know who I am? I can do it in eighteen months," William said.

Maybe it was the wine, or they felt particularly cozy in the old college haunt, but they continued for hours ending with nine empty wine bottles and twelve chosen crew.

CHAPTER 9

ENDURING GOVERNMENTS

In the stuffy Cambridge lecture hall, even the sleepiest fifteenth cycles raised their heads when someone asked. "Professor Gates, why do you believe the World Council won't endure?"

Young minds, drifting off a moment ago, were suddenly alert.

Professor Dr. Aubree Gates peered through her spectacles at the young man in the second row. The eagerness was commendable, but he was trolling. Gates was famed for her contempt of any who held the Council in undeserved esteem.

"What is your name?"

"David."

"David, do you know of any governing body in history long-able to maintain control over an intercontinental state containing a diverse population?"

His attempt to contain an assured smile signaled a prepared answer. "The Chinese, for one, ruled..."

"Over a fraction of the world. China, Rome, Carthage, Mayans, Assyria, Alexander, Persia, Huns, Mongols, Spain, Portugal, France, England, Napoleon, and *Nazis*. All rose; all fell; all bit off more than they could chew."

A chewing girl in the eighth row received Gate's damning glance. When she quickly swallowed her gum, there were chuckles.

David, meanwhile, tried again. "Isn't it too presumptuous to talk with certainty about the future?"

Gates sighed. "Why? The factors influencing an individual may seem random, protean, even chaotic, but the more people act as a group, the more predictable they become. Knowing there are cyclic patterns to collective behavior it's reasonable to predict how a country will think, act, vote. Understanding the past is the best way to predict the future."

Catching a whiff of the wood burning in David's head, Aubree waited patiently as he formulated his next, utterly predictable question:

"If that were true, Professor, wouldn't war be preventable?"

She paced along the front row. "No. Knowing what will happen doesn't mean being able, or willing, to change it. For instance, we nearly go extinct, and once things get comfortable again, we act as if they'll stay that way. War is inevitable. So long as we remain confined to a single world, its limited resources will be depleted and scarcity will lead to conflict. It's nigh impossible to share when you don't have enough for yourself. The World Council is a successor to the United Nations, a world-mediating group that inevitably failed to prevent a major war because it was too weak. The W.C. will inevitably create a major war because it's too strong. Consolidating nuclear stockpiles, not destroying them, has simply provided a single, bigger target. And who exactly decides to use them? And now, since Earth is all one nation, does that allow using them against your own countrymen? Even if it works for a while, given enough time, even a seemingly successful government will succumb to corruption."

She looked to David for another question. When all he did was gulp, she went on. "So, to return to your original question before we so delightfully tangented, World War III gave humanity a wakeup call. Having reached unsustainable numbers, we survived three brutal years of conflict, a "light" nuclear exchange, famine, a pandemic, and *The Darkness*. By the time we came to our senses, two billion were dead. We needed the Council to streamline decisions for rebuilding basic infrastructure. During its first decade, space travel wasn't an issue due to the deadly radiation belts we created. But now the atmosphere is clear, and most *still* insist we focus on Earth, accelerating the development of the same planet, with the same limited resources that caused the problem in the first place. As long as we're stuck here, we're stuck in the same loop regardless of government."

The class was gripped, enchanted, minds soaring and expanding, save for poor David. Having unintentionally become a representative of the ignorant masses, he looked ready to flee, but she had to send a clear message about who the teacher was here.

"If the World Council should miraculously decide to utilize its unprecedented control of our resources to find or make other Earths, I'll reconsider its potential for endurance. But, David, don't expect me to hold my breath."

He gulped again and sat. A wide range of emotions scattered across students' faces: grins, anger, thoughtfulness. Some leaned forward expecting flame from her mouth; others were shocked at her blatant god-complex.

As it should be.

Aubree stopped pacing and addressed them all. "This isn't an easy elective; you all worked hard to qualify. At the same time, very few of you will actually pursue what I teach you. I understand. Recording history is tedious, tiring, thankless, never ends, and doesn't pay well. Besides, who needs it? After all, there's this vast, omnipresent oculus beaming data at you in real time making you feel like informed participants in the world. But how many choices do you still make based on preconceptions or information you've never verified? How can so many think so differently? What do they know? What do they not? In five, ten, fifty, a hundred years, what will anyone remember of today? What moments will be most crucial to record? Who decides what children learn? How will it affect our laws?

"This isn't an academic, abstract sentiment. Humans have done a lot of bad shit,

---

The Darkness

An extended period of weeks in 2072 during which most of the world was without electricity following a worldwide emp as a result of high altitude nuclear detonations. The Darkness was the end of World War III. With no supply chains or communications, fighting quickly changed to starvation. The effects of the Darkness were lasting, with some regions of the world taking years to reestablish electricity and proper civilization. The newly formed World Council helped end The Darkness.

and we work very hard to gloss over it. We've also made many beautiful things. History, unflinching, unedited, preserves the good and the bad, telling us what deserves fighting for, and what deserves shame. Is it worth it to be part of that? I think so. To paraphrase Hemmingway, it's not about becoming superior to one another, it's about becoming superior to our former selves. Light stuff, really."

Mic drop.

The bell rang. She'd timed that nicely. Some sprang to their feet, but it was those who lingered, rose slowly, or remained seated who passed Aubrey's litmus test. They'd taken her words seriously; they were the ones to watch.

"First assignment due Thursday, 500 words or less on *What Caused the Demise of the Soviet Union*. Since you *will* need help, my office hours are Tuesday, Wednesday, and Sunday, 5:00 to 7:00p.m."

Smirking a bit, she packed her tote with pens, pencils, phones, data tablets, her journal, and a hard copy of Marcus Aurelius' *Meditations*. Feeling watched, she looked up to see an attractive, spectacled girl in a sweater and suede shoes standing before her—one of the lingerers.

"How can I help you, Ms...?"

"Deloytah. Amy." She extended a confident hand.

Aubree shook it firmly. "Pleased to meet you, Ms. Deloytah."

"I want to ask about your answer to David's question... about the W.C."

"Go on."

There was an expected pause as Amy mustered her courage, then... wait for it...

"Predicting the growth and collapse of a civilization is one thing, but what about a specific event?"

"Such as?"

In three...two...one...

"You mentioned knowing how a nation would vote. Can you figure out who'd win a specific election?"

And there it was. To avoid appearing responsive, Aubree smiled inwardly. Amy's head was in the right place, but they wouldn't get to the topic for weeks, and she wanted the class to proceed at the same pace.

"I can provide an excellent estimate of public opinion, based on recurring socio-economic and geopolitical events in the year before the vote, but candidates are individuals, protean, as I also mentioned, meaning the results can change like the wind."

A brief disappointment, was followed by—what? Disbelief, suspicion, annoyance? Before Aubree could figure it out, the girl put on a cheery face.

"Thank you. See you Thursday, professor." She bolted.

Definitely one to watch. No doubt she already knew Aubree had successfully predicted thirteen consecutive UK and eleven US elections before the war—and every W.C. election since. The girl was probably hoping to learn the formula for her secret sauce, but that was classified. It made her valuable and dangerous, providing the leverage she needed to pry certain truths into the light, generally kicking and screaming.

Packed, she headed out of the hall snapping her fingers to turn off the lights. Surveying a gloomy sky, she opened an umbrella and continued to wonder about Amy.

Could she be a spy? She wouldn't be the first or the prettiest. Aubree's career made *The Da Vinci Code* look like a library sleepover. But it'd been years since she'd been tasked with uncovering a conspiracy or courted by a foreign nation to influence which party would come to power. Good times.

Despite climate change, it was a classic English rainy day. Dodging puddles, Aubree headed across the courtyard to her office. The tango of academia was a nice break, but now and again Cambridge offended her. Even its most logical minds took the stone walls and science monuments as supreme and everlasting, denying the obvious.

All of this has happened before, and all of this will happen again.

Someone said that long ago... on TV? Embarrassing that a historian didn't recall a source.

In the faculty building, she left her umbrella at the door to dry and headed up the stairs passing glorious portraits of scholars, poets, philosophers, and visionaries. Her assistant, Michael, skipped down to meet her halfway.

The overeager look meant news. "Professor! Jordan and Askar found more carvings beneath the eucalyptus grove. It makes the map at least 30% larger than we thought. Isn't it incredible?"

She made it a point to never appear excited. "Hm. And it corroborates the bracelet."

"I KNOW!" Michael was practically bouncing.

"I'm headed up. I'll call them back shortly."

Michael pivoted to follow her. "There's more. Kesandu found something related to the Rasputin Case, and there are two messages from the COO of Brighton Printing. He wants to talk about..."

"I know. The 18th edition of their fifth cycle world history text failed my audit three times. Somehow, it doesn't bother them to reduce first millennium African history to a single page. Since they refuse to correct it, they can wait to talk in front of the Scholastic Quorum."

At which point I hope to learn if their staff is ignorant, racist, or both.

At the landing, she paused to catch her breath, a reminder of how badly she needed to get back to the gym.

The beaming Michael hadn't finished. "One more thing."

"Yes?"

"An Alex Hamilton stopped by. He said he was from the Smithsonian Archives, but... well, he didn't seem academic."

"Did he say anything else?"

"Only that it was important."

"Hmph. Probably my callback from budget dispensation. They want me to consult."

"Have to run to class. I'll touch base later."

Part of why Aubree hired the always-earnest, often-goofy Michael was the way he absorbed her every word. The devil, and the truth, being in the details, she liked proteges with steel-trap minds. That over-the-top enthusiasm he and other data linkers shared seemed a cosmic tradeoff for their retention capabilities. She watched as he bounded down the stairs.

Look at that boy run. I really do need to get back to the gym.

Aubree's eyes lingering on his tight backside, she decided it was a good night to have him over for dinner and help keep the bed warm.

Reaching her centuries-old-office, she unlocked it with an ancient key. The door creaked open on a cozy lair piled high with books and scrolls. Before entering, she waited until a pleasant male voice asked:

*"What occurred on the **thirteenth of Cheshvan, 5361**?"*

"The Battle of Sekigahara."

Only then did she enter, closing, but not locking the door behind her. Auto-candles flickered to life; overhead lights dimmed. Removing her journal and a tablet, she dropped her tote on a chair. Setting the kettle to boil, she removed a teabag from her pocket and placed it in a suitable mug. Cradling the completed drink in her hands, she entered the adjoining room illuminating a central hologram table. Rather than books and scrolls, this space was lined with data discs. She took one, labelled PAN OCEAN MIG, and placed it on the table. As it spun up, a map of the Pacific Ocean appeared so vast the hologram's edge revealed the earth's curve.

"Play simulation starting at 7000 BC."

Centuries ticked by: lines crossing from island to island.

Sipping her tea, she wondered what Alex Hamilton wanted and why he pretended to be from the Smithsonian. It didn't bode well. She hadn't seen the NSA, now dubbed "WSA," liaison in four years. When her predictions nearly caused a rigged election, she'd nearly imploded her career to expose the truth. That was when she told the Agency she was done and did not want to have that fight again.

"Call Jordan and Askar."

The field team answered in three rings. Their FaceTime windows had barely appeared when their virtual shouts filled the room. Jordan had tamed her wild Maori hair into thick dreads, undoubtedly brutal in the South Pacific heat. But, almost as giddy as Michael, she ignored the sweat pouring down her face.

"Professor, this is huge! I'm still eyeballing it, but the additional carvings seem key."

"Details?" Aubree inquired patiently.

Askar chimed in. "The wall was within twenty feet of where you predicted... perfectly integrated with local building patterns. We're sending the data package now."

Four holograms of ancient cartographic wallscapes appeared atop the ocean at the sites where each were found. A fifth loomed large above the rest.

"Superimpose new data."

Rotating and scaling, it descended and overlaid the Pacific. The carvings were now loosely aligned with several small land masses.

"See how the new one adds seventeen islands?" Indicating one group, then another, she said, "Those five are likely part of French Polynesia, section 879. But *these*, over here, don't correspond to any known landmasses."

"Any *current* landmasses," Aubree corrected. "Computer, add location of the most recent bracelet find from site 22 Kappa. Rollback migration sim and replay, accounting for new jump points."

Lines once more traced the ocean linking island to island until the trail reached from Asia to Patagonia. The computer crooned. "Simulation accuracy rate has increased to 74%."

"Professor, the pace and degree of early expansion we're seeing totally throws accepted models."

"Indeed. And…"

A shadowy man entered quietly but still dominating the room.

Aubree dismissed the call. "Sorry, too much tea. I'm going to have to call you back after a quick bathroom break."

As she broke off, Alex Hamiliton removed his hat and placed it on the table scattering the holobeams. She greeted him with the usual sarcasm.

"This is why I typically leave my door unlocked. It's considerably less disturbing than finding you behind a bookshelf. It also saves me the time of having to reset the traps."

He remained maddeningly impassive. "I did wait outside a bit. It sounded like what you were discussing was important."

She glowered. "Apparently not enough to keep you from interrupting."

Waving him back to the outer office, she powered down the table and grabbed her journal. It held a razor-thin blade in the binding…just in case.

Alex moved her bag from the chair before sitting.

"Make yourself at home, why don't you? Just like old times."

"No need to be completely salty, Aubree."

"I disagree. Why are you here, Alex?"

"Two reasons." He tossed a small folio on her desk. "First, the Agency wants you to monitor a potentially rigged election in the Turkish Zone."

"*No* means *no*. I'm not coming back." Aubree scowled, rounded her desk and leaned against the window frame, a position that kept her on her feet, and elevated above her uninvited guest. "Last time, it was North America trying to destabilize South America to incentivize the anti-W.C. movement."

"Which aligns with your current views on world governments, yes? Or did I mishear your little speech in the lecture hall?"

"You know damn well that deceiving the people, even if the truth shows the W.C. in the wrong, defeats the whole purpose."

Ignoring her flat refusal, Alex went on. "The second reason involves your Recurrence Theory. Top brass wants a debrief on any new developments. I have strict orders to take you to Iceland."

What? Why be interested in that? The Recurrence Theory codified her belief that the cycle of civilization was millennia older than suspected. It was widely considered inconclusive and certainly unconnected to politics.

"And if I won't go?"

Alex sighed. "Unfortunately, I was told to let this man convince you. You might want to brace yourself."

"Why? Do you think that at this point some WSA goon can..."

The office door opened and William Hunt walked in. Seeing her dead husband striding towards her with open arms, Aubree's dropped teacup shattered against the floor. Her vision swam. Suddenly, a big part of her was back holding Ken's hand watching the cancer slowly take him. At the same time, he was here—right now. A fog engulfed her senses she could hear herself screaming.

Alex managed to catch her before her head joined the teacup.

Ken's face appearing above her, she reached to touch him.

William gently gripped her fingers. "Aubree, Kenneth is gone. I'm sorry. I can only guess how hard it is for you to see me walking around with his face, but this isn't just important, it's vital."

It wasn't Ken. Up close, she could see it was Kenneth's twin brother, William. There was a difference in the light behind his eyes. Understanding cleared her vision. She pulled her hand to her mouth and sobbed.

THE GALACTIC STAR ALLIANCE
KARANDU GALAXY

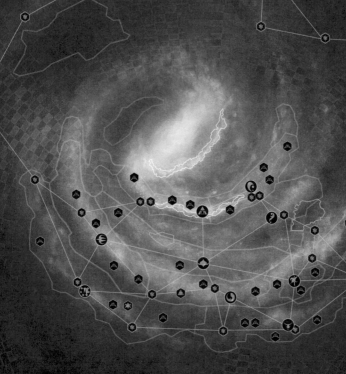

KEY

— NATURAL PHENOMENA

— SAARKI EXPANSION

— GSA EXPANSION ZONE

— VOID

— SECTOR

— WARPGATE SYSTEM

Humans refer to the Karandu Galaxy as the Milky Way Galaxy.

WARPGATE

A transportation construct created by the Builders, an ancient species that dates prior to the Classical Era. The gates are capable of moving matter across vast interstellar distances at near instantaneous speeds. The Warpgates are 100 rudon wide polyhedral structures through which each facet is an entry point to another gate in a connecting system. Ships entering move along a vector of space called a Warppath. A Warppath is continuously stretched and compressed allowing for faster than light travels while shielding the travelers from any outside objects or forces. The Warpgates were planted in Star systems across the entire Karandu Galaxy over 100 million turns ago and then abandoned for millions of turns before being re-discovered by several alien species at the start of the Classical Galactic Era. The group of alien species that stumbled upon the gates were able to use them but never replicate its true technological potential. The gates served as the only faster than light transportation until several Warpgates and the entire Warppath system were destroyed to save the galaxy from a self-replicating robot army millions of turns before the birth of the Galactic Star Alliance.

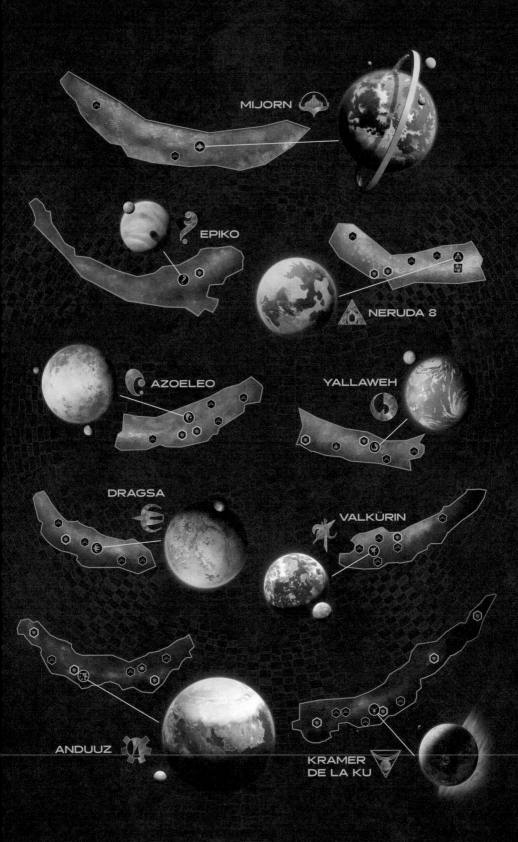

MIJORN

EPIKO

NERUDA 8

AZOELEO

YALLAWEH

DRAGSA

VALKÜRIN

ANDUUZ

KRAMER
DE LA KU

CHAPTER 10
THE GALACTIC STAR ALLIANCE

At first, Kruk was impressed that the GSA had dispatched a speedy *Mayad* class cruiser with fighter support to escort him to Mijorn. Even at *Patch 4*, though, the 21,000 *kulon* trip would take 39 prikes, and the journey so far had been lonely and uneventful. He thought he'd spend more time with Captain Paradon catching up on studies, getting tips on his Recall training, but they'd only had two brief conversations.

For trips this long, passengers were usually kept in cryo. Kruk was not only awake, he was confined to quarters for "security purposes." Mute guards were ever-present at his cabin door. Meals were brought to him. There was a *Resistor* for physical training, but his network access was limited to a scrubbed internal military hub. As the prikes stacked and he tried to guess at the reasons, a sickening dread crept over him.

Forever eventually ended; his solitude broken by the arrival of multiple soldiers, and an order to get dressed. They took him to the main hangar. The *artgrav* had dissipated, meaning they'd landed. For an instant, Kruk saw Paradon arriving, but the hatch opened and he was blinded by warm sunlight.

The 24th Generation Mayad Class Cruiser
A GSA battle starship measuring 0.4 rudons long with a crew of 14,000. They are commonly a GSA military Kuadron (Battle Group) command ship. Equipped with a reinforced, regenerating hull, shields, railguns, beam cannons, plasma torpedoes, ship to ship nuclear ordinance, and 150 Suppressor fighters. Take on average 40 turns to construct. Most are over 3000 turns old. They are usually deployed close to or within star systems.

Patch 4
A flowspace speed, 550,000 kulons/turn (or 736,000 light-turns/turn), a restricted flowspace used by GSA Military, Policing, Investigation, and Disaster Relief.

Resistor
A polymorphic athletic suit that molds itself in metal ribbons around the wearer to create a flexible framework that will resist the wearer's every motion. They are used to provide dynamic exercise for limited quarters and low and zero gravity.

Sweet, real air breezed over him filling his lungs. As his eyes adjusted, he saw buildings, lines of flying ships, and, further off, the massive skyscrapers of an oceanside city. At the horizon, the land rose into mountains; their peaks seemed to touch a giant halo in the sky. He'd arrived.

- - -

Not far off, KruktuskenBor stepped off his starship, *Nadisir*, and took in the scent of alpine *runyaya* and *blue varoon*s. The hangar for the The GSA's Council of Worlds' regional office overlooked ice-laden peaks so tall that snow never fell on the summits. Through the atmosphere's purplish haze, he saw *The Ring* encircling the planet—an ancient reminder of a civilization long gone. Bor had returned to Mijorn, original home of the GSA.

He only wished it was under better circumstances.

An attaché approached: a lovely specimen of the *Zundrilla*, with rich, vermillion scales, and metal protrusions.

"Councilmember KruktuskenBor, this way, please." Cricking nervously, she motioned him toward an exit. "I'm afraid I must apologize. Normally, we'd have significantly better accommodations, but our site lead is off-world and notice was short, so we've prepared your old office."

Wherever Bor went, he received respect. During his 270 turns in the government, he'd rotated ever higher, finally reaching the top of the Communications Department. Now he was a Prime, a Sector head, and a World Council member. Though it meant never again living on Dragsa, his home world, serving the galaxy had always been his sole ambition. Required to move every eight turns, he'd lived on 33 planets and had experienced at least as many cultures, traditions, lifestyles, ecologies, and reasons for living.

He gave the attaché a moment to sweat what his response might be, then smiled politely. "Not a worry. I prefer the high altitude. It provides clarity, not to mention a break from the usual hustle and bustle of a government center."

Nadisir
Bor's personal transportation vessel, it is a Frija Class Starship, 15 tradons long, used for the transportation of high level GSA members, patch 5 capable with kinetic absorptive layers, double shields, flares, drones, defensive railguns, and artillery. Built by Sector 7 Enterprises, the Frija Class Starships were utilized to dramatically reduce the need for military escort of Primes and Assembly members.

Runyaya
A dark grey, ground covering plant that spreads in sticky, geometrically faced spherical nodes that contain a seed. They emit a delightful odor to most GSA species, are notable for their seed husks, and, if nutured properly, can be used for an adhesive for forging weapons.

Hooting happily, she led him onward. At the exit, Bor touched the stone wall allowing the tactile sensation to stimulate his memories. Recall was a skill few Dragsan's had mastered at his level. How long had it been since he'd visited Mijorn as a Tier 3 Comm Officer? 45 or was it 48 turns? Regardless, he remembered how exhilarating it was being this close to the action.

Being part of the inner circle granted access, and, thankfully, a privacy that few could imagine. Because of who he was, his son's message had been sent on a hidden channel only he and his predecessors knew existed. More than that, he was able to destroy all record of it by sending scrambling waves, disguised as interference from a supernova, through every galactic relay it passed.

His son's first words conjured a ghost he'd prayed would remain dead:

The Creators of Space have returned.

He didn't doubt it. Kruktusken wouldn't use the channel if he weren't certain. The boy's summons to Mijorn only confirmed that the threat was real. The rest was more personal.

"Farraf, I don't understand. In the stories you told me as a child, good triumphed. But an evil rises and its armies live. Command thought they wanted Earth, but I realized they were after one of the probes I monitor. I had to warn them. Even so, the attack was flawless. They not only got the probe, our containment procedures failed to maintain the quarantine."

His son's actions conjured dual emotions. He'd acted admirably under immense pressure, but there was a cost. To convince Paradon, Kruk must've mentioned Loronzon.

It had been five turns since he'd seen the boy. Galactic service was a family tradition, but strict anti-nepotism laws banned them from serving together or even residing on the same planet. As a result, the family was rather fragmented, including his relationship to Kruk. Sometimes, Bor envied his brother, **DraktuskenDor,** for staying home. Dragsa's shining Nedsewa Sea sang deep in his heart, regardless of

---

Blue varoon
A Mijorn alpine mushroom, which if taken properly can help induce Recall for some non Dragsan. This property was discovered in the Second Dark Era by Dragsan Science Lead, Forthensertkor. Taken improperly will result in imminent death causing most species to not risk its secret gifts.

Zundrilla
A member species of the GSA from the planet of Zundril in the 6th Sector. They are 1 tradon tall, with 4 appendages, covered in reptilian-like scales, and have metallic-crystalline spikes that grow from their upper body.

DraktuskenDor
Dragsan names are broken into three portions: personal name (Drak), family name (Tusken), and title (Dor), which is sometimes granted later in life for certain status. In this case, Dor is the head of a great house.

time or distance.

The Inner Council's choice of Mijorn told Bor they were attempting to maintain tight control. If the government intended to be transparent, he'd have been summoned to Primidous for a full-scale Council meeting. It was easy to understand why. The revelation of Spek's return would fracture the lovely peace that they'd kept for so long. But the truth, like death, was subject only to delay.

Nothing lasts, not even the stars.

After navigating genetically coded locks, laser, and psionic evasion fields, they arrived at a very familiar set of semitransparent sapphire corundum doors.

"Is there anything else you need, sir?" His eager attaché was still lightly hooting. Must be new. Experienced support staff were practiced in being deadpan and nigh-invisible, whether your boss wanted atomic launch codes, fine *Samonca* prostitutes, or a snack.

"Would you find Thyron pre'Ducator for me? I believe she's still facilitator for this office. And send a formal Type 96 to Prime Abbotkrine requesting an immediate audience." To maintain secrecy, he added a half-true explanation. "He's an old friend, and we haven't seen each other in some time."

Not that it seemed to matter. More than familiar with the name of the *Effective Force Prime* for the Sector, the attaché made a squeaky gulp and hastened off to do as asked.

Bor pushed the portals with his palms revealing the room in which he'd spent so very much time controlling what the galaxy read, heard, and thought. Three sides of the hexagon were set in the mountain; the other three were composed of the same corundum as the door. More fully transparent, they revealed a sweeping view befitting the workplace aesthetic Primes shared.

Despite the grave reasons for his return, the full-circle made him chuckle.

There were, of course, changes. The *Clykwordol* sculptures were conspicuously absent as was the Tusken's familial tapestry of the first star map, the *Dra Ma Kun*.

Samonca
Sensual species with limited shapeshifting ability and powerful pheromones. They are considered the most exceptional of sexual companions and have their own working union: the League of Pleasure.

Effective Force Prime
GSA Sector head of the Department of the Military. There are 9 EFPs, one representing each of the 9 Sectors. The EFP's must be unanimous for any galactic war efforts.

Clykwordol
Were an ancient, intelligent, pre-industrial species that predated the Dragsan on Dragsa. They were estimated to have gone extinct 150 million turns ago. Their most enduring legacy was a rich culture of abstract statue making.

It had been mounted alongside a replica of the translation construct that was passed from one world to another heralding the end of *The Great Silence*. He assumed both were in storage.

Once he scanned his implant, the system instantly presented his correspondence matrix and divisional status reports. There was no pressing work. Then again, he couldn't imagine anything capable of shifting his mind from the return of the Creators.

To think, I sent Kruk to the Nova System as a safe start to his career. Still, sooner or later, he'd have needed some battle experience. The irony brought a deep, mournful trill. Now, he may have more than he'd ever need.

The vast, intricate web of lies Bor helped build successfully concealed the rebellion of the Voidwhisperers' original alpha squad, The Darkness Matters. Now, the falsehoods would collapse. Odian Spek's return would herald rebellions or, worse, wars of planetary secession. The inner circle had fifteen contingency plans, but even the most optimistic were well aware that many of the consequences of their lies would be irreparable.

Right or wrong, it's far too late to turn back.

Nebula whale chimes signaled his former staffer's arrival. "Come in, my dear."

"Prime KruktuskenBor, it is my pleasure to serve you again. This office has not seen someone of your stature and ability since you departed."

Thyron pre'Ducator was the lady who would pour his morning skrava or shoot someone, depending on his needs. Neither the passage of turns or the burden of a thousand secrets seemed to have aged her. He wondered if the same might be said of him.

"You're far too flattering, as always. Are we ready?"

"There's a *slipsphere* at port 19 waiting to take us to Councilmember Abbotkrine's residence." Bor smiled at the expected efficiency. It was good to be back.

Soon they hurtled down and away from the mountain. Unlike station sliptubes,

---

Dra Ma Kun
The first Dragsan starmap: made during the Classical Era after the Warpgate system was fully mapped. During the Second Dark Era, the Dra Ma Kun was used by the surviving ArchDragsan to locate their off-world colonies and bring them home.

The Great Silence
Also called the Second Dark Era, the 1.1 million turns following the destruction of the Warpgate system during which 90% of sentient life died out. With no faster than light travel, civilization and communication ceased leaving each world isolated.

Nebula Whale
Giant space creatures from Sector 8 that live in vacuum. They spend their lives in the gas clouds of the Lagoon Nebula consuming hydrogen to live.

in which crew traveled short distances suspended in air, slipspheres moved in a vacuum allowing shockwave-inducing speeds. In seconds, they were rushing past the beautiful habitations of the wealthy on the outskirts of *Rikjia*. The indigenous Metra built Mijorn's oldest city at the base of the tallest mountain peak. Its modern counterpart, and GSA headquarters, sat across the bay.

They zipped past stone-walled gardens and orchards surrounding lavish estates. As the sphere decelerated gracefully, it allowed for a better look at boulevards lined with ancient palaces and monuments. All were made from the same corundum as his office doors and windows but on a scale no one had been able to replicate for millions of turns.

They came to a stop at the local station, a central ring hub, where additional tubes undulated outward like petals. The sphere opened, leaving them standing at the head of a spacious avenue lined with broad *Namasaldra Trees*.

Bor walked quietly down a starkly empty street, Thryon shadowing him respectfully. The lack of inhabitants was Pias' doing: partly standard security, partly a need to keep their meeting secret.

With a quick glance from Bor: Thyron took a holocom from her belt. "Kimora, please let Prime Abbotkrine know Councilmember Bor is here."

A lush fountain in the middle of the boulevard engulfed Bor's vantage: crescent walls of cascading water still falling, flipped over, revealing circular steps.

"Prime Abbotkrine welcomes you to his home," Kimora announced.

The stairs took them to a state-of-the-art tunnel system and four waiting Hammerguard. They were escorted past two junctions, a set of blast doors, and into a maglift. Fearing what lay ahead, the railing forcefield felt like the universe closing its grip on Bor.

Pias had been the Voidwhisperer program's strongest advocate. Once he found out Spek was alive, the touchy subject could become volatile. Whatever strategy he settled on, Bor worried it might not be fully objective.

Slipsphere (Occurs on page 127)
A transportation capsule that carries occupants along a sliptube at high velocities. They were invented by the Baleen to move in a sliptube underwater at much higher speeds than their bodies could naturally tolerate the drag.

Rikjia
The original capital city of Mijorn. Location of the formalization and signing of the TAOTA. Considered holy by some, the city of Rikjia is a sacred land that factions like the Creators Of Space respect.

Kilrillian
A furry, humanoid species from the planet Kilril. Their docile, obedient nature makes them sought out for service and hospitality in the GSA.

The lift emerged in a huge underground structure with vaulted angular ceilings and spectacular floor mosaics. These were the halls of Ridius Ek, built to honor the great Metra leader who'd helped unite Mijorn and the galaxy. Knowing that legacy was at stake, Bor passed his stoic, cast diamond statue with a deep sigh.

Right, left, then right again, they finally reached the entrance to the quarters of the Effective Force Prime. The *Hammerguard* stood down, about-faced, and froze at their new posts. At KruktuskenBor's knock, Kimora called from the other side.

"Come in, please."

Kimora, a *Kilrillian* dur-female, stepped cheerily from behind her holodesk to greet them. "He's been waiting for you, sir."

"Pleased to see you in good spirits," Bor said. "Is your brother well?"

"Yes, thank you. Katron just left for a relief and rescue mission on Gradius 7, the old mining colony in Sector 7's echo quadrant. It should be an easy extraction, but with exiled *Harbitorats* inhabiting neighboring moons, Pias thought it wise to send the Zuni 88 Planet Guard with him. The 'Rats haven't exactly been cooperative since the GSA removed them. Unfortunately, we had to act. After all, their stewardship left the planet an ecological disaster."

"It's good to hear that Katron's part of the solution, then. He's a bright, determined young Kilrillian. I always knew he'd find his path. Speaking of which, heading back to Kilrill anytime soon to see your family?"

"Actually, yes. I'm planning to go for thirty prikes at the start of next turn."

"Splendid."

When Bor made no further small-talk, Kimora got the hint. "Go on in. He'll be there soon."

As he entered, Thyron stayed behind with Kimora. The office of Mijorn's Effective Force Prime was a spectacle. Great pillars, encasing projections of every past Prime resident, rounded the room creating a stream of faces. Hanging on the only wall they didn't cover and behind the current resident, the gallant Pias Abbotkrine,

---

Namasaldra Tree
Known as "Nature's Doorway," ancient species thought the portals created by the ring shaped trunks were used by magical spirits to travel between the worlds. The seeds are capable of surviving vacuum, extreme heat, and pressure for sustained periods. They are proven to have travelled from Neruda 7 to Neruda 8 on a piece of crust ejected from an ancient asteroid impact.

Hammerguard
Special division of the Dept. of the Military that protect planetside government installations. They began as a group of GSA soldiers who defended the capital complex against an insurrection by the Yarus (a native species that has since been extinct) on Kramer De La Ku 3 million turns ago. Using only battle hammers after an EMP detonated, their heroism lasted for 4 prikes.

Harbitorat - See page 132

were framed, elegant two-dimensional ink maps of space-combat maneuvers from the *Classical Era.*

Pias was a full tradon in height and usually bipedal. As a six-limbed Anduuzil, though, this was entirely optional. Head broad, his face flat and noseless, two eyes sat atop a narrow mouth able to expand into a head-splitting, fearsome, toothed smile. Each set of limbs were dinosaur-like, but the dexterity of the digits increased from feet to upper extremities.

A GSA founding species, the Anduuzil had millions of turns experience dealing with other sentient species. Its individuals also had the time to develop their skills. Anduuz was part of a rare three-star system that provided stable orbits. The unique radiation environment this created evolved a cellular structure that led to extraordinarily long lives. Pias Abbotkrine was four-hundred fifty-one turns.

"KruktuskenBor, so good to see you. What's so dire it brought you all the way to this side of the Sector for a clandestine get together? I hope there isn't some intergalactic war I should be prepping for. Ha!"

"Well..." A cloud swept over Bor. "... Much as I wish you were further from the truth, in about twenty nolaprikes you'll receive news of a quarantine failure in the T-Class Nova System. What it won't say is that the failure was caused by an attack. Worse, a comm officer recognized the tactics as unique to the Creators of Space. A First Contact escort was dispatched to retrieve him. A contingent is on its way here for a military council debrief."

Pias' head-splitting grin went into freefall. "What?" He rose, accenting his height, clasped one set of arms in front of him and the other behind. "Bor, how is it you had to travel so far to tell me what I should have known before you?"

"Communication is my job. To state the obvious, this confirms what we long suspected. Odian Spek isn't dead. He's back."

The words ran a shiver down Pias's malleable spine. His firm voice shook. "Are you sure? We found his arm floating in his cruiser's wreckage at the Loronzon

---

Classical Era
The second period of galaxy spanning civilization from 19-9 million turns ago. During this time sentient species could only use the Builder Warpgates (The Builders were the first known civilization and are widely considered the ancient fathers of the universe. Their ingenuity created an interstellar network of Warppaths, along which ships could travel faster than light. To date, no GSA species has been able to replicate the Warpgate technology). Eventually thousands of worlds joined together in The Cooperative, which existed peacefully for millions of turns. This included The Dragsan, Anduuzil, Valkon, Fandaxians, Baleen, Metra, Rakilla, Ulron, and Droteans. But expansion could not keep up with population and the Cooperative rifted over fights for resources. A galaxy-spanning war followed in which trillions died. This era ended when an endgame device was activated that created a vast self replicating machine army that destroyed many civilizations. Faced with annihilation, the surviving species banded together to destroy the Warpgates and saved the galaxy. A 1.1 million turn Dark Age ensued.

incident, ripped at the socket and melted by plasma. You and I both saw it, Bor."

Bor nodded at the memory. "True, but many have survived the loss of a limb, and I don't know who else could pull off an attack like this. They knew about the Nova System and how to beat our monitoring defenses. Also, the comm officer is my son, Kruk. He recognized the tactics from Loronzon and... told the assembled control room."

He raised a powerful hand and gestured, palm up. "How much did you tell him?"

Bor had to tilt his head back to look his friend in the eyes. Despite knowing Pias for ages, he was still surprised how terrifying he could be. "Everything, well almost everything."

The room vibrated with Pias' low frequency growl. "Why?"

Bor shrugged. "The continuity of secrets has always been part of the plan. We have to ensure that competent, prepared people know the full truth in case they have to deal with it. The Council won't see it this way, but a breach was bound to happen. We should expect another attack on any planets being considered for a Class S. At least we have a warning, thanks to my son."

Pias snarled. "Thanks to your son, this is a catastrophe."

Afraid he might panic, Bor became adamant. "I'm handling it."

"Are you now? How are you managing the information flow?"

"Per *Code 54*. No comms in or out during the investigation."

Pias balked. "That won't erase the memories of everyone at the Quarantine."

"Steps are being taken to ensure there are no... misunderstandings."

Still dissatisfied, he growled again. "Cut the *luukmarm* bureaucratic fluff. What have you done about the officers who actually heard your son?"

Trying to appear menacing himself, or at least cold and calculating, Bor nonchalantly looked at his fingernails. "I haven't come this far without knowing how to tie up loose ends. Paradon's been stripped of his rank and reassigned to a mining colony.

Anduuzil
A large, 6 limbed, longevinous species from the planet Anduuz, a founding member of the GSA from the 8th Sector. They are usually alpha, imposing, authoritative, and stoic. Anduuzil are commonly in positions of high authority, military, policing, and physical labor.

Code 54
GSA protocol calling for full communication blackout during investigation of an attack on a restricted government facility.

Luukmarm
Anduuzil word for "feces," commonly used as an insult.

The far more cooperative Aroxia has been promoted. Entok… Well, unfortunately he sent an unauthorized transmission to his wife. They were both executed, along with significant relations, as per *Article 37*."

Pias squinted slightly, his lips pursed indicating he'd let it go… for now.

This allowed Bor to bring up more immediate concerns. "Don't get too comfortable, yet. There's more. The Voidwhisperers couldn't stop the invaders from reaching Earth, so the planetary fail safe was activated."

"Did they get through?"

"No. But the humans were testing antimatter. There was an explosion. It was significant: visible from lookout SQA12. Luckily, even with the concurrent loss of their probe, the humans are still too devolved to realize it was something from space. I have been carefully monitoring their communication channels."

Surprisingly, Pias laughed. "KruktuskenBor, my dear friend, how long have you been aware that thousands of civilizations exist on worlds other than your own?"

Bor was puzzled. "All my life."

"All their lives they've believed the opposite. Last I checked, humans pray to gods they've never met and think themselves unique. Trust me, they'll make any excuse necessary to maintain that illusion. It won't be an issue. Our real focus has to be Odian Spek."

The cavalier attitude disturbed Bor, but he moved on. "Alright, then. We'll have to inform the rest of the GSA soon. If we don't stay ahead of this, it'll look like a coverup.

"We'll do no such thing. We'll simply deploy Voidwhisperers, quietly, to each of the nine sectors to assure the GSA we're aware of a threat and are taking the proper precautions."

Bor's face twisted. "All due respect but do you think it's ethical, or even possible, to hide this? If—when—Odian Spek attacks again, we need to be prepared. Besides, given his history, wouldn't it be wiser to scale back Voidwhisperer involvement?

Article 37
GSA protocol dictating the termination of any GSA personnel who disobeys a Code 54 communication blackout. Article 37 includes the termination of the offender's family.

Harbitorat
A prolific, sentient species that look like a turquoise and pink rodent, has a venomous bite, and are experts at ship and station repair due to their small size and engineering skills.

Artgrav (occurs on page 123 paragraph 3)
Artificial Gravity is produced on most GSA spacecraft to allow for ease of motion and prevent health damage of prolonged low gravity environments. Gravtiles produce a unidirectional graviton stream perpendicular to their surface when powered. Commonly square plates, they usually tile the floors of ships.

The only other time they've ever failed us was when they defected to his side."

To his credit, Pias gave Bor's position some thought. Then, he stuck with his own conclusion. "Panic gives us nothing, and there's no reason to assume any conspiracy runs deeper than the one we share. Spek's smart; Bor, a zealot, but he believes himself a liberator, not a terrorist, and he's not suicidal. Other than the forces we use to protect T class planets, he's never attacked any GSA. With the Nova System reinforced, he won't attack there again."

"What if you're wrong?"

"I'm not. What makes him so dangerous also makes him predictable. He thinks he's right. He craves legitimacy... wants the COS positioned as a political movement. He knows he'll never widen his support if he targets the GSA. Plus, he's getting old. I suspect he's tiring of the crusade. Age tends to bring moderation."

Bor shook his head. "It can also bring desperation. If he thinks the humans are a perfect way to prove he's right, it could be disastrous."

Pias waved him off with two hands. "Enough. We'll wait until your son is debriefed, then summon the Council of Worlds. We dictate what we reveal and when."

Considering the conversation over, he turned back to his desk issuing commands and loading holoscreens. Bor wasn't quite done.

"I know you feel responsible for the death of billions of Loronzons, but I'm concerned that you're underestimating the military threat. Odian led the best VW squad in history."

Pias' eyes rolled. "You mean well old friend, but the Loronzon incident set system integration back generations. That's the bigger threat. If the newer worlds find out the COS came from our black-ops, it would weaken trust in the GSA and feed Spek's rebel mystique. I do fear the Valkon, I'd be a fool not to. He rallied an armada under our noses, but I don't fear his prowess half as much as what he stands for. Our existence requires we maintain interplanetary faith in the GSA. Until we

---

The Ring (occurs on page 124 paragraph 2)
A giant, artificial structure 5000 rudons in diameter encircling Mijorn and made by the Builders about 68 million turns ago. It's entire inner surface is inhabitable. With an atmosphere and filled with natural ecosystems, the outside of the Ring has been modified by the GSA into a massive orbital defense platform.

know more, the less the public knows, the better." The conversation truly over, he dismissed his guest. "Thank you for your time, Councilmember."

Bor nodded, bowed, and embraced Pias before exiting, deep in thought.

Stopping at the door, Bor turned back with a final thought. "Shed a tear for my son."

For millions of turns a handful of sentient species made the GSA what it was today; enormous, efficient, but anxious. The Loronzon incident, the Quarantine on Dimur 7, *the massacre of Giyan Prime* had steadily eroded confidence in their ability to assess new species. They were no longer so sure how to tell if a given culture had good intentions, whether at heart they were interested in preserving life or destroying it.

Unhappy, he rejoined Thyron. The two made their way to the maglift in silence.

On the other hand, Pias was usually right, and, speaking of faith, he trusted his friend. Still, times were changing. Nova and Odian Spek were at the center of that change, and, despite the GSA's advances, life remained a fickle thing.

Massacre of Giyan Prime
5.4 million turns ago, the GSA was monitoring a rare system with two intelligent species evolving concurrently on different planets. When the Gorg, the more developed, went to colonize the other, the Hleesa, the GSA intervened. But when the Hleesa were given Class-S first, the Gorg became resentful. They attacked the Hleesa before their GSA status was finalized by throwing a nuclear arsenal into the atmosphere before GSA forces could stop them. The resulting battle within the system took heavy GSA casualties and ultimately led to the extinction of Hlessa and Gorg. The GSA changed its first contact rules after this event: if there are more than one intelligent species within a system, both must qualify for Class-S before first contact.

CHAPTER 11
OWL POST

A light morning wind flicked autumn leaves across campus. Behind older, more traditional buildings, an impressive array of cutting-edge architecture sat in a unique formation. Along the top of the tallest, the evenly spaced windows varied wildly in size and shape. The polarized *polyResonate* plates could expand or contract on command: their fluid geometry directed by magnetic fields. The first of their kind, they were designed by Dr. Lisa J. Hubert, director of MIT Labs.

Below, a young blonde student led a group of Kepler sixth cycles on tour. "The northwest lab holds the largest concentration of nanotechnology on the planet."

There was a question. "Kepler's nanotechnology lab is pretty extensive; how does that translate into getting accepted here?"

It was a good question. Kepler funneled over 20% of its best and brightest to MIT. Even more impressive, 40% of that group who graduated MIT went on to work at Outer Limits labs. The relationship between the three institutions was deep and enduring.

"We suggest a minimum of 4 robotics courses, three independent projects...." Her gaze caught by the appearance of an elegant woman, she stopped mid-sentence.

---

polyResonate
Type of material that can be vibrated into different atomic configurations using magnetic fields.

"Dr. Hubert! Wow! How are you?!"

"Mary, great to see you." Lisa Hubert was formidable, but her tone was open and friendly. "These our latest Keplers?"

Pleased to have the director remember her name, Mary beamed. "Yes, they are!"

Lisa took in the group. "I remember when I was at Kepler. These years of care-free exploration will be the best of your lives. I don't want to interrupt, but if any of you have questions for me, I'm happy to indulge."

A girl's hand shot up. "I'd like to ask about CERN. What..."

Dr. Hubert cut her off. "I'll stop you right there. Every student asks about CERN, so I'll tell you what I tell them. The explosion was tragic; the lives of many friends and colleagues were lost. As to the cause, the extensive, relentless investigation into my family and friends made it abundantly clear my husband was in no way responsible. Now, I'll throw in some free advice: learn, create, experiment, inno-vate. Don't waste time assigning blame where it doesn't belong. It fills your head with hate, leaving little room for anything else, and it certainly won't get us off this planet any faster."

She headed off knowing the answer wouldn't discourage them from pondering the big question: What really happened? She hoped Bernard's CORE break-throughs would soon lay waste to the endless suspicion they'd endured. Time would tell.

Drawing closer to the lab, Lisa noticed a peculiar bird atop the registration building. Given the daylight and the familiar black and gold patches on its feathers, she chuckled at her husband's nerdiness.

"Ah, Bernie, you're back to communicating by owl."

The mall was well-trafficked, but this was MIT, so no one batted an eye when the *owl* flapped down and spoke to her. "I'll meet you in your office."

Once there, Lisa threw open the window. The owl flew in and perched on the coat rack. Not bothering to face it, she set her things down. "So, what've you been

---

Owl
Science geeks in the future enjoyed paying homage to their favorite late 20th century childhood inspirations with these drone styled messaging systems.

up to?"

It took the feathered friend a while to encode and transmit her words. It must be a new prototype. Bernard's response came half a minute later.

"Oh, the usual, making interplanetary travel a reality, saving the world, and so on." She was stunned. "The Mayflower was a success?! But the reports said..."

The delay somehow resolved. The answer came quickly, "Don't believe everything you read, love. I am sorry I've been away, but I'll be home this weekend, at last! Isn't that fantastic? I can even grab you from the airport." Abruptly, he took on a more serious tone. "I do need a favor. Would you invite Ava and Galena for dinner tomorrow? I have a business proposition for them."

To mask her anxiousness, his better half feigned mild amusement. "I don't hear from you for two weeks, you make a major scientific breakthrough, neither of which is unusual, but your first request is for a business dinner with my best friends? What could possibly be happening in St. Bernard Hubert's world that he must wine and dine Iron Man's Maya Hansen and the 21st century Leonard McCoy? Oh, never mind, I'm sure it's a long story. It can wait until we're together along with my more personal congratulations."

"Sweet Lisa, I commend your wit and thank you for lowering yourself to my level. Oh, I met with Angie and Will. They agree we have..." Suddenly realizing the match he'd lit, his voice trailed off.

"Talking to Angelika On, are we?" Lisa dropped her sweet tone. "Getting fired and left to the wolves wasn't a big enough deterrent?"

The delay returned—conveniently. It was a full, long minute before Bernard spoke through the owl again. "You know what the fusion drive means for the world? For our family? We need Angelika, we need Will, we need Godric, Galena and Ava, too."

Looking down at her quantum entanglement papers, she briskly took note of her counterparts' argument. "I'll make sure Galena and Ava are there. 19:45?"

"Perfect. I'll cook my famous four-cheese serrano alfredo."

She laughed genuinely. "Why didn't you start with that? It'd have made the conversation easier for you."

The owl winked and flew off, leaving the MIT lab's keeper of the keys with a whirlwind of emotion: happy, proud, anxious, sad. She always knew about Bernard's plan to clear his name and theirs, but the price, a five year space voyage, had just grown much more real making it increasingly hard to swallow.

Morning blended into afternoon as she reviewed the weekly lab report, answered 237 emails, and texted Isaac. When her watch struck 18:00, she jumped behind the wheel of her *Newton 7GRX*—and headed for the *New England Intercontinental Airport*.

The flight to the Carolinas particularly dragged painfully lengthening the hours until she could see her partner and equal. Nibbling an edible to calm her nerves, Lisa nodded off and, thankfully, didn't come to until the plane touched down in the fading twilight of purple rolling mountains. For a blissful moment, her worries about the months and years to come faded.

The cylinder seating carriage detached from the fuselage lowering passengers to the wet ground. She stepped out and there he was—her knight—leaning against the car hood cleaning his glasses. The choice to bear the weight of the world had aged him considerably, but he remained as handsome as he was on their wedding day.

He met her eyes and smiled. "Hey, sweet young lady, I think I used to live here, but it's been so long I don't remember." He pulled a piece of paper tucked in his hat, bowed, and presented it. "Can you decipher this map I wrote for myself? It's super intuitive."

Seeing the blur of vector equations, she returned the smile. "If I recall, kind sir, there's nothing more stimulating than a woman who's good at math."

With practiced precision, she folded the paper over and over until it became an origami flower. The last corner in place, the compass bearing for their home

---

Newton 7GRX
"The "grand pumba" of racing cars and more powerful than the Newton 200, the 7GRX is the rally model of the 7th iteration of the Newton and encompasses style, muscle, and efficiency in one fully automated sportscar.

New England Intercontinental Airport
Formerly known as Logan Airport in Massachusetts, it was renamed under the W.C. and services nonstop flights to every continent but Antartica.

became visible in the math. A sucker for their old method of passing notes in Kepler classrooms, she handed the flower back.

"You seem to be on the right track, sir."

Bernard wrapped his arms around her waist and engulfed her in a hug. Thinking this might be the last time things would be so simple, Lisa tried to make it last giving him an extra squeeze before letting go. The warm, secure feeling lasted until they were on their way home.

With a slight sigh, she said, "Start at the beginning."

The recap occupied nearly all the hour and twenty-minute drive and left her agitated. Looking away from her husband with arms crossed, she said, "You couldn't have updated me on anything? You even went to see Isaac, and he said nothing. His own mother."

Bernard pursed his lips. "I'm trying to keep a low profile. We have to assume our communications are still tapped."

"Seriously? You hid an entire second fusion drive from your own company, but you're worried about our phones? This over-compartmentalization is too much, Bernard, even for you."

He reached over and held her hand. "I know. I need help; I admit it. That's why this time I'm asking for it."

Lisa kissed his knuckles. "Bernard William Hubert, I know you better than you do. You'd much rather carry the world by yourself. Your ambition is breathtaking, one of the great things about you. Please be careful that it doesn't become your undoing."

He broke his gaze from the road to look at her. "Undoing? Lisa, we're already undone. I'm trying to stop the human race from stalling out."

"I know, but don't think seeing the logic makes the conclusion any easier for me. You haven't shown the slightest regret at the thought of leaving us. It's hurtful, Bernard."

The tires clacked as they crossed a small bridge overhung by tall sycamores. "I'm not lacking in feelings, my sweet; I'm full of purpose. History has scores of couples separated by extraordinary circumstances and a shared duty to better the world. Today, we're that couple."

She let go of his hand. "Yes, but you actually want us to be that couple."

"Destiny demands it of us."

Oh, she understood; she'd understood completely since that night at Kepler. They were lying beneath the pines, gazing at stars, debating the existence of intelligent alien life when she asked.

"What if they are out there, but they don't want to talk to us?"

The idea upset Bernard deeply. He went on about it for hours lamenting how all the joyful products of humanity might never be shared. He was terrified that our species might remain alone, not for a lack of effort but a lack of worth. The implication was unspoken, but Lisa heard it clearly enough: *If humanity wasn't worthy, how could Bernard Hubert be?* He'd vowed to find the answer, and the quest had driven their lives ever since right up to this moment in the car.

"You're angry."

Sometimes the great genius was adorably clueless, particularly when it came to emotions.

"You're perceptive."

"We've had this conversation, Lis, many times. We've agreed."

"I still don't see why I can't come with you."

He gave the standard answer. "Because your abilities cannot be taken out of play on Earth. The world doesn't need another astrophysicist, but it does need your nanotech expertise."

When he tried to clasp her hand and kiss it, she recoiled.

Bernard looked her dead in the eyes. "And one of us needs to be here for Isaac."

She let him think he was being chivalrous but only for a moment. "Your beautiful arguments are utter bullshit. Isaac isn't a child anymore. You've seen him. You know. You also know damn well that five years in space could bring a century's worth of nanotech discoveries. Will you please finally tell me the real reason?"

He forced a half-smile. "At least you know it's not Angelika."

In an effort to be witty, he'd skated onto thin ice. Her eyes threw daggers. "Yes, how very reassuring of you not to include her in the crew."

Bernard's surrender came in the form of a long exhale. "All right, all right. We both know there's a very good chance I won't be coming back. One of a thousand possible reasons is that the aliens will be hostile. In any case, if I fail, Isaac has to carry on and lead a second expedition. Yes, he's no child; he'll thrive on his own, but he is young and losing both of us could set him back. He has to be fully prepared, sooner rather than later, in science, politics, business, and warfare. You have to ensure that happens, Lisa, that he has the discipline to know when to act and the courage to do so properly. Can you see that I can't possibly trust anyone else to do the job?"

Lisa smiled at the sincerity and endless trust. Here was the man she loved, following his destiny, convinced he could change things for the better. She believed he could too. Knowing if the roles were reversed, she'd have asked the same; a tear rolled gracefully down her cheek.

He was tearing up too. "I love you more than you can imagine. I love you more than I can imagine."

Eyes ahead, they held hands snug in the conclusive silence until Bernard turned onto their street. Lisa cleared her throat.

"There's some good news. Ava's flight doesn't get in until tomorrow."

Pleased by the dangerous look in her eye, Bernard sped up. That night they made their own universe: exploring its depth and breadth until the sun regretfully rose.

Dr. Galena Hunter jogged out of the airport, wheelie in tow, to a familiar shout and a frantic wave. Lisa called from a top-down convertible: "Get in, gal! We'll be late!"

"Coming!"

She tossed her bag in the trunk. "I was half-out the door when a student group returned from Africa claiming they'd been exposed to Ebola. If you're going to make yourself sick to skip school, at least do the research. I actually had to remind them that if you're not vomiting and shitting blood after twenty-four days, it's not Ebola; it's dysentery. Go drink some fluids and stop wasting my time. Anyway, the initial tests were negative, and there's nooooo protocol dictating a full quarantine, so here I am."

Galena hopped in, hugged Lisa, and buckled up. "Amateurs. At that age, I was selling four-hour flus out of my *Hubble* dorm good enough to fool Kepler nurses."

Lisa gave her a look. "Oh?"

"Oh, right. You're a Kepler, aren't you?"

"Loud and proud. Loud aaaaaaaand proud," Lisa said. "Well, I may not have been able to fool your test."

"Hey, I'm sorry you weren't there so I could buy your flu."

Laughing, they drove off amidst fiery, autumnal colors; yellow-leaved tulips, orange hornbeam, shining red dogwood, and oak. Forests stretched all around, their isoprene giving the Blue Ridge Mountains their name. Boston's industrial smell was one of the few things Lisa didn't like about MIT. Here, the fresh air whipping by was intoxicating. By the time they reached the Hubert homestead, they were in a perfect mood for a jovial dinner and meeting of minds.

Galena stared. No matter how many times she visited, she couldn't get over the design. It was straight from Kepler's campus. The sixty-meter house had no corner or end. Glass from floor to ceiling, its two levels, linked by sweeping staircases, flowed and warped around one another forming an infinity symbol. Despite the

---

Hubble
The Hubble Academy is a rival SETI school to Kepler founded by Aiden Alexander.

edgy design, it had a cozy, inviting air.

"Bernie, we're home!"

"In here, darling. Ah, Galena, excellent! Ava and I were just getting into the uses of nanobots in microbiology. Oh well... to be continued."

The renowned biologist, who was also a maid of honor at their wedding, had been chatting with her husband in the study. The half-empty glasses of '44 Malbec from Buenos Aires had no doubt put some of the gleam in their smiles. Bernie raised his to their guests.

"I appreciate you both being here, especially on such short notice."

Ava snickered. "Thankfully, travel and meetings involving Lisa Hubert can be expensed as research. Perks of being an O.L. contractor."

"Some of us didn't go to Kepler," Galena said making it clear she'd paid for her trip.

"Right, Hubblepuff."

Lisa snorted at the old school rivalry. Bernard moved quickly to restore the peace with wine. "Malbec or Pinot, my dear?"

"Pinot, please."

"I'll have the Malbec," Galena said while removing her travel boots. "Thanks."

Bernard met them in the foyer where he exchanged freshly poured glasses for their bags and waved them into the study. As they sat, he disappeared into the kitchen to retrieve appetizers.

The instant he was gone, Ava cornered Lisa. "Is it true?"

"Is what true?"

Galena rounded on her. "Stop it. You know exactly what." Lisa put her nose in the air. "I'm sure I've no idea."

"Drop the act, Lis."

"Tell us now, or we're leaving."

Begrudgingly, she gave in. "Of course, it's true. Why else would he be making the alfredo? You're here because he has a business proposition for you."

As if she'd won an award for guessing, Ava exclaimed. "I freaking knew it!" "Interesting," said Galena. "So, are you going?"

Lisa started at the question. She despised having to answer, but her friends were keenly waiting.

"One of us needs to stay... for Isaac," she said, in a tone that dared them to challenge her motherly instincts.

Oblivious, Bernard reentered with pigs in blankets, caprese salad, and his famous portobello french fries.

"We have much to discuss." He looked around to be sure everyone understood the gravity, then added, "And none of it should be done on an empty stomach."

Wasting no time, he grabbed a handful of the finger foods and stuffed it in his mouth. Appropriately amused, the others joined in. After making short work of the appetizers, they took their glasses to the dining room.

Ava dove right into the unspoken subject at hand. "Lisa says CORE is working through some pretty exciting discoveries."

Galena confirmed it. "Yes. Yes, she did."

"Did she, now?" Bernard raised his eyebrows and turned to his wife. "Well thank you for warming them up. Might as well get straight to it, then. The fusion drive is real. It can get us to the edge of the solar system in two and a half years. I'm planning a mission comprised of myself and eleven other exemplary examples from key fields to reach the Kuiper Belt and investigate the disappearance of the Voyager probe. In the extremely improbable event we'll encounter intelligent life we'll be acting as a first contact team representing our species."

Galena gulped the remains of her glass. Though trained in medicine, her understanding was superior to most physicists. "How? The energy requirements to contain a reactor that size would be staggering... debilitating. William Hunt couldn't solve that problem and it was *his* theory."

"Isaac figured it out. I don't quite get the math, myself, but we tested it, and it works."

"Hmmmm." Galena murmured with a keen interest. "So, Angelika builds it, you captain it, and we go explore the stars?"

Ava's brow twisted. "Do you hear yourselves? Bernard, I love and respect you; we go back a long way, but are you serious?"

"Completely. We're calling it W.C.O.L. Nomad -A, in honor of Darren. By we, I mean William Hunt, Godric Adams, Angelika On, and myself. Ang will stay on the ground with Lisa. Will, Ric and, I hope the two of you are coming with us."

At the name Ang, Lisa looked briefly irritated but still nodded her head in agreement.

Taken aback, Ava's voice trembled. "Honestly, I... I didn't actually believe you until you mentioned Darren. Did he have something to do with the fusion drive? Was that what you were working on at CERN? Darren died for his work so did a lot of our classmates. We could too. Is it really worth it?"

Noticing the exchange of looks, Galena asked, "Darren also went to Kepler?" Lisa nodded. "We were all close."

She didn't mention that Ava and Darren had briefly been a "thing" back then. First loves were not easily forgotten.

Ava repeated her question. "You want us to give up five years of our lives? No. You're asking us to risk it all... our lives. Why? What can we gain from this?"

Bernard had to be laser focused, give enough to satisfy but not expose a truth too dangerous to share until they were actually in space. "The short answer, Ava, is we don't know. We don't know what's out there; we don't know the risks. What we do know is that we will be the first humans past Saturn: the first to behold Neptune, the first to leave our solar system. William, Godric, and I have hand-picked the nine we want to join us. We choose you two for your ability to see the bigger picture.

Galena's vaccine research contained the *tuberculosis epidemic*. Ava's work on limb regeneration is revolutionizing biology. Between you, there are dozens of patents, papers, awards, and millions of saved lives. We need you. Humanity needs you.

"Girls, cut the crap," Lisa said. "You've already sacrificed everything for the greater good; you both want more out of life than Earth, and you both know if anyone can do this, it's Bernard, William, and Godric."

Ava and Galena knew Lisa would never blindly oblige her husband. Her support was the cherry on top. They'd often seen her put Bernard in his place when she disagreed. They raised their glasses and mutely toasted her.

"I have a million more questions," Ava said, "but I didn't fly all the way here on Angelika's dime to not enjoy that alfredo."

The mood shifting, Bernardo ran to the kitchen and returned with a beautifully plated bowl of pasta smothered in a creamy, golden sauce punctuated with bits of crispy ham.

Ava smacked her lips. "I thought you were exaggerating, Lisa."

"Oh my god! This is everything!" Galena blurted.

They ate, drank, discussed, and planned. When the three women were deep in conversation about a nanotech biometric signal monitor to install in the suits, Bernard took a moment for himself.

Next he knew, Lisa was shouting snapping her fingers in his face. "BERNARD! Anyone home? Hello?"

"Yes! Sorry. What were you saying?"

"I asked you to tell them about the NanoCube you and William created at Kepler. He still uses it, doesn't he?"

Bernard winced. *I'd have preferred you hadn't brought that up. You were right, Will. Touché.*

"Uh, yes. Security-wise, it's the safest place on Earth. In fact, he keeps all the

---

Tuberculosis Epidemic
The African Tuberculosis Epidemic of 2079 was contained to the continent by the World Health Organization, but 50 million people died.

Nomad schematics on it. In the next few weeks he'll bring it to Outer Limits to begin construction. You're more than welcome to come have a look."

"A NanoCube... fascinating," Ava said. "Everyone thinks they're only theoretical."

"And we'd very much like to keep it that way," Bernard said.

"Understood."

Galena thought out loud. "Can we use it to store some sensitive medical research I'd like to bring?"

"As long as it isn't an infectious disease blueprint, I don't see why not. I'll clear it with William."

"Excellent!"

The course was set; Lisa played her integral role perfectly, and the crew was two stronger. The next morning as Bernard packed the car, Lisa had a final tea with her friends. Once certain he was out of earshot, Ava spoke for both of them.

"This is the most exciting thing that's ever happened in our lives. We can't imagine what you're going through—how strong you must be to let Bernard do this."

Lisa drained her tea. "We're scientists, Ava. The needs of the many..."

CHAPTER 12

REDACTED

Godric screamed into the phone. "She already has her O.L. security! And there's no way you'll convince her to get on a helicopter with W.C. personnel!"

A surly dark voice responded. "If you want him, if you want even the thought of your Nomad to have any hope, that's how it's going down."

"General, this is not W.C. jurisdiction."

"It is if I say it is. The man you want to chat with made a dead city sustainable with a few nuts and bolts. We're sending back up." A buzz, a click, then silence. Smith had hung up.

She's not going to like this.

Dreading her response, fearing for his safety even at this distance, he called Angelika. Indeed, her rage against a man she'd never met made his chest hurt.

"SMITH SAID WHAT?! Agh. If he wants to play games, let's send Bernard and my head of security. We'll see who's the better chess player."

"Understood, Angie." Thankfully, she hung up as well.

Shortly after, Bernard was sitting in a briefing room in Moab. He completely

---

understood why the excessive oversight boiled Angelika's blood. She hated playing by another's rules. He didn't care for it himself, but he understood that Godric was being thoughtful in positioning his chess pieces. If he believed having two knights, such as himself and Security Chief Roy, engage these pawns would help Nomad's chances for approval, Bernard was all for it.

Roy was Angelika's muscle: Bernard, the brains, the secret weapon she'd sorely missed. Analyzing the room while appearing zoned out was child's play for the Kepler K.I.N.G. Aside from Roy and himself, there were two Peacekeepers; Moab *Consul* Cheyenne Martin, a Council attorney, and two women who were clearly intelligence agents. It wasn't the sunglasses that gave them away; everyone wore those to ward off the desert sun. It was their constant displeased expressions.

Bernard managed to keep a low profile until Peacekeeper Commander Williams felt it necessary to read Ilya's file aloud. Everyone present already knew plenty about the man; his image was enshrined on two walls of the Moab regional office building they were in, not to mention the courtyard statue that looked like the Pietà. The grand irony made Bernard chuckle, which, in turn, caused P.K. Williams to snap at him.

"Something funny, Dr. Hubert?"

"No, Peter, not at all. Please continue."

Williams' death-stare lingered a bit, then he read. "Ilya O'Connell, born 2051, Framingham, Massachusetts. Older brother, Patrick, younger brother, Jacob. At the age of seven, Ilya displayed prodigal engineering skills."

Reminds me of Isaac, but Ilya sadly lacked the framework we provided for my son.

"At fourteen, Ilya's father, Jack, died in a construction accident at which point his mother, Ruth, moved the family to Denver. He declined three full scholarships from Kepler, Hubble, and Jefferson Hall and chose public school instead. An incident with CU Boulder followed. The details have been redacted."

He was building his first zero-shock matrix, Kepler-level work; making it more

---

Consul
The elected leader of Moab. The office is similar to a mayor but has broader authority that includes imprisonment, sentencing, command of the police and civilian troops, trade negotiation, treaty creation, educational duties, and engineering appropriation. Ilya O'Connell was the first Consul, serving from 2072 to 2074.

the pity Ilya had turned them down. Bernard heard all about it from Ilya himself. Not that they were good friends, but shining intellects tended to draw one another's attention.

They'd been introduced at the 2078 *NE01 Sector 5 Nanotech Symposium* following Bernard's keynote. The misunderstood hotshot seemed worthy of his time, so they talked—for hours. They started at the rebuilt Hayden Planetarium but following a joint and a bottle of mezcal, somehow ended up on a rooftop in the former Brooklyn. Bernard heard Ilya's side of the story that night providing clarity amongst the many black lines scrawled across the document in Commander Williams' hands.

"Following his expulsion, he moved to Moab, worked as a vehicle repairman while experimenting with battery efficiency, solar power, and lightweight structures."

Bernard grunted—A crude and circuitous way of saying he'd revolutionized off-grid travel.

"During the Darkness, he ran the municipality for eight months, with full autonomy."

Another glossing-over. Borderline blasphemous. Ilya's a hero here.

He made Moab's power grid self-sufficient in days, then shepherded a series of conservation projects that kept the town virtually unchanged throughout the global crisis. Greenhouses were rapidly built while wing-suited scouts mapped out local resources.

Bernard originally heard of him when P.K. forces began moving east from the Pacific. Finding mostly desert and a few anarchists when they reached Moab a bluegrass band was playing in the town park.

"Asked to join the W.C. rebuilding effort—he declined. Crashed non-sanctioned quadcopter on restricted W.C. military outpost—redacted—August 24, 2074. Passenger Naomi Barnes, girlfriend, was killed. Additional details have been redacted. To avoid prison, he accepted a plea deal to work with the W.C. Science

---

NE01 Sector 5 Nanotech Symposium
Largest annual engineering and technology conference in North America that started in the year 2073. Representatives from all major STEM companies participate in four days of presentations, workshops, recruitments, business deals, peer review, and ethical debate.

Division. For the following five years, he... redacted, redacted, redacted, redacted. 2080, he married Michelle Hostford. 2082, he stole a battery prototype from a World Council R&D facility. It malfunctioned, destroying his home and seriously injuring his spouse, who divorced him shortly after the incident. He denied any involvement whatsoever but made another plea deal. This time to work for— redacted—but was let go in 2086 and has spent the last five years here." Williams snapped the report shut. "Questions?"

Bernard leaned over to Roy. "What a painfully simplistic description of a great man."

He nodded. "He was certainly... ah... misunderstood."

Council attorney Wolf piped up. "I have a question. Why don't we just ask him to come in?"

Even P.K. Williams laughed at that. "He doesn't respond well to invitations. He has a strong preference for not being contacted—at all. If that's it, we're done here. Boots up in two hours."

And so, Bernard found himself strapped into a repurposed Black Hawk along with the other attendees. The personal touch, face-to-face contact with each candidate, was essential. Still, most of the others were a plane ticket, rental car, and door-knock away. This extreme greeting reflected fear. Not that Ilya was a murderer, no. His capabilities went far beyond killing.

This feels like a movie. It's not about simply bringing in an asset. It's more like Professor Moriarty hunting Sherlock.

It was a beautiful day in NA Zone 3, Grid 37, formerly Utah. No wind, the desert simply baked. A gecko, one of many on the ground, basked luxuriously atop a sandstone outcropping. The sunlight refracting off its dull green scales made it seem black. On its left were the distant snowcaps of the La Sal Mountains, on its right, endless winding cliffs, buttes, and mesas undulated towards the horizon.

Content, the gecko prepared for a long, midday nap when a subtle vibration pulsed through air and ground. The reverberations intensifying, the gecko frantically spun about, searching for an oncoming predator. But there was none.

The Black Hawk burst over the ridge. Its green and purple O.L. insignia shining, it zoomed beneath an arch scattering the gecko and its fellows.

The extraordinary speed of the fleeing reptiles impressed Bernard, but, mostly, he was thinking. *Ilya knows we're coming.*

Irritated by the length of the trip, one of the intelligence agents used her headset to address the Moab Consul. "You told me he was eighty-seven klicks from Moab."

Cheyenne smiled disarmingly. "Roughly. It's not as if he carries a transponder or a calendar. He was headed towards Capitol Reef and said he'd be back in a few weeks."

The agent tsked. "Pilot, can you do any better than that?"

"Sorry, Ma'am. Can't radar track in this topography, and the relays are still shoddy."

The agent sighed. "Christ, what i wouldn't give for the old, full-spectrum, prewar, spy-sat constellations."

Her counterpart shrugged. "Be a few more years before we're at pre-war standards."

Bernard laughed inwardly. Ilya wouldn't be found until he wanted to be. No doubt he was the one tracking them. Rather than share his opinion of their futile efforts, he tried to add to their conversation about pre-war technology.

"All that will do is return humanity to that tiny place where we think we're living the high life because we can see and hear each other all the time—ignoring the developmental cost of never having a private moment. It never ceases to amaze me how so many derive so much comfort by mistakenly believing their minuscule corner of the universe is so important. I'd much rather know how to reach another world than another nearest Starbucks."

His words were met by two haughty sneers, but Cheyenne's shoulder tap pulled him from further confrontation.

Rather than the headset, she yelled over the chopper roar. "You'll want to look out the window for this!"

The helicopter cleared a cliff the ground dropped away. Flocks of birds scattered... their cries drowned by the swooshing rotors. They were above a vast gorge cut deep into the earth. The Green River Canyon was the Fiddler's Green of the American West: it's ancient waters having eroded enough rock to reveal thick, distinctive bands, rusty Wingate sandstone stacked above thinner, lighter Chinle, and below that, Moenkopi.

The river was a serpentine mirror reflecting blue sky. Cottonwoods dotted the banks, and wherever the water bent sharply, lines of reeds created an oasis in the otherwise harsh landscape.

Bernard nodded to Cheyenne. "Thank you. I can see why he retreats here."

Cheyenne smiled. "Never gets old. The desert calls the eccentrics most of all. He deserves some peace after all he did for us and all he's endured." She gave the P.K's a cold sideways glance, then eyed Bernard meaningfully. "I imagine you can sympathize."

If she means we were both misunderstood in our own right, then yes, but I faced my accusers while Ilya ran. I couldn't bear the thought of such loneliness.

They flew across the capricious landscape bearing west towards their target.

Preparing himself for what lay ahead, Bernard looked back on his previous recruitment trip. It was significantly less complicated yet, perhaps, more difficult.

- - -

He'd heard of the legendary Eurasian Steppe winters, but actually feeling the icy winds burn his skin was another thing. Otherwise, the journey to Asia Zone 27, Grid 9 (formerly Kazakhstan) had been uneventful. It was here the World Council established the new **Chokin Regional Science Academy**. Taking advantage of all the post-war reconstruction, they'd decided to build key tech and research facilities in the lesser-trodden areas of the world.

Watching the city zip by from his **mechataxi**, Bernard fretted about the coming

---

Chokin Regional Science Academy
Founded in 2076, this World Council research institute is named after the Kazakh scientist Shafik Chokin. The Academy is located in Nur-Sultan, the former capital of Kazakhstan, and focuses on material science, nuclear science, kinetics, chemical engineering, eco-mass agriculture, and infrastructure design.

meeting. So far, the crew consisted of a close circle that shared his vision: William, Angie, and Ric. He had no strategy to sell the Nomad to an outsider. He felt it shouldn't even require an explanation. Any effort to pitch it like a product in some ad campaign seemed facepalm-worthy.

By the time he ascended the stairs of the Chemistry building, he was still clueless but had settled on thinking: *Best not overpredict it.*

Justin's nasal drawl reminded him that he wasn't alone. "The information logs say the main research lab is on sublevel 4."

"We could just ask someone, Justin."

Angelika's O.L. tag-along was all network interfaces: totally lacking people skills. Bernard expected Angie to keep a close eye on him, but she was ruining her cool with this toad.

"What are you going to do if she says no?"

He was impertinent too. "Young man, I do not fail. That's why you're here answering to me, not the other way around. Now, go find us an elevator."

Passing through several airlocks, they arrived outside the thick shock glass of Advanced Kinetic Chemical Lab 1. Beyond it, about fifteen chemists toiled. Some working with beakers, flasks, microscopes, and other lab accoutrement. Others manipulated test equipment that pulled, punched, deformed, skewed, and otherwise tortured the dark licorice strands of some new polymer. On the far side, three interacted with a holofield, much like the one in Williams' office, teasing apart molecule images and recombining them into strange atomic tectrices in an effort to bend electrons into a stable form.

Bernard pressed the intercom, and its chime brought all activity to a halt. He cleared his throat. "Ah, may I speak to Dr. Medina Karimov?"

An attractive, dark-haired thirty-something woman stepped from the circle of three. "Bernard Hubert?"

As she wove across the room passing her colleagues, their activity resumed. She

---

Mechataxi
A common Eurasian term for a self-driving car. These came into common use in the year 2075.

opened the inner airlock to greet them and quickly sealed it behind her.

"No worries, there's nothing harmful in there." She pointed at Justin. "But allowing an O.L. employ to see any of our proprietary work for Space Oasis would violate dozens of contract clauses. What say we continue this in my office?"

Bernard liked her already. "Lead the way."

"And, by the way, welcome! It's a pleasure to finally meet you, Dr. Hubert."

"You, as well, Dr. Karimov. Please, call me Bernard."

"Well, Bernard, I must confess. I already know why you're here."

Is security this bad already? The crew isn't even fully recruited. On the flip-side, this could be another easy chat.

Despite some slight surprise, Bernard remained poker-faced. "I see, and how did that come to pass?"

"Ava gave me a call about ten minutes after she left your dinner."

Once again, he wasn't terribly surprised. "Funny, I didn't say anything about you to her."

"No, but it stands to reason that the world's best natural scientist would want the best physical one to develop the ***neurodigital interfaces*** you requested."

"My, no matter how big the work, we travel in small circles." He gestured toward the glass. "Since you know my secrets, can you tell me what you've got going here?"

She appraised Justin with a dismissive nod. "As I said..."

Bernard liked her more and more. "Justin, how about you give yourself an extended tour of the center."

"Why? I already I have a full rendering available digitally..."

Bernard raised a finger. "Exactly! You won't need a guide."

He stared at Justin until he wandered off scowling, then turned back to Medina. "Where were we?"

Neurodigital Interface
The theoretical construct that will allow for seamless transition of thought and consciousness from synaptic signals to electronic data. Darren Parsons is the only known publisher on this subject.

Without missing a beat, she said, "It's a kinetic absorption weave capable of deflecting or absorbing physical impacts and redirecting them outward in controlled bursts. Basically, what that comic book character, Black Panther's, vibranium suit is made out of but for real."

"Intriguing. I can already see about seventeen different applications for it."

"Oh, we're well beyond a hundred."

They passed a second viewing window that looked in on a centrifuge with a male test subject strapped to its arm. As it spun, Bernard paused to read the g-force on a large screen against the back wall: 4gs, 5gs, 7gs, 8.5gs. The volunteer was still going strong.

Medina kept moving. "I have a second team working on a g-force reinforcing serum. The biggest initial hurdle was toxicity."

If that was some sort of warning, it didn't work. The useful discovery itself made Bernard gleeful.

Another step and they reached her office. "You didn't dismiss that lackey to talk shop. This is a recruitment. So, recruit me!"

He waited until they were inside. "Ava gave you details?"

"A five-year space mission to Kuiper. Assuming you know I have two small children, a husband, and a billion dollar playground lab, how could you possibly think I'd say yes?"

She really is cutting to the chase. Alright, then.

"You are the best chemist in the world, are you not?"

She easily agreed. "I am."

"We're gathering the best to represent humanity at its best on the most important journey our species has ever undertaken."

Medina waved a hand deflecting the monologue of humanity. "Bernard, I took this meeting out of respect for you, but, clearly, my answer is no."

If you think that will stop me...

"If interstellar travel is to become a reality in a hundred years, then we need to develop cryosleep, and what better multi-billion dollar zero-g lab is there for your research than the Nomad?"

"You're saying without me the mission can't happen? That I'm indispensable?"

Was the show of ego a chink in her armor? "No. I absolutely want you on the team, but I wouldn't design anything that hinged on a single-point failure. No one's indispensable, not even me."

"Do you have children, Bernard?"

"Isaac, a son."

"What did he say when you told him you'd be gone five years?"

"That he loved me, that he was proud of me, that he knew he couldn't stop me. Then he got to work helping design our ship." Bernard started out matter-of-fact but was surprised to feel a tear trickle down his face. Pretending to clean his glasses, he brushed it away.

Medina was incredulous. "Really? You're ready and willing to abandon those you love and blithely expect others to do the same?"

"It's bigger than me, Medina, bigger than any of us. This is about defining the future for our children. Love isn't an obstacle; it's a motive. I'm doing this because I love Isaac. If missing your family is what holds you back, I don't see that as a legitimate reason."

"Then you've read too many science fiction novels."

He hadn't expected that. Did she see him as a foolish child, some sort of robot, or a ridiculous combination? "Medina, don't you understand? This could be first contact. Fate is calling as it has to only a handful of humans. Do it for your children. Do it for Earth."

She was moved but still shaking her head. Under other circumstances, he'd admire her stalwartness. Impatient, he clicked his tongue.

"I'm not going to drag this out. I can't force you to come. But we both know that at the end of the day it's the things we didn't do that we'll regret, not the things we did. All the earth bound breakthroughs are nothing compared to knowledge of the universe. If you turn this down, mother or not, will YOU be able to sleep at night?" Growing emotional again, he lowered his voice. "Truth to tell, I fear that thought more than the thought of never hugging Isaac again."

That was it. He said his piece, perhaps, too honestly. The silence lingered.

"My choice is my own." Her words sounded final.

Bernard nodded. "Then, thank you for your time. Good day, Doctor Karimov."

Without a backwards glance, he strode toward the door. Maybe he was wrong; maybe even great minds couldn't see what was so plain to him.

His hand was on the doorknob when a voice called from behind. "Five years... that's it?"

He smiled at the door admiring its wood inlay. The beautiful grain caught the light in golden, flowing layers. "Five years. That's it. This isn't Interstellar after all."

- - -

As the helicopter zoomed above mesas and canyons, he wondered how William and Angelika were faring. Godric drew too much attention to take part in the invitations, but having the CEO of Outer Limits, a famous mathematician and a world-hated astrophysicist, move about covertly was no small task, either. The last few months, they'd been scattered across the globe: communication strictly limited until they reconvened.

Still, Bernard could easily picture what they were up to. Right now, Angelika was tromping through Borneo, deep in the Kayan Mentarang rainforest, to find Odin Tiberius King. Part of what made him the foremost botanist was his endless field work in uninhabited environs. That meant he was in a jungle months of the year and hard to find.

Angelika wouldn't mind. There always was a wildness to her that office walls could not contain. She loved driving her board crazy by dropping off the grid and leaving nothing behind but a pickup time and location—her "mental health days" as she often joked. Amongst the trees, she'd feel alive and unburdened.

He imagined her quadcopter touching down in a sweltering meadow surrounded by dense forest. As she trekked through the thick growth, her perfect hair would frizz into a wild blonde mane. She'd have to manage a tropical waterfall or two before finally finding Odin King.

Tall and handsome as his Viking namesake, he'd be in a tree delicately collecting seeds. Surrounded by serenity, they'd talk for hours about his work with the Regrowth & Restoration of Original Species program. It wouldn't be their first, second, or third time. They'd met in Finland while rescuing a seed ark from the glacier melt and kept in touch ever since. Not that they were together, per se. They existed, by preference, in occasionally crossing orbits which made each reunion an oasis of passionate simplicity.

He'd give her a dazzling blossom from a new plant he'd yet to name. She'd tell him about Nomad: the journey of a lifetime. No matter how many different ways Bernard imagined it, there was no variation in which King refused.

William, meanwhile, was in the Sinai where the **New Alexandria Library** had been constructed over St. Catherine's Monastery protectively conserving the world's oldest continuously operating library. It was a center for ancient languages as well as chief verification site for recovered artifacts. After the looting during the Darkness, many forgeries appeared necessitating a cautious evaluation.

He'd be alongside the Linguist Premier, Nawal Hawass. Wearing those absurd cotton monogrammed gloves Aubree gave him many Christmases ago, he'd be handling manuscript fragments from the original library. They alluded to some tantalizing ancient mathematics, his stated reason for making the trip, leading to a debate on whether mathematics was a universal language.

"But it could never convey the emotion that makes us human," Nawal would say

---

New Alexandria Library
The largest library in the world constructed in 2075 by the World Council to act as a new bastion of knowledge, translation, and base of operations for the recovery of antiquities stolen during World War III.

over Turkish coffee.

William would agree, to an extent. "But to presume another species' consciousness would use human emotional constructs is a big leap."

"True. At the same time, if we're talking carbon-based life crawling out of the mud on another world and developing sentience, I'd bet my copy of the Magna Carta they didn't start out talking in numbers."

By then, she'd know he wasn't here to see the fragments or chat hypotheticals. So, he'd tell her he was going to space possibly to meet the otherworldly life she'd mentioned.

She'd joke how science fiction had such a childish, oversimplified view of inter-species communication and ask. "William, how would you try to talk with them?"

"Why, Nawal, that would be your job." He'd smile and drain his cup.

She'd smirk, argue against the idea for a while, then give in to the boyish charm she could never resist. It was why they sent William after all.

"There's a ping on the infrared!" The pilot's announcement snapped Bernard back to the moment.

What would this meeting be like? Was there a strategy? A simple hook? A key? Would emotion hold Ilya back, or would they play chess? Not knowing set his adrenaline pumping.

The helicopter followed the signal, on and on, until the pilot pointed to a rock column. "To the northwest, atop one of those spires, I can see a small figure. It's him."

Aghast, one P.K. whispered to the others. "He must have climbed 300 feet on vertical slickrock to reach that spot. Unreal."

As the chopper approached, Bernard made the figure against the desert horizon. Sunlight glinted off his goggles and some odd metallic portions of his faded clothing. Unphased by the noise or the wind whipping the sand at his feet, he raised his arm and waved.

P.K. Williams grit his teeth. "Bastard picked a spot too small for us to land."

Bernard sensed a will to rival his own. He chose his board well—a chess game, then.

"Maintain a close perimeter," Williams barked to the pilot.

Below, Ilya raised a radio and pointed to it. Signaling, he raised three fingers, five, then two. Cheyenne figured it out. "Go to open channel 123.5."

After a crackle of changing frequencies, they heard a loud yet smooth voice. "Cheyenne, that you?"

"Yes, Ilya. I'm with… some officials who'd like a word."

"Goodness me." Despite the noise of the chopper blade, the sarcasm came through clearly.

"This is P.K. Commander Williams, Mr. O'Connell. We'll need you to come with us."

Ilya waived gaily. "Phillip, how've you been? Didn't think you'd be back. Thought you knew better. I made it very clear last time I wanted to be left alone."

They were close enough for Bernard to see Ilya hiding a smile.

Williams' face soured. "My orders are straight from the top."

"Ah. In that case, my friend, I'm sorry to say, it'll be another disappointing day for you."

What did Ilya do last time?

Fearing things could go sideways, Bernard hit his mic. "Ilya, this is Bernard."

There was a pause. Ilya frowned. "Hubert? That really you?"

"Yes. In fact, I'm the reason we're here. It's important that I talk to you, Skil. Think of it as another Brooklyn rooftop chat."

As the agents and Peacekeepers tried to decode his remarks, Ilya's interest was piqued. He hadn't heard the nickname since Brooklyn.

"I'll only talk to you, Bernie. The rest can stay on the chopper, high in the sky. Option two, you can all leave, and there's always option three. You can ask Phillip about that one."

Bernard turned to the commander. "What is option three?"

Williams hissed. "Last time, he remotely disabled the chopper. We don't know how."

"Since he's clearly holding all the cards, I'll go down alone, yes? It is why Angelika sent me."

After the commander's begrudging nod, the Black Hawk descended low enough for Bernard to hop out. Then, buzzing like an angry wasp, it dipped, pulled away from the rock, and hovered high above.

Ilya gave Bernard a strong handshake, then removed his goggles for a clearer view. Hubert looked a lot older since he'd seen him last—not surprising after what must have been some very stressful years, but his eyes were still just as fiery. Whatever this was, it was significant.

Still, men with causes had a habit of stepping on, or through, anyone in their way.

"Dr. Hubert, it's been a long time. Hope you brought more mezcal, or at least a joint."

Bernard removed his sunglasses. "The mezcal wouldn't fit in my pocket, but it just so happens..." He pulled a thick, rolled tarantula from his pocket. "I have this old thing we can smoke."

Taking the joint with a smile, Ilya took out a four-centimeter glass sphere and used it to focus sunlight on the tip. Once it ignited, he took a massive hit. He held it for the longest while exhaling as he spoke.

"So far so good. How about we start our rooftop chat with why you're in an O.L. Chopper with W.C. Peacekeepers? Not your usual company. Unless... things have changed? Oh, I took the liberty of activating a localized jammer in case you were bugged. You can speak freely."

"I will, then." Bernard gestured at the naked sandstone. "But where should I sit?"

"Ah, where are my manners?" Ilya took two small metal rods from his pack and tossed them. At the peak of their trajectory, they unfolded and snapped into place like tent poles over and over. The rods grew, hinged, and clicked. By the time they landed, they were semi transparent chairs composed of scores of tiny struts that made their solidity seem almost an illusion.

Surveying Ilya's handiwork, Bernard took a puff, passed the joint back, and sat. As the smoke curled from the desert man's mouth, he couldn't help but admire the show of force. Clearly, Ilya assumed Bernard had become beholden to higher powers. While it was a reasonable assumption, it wasn't helpful. Keeping their brains from those who might misuse them was a shared ideology.

Ilya's desert freedom must be his own doing. Why else be so assured in it? He was also the type who'd screw up the world's most important mission just to stick it to the powers that be. Bernard had to be careful how he framed things.

"The P.K.'s weren't my decision. The Council seems to think contacting you requires... precautions."

"Do they?"

"As for O.L., well, sometimes the devil you know is the only one who can do what's needed."

Ilya gave him a sideways glance. "Excuse me, but I'm having trouble imagining any scenario in which O.L. would risk the PR nightmare of bringing you back onboard."

"Probably the same sort that'd make the Council risk using you again."

Ilya gave off a jovial hoot. "Touché! Okay, next question. You said you wanted to talk, but the jarheads above are laboring under the delusion I'll be leaving with them. I like it here. Why would I need to go anywhere else, Bernard?"

"Because I'm leading a group of very smart people, and we need a mechanical engineer. Your name came up as the best for building... well, quite honestly, anything but more specifically, an interplanetary ship. Oh, and you'd be part of the crew for a journey to the edge of the solar system."

Ilya raised an eyebrow. "To do what, exactly? Play Bob the Builder on Titan?"

Bernard smirked. "Ha! Yes. That and, you know, search for extraterrestrial life."

Ilya took a long drag and closed his eyes. He appeared to be doing something Bernard most definitely knew he was not—praying.

Rather, he was taking the pieces he had, putting them together, and making highly educated guesses about what was missing: *O.L. must be providing resources, but even if he gave Angelika a Klingon phone number, she wouldn't stick her neck out without something big in return. Whatever it is, she wouldn't share it with the W.C. So, what's their angle? For a government pushing an earth-centric agenda, a big space trip would be seen as a waste of resources. Which means... Bernard has some heavy hitting political support, too. Not an astrophysicist's usual pattern. This has long-game written all over it.*

He looked directly at Bernard. "This is about clearing your name."

Unexpected but Bernard managed to compose himself. "Slightly. It's true that opening the next chapter of human history comes with the chance of clearing my family name, but that's further than Kuiper from the big picture. It's about exploring further than any human in history. I cannot abide space being ignored because of fear and lies. It's also, I hope, about finding some answers. The 4,000 dead at CERN and our species deserve more."

Using his holopad as visual aid, Bernard presented his tale of the retrieved lunar station data and the omnidirectional signal.

When his careful presentation and the joint were finished, Ilya leaned back into a pleasant buzz. The spindly filaments supporting him morphed to accommodate his new position. He was inwardly impressed how far Bernard had gotten, especially since he lacked some key information that Ilya just happened to have.

Keeping his cards close to his chest, he interrupted the calm oasis. "Heard your son's doing a lot of good work."

Ilya's ability to place Easter eggs reminded Bernard of a simpler time. Appreciating the breadcrumbs, he played along. "Yes. He'll need your help finishing the ship designs. Williams' math could only get us so far after all. If you come, you'll get to meet Isaac. I suspect you'll like him. He reminds me of you in many ways."

"Then he must be a pain in the ass."

"Many, not in every way. His imaginative mathematics and practical creativity reminds me a lot of you. However, unlike present company, his discipline is unparalleled."

"You obviously love him which means I've misjudged. You're not doing this for your name, you're doing it for his. Okay, but fess up right now; is what you've just told me everything we're risking our lives for? There isn't anything else?

We. Ours. Interest percolated from Ilya's candor.

"I've told you all I know."

Ilya scanned him cautiously but found no tell. He laughed. "Well, you can't go without me there to fix things when everything goes to hell. As long as it doesn't require indebting ourselves to O.L. or the W.C., I'll be there. But to be clear, even space flight's not enticing enough for me to cross that line."

Ilya seemed to enjoy the change on Bernard's face.

So that's the roadblock Ilya will hide behind, his idealism? Or is he just messing with me? To think, I'd complained about Medina.

Bernard snapped at him. "Don't be so simplistic, Skil. Nothing's black and white, including your own crusade against your past oppressors."

"Hm. Sounds like your vague way of saying compromise is inevitable." Ilya's eyes narrowed at the hovering chopper. "Bottom line, in this case, compromise means working for them—and they will always screw you. You know they'll make you take one of their people along. Besides, the Bernard Hubert I remember would never make deals with those who betrayed him."

Ilya hoped Bernard wouldn't notice, but he was stalling for time trying madly to figure out what piece was missing from the puzzle. *The mission, his son, the ship... what had Bernard promised Angelika? It must be sweet, even if Bernard thought he was getting something sweeter.*

Ah, the Mayflower launch.

Likewise stalling, Bernard removed and polished his glasses before responding. "This isn't the usual scenario and you know it. Of course there are days I want to burn O.L. to the ground for leaving me in the cold, but it's so much better having them build my ship for me. Once we're out there, we can do whatever we want, go wherever we please, be whoever we like."

He eyed the lenses and placed them back on his face. "Come on, man. You were a leader making difficult choices for the greater good. The ethics here are the same—the good far greater."

Ilya snorted. "Come on yourself, Bernard. It's not like the Council of Elrond picked my name from a hat for my leadership skills."

Bernard chuckled. "No, friend halfling, you were chosen for your engineering prowess, intelligence, tenacity, and, frankly, because you're a wildcard. The fact that you don't serve the government or big business makes you utterly trustworthy and, hence, more valuable." He leaned forward, elbows resting on armrests, hands clasped. "Join. Let's be masters of our fate for a time."

After a light whistle from the wind, Ilya said. "Fine. I'm in." He rose, stretched his arms and smirked. "Do tell me, though, when did you realize Angelika didn't betray you?"

Caught off guard, Bernard froze. In so doing, he gave away his hand.

"There it is." Ilya nodded. "Like I said, the Bernard I knew wouldn't go back to anyone who betrayed him. It's clear you're the same guy, ergo, you must have realized she didn't betray you. Something deeper was going on. Ah, don't worry. You can keep that secret for now, but understand I will want the truth before we pass Jupiter."

Bernard not only admired the rugged outlaw's attitude, coupled with brain, sometimes, he downright envied it.

Ilya checked his watch. "The way I see it, you'll need my help, anyway."

It was an aloof, curious statement. As much as it nagged at the man who hated uncertainty, the conversation was over. The two men atop the high flat rock faced each other in the late afternoon light and, again, shook hands.

Ilya hauled on his pack, secured a harness, then pressed a hidden button woven and wired into the strap. His radio crackling to life, Ilya again spoke in a smooth voice. "You can come get him now, Phillip."

"Dr. Hubert? Report mission status." Commander Williams sounded anxious.

"Mission successful," Bernard reported.

"Fantastic. We'll scoop you two up and head back."

As the helicopter descended, Ilya laughed. Pulling the goggles over his eyes, he whistled a five-note tune. The chairs snapped back into small rods, which he returned to his pack. Facing Bernard, he clasped his shoulders and shouted.

"See you back in town. There are a few things I need to take care of. Tell Phillip to give my best to his wife. That'll annoy him. Let's go free the world from itself!"

Bernard tapped a finger to his head. "Two days, Ilya."

Behind them, the two Peacekeepers jumped from the chopper. Presenting them with two middle fingers, Ilya hurled himself off the edge. The soldiers pushed past Bernard reaching the mesa's edge just as Ilya's majestic bronze-colored wingsuit unfurled.

He soared like an eagle, east, back from whence he came, no doubt. Above the sound of the rotors, Bernard heard his laughter echoing amongst the sandstone walls.

What did he mean by, "You'll need me, anyway?"

An invigorating wind whipping his face, Ilya knew his desert solitude was at an end. He also knew things Bernard did not. This journey on the Nomad would be the perfect time to enact plans of his own.

CHAPTER 13

THE DISTANT ZONES

"Did you hear?!"

"No. What?"

"The Council of Worlds is meeting on Primidious in ten prikes."

"The COW?"

"Yes, the COW!"

"So? They meet all the time. What's so special?"

"Rajav, the WHOLE Council is meeting."

"WHAT? Mikal, are you sure? The full COW hasn't convened in over two hundred turns."

Noshing on *fried equak*, Mikal answered flatly, "I'm sure."

They were in esta De u, a corner diner on *Neruda 8*, in the *Liyathin 7 system*. Mikal was a bipedal, blue-haired, silver toned Maruuvean. A curious breed, Maruuveans were known for their high energy, big mouths, and three stomachs. All three were on display for his Potonian table mate. Watching from eyes in the palms of his hand, the more humanoid Rajav waited as Mikal used the utensil held in his

---

Fried Equak
Popular Ulroni street cuisine. The equak is a small, lizardlike invertebrate that taste delectable when seasoned, dipped in batter, and cooked in burning oil.

Neruda 8
The homeworld of the Ulron since the Classical Galactic Era and the Capital of Sector 3. Its natural ecosystem once allowed the Ulron to live in relative immortality during the Second Dark Era. When the Reclamation Era rejoined the Neruda System with the galaxy, the garden of immortality was poisoned. Within a few generations, the Ulron had sacrificed their long life for a more ubiquitous civilization. To mitigate this, the planet is divided into hemispheres by a giant wall. One half of the world is industrious and a massive GSA city; the other half is preserved wilderness. 97% of all Ulron are born here. Their nascent forms are highly sensitive to toxins.

Maruuvean - See page 177

tail to shovel more equaks into his prodigious mouth.

It was exasperating.

"Mikal! Why are they meeting?"

His friend threw a copy of the *Starry Prikely* at him. "Here."

Removing it from his face, Rajav saw the headline currently circulating the galaxy: Council of Worlds to Meet in Full: Rumors of Galactic Threat.

Beyond that, the piece was mostly propaganda meant to reinforce the image of the GSA as a peacekeeping organization. As a painter, Rajav tried to read between the lines. Art was more than aesthetic on his home world of **Ponton Prime**; it was a chief means of communication.

An ardent follower of the ways the GSA conversed with member planets, he felt he should be able to glean more. It said the Primes arrival at **Primidious** was imminent, meaning they were desperate to control the narrative. Which meant... tides were changing. But how?

"Mikal, interstellar space in this Sector has been quiet for over a hundred turns, at least. Not a peep about any threat. They're hiding something something big."

Mikal swallowed a half-equak. "They are a government. What do you expect?"

"True. Still, it feels like more than that. We'll have to wait and see, I suppose."

Most who read the piece felt the same creating so much unease. Answers to the unknown threat were demanded but few were available. For the member worlds, the meeting couldn't come soon enough.

As Rajav and Mikal continued their meal in ignorance, Bor and Pias prepared for their journey to Primidious.

- - -

15 Prikes Earlier

Bor barely waited for the office door to close. "How did it go?"

Pias cracked four sets of knuckles. "Not well at all, which means exactly as

---

Pontonian

A bizarre, humanoid species that have their eyes in their hands. They are native to Ponton Prime of Sector 3. They are uptight, snobbish, and are usually wary of physical confrontation due to their limited ease of holding weapons but are known to be unrivaled kickboxers.

Primidious

The capital planet of the GSA, home of the Anador, and currently the most advanced Udarian technology ever weilded by the Alliance. It is a government center with no permanent residents created on a terraformed world in an unoccupied system in Sector 5 to provide the greatest neutrality. It is a meeting place for many high level GSA functions involving Primes, including the Council of Worlds.

expected. The evidence gathered from the Nova System has already been distributed to the other EFPs. No doubt you've seen the headlines."

Bor nodded. "The latest reports from Epiko indicate a threefold spike in military chatter."

Pias continued. "I submitted the formal request to summon the full Council. But, there's a complication; Kruk's being taken to Primidious for a full interrogation by the Military Council."

Bor was livid. "What!?"

Pias raised two of his left arms in a placating gesture. "It was out of my hands. The members of the Investigation Council were planetside. Once they heard your son had mentioned the Loronzon Incident and the Creators in the same breath they became rather... alarmed."

Bor was silent for a moment. "He understands exactly how dangerous the Creators are. In the heat of the moment, he made a judgement call."

Unhappy with the response, Pias puffed to his full height and crossed four arms. "And I learned exactly how he made that judgement—using a Prime-level override code to commandeer station sensors. You left that part out."

Bor paled slightly but stood his ground. "Kruk's trained to resist psychic probes, but I'm not a complete idiot. Even if he talks, he won't be able to tell them Odian is alive. You know, the point of compartmentalization."

"You endangered so much." Despite his obvious irritation, Pias backed off. "Still, I suppose you've protected the larger cause."

"Exactly. And he gave us a warning, when otherwise we'd have none." Bor gave him a smile. "Shall we take my ship? It is faster."

"Faster, true, but since your son's already such a hot topic, travelling with less attention will be easier in mine."

"Agreed. The **Bridalgo** it is."

Bridalgo
Pias Abbotkrine's personal transportation vessel, a Nuukon Class Starship, 25 tradons long, patch 5 capable, with cloaking, double shields, flares, drones, and defensive railguns. The Nuukons were developed to dramatically reduce the need for military escort of Primes and Assembly members due to their incredible speed.

Maruuvean
A fast, high energy species that move by taking powerful leaps with telescoping bone legs propelled by coiled, springlike fibers. They are also known as "tree walkers"; their method of transport evolved from safely jumping between trees on the predator filled plains of U'uvea.

Pias's official call for the full Council of Worlds rang a cosmic bell. Communication relays strained bandwidth to accommodate the interstellar talk. Galactic trade dipped ten percent as planets stockpiled resources. Trillions who were usually occupied with their own corner of the universe, suddenly remembered they were part of something larger. Still, while previous, full meetings had been indicators of coming war in much of the GSA, mass conflict was such a distant memory few who still lived remembered.

During the voyage, Pias and Bor, with little sleep, struggled to keep the Nova Incident quiet. Bor scrubbed and jammed comm lines and slanted Sector news. Pias used loyal subordinates to keep data sealed under galactic security protocols —for now.

The shared work kept them together, but Pias' coldness made it abundantly clear he was still upset. Nearing a twenty-seven prike trek, the Bridalgo finally reached the edge of the Primidi System.

Without turning from the observation panel and its star-strewn sky, Pias asked, "Have the others responded?"

"Yes, but not all directly. I received acknowledgement echoes from everyone through the usual backchannels. Scalipio's already on Primidi coordinating arrivals on the ground. I left encrypted instructions to meet at Sanctuary 19."

Pias eyed him dubiously. "The Communication Council Island? A bit too close to home."

Bor scowled. "It's not as if we can escape notice entirely. The Communication Council held its quarterly gathering there forty prikes ago, so we know there'll be no other assemblies at Sanctuary 19 prior to the full Council meeting. That means it was available and, importantly, the only place on Primidious where I can override and plant a loop in the automatic recording system."

Pias shook his head. "I suspect you'll have a lot less control than you think. This is going to look bad in every way, more so with your son involved. There's a very

---

Liyathin System (occurs on final paragraph of page 173)
A single G class star system that contains an unusually high density of naturally occuring habitable planets: Neruda 6, 7, 8, and 9. It is scientifically proven that an ancient impact shaped the unique system when Neruda Prime, a super massive rocky planet, was impacted 900 million turns ago shattering and reforming into Neruda 1 through 9. A later impact ejected Neruda 7 life onto Neruda 8.

narrow space between claiming his ignorance and the obvious level of knowledge he's shown."

"I am painfully aware. Right now, I am attempting to arrange a meeting with him."

"It'll have to be after the Council meeting. If you meet beforehand and anyone finds out..." Pias let his voice trail-off.

He didn't have to finish. It was obvious KruktuskenBor was, for the first time in a very long while, vulnerable.

Moving through the Primidi System, Bor fell deeper into **Recall** finding himself back in The Halls of Ek. In his entire political life, he'd never been as uncomfortable as he'd been while waiting for Pias to return from Kruk's debrief. Pias' Anduuzil physiology and theatrics were more than enough for Bor to feel as though he had a front row seat at the hearing.

It was held at the far side of Rakaja where the seas converged on The Falls of Q. The dungeons awaited Kruk; the Sector 1 Investigation Prime would be met by Pias for the gathering.

"Pias, before we leave... a river of tears?" Bor inquired.

"You do not deserve that honor, nevertheless Kruk acted honorably. Be assured, if he had not, you would not be standing here now. Never in all my turns have I seen such foolhardy, whimsical..."

"Is that so Pias? Our heroism on Irikus 4 and the peaceful reckoning on Ja'dor is not enough to cement a lifetime of trust?"

"It is only for those reasons that I did not invoke Article 37 on the Tusken family," Pias boomed. "Inner Council training or not, it was foolish of you not to have prohibited him from using those overrides! At the very least, you should have explained the ramifications."

Not wanting to test the might of the Anduuzil, Bor's voice retreated into a more placating tone. "Very well, Pias. Did you record the interrogation as I asked?"

"Of course." He pulled a vial of translucent blue liquid from his shoulder patch

---

Recall
A Dragsan ability to fully and consciously immerse into memories. Thus, the observer may relive past events with perfect clarity and find details that were unconsciously gathered but yet to be realized. Recall was practiced by all Dragsan through the Second Dark Era but is now performed by less than 1 in 1000. Only those with genetic aptitude towards the ability, coupled with turns of training, are able to Recall.

and handed it to Bor. "Take it. I'll await your return."

Pias pulled out a throne-like chair for Bor to sit in and withdrew.

Bor absorbed seven drops of Anduuzilian tears in each eye. The memory transfer was blurry and imperfect, but it was enough. With their aid, his Dragsan Recall flared to life. The room dissolved... replaced by a dark, opaque mist. Gradually, it coalesced into the shapes and sounds of an interrogation room populated by shadowy figures that flowed in and out of focus.

"Silence!" The voice of Investigation Prime Sector 1, Surenik Lamos Bink, slithered through the room like a venomous serpent. A petrifying feeling deep in his naval moved through Bor's body as it hit his senses.

A light flickered from a central node christening the room with a golden hue. He scanned the room. It was bare save for five otherworldly chairs circling a single, standing figure—his son. The chairs, gleaming fluorescent purple striped with dark metal, each threatening in its own way, were alien even to the cohort.

Bor stepped around the shadowy figures; their detail and intensity varied whenever Pias shifted his focus. Kruk looked nervous but steady. Reflexively, Bor put a hand to his son's shoulder, only to have it pass through. Much as he should have expected it, he was disappointed.

Prime Abbotkrine spoke with the regulated calm only the fiercest warrior could muster. "Prime Bink, while I enjoy your tactics, let me remind you this is a debriefing. Kruktusken is not a criminal."

"Interesting you would say that after what you did to the Entok Family."

The *Metra* stood and circled the Anduuzil; a tension mounted that could bring the entire building to its knees.

Pias was unperturbed. "While the accusations of a Prime should be taken with gravity, need I remind you who you are speaking to Surenik Lamos, Daughter of Euek, and House of Bink? You will address this member of the Council with the respect he deserves."

Metra
"Those who live in the shadow of the Ring," are the proposers of the TAOTA and first founding species of the GSA. The Metra are: humanoid, calm, calculated, highly intelligent, never quick to violence, and have an interlocking exoskeleton. The Metra understood the necessity to destroy the Warpgates to save the galaxy at the end of the Classical Era. They protected and preserved a large portion of galactic knowledge through the Great Silence.

Picking her battles wisely, Surenik continued. "Very well, Prime Abbotkrine, very well. Kruktusken, you know why you are here, yes?"

The blue on Kruk's face flushed from stress. "Yes. In the heat of an attack, I used my father's override code. The intruders were already inside the quarantine..."

"And how did you come about such a code?"

A long silence followed before Kruk went into the full details. When he was finished, Bink made a noise that clearly indicated disapproval.

"I see. While we understand the how, the question becomes why jump to the conclusion that it was the Creators? The litany of information you'd need to have accessed would be..."

Fearing things would spin out of control, Pias broke in. "Enough! Bink, let's be corundum clear about this. We know where Kruk got his information, we know how. Continue down this road and I'll call for a Routine 81 and end this debrief due to military security."

"I will not have it, Pias; I will not! The House of Entok was issued an Article 37; why not Bor and the House of Tusken? It's outrageous! I should call for an investigation on you!"

Pias retained his cold killer tone. "Just because Entok and his wife were your classmates at the Academy doesn't give you the right to speak to me this way. His execution was warranted. If you knew half the things he was saying, you'd agree. Investigate me? No. A *plop* like *you* should know her place in the galaxy. It's your family who'll be investigated; if you'd like."

Kruk brought the conversation back to his debrief. "Primes, if I may? Nova's attackers were systematically evasive. The subroutines they used fit only one other known assault in GSA history."

Bink raised an eyebrow. "Which was?"

Even through the memory, Bor felt Pias bracing for the inevitable.

Kruk shifted uncomfortably. "The Loronzon Incident."

Plop
An Anduuzilian derogatory term for a migratory Anduuzil who has never lived through a true winter.

Bink blinked. "Excuse me?"

To the Metra's right, Nimaguardian NamaruldanBor glanced at Pias. His look was all she needed to know that he might call on her at any moment to act swiftly and decisively. Turning toward Bink, the female Dragsan subtly slipped into an attack stance. Bor, stepped closer to Bink. Even through the tears, he felt the same satisfaction as his fellow Dragsan felt: the scent of fear.

Kruk did not seem to notice. "Given the incident, the only logical conclusion was that it was the Creators. Primes, if I also may, the object the escaped ship took with it, the probe, carried important data on the history of the Humans. I believe the Creators are gathering information for a judgement."

"I am officially calling for a Routine 81," Pias commanded. "We're now in an Article 37 lock down. Anyone who relays, discusses, or disseminates what we've heard here will be executed along with their friends and families." He shot a withering look at Bink daring her to inform Tordok. When she was silent, he added, "Then it's settled."

Bink found her voice. "Not so fast, Prime Abbotkrine. You are blocking this inquiry. This Duraguardian possesses information about an enemy that's not supposed to exist. I may be new, but I am aware of yours and Prime Kruktusken-Bor's long history of collaboration."

Bor's vision darkened and blurred as Pias focused his attention on the rookie Metra Prime until she all but glowed. It was the closest someone had come to threatening the mighty Anduuzil in a hundred turns.

Unphased, Pias raised his two left arms. "Hopefully, Surenik, you are not so new to be unaware that I don't need your permission to declare this a military matter. Since you're looking for consensus, I'll defer to this Investigation Panel for a final decision."

Bink seemed smug. "Very well, let us vote. All in favor of blocking the Routine 81 and continuing this interrogation?"

Only one other voice joined her own.

Her shock and rage filled the room. "IS THIS THE ALLIANCE OR AM I SPEAKING TO SOME BACK PLANET DICTATORSHIP? Not a word from First Contact or the SAC? An entire quarantine threatened and you don't want to see how far the Gargaric Snow Buffalo goes?"

Sector 1's First Contact Prime, Blika Randu, leaned forward. "I speak for myself and Nimaguardian NamaruldanBor when I say that maintaining a T-Class system's secrecy is crucial. If you let this Nova attack go public, we'll be fighting off a lot more than just the Creators."

Pias turned to an unknown figure that Bor could previously only identify as *Fandaxian*. "Olbera'n, I'm surprised at you."

The intelligence officer met his superior's gaze. "Apologies Pias, but we need to know about the Creators; gathering the truth is of the utmost importance."

"I agree that the truth must be regarded above all. There must be reasons everyone in this room has been unaware of this new information. Very good reasons. Reasons that merit discussing before we do anything... rash. Per our vote, this is now a military matter, and the five of us do not have the authority to declare war. A decision of this magnitude requires the Council."

Bink nodded darkly. "In that, we are agreed."

The walls turned black. Shadows rushed in. The vision collapsed. Bor caught a final glimpse of the fear on Kruk's face before his son dissolved as well. Then, Bor rose physically pulling himself from the Anduuzilian vision. His head ached from the synaptic mismatch, but at least now he knew how they'd survived this first hurdle.

The ship depatching, he looked over to Pias knowing he also felt the strange sensation of passing through water.

Pias nodded through the window at a bright blue dot visible far away amidst the firmament. "We're here."

Fandaxian

One of the nine founding species of the GSA. The name translates as "keep your mind and claws sharp." They are a therapod looking creature: orange, covered in scales, and native to the hot scrublands and jungles of Azoeleo. They have a powerful, whiplike tail, excellent smell, acidic tears, and are compatible with Voidwhisperer implants. They are fiery, passionate, and determined. When the Warpgates fell, Azoeleo was overpopulated, and they fought a 700 turn war against an alliance of Rakilla and Droteans for control of their system, in which they ultimately triumphed. Then, the Fandaxian WarKing declared the Fandaxians smash every egg before 30 frikes old. This took a small dent out of the population and continued periodically, but at random, until the Reclamation Era by which time their population was reduced by 80%. By that time, they had rebuilt their sublight interstellar civilization to 39 other systems; 11 of which failed, and 7 others suffered an atomic ending, but Azoeleo and 21 colonies thrived.

A brief chime signaled an alert from the ship captain. "Sir, we are being hailed."

"Put it through, Captain."

"Attention GSA Class 1 Military vessel," the steady voice announced. "You are within one endon of Primidious: a restricted space. If you are here for the Council of Worlds meeting, please transmit your authority codes now; otherwise leave immediately."

Pias responded, "Sending codes now."

"They wasted no time getting battle ready." Bor muttered. "If I didn't know better, I'd say they already know the COS is back. Not that Odian would be so stupid."

"Authority codes confirmed. Welcome Effective Force Prime Abbotkrine & Effective Communication Prime KruktuskenBor. Protocol requires Prime council members be escorted to the surface. What sanctuary zone will you be landing in?"

"That would be 19, thank you."

Several drikes later, in the company of six **Roarlan Class combat ships**, the Bridalgo entered Primidious orbit.

Pias' wide smile gleamed at the sight of the shimmering turquoise oceans. "It's been so long, I almost forgot what she looked like."

Bor seemed distant, pondering the growing skyline as he clutched a small crystal. "Doesn't it seem strange to come to such a remote place to debate the path of the galaxy?"

"Eh, it's good for the process. Keeps the politics away from the populous. Removes the complication of having everyone want to attend, not to mention the fact that council Security vehemently deplores the extra measures needed to safeguard anyplace else. Bigger cities means more opportunities to hide attacks."

As the Bridalgo descended through its assigned orbital shield portal, the escort broke off. Bor couldn't help but be impressed by the technology.

As if reading his mind, Pias rattled off the specs. "That Class 4 Planetary Shield

---

Roarlan Class Combat Ship
A 75 tradon long light frigate built by Pelkon-Intok, the Anduuzilian conglomerate. They hold a crew of 400 and are commonly a GSA military escort ship due to their speed and maneuverability. They are equipped with a reinforced hull with kinetic absorption weave inner layers, shields, railguns, laser cannons, plasma torpedoes, and 10 Suppressor fighters.

can sustain the kinetic shock from a collision with an eight rudon-wide asteroid, assuming one made it that far. Given the fifteen battle group patrols and five independent Dark Energy Arrays on orbital platforms, that would be highly unlikely."

"Rooka! Why? Is someone planning an assassination?"

"With all of the Raa'Tiki in one place? I'd like to see someone try."

Pias was right to be confident. Bor shivered at the thought that right now in this ship cabin, one of the Raa'Tiki, the Council's personal security agents, could be present. Naturally cloaked, they served invisibly. Though he never saw them, he was certain this Raa'Tiki voyaged with him to Epiko.

The inability to see them until they struck suited him fine. After only a brief view of their therachnid physiology, he couldn't forget the way their segmented shells failed to completely cover the pulsating organs beneath. Their six appendages, used as hands or feet, connected to a body covered in layered carapace. Worse, the partial exoskeleton was crisscrossed with patterns that had evolved to be unsettling for potential foes or anyone else.

Whether the Raa'Tiki were capable of emotion recognizable to any other than their own kind had long been debated. The answer wasn't made easier by the lack of facial expressions. Brr.

As the Bridalgo dropped through the last cloud layer, the **Anduri** Archipelago, dozens of islands set across hundreds of square rudons of ocean burst into view. Many of the elegant land masses had impossibly high mountains: peaks visible as pinpoints that ran down to the sea. One was an active volcano: another encased in polar ice. Each also held an identically shaped tower that simultaneously blended with its surroundings, yet stood apart.

"Amazing what **World Shapers** can do," Pias remarked.

Bor shared his appreciation. "Indeed. **Yurra Hu** has a way with bringing lifeless planets to a state of wonder."

"Yurra Hu? Isn't she from the Quadlox system?"

Anduri
The largest island and namesake of the Anduri Archipelago on Primidious. It was built by the World Shapers 400,000 turns ago. The island is a former supervolcano with crater walls over four rudons tall, home to dozens of ecosystems, and harbor a central lake: the cradle of the Anador.

World Shapers
The topmost operators of the GSA Department of Terraforming. They make all final decisions regarding planet creation.

Yurra Hu
The Ulron Transformative Terraforming Prime of Sector 5. She is the senior member of the World Shapers, the uppermost level of the GSA Department of Terraforming.

"You know, I think she is."

Suddenly realizing that Hu, an Effective Prime, would be livid at the news that Odian wasn't only alive but close to her homeworld, they looked at one another.

The Bridalgo flew above all manner of ecosystem: deserts, forests, jungles, swamps, grasslands, crystal fields, sand pits, and more. Passing a particularly magnificent volcanic lake, the ship circled a lovely island covered in *julonga trees*. There, on a small peninsula, was the meeting tower called Sanctuary 19.

Bor jabbed his companion. "There it is."

The Bridalgo's landing thrusters engaged rustling the enormous julonga fronds as it dipped below the canopy. The landing pad, previously obscured by the foliage, came into view. They were already at the hatch when a lurch from the Bridalgo indicated their arrival.

As the doors opened, a slight breeze seemed to come from within the ship. Bor realized the Raa'Tiki must be about scanning for danger.

"So much to discuss and so little time." Pias activated his body shield. The only noticable result was a humming so slight, it was only audible at close distance.

Bor followed suit, then, slightly overwhelmed, grasped the lower forearm of his companion.

Pias looked at him. "We'll make it count, old friend."

They were greeted by a tall, winged, quadrupedal woman: a Rakilla from Epiko. Rakilla, another of the nine GSA founding races, had sharp beaks, clear eyes, and powerful, clawed hands at the tips of impressive wings. Immensely intelligent, they'd existed since the Classical Era.

"Scalipio," Pias said. "Too many turns and endons have passed since we were all together."

"True. It is, Pias, though I wish it were under better circumstances. Come. Many are here already."

Raa'Tiki
The hidden protector of the Primes. The species are Theracnids, a loose interspecies classification of beings who possess common anatomical insect-like traits with a 6 limbed segmented body, head, mandibles, 4 eyes, partial exoskeleton, and an armored carapace. They are capable of surviving in extreme heat, cold, pressure, radiation, magnetism, impact, and short periods in vacuum. Naturally invisible, they proved a formidable enemy when the GSA accidentally colonized their world In'dika. In return for a cease fire, they offered their best warriors to be the lifelong guardians of the Primes. Their decloaking creates an immense energy field so unique that it is coincidentally a perfect natural frequency to program the Valador access within The Andador. It is hypothesized that the Udari and Raa'Tiki were allies before the formation of the Alliance. This has yet to be confirmed.

Julonga Tree
Giant plant native to Azoeleo. They have giant elliptical fronds 2 tradons across with a crescent hole through. The Julonga Tree produces 10 times the amount of oxygen as a standard Earth bearing tree.

Once they were beneath the trees, the tower could barely be seen. *Trillsuckets* chirped and chimed filling the underbrush with music.

"How much time until the countdown?" Pias asked. "By law, it started the moment 85% of the Primes checked in with their authority codes. The Council of Worlds will commence one prike after that. We don't have much time; let's begin."

"1.15 drikes." Scalipio, Effective Educator Prime of Sector 7, didn't have it in her nature to be vague.

"Should be plenty."

At the tower door access panel, Bor suddenly stopped. He inserted a data chip, raised his hand for scanning, and entered his Prime Level comm code.

Before the others asked, he explained. "I'm uploading the Nova debrief to the personal mainframes via the tower share for the others. It's a closed network, so we're safe. Even if that's not secure enough, the file is read-only and self-corrupting if taken outside Sanctuary 19."

A moment later, a ding from Scalipio's reading screen indicated the document's arrival. She was already reading it as they entered the main sliptube. The journey to the top of the tower was swift and, surprisingly, quiet.

Though each tower appeared similar, their design was dictated by the section stationed there. Bor had chosen 19 specifically for the extra privacy measures installed by comm Sector leaders; sonic inhibiting fields, surveillance jamming, eavesdropping alarms, and quantum entangled local comm stations.

As they zipped through the corridors, Scalipio commented on her reading material. "Hmm. This is disturbing for a plethora of reasons."

"Such as?" Bor asked.

"First, there's no proof Odian was there just your son's supposition. Given that, why was the situation escalated to the highest level?"

Bor bristled. "Do you really think it wasn't the Creators? That Spek wasn't there?"

Trillsucket
A common, small, flying forest creature of Azoeleo that communicates through singing. They have a birdlike appearance; beak, feathers, end claws for grasping, and four, winged limbs.

"I'm a teacher of teachers, Bor. Don't dodge the question."

"I, for one, don't think Odian was there," Pias interjected. "If he's alive, he'd never risk his own death. But the tactics do point to the Creators. Mercifully, or so it seems, they didn't make this attack a public spectacle. If Odian is alive though, we can't risk him doing the same with whatever their next move is. We have to control the narrative. But this discussion should be saved for the quorum."

Exiting the sliptube at the top level Scalipio asked, "So, what is the plan?"

Pias gave his toothy smile. "We tell the whole Council the truth, naturally."

The light green Rakilla took the news better than Bor imagined. She folded her wings, thought a bit, then calmly inquired, "You're confident stepping into the light won't backfire?"

"The COW's will be upset, but in the end, they'll agree that limited transparency is the best option for continued stability."

On the main door, an interlocking linkage of spiral metal spikes unraveled allowing their entry. Inside was a small, circular amphitheater with intermittent walls and a breathtaking island view. Above, an oculus capped the domed ceiling. A large refraction crystal suspended from its center lit the room. Below, concentric rings of steps descended to a central floor.

Scalipio nodded to her companions. "You have my support."

Three inner circle members were already present; Socrula Paru, Sector 5 Transportation Prime; Mattrolo Kuskar, Sector 1 *Archivist Prime*; and Jedareg Rojhov, Sector 6 Investigation Prime.

"KruktuskenBor and Pias Abbotkrine." Socrula Paru greeted the new arrivals with a four-armed salute. "Caught in the middle of everything again, I see."

Bor nodded at each. "Socrula, Mattrolo, Jedareg, good to see you've all made the journey."

The sliptube, visible through the now-open door, ejected more attendees—their hasty steps likely spurred by Bor's uploaded file. He tried to ease into things.

Archivist Premier Prime
A Sector Head of the Department of Archiving. They are responsible for recording and indexing all events within the GSA, preserving artifacts, and creating and managing museums. They are the watchdogs against the degradation of time. After the reintegration of the galaxy during the Reclamation Era, the Metra group, Ka'fla-em (Translation: Keepers of the Flame) realized how little information survived the Great Silence outside of their care. Determined to ensure crucial galactic data would never again be lost between eras, The Assembly of Planets quickly proposed Amendment 12 to create the A.P.P position.

"Before we delve into weightier topics, it's been a long time. How has everyone been?"

Jedareg gave his standard, fang-filled, terrifying smile. "Oh, you know, holding the galaxy together through the force of sheer will... the usual."

Having weathered many threats together, the others chuckled. The laughter took Bor's disciplined Recall to two-hundred turns ago when many worked in various positions: some Primes, others not. Whatever the rank, back then, they'd kept the Voidwhisperers and the Creators off the map.

Jedareg, scanning the debrief, ended the too-brief niceties. "Bor, what is this about your son divulging secrets he shouldn't even have?"

Having spent much of the journey preparing, Bor was ready. "It's true; I did share some key information in the hope that it would prepare him for this council."

A smiling Pias stepped in. "It's not news, Jedareg, to you or anyone else here. It's in complete alignment with the historic yet vague directive we voted to uphold 141 turns ago to ensure personal continuity of information in case of disaster."

Despite her stated support, Scalipio reframed Jedareg's point. "But, Bor, why did he tell others what he knew?"

"It would be wrong for me to speculate on Kruktusken's reasoning, and we haven't had an opportunity to speak yet. It is one of the items I wish to cover here."

"We're already getting sidetracked." Lead archivist Mattrolo spoke adamantly. "The far more important question is how did the Creators find the Nova System in the first place?"

In the contemplative silence that followed, the amphitheater filled with 31 galactic leaders: among them Khan Panda and Trinna Tau. Exploration Prime Tordok was running late, as usual. He had, though, notified Bor of his considerable distance. Otherwise, the Inner Circle had gathered.

Pias stretched to his full height and let out a harmonious sound: part burp, part chime, impossible to ignore. "700,000 turns ago, our predecessors understood that the Council of Worlds was vulnerable to incremental manipulation of our choosing computers. As a result, the 32 most senior members began, in secrecy, shaping GSA decisions for the greater good. We all know why we're here now. Has everyone reviewed the military debrief from the Nova System?"

Hands, talons, paws, flippers, wings, tails, and tentacles reached for their voting talismans and flung them in the air to hover above. The bright, fluorescing crystals then produced floating points of green above each member indicating affirmative answers. An orange spot would have indicated a negative response, but there were none.

"Excellent. Let's submit formal queries."

More dots, now glowing different colors, floated into the amphitheater's center and grouped themselves into constellations of similar hues. Once the shapes stabilized, each beamed a golden light to a particular Prime. Talismans had a consciousness of their own choosing speakers as they saw fit.

As Khan Panda's talisman grew brighter, the others dimmed focusing everyone's attention. "The first question is what do we tell the Council of Worlds about the Creators of Space and Odian Spek?"

As he sat, the talismans glowed equally—until Pias stood and they, again, shifted brightness. "We tell them everything. All the facts be laid out; Odian's escape after Saaryki, every COS-related event since, every systematic coverup all the way through the Loronzon incident, and, now, what happened in the Nova system."

Pias sat; Mattrolo rose. "The larger council will be angry, but they also know that admitting past, illegal coverups to the *Assembly of Planets* would likely result in the dissolution of both bodies. The Council won't risk that. In addition, admitting the COS has endured would subsequently lead to the uncovering of the still active Voidwhisperer program which is technically criminal and certainly divisive."

He was followed by the First Contact Prime of Sector 4, Luman Ontares. "Looking at the proposed revelations from a positive standpoint, we only need the council

---

Assembly of Planets
One of the two main governing bodies of the GSA (containing 3,756) with each member representing roughly 160 planets. Representatives only increase in numbers once all Assembly members reach more than 175 planets of inclusion. It is equal in stature to the Council of Worlds and votes if laws proposed by the opposing body will go into effect. The AOP meets on a remote asteroid at an undisclosed location. AOP representatives are provided with a Metra native company, Tejia Flight's Space Bus X61. The X61 is equipped with a giant hexagonal Kalean steel plate. When all 3,756 ships engage their steel plates around the asteroid, an orb-like planet is formed creating a secure location for the proceedings.

to see the logic of containment. Our long record of success is attributed to our reliably closed information loop. Once the COW as a whole are read in, they will understand. More important, they should be reminded how public engagement with a self-made enemy destabilizes us. That history speaks for itself."

Jegareg responded. "Information leaks also speak for themselves, which is why, I'll remind you, we're here in the first place. Trust this data to the larger group and keeping it contained will be like threading a starfighter through an asteroid field. It's hard enough to quarantine Class-T planets. This would require making records disappear, altering historic records, forging manifests, jamming signals, hiding missions, crews, and much more. With so many moving pieces, one is bound to fail. While I admit that the execution of this massive effort would be far easier with the full council's cooperation, ultimately, it may not be our choice at all. The Nova incident has already involved too many outside Primes to ever close this box again. We move now, or we'll be exposed forcibly—and that would be far worse."

When Jedareg sat, the lights balanced indicating the discussion was over. Mattro-lo's booming voice echoed against the domed ceiling. "All in favor of revealing what we've done and what we know to the Council, including all we know about the Creators, please vote now."

As the members complied, the cloud of floating talismans glowed green: no orange to be seen.

"It's unanimous, then. Moving on. "

Manti La Scal voiced their second issue.

"What shall we recommend to the World Council regarding the fate of Bor's son, Kruktusken?" After a long, awkward silence she added, "Bor, it's appropriate you have the floor."

His talisman glowing, Bor felt the weight of many eyes as he took center circle.

"Kruk's intent was righteous. While I admit it wasn't handled perfectly in the heat of the moment, he provided a warning we sorely needed. Punishment should fall, not upon him, but me for mishandling his education. I submit we recommend Kruk return to a normal GSA rotation, far from any Creator-related activity, and distance himself from future involvement in high-level politics."

All the grunting didn't bode well. Bor was relieved when Trinna Tau rose but not for long.

"The penalty for revealing Prime-level classified information is to be stripped of any government rank and be imprisoned long-term on a mining colony. And some can argue this is an Article 37."

Bor opened his mouth, then, too disciplined to break protocol despite his shock, he closed it.

Noticing his reaction, Trinna gave him a supportive glance before continuing. "However, since the information was technically not classified by the Council of Worlds, Kruk's actions were technically not illegal. Kruk did everyone a tremendous service by alerting us to the Creators. My recommendation is that he not be punished."

Bor was relieved but, again, not for long. When his dear friend Pias spoke, he was choosing his words too carefully for them to provide comfort.

"Bor, I know I speak for many when I say that removing Kruk from the Nova system is a bad idea for an abundance of reasons. Foremost, we cannot show any further favoritism. Second, we need a trustworthy source there; undoubtedly, there will be information we'll need access to. I feel we should recommend that Kruk remain there. It would highlight that he performed an important service to the galaxy and will continue to serve the GSA loyally."

Not entirely under the individual's control, the talismans were also created to prevent silent dissents. When Bor pulsated an angry orange-red indicating his feelings on the current subject, it drew nervous glances.

Pias took no notice. "Lastly, if Kruk is removed from government, as you suggest, all Bor's efforts at grooming him for the Inner Council which we agreed to will be wasted."

As Bor weighed his fear against the logic and his son's restored career, his talisman returned to its neutral color. When it came time to vote regarding Kruk's return to the Nova System, his vote was absent. The Inner Council followed all larger GSA statutes, and Article 81 was clear on nepotism. His dejected face said all that was needed with a green hue illuminating all around.

"Moving On."

Jedareg presented the third question. "How did the creators know about Nova?"

Each relevant department Prime provided what they knew.

Socrula Paru presented transportation intelligence. "We have had no record of other ships of any kind in the region. That rules out direct recon which was unlikely to begin with."

Archivist Mattrolo said, "There's nothing in the public domain that could have led them there. We'd already removed any traces of god-impersonators who'd visited Nova."

Bor spoke for communications. "There's no record of any unusual comms to or from Nova. But, I assure you, there are ways of transmitting without detection."

Jedareg finished with an obvious conclusion. "Only significant operations knowledge could allow the Creators such a success. They knew the precise location of the probe, so that intel had to be current. Therefore, it's highly likely the Nova quarantine program has a mole. Nova has been locked down, so the mole must still be there. A full Council of Worlds investigation will find them. I'll lead it myself."

Bor, realizing how he could further solidify Kruk's position, spoke up. "May I suggest deflecting two asteroids with one collision? Undoubtedly, Jedareg's efforts will swiftly find the mole, but simply capturing them might be a dead end. Since Kruk will be there, may I suggest that if he quietly seeks out this mole, we may be able to learn more?"

Voting commenced; the talismans glowed green.

Scalipio asked the fourth and final question. "What do we do with Odian?"

Pias himself answered. "Using whatever means necessary, as quickly and quietly as possible, remove him and all of the Creators from the galactic equation. I know some may fear that doing so may lead sympathizers to revel, but, I promise you, allow him a single breath of diplomatic air and he could unravel our control from planet to planet. This is far from an unreasonable assumption."

He projected the Nova debrief across the amphitheater. "In case you missed it, analysis of the disabled enemy ship showed it was machine-piloted. Unremarkable in itself but there's more. As expected, by the time we pulled the pilot from the craft, its kill switches had wiped the navigational logs. We thought the same happened to its strategic mission programming, but further analysis revealed it never had any. Meaning, it wasn't programmed to attack; it did so, for lack of a better word, voluntarily."

He gave that a moment to sink in. There were no questions, no grunts, just thoughtful silence and, from those who had faces or other emotive organs, reactions ranging from bemused to grave alarm.

"Odian Spek is capable of appealing to machines. If he can convince them to join his cause, he can convince anyone. Intentionally or not, he may incite another *machine uprising*. My people remember what that cost the galaxy. I, for one, do not wish to test the Kaleans' loyalty to the Alliance."

Seizing the opportunity, Bor initiated the vote. "All in favor of removing Odian Spek and any members of the COS by any necessary means for the good of galactic stability?"

For the final time, all the lights burned green concluding the Inner Council gathering.

Pias wrapped up some ancillary details. Bor, wanting a moment to himself, was among the first to exit the Sanctuary 19 tower. Despite his and Kruk's missteps, they were still intact. Despite the looks he imagined he was getting, he felt comfortable

---

Machine Uprising

Refers to the recurring danger of an AI rising to dominate all other life. The most notable instance of this is the event that ended the Classical Galactic Era. A vast, self-replicating machine army was created as an endgame device to stop thousands of turns of resource fighting wars over the limited worlds in the Warpgate system. Instantly growing beyond control, the machines devoured planets and stars travelling along the gates. The Warpgates were sacrificed to send a galaxy spanning blast that disabled all of the robots.

they were on the right side of history. He was even getting used to not knowing whether things were happening because or in spite of his errors.

As ships rose through the canopy and headed toward the archipelago center, there was a momentary atmospheric dimming: an unnatural aurora that cascaded across the vector right above them. It was the signal that the Council of Worlds was about to begin.

Despite the imminent deadline, Bor saw one vessel screaming toward the isle. It was Tordok, of course. Late as usual.

Instead of landing at the tower, though, he veered off and touched down on a lower jungle platform. Perplexed, Bor headed along the trails to bring him up to speed. Someone had to.

He was greeted by a sleek, dark, glowing craft. Definitely not standard GSA issue, it was a *Quasar Screamer*. They were terrible on interplanetary maneuvers but one of the fastest flowspace fliers in existence. Not necessarily a ship you'd expect an explorer to use.

Tordok leapt down from the cargo bay before the ladders telescoped.

Bor moved to meet him. "Well, at least you're consistent."

Out of breath and clearly disturbed, Tordok grabbed Bor's shoulders and whispered as if there were someone around who might hear. "I know full well we have to get to the Council meeting, but I had to delay leaving as long as I could. We found something in the *Distant Zones*: evidence that the Creators have been out there tampering with unmapped worlds."

The considerable catalogue of Bor's previous worries were instantly overshadowed. Looking deep in the Metra's eyes, he saw his own fear reflected back. The only sound was the tropical breeze rustling julonga fronds until he asked.

"Are you sure?"

Tordok dropped his arms and spat indignantly. "Am I? I've dedicated the entire 3rd Expeditionary Fleet to this. They're deployed and monitoring beyond contact

---

Quasar Screamer
Built for maximum speed, it is a patch 5 capable starship with a quantum vibration dampening hull for rapid patch transitions and some flowspace maneuverability. Seated for 1, they have triple redundant inertial dampeners and can reach up to 30% of the speed of light. The first generation has been the winning starship in the Neruda Circuit and the Sector 6 Loop 8/10 times for the past 400 turns.

The Distant Zones
The vast, uncharted regions of the Karandu Galaxy (Milky Way) that are beyond the edge of Alliance controlled space. This area comprises over 60% of the galaxy, including the galactic center, and remains largely a mystery. It is unlawful for Alliance civilians to travel there; it is where political exiles are banished, and it is rumored to contain hidden civilizations. Ancient maps indicate portions of the Builder Warpgate system extended far into this unknown space. The Department of Exploration conducts missions into this realm to learn and discover new worlds, beings, and resources.

range. Of the last four sentient systems we catalogued, we found three confirmed encounters between the Creators and the indigenous sentients—all within the past thirty turns."

He briefly displayed the contents of a data chip on a tiny holoscreen. "Even with combuoys, I couldn't risk transmitting information like this, so our messengers relayed this on Quasar Screamers. It was my turn when I got the Council summons, but I had to wait for another runner skiff with a mission update."

Bor's mind raced like a Screamer in flowspace. Spek had been busy in death. Had he just been toying with Nova?

"There's more. Unsubstantiated, but we've heard rumors of a planetship."

Bor relaxed at once. The very idea was so insane Tordok must have taken too many stims or hadn't gotten enough sleep. He was just babbling nonsense. Still, the data looked real, and the fear on his face was sincere.

"I came to you directly because sensitive communication is your strength. No one knows about this other than my personal Explorers and you and I. Honestly, I... don't know what to do."

His own head spinning, Bor managed to put a comforting hand on Tordok's shoulder. "You were right to come to me. It's far too important to throw out into the universe. We'll figure out how to proceed but not here. Get to the *Anador*. We'll contact the Inner Council after the meeting."

Dubious, Tordok turned off the datachip. "This can't wait long, Bor."

"I know. Trust me, I know. A lot's happened here, too. Just to bring you up to speed, Odian Spek is alive and the Creators attacked a T-Class quarantine planet."

The Metra Prime looked about to faint when another countdown aurora arched across the sky drawing his attention upward.

"Go," Bor urged. "Now."

Jogged into the moment, Tordok made a formal parting gesture before running back into the Quasar Screamer. Bor ran back, arriving at the Bridalgo just as Pias

---

Anador

Called "Place of Power" in Udari, this giant crystal structure was grown from an Udari crystal that was crashed into Primidious by the World Shapers 400,000 turns ago. To this date, its composition is still a mystery; however it is known to be of a material that even temperatures within a star's core cannot harm. It contains a temporal chamber, the Valador, where the Council of Worlds takes place. It is also a sleeping consciousness that has refused to wake even after being explored, partially decoded, and reprogrammed by GSA scientists and the Kaleans over thousands of turns.

broke away from a conversation with Scalipio and Manti. They two saying goodbye, they headed for the paths.

"Tordok?" Pias asked, bemused. "That why you're late?"

"Yes, I was giving him an update. We're all in agreement. He'll meet us at the Anador."

"Excellent. Time to go shape history!" Noticing Bor's dark expression halted Pias' excitement. "Now what?"

"Pias, circumstances have grown immeasurably more complex even from nine nolaprikes ago..."

"What did Tordok say?"

"The Creators are recruiting from the Distant Zones."

Whatever calamity Pias expected to hear about, it wasn't this.

The engines roared to life, but the two of them sat in silence as the Bridalgo took off soaring over Sanctuary 19 and onward to the Anador.

CHAPTER 14

THE ANADOR

U nwilling to let any opportunity to enjoy a vast body of water slip by, as they
approached the center of the Anduri archipelago, Bor asked the pilot to take
the ship as low as he could. With the Bridalgo practically skimming the turquoise
waves, a wondrous menagerie of marine life could be seen below the surface. Vast
schools of Crimptons played in the shallows' colorful corals. In the deeper water,
cinkplods, alerted by the ship's magnetic field, flung themselves from the sea into
the air.

Abandoning the observation deck for the cargo bay, he slid the hatch open. A
vertical bar of sunlight entered accompanied by the hissing, salty ocean breath.
Bor eagerly gripped a handhold and leaned out letting the cool spray flash the
fingers of his free hand.

The sensation brought him into Recall—conjuring a childhood family trip to the
purple *Sea of Nedsewa* on *Dragsa*. He and his cousins were on *surfskimmers*. Led
by Uncle NooktuskenDor, they spent long drikes looking for *rudiathens*. When
they breached, the gargantuan creatures generated massive waves twenty tradons
tall. Leaping to them with their *glideboards*, they'd surf the swells for rudons.

Dragsa
The Dragsan homeworld located in a trinary star system. One of the stars went supernova 1 billion turns ago and left a neutron star at the system center
orbited by two K class stars. The supernova stripped Dragsa of half its oceans but seeded the planet with enormous quantities of rare elements. The
unique radiation of their neutron star is what has been pinpointed as the direct cause for the evolution of Dragsan Recall.

The Sea of Nedsewa
Large body of water in Dragsa's northern hemisphere: roughly 7 million sq rudons. Named after an ocean goddess from Dragsan mythology, the Tusken
ancestral home is located on its shores.

"Close that hatch! We're about to pull up and the anti-grav can't kick in unless we're sealed!"

Bor swung back to see Pias' disapproving look. The Recall faded. It was, and felt like, a lifetime ago. Epiko didn't have oceans, and Primes lacked the luxury of vacations. A brief assignment once took him into orbit around the water world Yallaweh. He thought back to when he heard the beautiful symphonies of the Murakoor whales. Even the view from space of that endless blue expanse brought him overwhelming happiness.

He hit the close button and, smiling happily, headed toward a grunting Pias. "Your behavior is quite unbecoming of a Prime."

Bor's response was guiltless. "I know. That's why I'm doing it in the middle of the ocean. Don't worry Pias; I just needed a moment."

On their way back to the observation deck, his friend's objections faded. "I understand. The immediate stakes are personal for you."

Though still distant, Anduri already loomed large. The archipelago's namesake and largest island was once a supervolcano. Its absent peak suggested a massive eruption collapsed it long ago. The coast was a mix of blinding white beaches and monolithic stones standing defiant against the waves. The shore gave way to dense jungle that climbed high up the mountains before finally yielding to their snow-capped peaks. There, the reflective ribbons of waterfalls sluiced down the slopes.

Pias tapped his comm band. "I just sent alternate coordinates for a more scenic route, Lydon. Take note, you may never see this again."

The *Tycan* pilot responded with a stiff, "Thank you, sir."

Though Lydon was the product of strict military training, Bor could still sense his excitement. It was a feeling shared by all, except perhaps the Raa'Tiki.

Adjusting course, the ship slowed and moved parallel to the ridgeline. Pias had directed them through a magnificent fjord roofed by crisscrossing, 400 tradon length *Junadian* tree boughs. Their multicolored leaves created a magical, prismatic

---

Cinkplod
A ray-like alien creature that hails from the tropical oceans of Ond'Yallaweh. (An expansion world of the Baleens.) With a "wingspan" of 1.2-1.5 tradons, it can leap and glide over the water for over 40 tradons at a time by rapidly expelling pressurized air from twin chambers in its body.

Surfskimmer
A low altitude hovercraft that uses a compressed air cushion to fly at a max altitude of one tradon. It is extremely fast on water, lightweight, and uses negligible power, thus excellent for extended duration ocean voyages. It was designed by BriksandenLur during the Classical Galactic Era as a school project to help her older sister with her new fishing job. This new type of ocean hovercraft soon became commonplace in Dragsan culture.

NooktuskenDor
Was the head of House Tusken and uncle to KruktuskenBor and DraktuskenDor.

glow.

"A bit more grandiose than I remember," Bor mused, "but stunning."

"It's the single best replication of nature ever created," Pias said. "It should be grandiose."

A sudden mist left them in a nebulous, colorful, haze. Only the growing light above indicated the Bridalgo was still climbing. Once they rose above its source, a massive waterfall, the haze vanished. A giant caldera came into view; its crater, a vast lake feeding a broad river, ringed by barren cliffs and pristine forest shores.

Chuckling, Bor nodded.

The Anador itself sat in the middle of the lake. Some of it looked naturally jagged. Other portions had a too-perfect, too-smooth geometry. The central orange crystal, though, was riveting. Two hundred tradons wide, its hexagonal structure rose over a rudon skyward. Reflecting sunlight, the lattices and facets glinted occasionally creating a blinding flash.

Rather than built, the Anador grew from a single seed: a *Udarian crystal* sent here 400,000 turns ago by the World Shapers. After crashing to the surface it activated becoming the great hall of governance as well as serving as a reminder to the GSA that there were always technologies greater than their own.

The silicon-based Udari once created vast cities of unfathomable technology from these crystals but were tragically obliterated at the end of the *Reclamation Era*. The method of controlling the crystals was largely lost to time. Even if one could be drilled into, no one would dare. It had taken generations of collective effort to program only a few elemental functions. An *Ulron* pirate vessel crashed on Neruda 7 four million turns ago activating one of the rare crystals. Even with thousands of turns of research before the existence of the Kaleans, the GSA could not fathom the necessary skill and knowledge to functionally manipulate the Udarian technology. As far as any knew, only the Kaleans had completely learned its secrets.

Tordok's Screamer zoomed by followed by scores of vessels: some moving leisurely

---

Rudiathen
Called the "big sister of the deep " in the old Dragsan tongue. It is a massive sea creature that breathes in water, and lives on Dragsa in the Sea of Nedsewa. Towering at 100 tradons in length, it has four giant fins for swimming, and an endoskeleton, with hardened skin and segmented armor on its belly and back. It bears a massive mouth that never closes, filled with filtration structures and paralyzing stingers. Despite its size, it is gentle, omnivorous, and will ignore all but large ships and creatures.

Glideboard
A water platform traditionally made for Dragsan surfers from the fronds of the giant Kedsewa Palm Tree. Less expensive versions are made from wood, polymer, or light flexmetal alloy. However, the most expensive boards are from reclaimed Rudiathen bone. Their scarcity owed to the fact that it is punishable by death to kill a Rudiathen outside of ceremony.

enjoying the scenery, others swooping in from above.

The Anador base glowed; its light rose up the structure. Growing in intensity, it pulsed in cycles like a charging railgun becoming a flowing, humming stream that filled every crystal face. Reaching the top, it shot skyward until, high in the atmosphere, it hit some invisible barrier. Those on their first visit to Primidious grew afraid until the plasma waves scattered brilliantly outwards becoming the familiar aurora that announced the approaching meeting.

The Bridalgo spiraled down landing on a platform neatly concealed by the cliff ring. There were similar pads scattered about, often hidden from one another, adapted for that use wherever the crystal had grown large, flat surfaces. Three ships shared their pad bearing the markings of the departments of Health, Arts, and Mining, respectively.

The Bridalgo's landing gear faintly hissed. The ship's hum faded leaving an eerie silence. Pias, holding his voting talisman, remained motionless apparently reviewing some final details for his presentation. When Bor placed a hand on his friend's lower arm, Pias blinked, stored his talisman, and gestured it was time.

A flurry of activity ensued; the crew inspecting ship's systems, political aides gathering data blocks and making last-minute communications. While the Primes met, they'd have their own negotiating duties with their Sector counterparts.

One aide stepped forth with a small case containing two injectors and two blue *nanite* spheres. The nanites would absorb any waste material from the Primes during the lengthy debates ahead.

"Ready to not defecate for seventeen prikes?" Pias joked. Bor sighed.

Each took a set, loaded the spheres, and injected themselves. He'd done it before, but Bor would never get used to what felt like freezing lightning filling his body.

Ready, they exited with their entourage expertly in tow. Outside, the looming crystal dwarfed them bathing everything with the orange glow of its reflection. Used only for the full council, few trod the sublime paradise. Now, in a scene

---

Digestion Blocking Nanite
Are highly adapted GSA tools for extended duration tasks under restricted conditions. It is a microscopic machine that processes and breaks down bi-products of organic digestion allowing for food consumption without creating excrement. Versions of moderate success have been recorded since the Classical Era. The widespread Generation 1 was developed by the biosynth conglomerate, Pelkon-Intok.

Tycan (occurs on page 198 paragraph 8)
Translated as "The First" from their old tongue, this sentient GSA species hail from the desert planet Lumathaan. Evolved to sentience during the Second Dark Era, they possess excellent eyesight and reflexes, armored skin, 99.6% biological water reclamation, and a strong resistance to heat and cold. They appear grey with spiky neck frills and are usually stoic, obedient, emotionally reserved, and analytic. They were enslaved as a species by a rogue system of the Anduuzilian Protectorate, then liberated by the GSA during the Reclamation Era. Most are strong believers in the mission of the GSA and commonly serve in military, piloting, and security positions.

replicated across the Anador, Primes and their teams moved in formation disappearing into a tunnel that led to a crystalline staircase weaving through the rock.

There were no lights, no wiring—no signs of GSA technology of any kind. Everything and everyone were illuminated by an omnipresent surface glow. Within the crystal itself, strange energy crackled in luminous ribbons. Everything, even the smooth stairs, was made from a crystalline circuitry stacked in impossible matrices.

As they ascended, the groups mingled. For many, it was a reunion, but there were new faces as well. Not being politicians vying for reelection, the momentous occasion didn't preclude the preeminent GSA authorities from being themselves.

Trinna Tau, Sector 4's Archivist Premier Prime, floated ahead. Her deputy curators carried some sort of artifact, undoubtedly, from a world that the GSA had yet to understand. She and her team's ability to comprehend cultures through their relics had led to nine peaceful first contacts. It had also unearthed dark secrets.

Though in deep conversation with one of her team, she glanced back, briefly sweeping her eyes across Bor's face. He thought he caught a glimpse of a smile.

At the end of the lengthy climb, arrivals from various staircases merged in a toroidal antechamber. Along the outer curved wall, there were entrances to smaller chambers but no markers of any kind. No offices. No inhabitants. Like its smooth walls, the Anador was meant to be a blank slate: intended to have no sign of cultural, technical, or species influence when the GSA voted. Ironically, it made the Anador a very alien place.

Trying not to appear as desperate as he felt, Bor looked around for Kruk. They couldn't meet yet, but he hoped to be a consoling presence for his son. Kruk was nowhere to be seen, but the realization that there were no noticeable gaps in the crowd brought a shudder. Were the Raa'Tiki climbing the walls?

"Trinna Tau! As I crawl and flob." A seven-tentacled *Arpedime* undulated their way. "Kud Mora Laru, as I paint and judge," she responded.

Kud Mora lay flat and curved her tentacles above her head creating an empty

---

Arpedime
A seven tentacled land species that hail from mudflats in the heavy gravity of Trantor. The Arpedime's cerebral cortex is unusually large creating heightened empathy which has evolved the species to have an elevated understanding of the arts.

Junadian (occurs on page 198 paragraph 10)
Called the "Roof of the World" in Osanii, this non-sentient lifeform is among the largest plant species in Alliance space growing up to 700 tradons tall. The leaves on a single tree grow in all known colors of the infrared, visible, and UV spectrum. Mainly found on its native world Monzama or on Primidious, it thrives with its roots in humid, tropical jungles and protection from the wind for its tall limbs.

sphere. Trinna returned the greeting by forming her many-jointed arms into an arc, holding it above her head, and then lowering it across her face.

Kud Mora was delighted and eager to share the latest trends. "We absolutely must discuss the Azeoleo-inspired Neorepetitive light sculpting movement sweeping *Obsidian 7.*"

Trinna was equally thrilled. "Tell me everything! Who are the stars? Are we talking intersector gallery tours, yet, or do we need to discuss grant funding?"

Bor chuckled at their friendly conversation, but it also reminded him of those who were missing. "I wish Merrit Lones and Redokin were here. We need all the strong voices we can get."

To Pias, any hint of self-pity was anathema. "It was their time, plain and simple. There's still much good they can do from *Havlangar.*"

Gon'dil Messeni, the Trade Prime of Sector 5, sidled up and rudely planted one of his two tails on Pias' shoulder. "Pias! We're all dying to know what grave events motivated you to summon us all. You must tell us!"

Bor never liked him. It wasn't that *Nithons* slithered, it was the first-rotation Prime's utter lack of subtlety.

The question was echoed by ten others forcing Pias to raise his arms in four directions. "I called us all because the discussion requires all of us. Any side conversations or speculation will only be an impediment. My reasons will be clear shortly."

The curved antechamber continued filling bringing a general sense of urgency. The galaxy was huge—transportation far from instantaneous. After the main meeting, there'd be many other negotiations piggybacking on the rare opportunity.

Pias, seventeen moves ahead, turned to an aide. "Schedule a military investigation and exploration meeting to follow the Council's gathering. Prepare a chamber."

The light from the inner wall pulsed indicating everyone was present. Attendants and support staff headed into the side chambers or disappeared down strange staircases and halls. Bor, again, looked for Kruk but apparently, not as discreetly

---

Obsidian 7
The farthest orbiting planet of the Obsidi System. It is a dark, moody, rocky world that was terraformed and became known as a retreat from the busy core. In time, the GSA founded the Sector 6 Academy of Arts here. Since then, the world has been an artistic hub from which come the main influences of fashion, art, and music for 10,000 kulons around.

Nithon
A snake-like sentient species from the planet Koorpal. They breathe oxygen, have four eyes, a mesoskeleton, and can grow 2.3 to 4 tradons long. They have two tails that split and create 1/3 of their body length. They are extremely strong and fast in close quarters, with toughened scales. They are generally too nice and are poor at reading social situations, while a few are sociopathic.

as he thought.

Without breaking stride, Prime Jedareg whispered as he passed by. "He's being kept by the Sector 9 Investigation delegation in a small chamber on the opposite side."

Once only the Primes remained, they spread along the inner curved wall until they circled it all the way around, faced outward, and linked to form a ring. Talking ceased, save for Pias who addressed the air in front of him.

He wasn't shouting, yet somehow his voice was heard equally around the antechamber. "Raa'Tiki, Guardians of the Primes, reveal yourselves and unlock the Anador."

Havlangar
The government retirement planet of the GSA located in the Skulvar System, Sector 5. Its name translates as "where knowledge sleeps" in Old Metra. It was chosen from an early census of newly explored planets 36,000 turns after the formation of the GSA. Barely habitable, it was special because it contained Builder ruins and a deactivated Warpgate, but it was not on any maps of the Warpgate system. Why the Builders had removed it from their society remains unknown. Some terraforming work improved the ecosystem, and it was decided to be the final residence of any life-term Primes. There, the GSA transformed a small continent and built the Citadel of Thought for the retired Primes to live in. As per Amendment 33, all "Life-Primes" are never allowed to return to normal GSA life after serving the galaxy. The Raa'Tiki still continue to protect their Primes there until their deaths.

CHAPTER 15
THE COUNCIL OF WORLDS

The air before them shimmered. Pixelated, golden motes appeared defining the contours of unseen beings. Coalescing, they flashed into solid shapes encircling the Primes. The light evaporated but not without leaving burning silhouettes on Bor's retina. In place of the glow stood monsters of legend. Six to a Prime, their appearance elicited screams, gasps, and squawks from the uninitiated.

The Raa'Tiki's dark, stolid features and segmented appendages were every bit as terrifying as Bor remembered. Their upside down, triangular heads had four eyes spread across faces covered in clicking scales and spines. Cobalt-bladed tarsi jut from each appendage capable of piercing thick, titanium plating. Seeking better balance on the crystal floor, they shifted their limbs from arm to leg, yet somehow remained silent.

Nothing about their appearance alluded to their inexplicable species' ability to become invisible. They seemed to carry no weapons or tech of any kind, but they were born killers perfectly suited to protect Primes. Two antenna stubs atop each head were a reminder of the loyal sacrifice they'd made to serve the GSA. Despite his queasiness, Bor knew this was probably the safest place in the galaxy.

Udarian Crystal (occurs on page 199 paragraph 6)
One of the most powerful objects in the known galaxy. Created from an Udari that willingly sacrifices itself, they transmute into a living silicate. These precious objects can be imbued with vast energy and programmed to grow into structures, ships, or whatever technology desired. The crystals contain a sleeping consciousness.

Reclamation Era (occurs on page 199 paragraph 7)
The time period heralding the end of the Second Dark Era (8.5 million turns ago). It began when the Dramurians discovered flowspace to escape the destruction of their planet from a supernova. They arrived at Zesperana, having sent messages ahead of time, and asked for refuge in exchange for knowledge of the flowspace drive. With flowspace, intelligent life again spread throughout the galaxy finding thousands of old and new worlds as well as species, most outside of the Warpgate system.

The crystals beneath them grew together raising the floor. As they moved skyward, the entrances to the antechamber and side chambers were swallowed beneath the rising edge. The ceiling recessed allowing them to ascend further.

"What's happening?" The question identified the asker as new.

Bor remembered wondering the same when he was a fresh Prime and the full Council met to decide the fate of the Saaryki. The tone had been equally somber then, but the novelty made it all so exciting. He wished his mind were as unburdened now as it had been then.

Someone along the circle answered the novice. "In the unlikely event that one of us were an imposter, the original's six Raa'Tiki would be dead. To safeguard against infiltration, opening the Anador's first door requires a unique energy burst that can only be produced by the simultaneous decloaking of all 1,026 Raa'Tiki."

With a light grinding, the upward movement stopped. The Raa'Tiki guarding their backs, the Primes turned to face the inner wall. Bor removed his voting talisman. It was hot, though he had not activated it, and glowing the same orange as the Anador.

He put his free hand out to the inner wall. Wherever his fingertips touched, weaving trails of light danced along the impenetrable surface. The other Primes did likewise: talisman in one hand or appendage, another touching the wall. Ribbons of light flowed from every point of contact snaking along until they connected with each other.

The circuit complete, it was echoed by a solid, lava-like river within the crystal. Pias nodded at Bor, then passed his hand through as if it were mist. Gliding, Trinna Tau passed through as effortlessly as a neutrino through a planet.

Bor took a deep breath and followed suit. His body phased through; he had a feeling, not unlike slipping into warm water. Held in warm, comforting energy, surrounded by what looked like the heart of a star, he had no sense of direction or place other than relative to the similarly suspended Primes to his left and right.

Ulron (occurs on page 199 paragraph 7)

One of the nine founding species of the GSA. They are the most peaceful, longest living, and the least populous of the nine, with most still residing on their homeworld, Neruda 8. Starting as a tadpole-like creature that evolves into a stronger, more durable body, they can metamorphosize up to 7 times. They have an extremely long childhood and are virtually immortal if they remain in their nascent stages. They must evolve into their final form to exist beyond their homeworld for any long duration, at which point they lose their ability to heal and can no longer breed. They possessed lifespans of up to 30,000 turns during the Second Dark Era due to a symbiotic relationship with their planet. But after the Reclamation Era, industry and commerce inevitably affected the ecosystem, and within a few generations, they sacrificed relative immortality for civilization. The Ulron now live to the ripe age of 1,000 to 3,000 turns.

The orange plasma flowed to the horizon shifting and bending along the planet's magnetic field lines. Tiny stars, carried in undulating patterns by the liquid winds, twinkled. The Anador was alive. He could feel it. How? One theory was that each crystal was the remains of an individual *Udari*, that they'd built their great cities from their dead. Whatever it had been, now it was an entire mountain: stoic, impassive to the miniscule beings temporarily touching its history.

Experience told Bor his goal wasn't far. Still, his lungs were burning from the lack of oxygen by the time he emerged into the Anador's heart.

The Zundrillian to his right likewise gasped for air. "Wow, I'd forgotten how difficult that was. The Udari must not have known many carbon-based lifeforms."

"True. On the lighter side, they did create a stable phasing field that doesn't disintegrate your DNA." Bor's tone expressed his admiration.

The heart was an amphitheater of sorts. A tall, cylindrical chamber, it reached nearly to the structure's top where brilliant sunlight filtered down. The floor here was composed of hundreds of stepped hexagonal terraces. The highest at the edges led down to the lowest in the center. While many shared the ambient glow, a sizable fraction were dim and colorless: one hundred seventy-one, to be precise, matching the number of Primes.

Arriving from various points along the wall, all together for the first time, they descended. As each Prime took their place on a terrace, it glowed. The hexes were more than adequate. Designed for beings much larger than Bor, even Pias comfortably fit on one.

Once the final terrace was occupied, a rumble, accompanied by a low whine, indicated the activation of some large machinery. In unison, the Primes bent and touched their talismans to the floor. Beneath his feet, Bor could see the cell and crystal structure stretching downward forever.

The rumble and whine rose to a fever pitch. There was an abrupt flash and then silence. As the walls and ceiling became solid once more, the sunlight darkened.

Udari

A rare, exceptional, silicon based lifeform. Called "The Foundation " in old Metra, they existed entirely on the planet Dumar Tar'Rain. They do not breathe oxygen, thrive in extremely high temperatures and pressures, "grow" from crystal "seeds," and can transform into sentient structures. They possess genetic memory, with no known natural lifespan limit. Many died; they were wiped out by a fatal, unknown disease introduced by first contact during the Reclamation Era. They never joined the GSA but were peaceful and indifferent to other species. They possess highly advanced, virtually indestructible technology that remains beyond most GSA understanding and is used at the highest levels of government. They are currently protected under the "Kalean Concurrence Act" of the turn 8,006,106.

This was now the place without time, a temporal bubble, known as *The Valador*. The council could spend a turn here while outside, only a few prikes passed. It was the Anador's true power—allowing full debate with no adverse impact on governing.

When the structure first grew, the Valador was unlocked: its walls permeable, its purpose unknown. After much analysis, and even more trial and error, the GSA managed to decipher its rules. Each hexagonal terrace a Prime stood upon contained a talisman that was a key. If any talismans were removed, the space was locked and could only be reopened by the same number of talismans. Everyone had to leave and arrive together, and the temporal bubble could only be activated or deactivated if all the occupants "keyed" simultaneously.

Some enemies of the Galactic Star Alliance thought the talismans were a weakness that they could be stolen or destroyed. But when a crippled Prime's cruiser was drawn into a star and pulverized, along with the talisman, the Anador simply grew another. As for theft, the Raa'Tiki ensured that would never happen.

The Valador activated; the Primes were free to move about. Most gathered in social groups near the low center. Many sat on the terrace edges... feet, tails, and tentacles dangling.

Across from Bor, a cheerful voice rang strong and clear. "Before we begin, does anyone need additional nutriment?"

It was the Kalean, Enareggario, the *Entropless Energy Prime* of Sector 1. Living machines, the Kalean's mostly humanoid anatomy shone like fine ceramic but bent and twisted like real tissue. In some spots, armored panels covered his body. In others, transparent plates revealed whirling, dazzling machinery. Importantly, they could morph their features at will.

At the moment though, Enareggario's face was absent until a Duma Prime announced. "I need a resupply. We practically ran out the door."

In response, a beautiful visage appeared wearing a Rakilla tribal mask. What

---

The Valador
Called the "The place without time" in Udari, is the modern meeting location of the Council of Worlds. It is a temporal chamber that resides at the center of the Anador. Time inside the Valador runs at a 200x rate in relative space. It was discovered 70 turns after the Anador was first explored, when scientists were sucked into the chamber and starved to death. The GSA slowly learned to reprogram the Anador, and The Valador was used for long duration, scientific experiments. After the Kaleans joined the GSA, understanding of the Udari construct grew considerably, and the Valador became the meeting location of the Council of Worlds. The Kaleans reprogrammed the Valador to create the voting talismans and interface with the Raa'Tiki's decloaking.

Entropless Energy Prime
The Sector Head of the Department of Energy. They lead and oversee a department that's operations generate and maintain power, repair planetary grids and infrastructure, as well as performing research into new methods of energy generation and capture.

features were visible beneath the stoic veil looked part Dragsan, part Valkon but with metal skin and glowing tattoos.

Enareggario claimed he changed faces often to gauge how people reacted to different species. Bor suspected he just enjoyed messing with the mortals.

Several Primes stepped up to the Kalean and presented their nutrient imbeds. Sufficient food and water were crucial for those inhabiting a room they would not be leaving for an unknown amount of time. Bor's implant worked with the nanites, leaving him no need to eat or relieve himself. The problem for those lacking this symbiotic biological advantage had been solved by the Kaleans. They could store nutrients and water as superdense energy and easily carry enough for all.

Enareggario's fingers morphed into siphons that he connected to each Prime's imbed. While Sprog Doorlig's pack was being filled, he jokingly asked, "If you can keep enough water for all of us in the tip of your finger, why haven't you conquered the galaxy?"

The Kalean chuckled. "There is no need for such violence, Sprog. Time is of little consequence. The Kaleans will exist long after the expected lifespan of your mortal civilizations. Once you're dead or have evolved beyond this plane of existence, the Kaleans will inherit this galaxy. It is an exciting future for certain."

Unable to read the machine's blank face, Sprog laughed and hastily turned away. "Next?" Enareggario asked.

"Bor, you're staring." Pias had walked up quietly behind him.

Bor frowned. "They're a race of sentient machines, with technology so advanced, it makes the Anador look like a brick, yet they treat us as equals. Why? Even after 300,000 turns of peacefully coexisting, I still don't trust them."

"No one does. That's why they're not part of the inner council," Pias whispered.

Once nutrients were supplied and recording devices calibrated, the Primes returned to their terraces. There, they removed their talismans and let them float to the center. Shortly, a hundred and seventy-one orange stars formed a revolving constellation.

When it changed to white, a pinwheel of beams colorful as an aurora, flew forth connecting each talisman with its owner. One by one, the beams trembled, then vanished until three remained. When they turned red, the corresponding talismans separated from the constellation and hovered over their owners.

The first, an **Onphont** named Brooznoor Ren, announced, "The Mediators have been chosen."

The second was a tall, poised **Kitta**, Pika Ru'Yak, veteran Agriculture Prime. The third, Barulka Nimitz, Effective Policing Prime of Sector 5. Recognizing him, Bor moaned. He was not a preferred choice.

The Mediators made their way to the central floor and proclaimed in tandem, "So commences the 5337th Council of Worlds."

Brooznoor continued. "The Council having been summoned by Effective Force Prime Pias Abbotkrine of Sector 1, he shall take the floor. Naturally, we're all terribly curious what matter of Galactic security he deems merits such a gathering. Not since the Creators of Space were a threat, have we held such a meeting."

Though Bor cringed at the comparison, he was all the more grateful his unflappable Pias would be speaking, not him. As Pias descended, his crystal floated from the constellation. They met in the center: the talisman floating a quarter-tradon above his head.

When it glowed white, Bor swallowed hard. There was no turning back. If Pias lied, the talisman would turn black and inflict pain. Not simply a shock, the discharge was designed to overload the nervous system, or circuitry, of any sentient being. Every dendrite or node would burn with phantom fire; each nolaprike would feel like a turn.

Within these beautiful walls, he'd heard screams otherwise found only in nightmares. If inflicted often enough, the pain could kill.

Pias cleared his throat. "Fellow councilmembers, species from thousands of

---

Onphont
A sentient species with a prehensile trunk that walks on four legs. Native to the planet of O'Khanda located in the 4th Sector beyond the Jagged Tooth Nebula.

Kitta
A sentient herbivore species from the planet Tun'Gara. They evolved from huge grasslands that cover the planet. They have an antelope-like head and a tall, thin body with four elongated legs. Their feet contain "hooves" that can lock or split into 4 fingers. They are known for being hypervigilant but are not easily startled and are one of the fastest sentient species in the GSA.

planets, leaders who help operate this great government, it is my duty to inform you that the Creators of Space recently attacked the T-Class planet at the Nova System quarantine program. Furthermore, Odian Spek is not dead as we all presumed but alive and, again, leading them."

When Pias's crystal remained white, Bor counted several lifespans worth of silence. He wasn't sure if anyone was breathing. Despite the lack of overt motion, the talismans revealed the wild subtext in violent, pulsing flashes of hues across the spectrum.

As the light show escalated, the room exploded. Voices and nonverbal sounds cluttered and rebounded along the walls as the members expressed what their talismans already showed.

"What is this nonsense?"

"I don't understand!"

"How could this be?"

"Why are we only hearing about this now?" "What proof do you have?"

"Rooka! Is this a joke?"

The constellation of talismans, struggling to find and filter common questions, blinked madly. The mediators tried to quell the cacophony, shouting.

"Order! Order! Order!"

When the three red beams once more connected them, a silence descended as if all the air had been sucked from the room.

Brooznoor roared. "We are the leaders of the Galactic Star Alliance and will behave accordingly! Questions will be presented according to procedure."

The color storm steadied. Though their brightness did not fluctuate, as the talismans stabilized, they sorted themselves into color groups. The hexagon beneath Barulka glowed; the others dimmed indicating he would ask the first question.

"Odian Spek was tried and convicted two-hundred turns ago. He escaped custody and has never been seen since. The Creators were a short-lived nuisance destroyed at the end of the Saaryki War, again, with no verifiable evidence of them since. Prime Abottkrine, how do you back up your claims?"

Studying the intent gazes, many with a stalwart belief in the GSA's perfection, Bor imagined kicking a pebble down a mountain watching it become an avalanche.

Pias made a sweeping glance at his audience before looking directly at Barulka. "To probe my claims, I'll begin with the fact that for the past two hundred turns, the continued activity of the Creators, along with Odian's involvement, have been covered up by the highest levels of our government. Thirty turns ago, convinced he was dead, we decided that to maintain stability, public knowledge of incidents involving the Creators of Space should be contained indefinitely. That was... until 64 prikes ago. "

Other than a few holdouts waiting to hear the rest, the shock and outrage was universal. Enareggario's face became a cartoon caricature of disbelief. Barulka's expression grew menacing. But, no one stopped Pias from continuing.

"There have been thirty-seven attacks by the Creators, mostly to harm T-Class planets. That's why our quarantine programs have been steadily scaled up. Many will recall that after Odian obliterated the Saaryki, he blamed the GSA for giving them the opportunity to accomplish their genocide and vowed to ensure it would never happen again."

Barulka raised his tail. "What proof did you have of Odian Spek's death?"

Uneasy murmurs wandering the chamber, "The tactics used at Nova were highly consistent with the peculiarities of their known strategies. For example, the theft of a native probe which the Creators are no doubt now using to decipher data from Nova. If they deem Nova unworthy... which they doubtlessly will, they'll try to sneak a bioweapon past our troops. We know this because they've done it before. Several planetary genocides have been falsely indexed as natural pandemics or concealed as ecological disasters. In one case, the Creators sabotaged first contact by inciting a war permanently removing the planet from Alliance consideration."

The second mediator, Pika, asked, "What war are you referring to?"

"The Loronzon Incident."

As Pias smiled darkly, his comm band projected a grizzly hologram. "This is Odian's right arm and a portion of his upper torso. They were found in the wreckage of his cruiser in the wake of the Loronzon Incident. Analysis indicated there was a better chance of two stars going supernova simultaneously in the same system than him surviving. We compared it with genetic samples taken during Spek's time in custody. It was a match. Not a clone, not code masking, not a quantum match tissue reprint, by any reasonable measure, this was him. It was over. Yet, because it was Odian Spek, we spent five turns hunting for any trace of the Creators and found nothing." Pias slammed his two lower fists together.

The murmurs grew louder, angrier, predictably so, given that he'd brought up the Alliance's most notable failures of recent times. The barely bottled rage made Bor anxious. Pias had to bring things to a point quickly before the debate accelerated away from him.

"Do you remember how many allies Odian gathered? How quickly? Many parts of the Alliance still agree with his central tenet that T-Class civilizations should be eliminated to make room for our own expansion. Numerous, scientifically-backed studies show that the resources required to cleanse a planet are insignificant compared to even the most minimal terraforming or, for that matter, the quarantine program used to protect these hostile species. How long will morality hold when we can, cheaply and more easily, play God? Given a voice, Odian could easily destabilize the peace. What happens if he finds a violent T-Class planet, perhaps Nova, to flaunt? How long before others decide to attack infant worlds? If his ideology spreads across the Alliance, how long can we ensure peace?" Pias smashed all four of his fists together. "This is why the Creators and their actions had to be concealed. This is why we need to act."

The sound echoed around looks of anger and agreement, free and begrudging—the intensity of the emotions varying from passion to blank expressions. Bor noticed that Enareggario's face had become a blank screen projecting a moving starfield.

Silence increasingly uncomfortable, Pias took a long, sweeping look at the representatives seeming to single out each one. "Every world deserves a chance. That's why we formed the Alliance: to prevent the long ages of destruction from revisiting us. Odian wants to undo all that."

Barulka gave Pias a nod signaling satisfaction with his answer. His crystal dimmed. The floor illuminated Pika Ru'Yak revealing tall, antelope legs made for Saroom's high grasses. She wore a simple, yet elegant duraweave bodygown. It hid most of her tricolored stripes but didn't obscure the scowl on her muzzle or the disdain in her voice.

"Prime Abbotkrine, by your testimony, despite your best efforts, Odian has already succeeded in eliminating more worlds. Don't you agree that those efforts could have been more effective if you'd called upon the full government's resources?"

Pika had worked with Pias over one-hundred turns and now suddenly found she'd been left in the dark. The Agriculture Department had no need for covert ops, but it clearly galled her that the secrecy granted the military had been so blatantly abused.

Pias was unperturbed. "Perhaps, but Odian is a Voidwhisperer, one of the best, and has given that technology to his army. Poetically, perhaps, the Voidwhisperers have been the only effective method of combating him. Full involvement of the Council would have meant public disclosure of the continuing Voidwhisperer program revealing we've all been lying for the past two-hundred turns."

Pika Ru'Yak had no response.

Bor exhaled. There it is. He's tipped the scales. Few things were as binding as mutually assured destruction.

"Next question?" Pias said.

Nimitz, the third mediator, hummed. "How was the Nova incident identified as a Creator attack when so few know of their existence?"

Bor's fate hinging on what Pias' said next, they briefly locked eyes. Bor occupied his final moment of uncertainty by contemplating the Valador's beauty, especially the way the light flowed around the walls like an endless river.

He heard Pias saying, "A Nova system quarantine analyst identified the tactics. As per protocol, he was debriefed by a military and investigative panel on Mijorn and brought here for further questioning."

The crystal remained white, but Nimitz found the vague answer annoying. "Allow me to rephrase, how did this analyst come by information so highly classified that most of this council, myself included, didn't know about it until just now?"

Watching the dance play out was agonizing. Pias was about to weave some half-truth to protect him and the Inner Council. What if it failed, and a stubborn Pias was tortured to death by his crystal? Bor thought of all the justifications they had committed to, and yet here they were. He angered at others protecting Kruk, even though he was the one to blame. In fact, he couldn't stand it anymore. As a master of communications, he knew that above all else you had to control the narrative.

The truth was a more powerful weapon than any lie. Having led himself into this mess, it was time to pull himself out. He touched his hand to the platform and shouted. "I invoke Article of Engagement 47!"

Instantly, the constellation locked a beam on him. The rest of the chamber cut to darkness; only the terraces beneath Bor's feet glowed as he descended to the center.

His move was so stunning, he was nearly at the bottom when Barulka shouted angrily. "By what right do you use such an archaic protocol? Thousands of turns have transpired since anyone dared resort to it."

They'd all be shouting at him if they could, but the silencing field prevented that. There were looks of shock, glares, disdain, disappointment, and offense. The voting crystals all went red with disapproval. A sea of twitching antennae, flailing hands, bioluminescent flashes, and thrashing tentacles accentuated the heightened emotions.

But *Article 47* gave Primes a once in a lifetime opportunity to interrupt proceedings without opposition, so he approached the Valador's center with open arms.

"I only take such action due to the greatest need. Allow me to answer your questions."

Pika looked down her snout at him. "Because the Article compels us, we yield the floor."

Bor stood equal to Pias. The Effective Force Prime remained stoic, but Bor felt his rage. Once Bor's crystal drifted down to float over his head and reveal his heart, he began.

"Mediators, it is only right these questions be directed to me because the analyst is my son, Kruktusken. I admit to aiding in the concealment of the Creators' activities. I also admit to grooming my son to be the best possible contributor to, and defender of, our government. When he was a child, I told him bedtime stories about the Creators. When he was older I taught him the reality and how to defend against our greatest enemy."

His opening was enough to disrupt the brooding energy disengaging the silencing field and allowing a buzz of angry mutters to flood the air.

He pivoted to face the other half of the crowd. "I only ask that whatever conclusion this council reaches, any penalties be passed onto me. If Kruk had been given all of the information, if he'd known and understood the coverup, if I'd been forthright enough to admit my part in it he would never have publicly implicated the Creators. He would have understood the importance of secrecy." Bor gestured all around the chamber. "Just as you all now understand."

At this, the room hushed. "Mediator Pika, you suggested it might have been wiser to involve our entire government. Well, I fully share Prime Abbotkrine's doubts that it would have worked. At the same time, as we naturally cycle, replacements must be aware of the truth to remain on the lookout for the Creators. But, who

---

Article 47

An archaic law in the GSA that allows a Prime to one-time interrupt a Council of Worlds meeting to present their case unobstructed. If a Prime invokes Article 47 a second time, they are automatically stripped of rank and exiled from the GSA revoking their citizenship to Havlanger.

to trust? Kruk wanted to be part of this government. Like us, he gave up his home world, travelled far and wide to understand how life can be different yet similar, that even as the peaceful protectors of a vast alliance we must never lose respect for viewpoints other than our own, lest we slowly slip into despotism. I strove to give him a greater understanding, so he could see that, so he could be better. In the end, what I did tell Kruk gave us a warning we would not have had otherwise."

The third Mediator raised his arm and a beam jumped to his grasp. "Prime KruktuskenBor, do you believe your disclosure of these secrets was lawful?"

Bor's crystal flickered giving him a slight sting. Rather than react, he contemplated the question further before responding. "I do, because by no definition were my actions technically unlawful. The decision to hide the COS was not made by the whole council. Therefore, the revelation was not lawfully banned. Given that, I believe Kruk should be spared punishment and reinstated at his post in the Nova System."

All waited, expecting to see Bor's crystal turn black and inflict its agonizing consequences. When it didn't, there was surprise from many—their crystals pulsing in shifting hues.

Pika's eyes narrowed to slits. "After Prime Pias' speech about the dangers of the Creators, you'd put your own son back into the line of fire?"

To avoid mentioning that the Mediator came from a group-raised species that hatched from eggs and never knew their parents, Bor bit his tongue. "For many of you, having a family was never an option. I love my son, yet I risked giving him information because this is that important. I'd risk his life again because we need him. Not only because we need those loyal to this government to watch for signs of Odian's ideas, but because there's a mole in the Nova System. It's the only way the attack could have been planned so well. Kruk can help find them."

He was sure to leave that last bit for the end. Much as empathy was a powerful persuader, danger was better. Indeed, the room buzzed. Bor felt Pias nodding behind him. The focus was shifting in his favor. Now if they'd only let him steer a little longer.

"And you'll vouch that your son, Kruktusken, is qualified for such a task?" Barulka asked.

Bor straightened. "I do."

The crystal did not strike. The room was silent. Bor hoped he had done enough. Maybe, if this all worked out, one day Kruk would forgive him.

The Mediators spoke in unison once more. "Are there any further questions on the subject of Kruktusken?" The crystals remained dim. "Then we are prepared to vote. All in favor of absolving Kruktusken, son of KruktuskenBor, of any crime and allowing him to keep his current position in the Nova system?"

Bit by bit, the crystals turned green or vermillion and joined their distinct group. There were too many changing too fluidly for Bor to count, but there seemed to be a clear majority—a fact confirmed by the announcement. "The vote is 127 for, 44 against."

Bor's heart leapt—his joy contained out of the need for decorum. For the first time since receiving Kruk's message on Epiko, he properly exhaled.

The mediators called a recess; the Primes, again, took to mingling. Pias stepped close to Bor and casually lowered his large head. "Well done."

Bor grinned. "Well, the hard part is over."

Pias was oddly cold. "No, it's not. We still have to see if you can save your own neck. I did have a plan to lift all of us out of this gracefully, I might add, but you decided to blow it up. Next time you interrupt me like that, I'll throttle you. Two hands suffocating you and the other two to bash in your skull."

He gave Bor that Anduuzilian head-splitting smile. Despite the warning, his stress continued melting away.

"Don't worry, I've got something to take care of us, just in case."

Pias's face twisted at the maddeningly cryptic answer. Before he could demand more, the lights called them back into session.

The Mediators raised their appendages. The talking stopped and the talisman beams swirled with new questions: the strongest coalescing. Watching, Bor wondered how far he could get without resorting to his backup plan.

Barulka began. "Prime KruktuskenBor, having declared yourself part of this coverup, this council demands you name any co-conspirators in addition to Prime Abbotkrine."

Pika added, "A sizable majority believe that as a consequence of yours and Prime Abbotkrine's deception, you both should be stripped of your titles and removed from government. While a smaller sector of the council believes Article 37's are in order."

Nimitz rounded it out. "Having lied about so much, you both only came forward out of necessity rather than ethical considerations."

"In consideration of those ethics, you'll get no names from us," Bor said flatly. "Do what you will, but those good people acted for the sake of the galaxy at great personal risk and no personal gain. Yes, necessity forced us to break the silence. The Nova Incident already known to many in various departments, it was inevitable that an effort to contain the information would fail. Now that the wider circle of this body knows, it's crucial we strive to keep this from the populace and the Assembly of Planets. Problem being, our removal would prompt them to investigate."

Ignoring the many hateful glares, he confidently looked to Enareggario. "Prime, how do you think this council would fare during their interviews with the **Kalean High Council** and the Assembly of Planets dissolution board?"

For a few breaths, the Kalean's face flowed before solidifying into a Dragsan child with mischievous, blue eyes perched above a cloth-covered mouth. The eyes twinkled merrily as he answered. "Much as I despise deception, if all Prime Kruk-tuskenBor and Prime Pias Abbotkine have stated is true, it would be ill-advised to pursue that route. Limiting communications is the more logical action."

Kalean High Council
An independent governing body that is the highest adjudicator in the Alliance due to its impartiality. It also acts as an arbiter between the Assembly of Planets and the Council of Worlds during constitutional disputes. If no confidence is called into question by either body, the KHC is activated. It consists of 9 Kaleans appointed randomly every 3 turns.

Bor nodded appreciatively but wondered if the Kalean was mocking him. Was Kruk's face under that scarf, or his? Resisting the urge to stare, he turned back to the Mediators daring to believe they might as well escape with no consequences.

As he looked up and saw the impassive judgement in Brooznoor Ren's eyes, that hope died. The Prime's prehensile trunk reached up. A beam appeared above him.

"Prime KruktuskenBor, while your logic may be impeccable, your arrogance is itself damaging to this body, and your lack of wisdom clearly does not meet the expectations of Havlangar. While I admire your honest desire to clean your own mess, since both of you refuse to name your co-conspirators, once your tenures are concluded I call for exile."

Bor's heart tumbled into his stomach. The present-day world began to recede; his Recall offered a tantalizing escape from this nightmare. This time, there were no shouts. No opposition. The talismans danced at a wild tempo, and when enough shimmered as green as the Valkürin forests, Bor realized they were being sacrificed to keep the morality of the Council intact.

Pias' expression, as usual, was stony, save for the single tear falling from his eye. What hurt worst was knowing that while this punishment was necessary, it would do nothing to stop the fracture of trust eroding the very fabric of government.

Barulka raised his voice at the lumination of verdant talismans. "151 to 20, so be it. Prime KruktuskenBor, Prime Pias Abbotkrine when your terms are at their ends, you will both be exiled from the GSA to live out the remainder of your lives on *Ramur 7* in the Distant Zones."

Bor turned to Pias and the flicker of a moment said all that was thought. They would die alone in the cold void far from the warmth of any familiar star, never to rest by the sea.

Bor slipped into a moment of Recall. From the first time he was selected a Prime to the last, he never thought himself deserving. He didn't even campaign for himself, but the system chose him again and again. It was only in defeat that the Effective

---

Ramur 7
A GSA exile planet in the Distant Zones where political prisoners are left with no resources to die slowly alone.

Communications Prime of Sector 2 finally felt his worth was not in question.

Bor stood tall. He felt a myriad of strong hands on his shoulders.

Pias stepped forward. "Very well. When the computer deems us finished, we will fulfill our sentence."

There were squawks of disapproval but not many, and they quickly died when neither's crystal struck him with nerve-gouging agony for lying. Instead, they burned bright and true.

The Mediators responded in slow unison. "Indeed, you will."

Enough about us, Bor thought. The meeting was supposed to be about fighting the Creators; instead, they'd used it to hurt them.

He cleared his throat to indicate he wasn't quite finished. "Until that time, I believe our skills, knowledge, and experience, like those of everyone here, will be crucial especially in light of the discovery that the Creators of Space have been recruiting from uncharted worlds in the Distant Zones." *The irony.*

His crystal, yet again, remained white. The superior looks dropping from faces all around provided a grim satisfaction enhanced by the ironic juxtaposition of Tordok's relief. It was a monumental card to play, but the right timing had presented itself. No gossipy chatter about his exile could overwhelm the revelation's importance.

As indicated by the uniform color of the talismans, there was only one question on everyone's mind. Prime Nimitz gave it voice. "Would you please...um, elaborate?"

Bor nodded at Pias. "If the Council permits, I respectfully defer to Effective Force Prime Abbotkrine, who is far more learned regarding Creator strategy."

The talismans green, Bor turned to depart the central floor. Passing Pias, his grimace filled the emotional void as he whispered, "That should give you plenty to work with."

Pias's fluorescence gave the appearance of a happy Anduuzil. "Why, you sly puppeteer..."

I'll be there soon, Kruk, Bor thought. *The hard part really is over... for now.*

- - -

Far below the Valador and its guarding circle of Raa'Tiki, Kruk sat alone in a small chamber weighing his choices. Running his fingers along the luminous crystal floor, he scoured his Recall for some familiarity but found none. The place truly alien, he'd never felt so far from home.

On one level, he was astonished to be at the famed seat of power and judgement. Trillions dreamed of seeing the Anador but only a handful did. Then again, here he was effectively a prisoner. At least he wasn't restrained, not that there was anywhere to run.

Well, if they kick me out of government, at least I got to visit, and I didn't even have to be a Prime.

Speaking of which, his father must be here too. Why hadn't he seen or heard from him? Kruk's first direct message had been their sole communication.

A bizarre hologram was imbedded in one of the walls. A guard explained that it was a clock displaying the relatively faster time passing within the Valador. If Kruk read it correctly, there had already been a considerable debate—nearly 93 prikes. How much of that was devoted to his fate? He wanted proper consideration, but not so lengthy as to unduly burden the Council.

A faintly familiar smell snapped him to his feet. He spun to face whoever had entered so stealthily. Initially, this quiet guard appeared to be one of the Fandaxians that accompanied them from Mijorn. But then, their body spread out shifting into a new form.

The biomorphic armor adjusted to suit its altered occupant. A vaguely familiar smile was visible beneath the helmet, but removing it revealed a face he'd seen over hundreds of gobbletek matches. "Maruk?"

The Station 19 suppressor pilot laughed. "Hey, Kruk, remember all that complaining about how bored you were? Look at you, now. I think this is what humans call karma."

Maruk might not be perturbed by the strange reunion, after all, the Drotean could impersonate anyone, but Kruk was stunned. "What are you doing here? How did you get here? I am so rooka'd happy to see you."

As they embraced, Maruk let out a full-blown cackle. "As you know, my physiology provides some unique opportunities to move undetected, so I came to check on you of course. Couldn't miss the chance to be Luke and save Han from Jabba. But what happened? I was told you helped save the day, and then—boom—you were gone."

They sat. "This will sound crazy, but my father told me the truths about the Creators of Space; I recognized them as the attackers at Nova."

Maruk was incredulous. "The myth? The ones who live on the planet no one can find?"

Kruk gave a hollow laugh. "It sounds way more ridiculous when I say it out loud like that, but as it turns out, not only are they real, the government's been covering up their existence for a very long time. The GSA thought they were gone, but they were wrong."

For most of Kruk's life, this information seemed insignificant, but Maruk hung on every word.

"They took me to Mijorn for a debrief because I used an override. At least that was the official story. Once I mentioned Loronzon, the department investigators took an alarming interest. The funny thing is, it felt like they were fishing more than debriefing."

Maruk stared. "What's that supposed to mean?"

"It means, I think they didn't know as much as I did. I think my father was part of a high-level conspiracy."

Maruk scoffed. "No way. How could they pull that off? Even if they could, how could the whole government not be in on it?"

Kruk sighed. "I don't know. It seems impossible, but the Galactic Star Alliance has been around for 8 million turns. That's plenty of time to get good at all sorts of things."

His friend nodded. "So, where does this leave you? If they already interrogated you on Mijorn, why bring you here?"

Kruk shrugged. "My best guess is that I'm a living, breathing, information breach, so they all want to analyze me personally. The better option is that Pias brought me to convince the Council that the Creators are a real threat."

"The EFP of Sector 9? You know him?"

"Not really. He and my father go way back."

Maruk made an impressed trilling sound. "Well, after seeing how the Creators or whoever got through a quarantine shield, consider me convinced."

They sat in a reflective silence. Kruk occasionally checked the Valador clock. What would he do if he was kicked out? Return to Dragsa? Would his family even accept him now that he'd tarnished the long, prestigious, Tusken lineage?

Apparently sensing Kruk's dark inner turn, Maruk patted his knee. "Is there anything I can do for you?"

Kruk studied his bare quarters. "Nothing I can think of. You've already done a lot just by being here. No way they won't punish you for being AWOL. You're a great friend."

Maruk's claws clasped his shoulders. "You might not want to, but when this is over, come back to the Nova Station. I miss our gobbletek matches. Plus, you owe me a drink."

Kruk had his first genuine laugh in ages. It was so hearty and heartfelt, a tear welled in his eye. "Get out of here, you crazy Drotean, before whoever you're impersonating returns."

With a flourish, Maruk redonned his helmet and morphed into a lanky Metra. With a backward glance and a smile, he darted out the entrance and disappeared.

Kruk pinched himself. Apparently that had been real.

Looking at the clock again, he realized it had stopped at 135 prikes. Was the meeting over?

He felt the slight rumble of large, crystal machinery grinding somewhere far off. The real guards reentered. Distinct, purposeful footsteps echoed from around the corner followed by the appearance of ECP KruktuskenBor: his father.

"*Farraf*!"

Kruk leapt to greet him. They embraced, then held each other at arm's length.

Still looking at his son, Bor dismissed the guard. "Leave us."

The time apart had brought changes. Bor looked older, weighed down by much heavier burdens, but there was also a hopeful aura.

"How are you?" Bor asked.

It was comically painful to hear the great communicator boil a thousand questions into one.

"I'm well. Everyone's really intense, especially the Investigators, but they're not exactly treating me badly." Kruk chuckled. "They even gave me my own room. I'm sorry about using your override code, but if I hadn't, we may never have known it was the Creators."

"Don't apologize. You did the right thing," Bor said. "I'm so sorry this happened. I should have been more diligent. I should have better prepared you. Then you'd have understood exactly how much of a threat the Creators are. I wanted to keep you safe until you were ready to be part of the Inner Council, but time ran out."

"So, what happens to me, now? I expect there'll be consequences. I know I'll be debriefed again at the Security Council meeting but not much else."

The question evoked a sorrowful look. "Son, there won't be any penalties, but you must do the GSA a great service. The Council wants you to return to your post in the Nova System to prepare for a second Creator attack and find a spy. Only a

---

Farraf
The personal, informal Dragsan word for "father."

mole could have enabled such a precise infiltration."

It was a bucket of cold water. "Farraf, I thought you'd had me stationed at Nova because it was so far from any combat."

Bor raised his hand. "It's part of the terms absolving you. I vouched for you before the entire Council, under the penalty of the crystals, because I trust you can do this."

Temporarily speechless, Kruk dropped to one knee, bowed his head, and extended his elbows sideways. He placed his hands under his chin, one palm up, the other down, completing the formal Dragsan salute of respect.

"I'm sorry I questioned you, father. This is an immense honor. I will show you that your faith is not misplaced."

Bor touched his shoulder and Kruk rose. "I suspect the mole is someone you've already met. They had the same Nova probe information you possessed."

Kruk's mind froze on the word met, making his father's remaining words feel far off. Maruk. How had he gotten onto Primidious? Into the Anador? The planet was restricted—guarded by an armada. The Raa'Tiki were here.

How much had Kruk told him? Kruk cursed inwardly... only valuable information that exposed his father. Should he tell Bor?

"Kruk, what is it?"

"I'm... trying to recall who was in the probe analysis program before me, but nothing suspicious comes to mind." If he was going to brand his best friend a traitor, Kruk had to be absolutely sure first. Death was the mandatory punishment.

If Bor questioned Kruk's answer, he made no indication. In fact, his father's mind had moved on. "I have to go. There is much to be done. The Council wants to use the utmost stealth in the matter. It will redirect a quiet, but substantial portion of Alliance resources to combat the Creators. There's a plethora of side meetings going on to negotiate the logistics. There'll be discussing new exploration missions as well. We know the Creators have been out there meeting civilizations we've yet to find."

As Kruk's mind exploded at the idea, his father grabbed his shoulders. "But before I leave, I'm going to tell you everything you need to know to fight the Creators."

CHAPTER 16

M.C.D.

At the end of the tunnel, the mouth of a vast cavern provided Bernard with a stunning view of a marvelous city of steel and futurism spread across acres. As he drove his Newton along the winding road, he couldn't help but think, *the prodigal son returns.*

For the first time in six years, the famed cosmologist pulled up to the gates of Outer Limits.

"ID... oh my..." The guard stammered when he realized who he was.

"Not sure I need one. I'm here to see Ms. On. I believe William Hunt and Godric Adams are already here?"

"Your son, as well, Dr. Hubert," the awed man offered.

"Ah yes. Well, that makes sense. I would like to get going. Is that alright with you, or should I call Angelika?"

Asking himself the same question as everyone else would that day, the guard motioned to his colleague to raise the gate.

Naturally, Bernard's return meant opening a lot of old wounds. The CERN disaster was a part of O.L.'s bones now: an extension of all he'd worked for. Accident or not, few within the inner circle here had forgiven Bernard for living.

It is a magnificent place, though.

To his left, an orb-shaped facility housed the nanotech labs. To his right, a towering observatory held a telescope that could pinpoint a crater on Ganymede. Ahead, past the Advanced Concepts Lab and the boundless shrubbery, laid the Tyson Planetarium, an homage to the great cosmologist of the early 21st century.

While the graceful structures seemed to have no end, just to the right of the entrance, a towering black mass disrupted the land's beautiful chemistry with the architecture. It was his former workplace: his theoretical physics and interstellar anomaly research facilities designed and constructed to pursue his vision.

Home.

No matter what taunting, snickering, or whispered lies he faced in the days and weeks to come, this moment was his.

A shout echoed across the grounds. "I knew I'd find you here!"

William Hunt strolled up; his long coat billowed in the winter winds.

"William! This place is magical, isn't it? Pure exploratory research and development."

"Don't forget the endless funding, my friend!" William cheerily added. "Did you get Ilya?"

Bernard smirked. "Of course, he couldn't resist."

"Medina?"

"Yup."

"Lovely," William said, but his demeanor could just as easily indicate he'd successfully ordered lunch.

Bernard looked at him sharply. "My turn. Walk me through your escapades with Nawal."

"I assume, Bernard, that it went exactly as you imagined minus the part where she hesitated. You do always underestimate my ability to sell."

"Maybe so, old friend, but in the end, you never disappoint."

"So, who's left?"

"Lily Parsons and a military strategist. Ang and I are still arguing on the shortlist for that one. It's not surprising that the expert furthest from our fields would be last." His voice grew a bit tense. "I assume you'll speak to Lily today?"

William looked displeased but said, "Yes."

Bernard nodded. "I think that makes the most sense to avoid initial conflict. We should get her read on the mission as soon as possible. Where's Angie setting us up? Did we get the hanger?"

"We did. Isaac's there now with a few engineers. It's incredible watching him work. He's more brilliant than we ever were. And that's saying something."

Bernard winked. "He takes after his mother."

They walked a path through small woods arriving at a second set of buildings designed for assembling and housing rocket ships. A massive structure connected the two facilities: a bridge overlaid the sky with architecture that ensnared even these dreamers.

En route to the entrance, four armed guards approached the two scientists. Realizing who they were, they broke off with a nod.

Other than that, though he saw many, Bernard reached the hangar entrance without interacting with any. It seemed they were willing to remain professional, for now.

Beyond the obsidian doors, a receptionist waited at a massive desk carved from a meteorite. Not recognizing her, Bernard assumed she was a recent hire. She eyed him with a mix of curiosity and preconceptions, no doubt trying to see how well he matched the office gossip.

"Dr. Hunt, good morning again, and good morning, Dr. Hubert. I'm Melanie. I have your badge right here. It will give you full access. I was also told to inform you that your personal items, vacuum stored since 2085, have been unboxed and placed in your old office. Ms. On saw to it personally."

"Excellent." Eager now, he grabbed the badge and moved through the next set of doors—William close behind. They walked through a long hallway, then badged through a sealed door marked AIRLOCK.

Bernard carefully felt for the NanoCube that rarely left his pocket, then put his keys, wallet, and phone in a locker. The two then ditched their jackets and donned white, cleanroom coveralls, caps, beard-covers, and booties. Once suited up, the airlock's second door beeped and, on opening, released a burst of positive air pressure.

Isaac met him before the doors closed behind him. "Dad, you're here! Isn't this place incredible?"

He looked like a kid in a candy factory, of course. The tech Angelika had waiting for him was beyond anything he could have prepared himself for. There were Nanoblades to hand-cut any metal, full-scale holographic mapping projecting their concept work, while AI robots called *Seymours* stood ready with their predictive algorithms able to help construct... whatever it is you're constructing.

Then there were the *Halo Builders*; bleeding-edge 3D Printers that could not only use hundreds of materials, they levitated as they worked. Integrated with the Seymours they could build anything humans could in a fifth of the time. Called "toys," they were unique to O.L., helping keep them ahead of companies like Iron Corp. and Space Oasis.

Isaac laughed out loud. "If Naomi and Howard could see me now!"

It hadn't taken much to convince Kepler's school board to grant his son a leave of absence. Angelika had even sent a hypersonic jet to retrieve him. Bernard thought it over the top, but she considered the boy's time too precious to waste.

Much as Isaac was pleased with his work and how awed and envious all his classmates would be if they knew where he was, his thoughts turned briefly dark. Claiming he was meeting his family, he'd slipped away during a vacation weekend.

Seymour
An AI robot programmed with predictive algorithms to understand and assist humans in building any unique structure, machine, or construct. This early stage AI began as a concept of RNA Industries, founded by Grayson Freedman of MIT, Candice Oliver of Harvard, and Aiden Alexander of CalTech. These founders of RNA & SETI Schools looked to create a bilateral, multi-functional assistant for labor intensive occupations. The project was later continued by Angelika On at Outer Limits starting in September of 2076.

Halo Builder
A bleeding-edge 3D printer that can build in hundreds of materials and levitate as they work. This includes fabricating high precision mechanisms with smooth finish and no build layers. When integrated with Seymours, they typically assemble hardware in a fifth of human time. In the early 2080's, Seymours and Halo Builders were brought in front of the World Council as amenable options for rebuilding off world colonies.

He hated lying and didn't know how long he could keep it up. It would only get harder, especially with the Explorer's Cup approaching. Lisa, Chelsea, and Marcus certainly wouldn't accept his absence from that—nor would he.

Hopefully, the public announcement of the mission wasn't too far off. That would put an end to any charades.

At the sight of his former lead engineer, Bernard's face lit up. "Fredrick!"

A close friend, Fredrick Johnson, and his family had defended Bernard throughout the CERN investigation at great cost. The man had been passed over for promotion twice. But, here he was, handpicked by Bernard as his personal project liaison for The Nomad.

"Bernard! I was just showing Isaac how to integrate the Seymour 4.0 and the Halo Builders. I have to tell you, the ingenuity of your design has held up spectacularly."

"Now, let's not get carried away. I only drew up the original schematic, not all this."

"Never one for accolades, are you? Well, your boy takes after you. Within two days, he knew how to operate the duality of a Seymour and a Halo Builder. I have engineers three years-in who can't grasp the symbiotic engineering."

"I expected no less." Bernard winked at his son. "Isaac, Fred, I'll see you later."

Transversing the gargantuan structure, he found his hair electrifying with excitement as he moved between facilities. Angelika waiting, he walked to the elevators leading to the offices. As the doors closed, a sense of deja vu came on strong. Muscle memory guided his hand as he punch-swiped his badge and pressed 9. As he ascended, a Carbon Based Lifeforms song played. As he passed the 7th floor, though, he remembered his office on the 8th.

He was already on memory lane; why not catch all the stops? And why rush to an office with an angry Angelika in it?

He slammed the button just in time. The opening doors presented the rare sight of O.L. employees caught completely off guard. Those who recognized him ducked into offices and conference rooms. The others just gawked.

Without a pause, he moved around one corner, then another—and there it was, the door to his old office... Darren's right next to it. Unlocking the room in which he'd spent over a decade designing the impossible, he saw boxes all around: on the floor, atop the furniture. There'd be time to deal with that later.

On his way out, he touched the entrance to his fallen friend's office. Feeling for the doorknob, he found it, incredibly, unlocked. Reverent, he pushed it open. It was exactly as he remembered: from the magnificent forest panorama offered by the floor to ceiling windows, to the stacks of aerospace books, to the Saturn V rocket model hanging gracefully from the ceiling. The open door provided just enough air to set it creaking.

He eyed the door between their offices. It was never closed. They perpetually walked back and forth, sharing and honing fantastical ideas. Once, they ordered maintenance to cut a hole in the wall so they didn't have to waste time walking around the wall and through the hallway.

Touching. Angelika must have left it untouched as a memorial.

Right. She was waiting. Finally, he headed up to the monolithic structure housing her throne and navigated the clear glass entrance to her office.

It wasn't *like* a science fiction story—it *was* one. The soaring ceiling high above the workshop floor engulfed the skies. Sitting atop everything like an Asgardian queen, Angelika screamed at some poor wretch on the phone.

"I DON'T CARE WHAT THAT SON OF A BITCH MARCUS TOLD YOU, WE CAN DO IT AND WE WILL!!"

When she hung up, Bernard bowed. "Afternoon to you, too, Angie. Who was that?"

He already knew the answer, but asked all the same.

"THAT LOWLY WRECK OF A HUMAN, RIC. HE JUST COST ME BILLIONS."

"I think it's closer to 700 million, but who's counting?"

Her face contorted with fury. She chucked her comm at him. "YOU KNEW? YOU KNEW! WHAT THE HELL AM I?! THE LAST ONE TO THE GOD DAMN PARTY?!"

Thankfully, both he and the flip phone were unharmed.

"Angie, you really think I can sway his vote on a political decision? You only count it a loss because you have to wait. It'll be fine. It's not like Marcus can innovate during the next five years anyway. Space Oasis won't have their core asset, Medina."

That snapped her back to some semblance of reality. As if she hadn't just been a raging, green monster, she nodded peacefully. "That does seem like a win-win for me, now, doesn't it?"

Angelika screaming at Godric, Bernard calming her down, William nowhere to be found, busy solving the next impossible math equation... It was as if the last seven years had been wiped away.

"How was the jungle? Odin doing well?"

Angelika gave him a rare smile. "Oh, exploring, thinking he's Indiana Jones. You know that one, don't you? Early, maybe late, 20th century pop culture? Anyway, he took very little convincing. It was as if he knew it would happen eventually and had already decided."

"Excellent. Fantastic work Angelika."

"Thank you, Bernie. Are you going to talk to Lily today?"

"William and I decided it would be best if he made the initial approach."

Bernard was wondering what that conversation would be like, when William barged in. "GUYS, highbay now!"

They both rolled their eyes. He had a reputation for making very minor breakthroughs feel like he'd just discovered a new God particle.

"Isaac and I finished the micro-water repulsion field! He found a complex wave generation sequence that intensifies the magnetic pulses without requiring additional energy! We can grow crops in zero g and not drown them!"

Now they were genuinely shocked. Sufficient food in space was a perennial problem. It had to be grown, for self-sustenance, but rather than drain in the absence of gravity, water pooled around the roots blocking oxygen-absorption. This new localized magnetic field would force the water from the roots. Even William thought this was a distant, future objective.

Bernard raced William back to the floor, shoved his way through some spare thrusters, and skidded around the wing to reach Isaac.

"Is it true? The magnetic energy required to move water is immense."

"It was really William's idea," Isaac said. "We were talking about what it would be like if you could shrink small enough to walk across water; how powerful the attractive forces would be as long as the water remained laminar. I figured, if the magnetic field harmonics were stabilized, we could deploy it anywhere, even inside a root ball. I know some mathematical patterns that can spiralize the magnetic field lines like a braid. That way, the field is knotted without outward interference."

Wildly impressed, Bernard shook his head. "Why I didn't think of that is beyond me. The simplicity in your logic is beautiful. Brilliant."

"Thanks Dad." Isaac beamed. "For larger scale applications, it can also reduce the hardware needed for a railgun or, theoretically, fly someone through the air in a hollow magnetic channel."

"I wish you and William were designing O.L. ships for me decades ago."

Angelika bellowed from above. "Bernie, come back here!"

"Give me a moment!" He shouted back.

"William, did you get Aubree?" Bernard said, turning his focus back to William.

"It wasn't easy, but I did. She'd do anything for me. You must have known that."

"I was counting on it."

"So, I'm another pawn in your game now?" William said.

"No. A bishop." Bernard smiled.

They ascended back to Angelika. "Took you long enough..."

"Oh? I didn't realize I still worked for you."

Angelika shot him a look of cold fury but spoke with considerably more control. "I'd like to think, Bernard, that I'm above your games, that I do not wait for you."

"Fair enough, Angie. What's so important it couldn't wait?"

"Our military crew member, the one who'll ensure everyone's safety."

He balked. "Is it seriously all that much a crucial rush? What's one human going to do if we encounter a hostile spacefaring race?"

"It's not just about aliens, Bernie. You're a group of civilians with very strong opinions. I want my assets protected."

Bernard sized her up. What she said was true, but it wasn't all she was thinking. This could well be the compromise Ilya predicted. Would Bernard accept an Outer Limits henchman on his ship? Not that it was a completely bad idea. They didn't know what would or could happen, and her private security was the best.

Thoughts racing, he decided in a flash. "I want Conrad."

She was a bit too pleased. "I heard you two bonded during Ilya's extraction. He's my choice too."

"Huh. Was that why you sent him with me to fetch Ilya? Am I one step behind you, or are you forever catching up to me? I never can tell, Angie. "

She stood and headed out, her last words fading softly. "And you never will."

Bernard stayed returning to the floor and working alongside Isaac for hours. Using the existing skeleton design, they outfitted a digital ship with a Hubert drive, then father and son started the design for a ***Surface Exploration Vehicle***. Piece by piece, they created a pragmatic yet elegant shuttle that could fit four Nomad crew and land on a small planet or moon. As they prepped the full-scale holographic projector for a look, William ruined the blissful peace.

Surface Exploration Vehicle (SEV)
A smaller, chemical powered spacecraft that attaches to the forward section of the Nomad. It can shuttle a crew of 4, has enough fuel to visit the surface of one planet with Earth like gravity, or visit two planets or moons with Mars like gravity.

"Bernie, so...um..."

"What is it?"

"I talked to Lily. She agreed, but..."

Bernard knew his tactics far too well, and he wasn't about to play coy about it. "Jesus, you told her I'd talk to her today, didn't you, Bill?"

"Yes, I did. Like it or not, her father, our lifelong friend, died, and you chose to hate her for acting human in a time of utter despair. Casting her out is a stain on your... no, our lives. It's time you faced it head-on."

Bernard found himself appreciating Ilya all the more. Some situations were so hard, running made more sense. But even the oft-fugitive rebel understood the need for this mission. Even he wouldn't let the past dictate the future this time.

With six years of pain palpitating his heart, Bernard left the highbay and headed toward the Nanotech lab. Aside from thoughts of Ilya, he found himself appreciating the vast layout of the campus. The thirty minute walk across the spectacular nine-square kilometer grounds gave him time to reflect on what he'd say to a woman who flat-out blamed him for the loss of her father.

Nanotech provided a hefty percentage of Outer Limits' revenue; they'd spared no expense constructing the lab. From the entrance, he could see how the halls adapted to each individual's mood shaping the colors and ambiance by reading the emotions of its occupants through nanofibers in the floors.

That alone could herald an ergonomic revolution, but he'd heard they were working on an upgrade that could cushion each step.

And it's based on my concepts. Lily must have found my hidden papers. Clever girl.

A cold, dispassionate voice emanated from the receptionist who looked and sounded like a machine. "Can I help you, Dr. Bernard Hubert?"

"Are you a Seymour?" He hoped so. He was eager to learn more about them.

"No. I am *the Alchemist*, an eternal machine created to help humanity along their journey. Your presence coinciding with Dr. William Hunt's recent visit indicates you are here to speak to Ms. Parsons. Our nanofloors have scanned your biometrics and determined that this has evoked stress in you."

Bernard was a bit amused. "That is accurate."

"Please have a seat. Would you care for coffee or tea while I inform Lily of your arrival?"

"Coffee, thank you."

A curious device rose out from the floor and built (or so it seemed) a small coffee mug out of nanotech pieces of the front desk. When Bernard picked it up, a small service drone flew over and filled it with Jamaican dark-roast. Intriguing.

"Alchemist, how did you know?"

"You wrote my code, or so I am told. The algorithm on which my AI is based draws from all accessible data, so I can better serve you."

Really? Have they forgotten what started The Darkness? This is far too advanced for O.L. to have developed without some major government oversight.

He'd have to give Angelika a stern talking-to before the Nomad launched. Dedicated humans started a nuclear war just to stop a rogue Chinese AI from fully awakening.

But before he could put too much thought into Angelika's early Skynet problems, deeper in the halls, voices talking one to another grew swiftly loud. Until a woman appeared, hand outstretched. "Dr. Hubert, I'm Joanne, Lily's lab technician and assistant. Please come this way. She's waiting for you in her office."

The Alchemist said farewell. "A pleasure meeting you, Dr. Hubert."

They walked at a good pace. Joanne remained silent until Bernard spoke.

"If I am not mistaken, you're a K.I.N.G as well—from your time at Kepler?"

She seemed unprepared for the compliment. "Correct. My sixth cycle. Unlike you, I only received it once. I found your accomplishments there fascinating."

The Alchemist
An eternal machine composed of trillions of nanobots created to help humanity along their journey. It pulls from all known data to better serve a person and can manipulate portions of itself to build objects. Darren Parsons worked on it as a side project in 2074, though the origin of the original schematics was unknown. When he realized he was on the threshold of creating sentient AI, and thus a hypothetical "Overlord" or as he would say "Skynet type event," he shelved everything and told only Angelika to burn the lab and its work. After telling Daren she would, she proceeded to store the work instead. In 2086, after Darren's death, Angelika revived the project and provided schematics telling Lily Persons it was her father's dream to bring the Alchemist to life.

Before he could tease out any subtext on that statement, they reached the metal doorway to Lily's office. It looked like it belonged in a spaceship.

"Curious meeting you, Joanne. A curious encounter given the circumstance. I hope we'll speak again."

She bowed and left. After three long breaths, he activated the entry. It split and disappeared into the walls. The room beyond was completely, ominously, dark.

"Lily?" Bernard was surprised at his own soft tone, not so much the icy voice that answered.

"Come in, Bernard."

The sound of it, not heard in six years, sent him plummeting back through a wealth of joy and sorrow, before he noticed how it had changed. It was sadder, perhaps, certainly more aloof tinged with long-smoldering anger.

This would be touchy. Her expertise was unparalleled. He needed her on the Nomad. William wanted her there too. More than that, though, they both wanted her there for Darren, a great man and one of the few minds Bernard valued more than his own.

Was it yesterday I passed him in the hall on my way back here? I waved farewell and said we'd do dinner next week to review the outputs from the Large Hadron Collider.

Moments later, he was safely in his Newton 7GRX heading for the airfield, when, in an instant, everything was gone.

Lily's voice, coming from somewhere far in the darkness, yanked him back to the present. "You actually sent William to do your dirty work?"

"You made your feelings about me abundantly clear, Lily. Publicly, I might add. I was... trying to respect your wishes."

"Really? And was thinking you could recruit me for your interplanetary voyage and avoid seeing me until launch day part of that show of respect?"

"Lily, truly, I didn't know where to begin. But I am here. You must realize this mission matters more than anything."

He still couldn't see her and had no idea if she could see him, but he covered his heart all the same hoping it would convey his sincerity. The only light remaining, from the hall behind him, disappeared when the doors snapped shut engulfing him entirely in darkness.

What the hell? His heart sped up, soon pounding in his chest.

And then, there was light. Sourceless, it dissolved the void but failed to reveal anything; no walls, floor, or even the door he'd entered through. Before him, behind him—all around—there was white, bright, infinite nothingness. He couldn't even tell if he was standing or floating.

This looks like the construct from The Matrix. He rubbed the back of his neck looking for a plug, then realized if this was virtual reality, he wouldn't be able to find one.

Little else to do, he walked, and as he did, the air split creating a square-shaped entrance in front of him with a jungle visible beyond.

Well, she's certainly winning the "most interesting recruitment" award.

He stepped in among the trees. Birds chirped; sunlight left dappled chiaroscuro patterns on his hands. Even the dirt felt real, all thanks to the nanofibers in the floor no doubt.

The door behind him snapped closed and another opened. When he moved through the new entry, multiple rooms sprung out; accordion-like, each expanded deeper and deeper revealing a wealth of extreme climates. He traversed from the tropics to the arctic—to blistering Saharan dunes.

Finally, a doorway opened to what seemed a normal room. Sensing this was the end, that the dreaded encounter was nigh, he almost hesitated before stepping through.

The office was at last illuminated. Its walls were circular, not unlike William's but windowless. In fact, there was nothing in the space except a raised dias supporting the two semi-circular desks Dr. Lily Parsons sat within. She wore a patterned, green top with matching floral skirt: her fiery, red hair pinned in an imposing Japanese style.

"Actually respecting me would have meant allowing me to look into the eyes of the man responsible for my father's death without having to ask."

The words and the angry fire in her eyes pained him. "Your father was my closest friend, you know that. I understand why you were hurt. I was too, believe me, but I had nothing to do with his death. It wasn't human error, either. Part of this mission is to prove that. To find out what did cause the accident... what killed our family and friends. Think about it. What possible motive could I have for hurting the scientific community so profoundly?"

"That's easy." Her eyebrows shot up like an Atlas rocket. "To pretend that first contact is upon us just so you can go adventuring in space."

He tried to remind himself this was Lily; this was part of his atonement. Even so, he couldn't resist. "That's absurd."

She dismissed the claim in a heartbeat. "Is it? You always want to be part of anything you consider important. The present situation only proves my point."

Far from calm, Bernard climbed the dais bringing himself to eye-level with Lily. "I tell you it's nonsense. You talk about respect? William shared the complete evidence with you. As a scientist you should respect the facts. Your father would never have sunk to such warrantless conjecture."

She became shrill. "Don't dare talk to me about what my father would and wouldn't do. If you cared so much for him, why didn't you reach out after CERN? His best friend? You weren't even at his funeral! Why didn't you come and talk to me, if only for his sake? WHY?"

The memory of Bernard's betrayal in her time of need was too much. He was speechless. William was right, his inability to comfort the family of his fallen friend was a dark stain. True, his absence at the funeral was for security reasons, but after that, he did stay away. The world already hating him, close friends were turning on him feeding his survivor guilt... the rift grew over time and he let it.

The EMF sculptor on her desk reminded him of when he and Darren built the first one. It somehow gave him the courage to speak, not with his usual chess-master tone, but with a softer voice that cracked with emotion.

"You're right. My actions in the aftermath of that horrific day were dishonorable. As assuredly as I did not sabotage the antimatter containment, I did nothing to deserve living instead of Darren or any of my fallen friends. I should have been here for you. I should have been there for a lot of people, but I wasn't. I lost everything and didn't know how to continue, so I hid my sorrow and myself in my work. I don't expect your forgiveness, Lily, but maybe, just maybe, this mission will shed some light for us all."

Through pitiless tears she gave him a piercing stare. "All I understand is that I lost my father that day. And yet, here you are, still alive fantasizing about how your next great discovery will erase your previous sins."

That was it. He had tried. "Were you just lying to William, then, when you said you'd join the Nomad to give yourself a chance to vent this bile?"

Eyes drying, Lily transformed her expression into a fearsome smile. The sudden shift reminded him of a calculating Angelika.

"Oh no, Bernard, I am going on this mission. I'm looking forward to it."

Uh oh. Where's this going?

Suddenly, she sounded dangerous. "I said yes because I want to be there when you fail. I want to make sure everyone knows the truth, to deny you any opportunity to twist the facts when you reach the edge of the system... and find nothing."

Angelika, we've found our dissenter. Congratulations.

Lily's eyes probed for chinks in his armor, but if she was going to announce herself as the enemy, he'd be sure she'd find none.

Already returned to his chess master persona, he answered with no affect. "Well, the little show you gave when I arrived makes it clear you've made progress in photon manipulation. The crew will be grateful for your expertise. I was hoping we could start again but, nevertheless, welcome aboard. William will be your liaison going forward. If there is nothing else, I have pressing work."

As he tried to leave, Lily grunted. "There's another reason I wanted you here."

That stopped him. Half expecting the room to become a desert, a dungeon, or a pit of lava, he turned back. Lily still sat at her desk judging his every twitch. Abruptly, she opened a drawer and pulled out an oceanic blue cube.

"This is my father's NanoCube. I can't open it, naturally, no one can. But I think he added a failsafe for you."

Bemused as much as surprised, Bernard looked at the cube, to Lily, and back to the cube. "For me? What do you mean?"

"After he died, I found this with a note. I didn't understand it at first, but over the years I came to realize it was meant for you."

She handed him a small piece of paper with one line on it.

"Forever a mote of dust. Forever and explorer. Forever a friend."

Bernard was flabbergasted. Only Darren and William had ever read the letter from Carl Sagan to his great-grandfather. Excited, he reached for the NanoCube thinking it would activate at his touch.

But a creeping suspicion made him hesitate. "Even if I could, Lily, why would you let me open Darren's cube?"

"Because whatever's inside must be important, and, regardless of my feelings, I am still a scientist."

"A scientist that waited six years..."

"Research takes time Bernard."

Is this why Angelika insisted on choosing her?

"Lily, Darren's NanoCube was protected by a tridimensional rotating code. I certainly can't... ah. No, wait. Of course I can. Hand me the note again."

Though confused, she obliged.

His clever friend left the clues in plain sight—voice, print, touch, they were all there. Without wasting another moment, he gripped the cube in his right hand and said.

"Forever a mote of dust. Forever and explorer. Forever a friend."

When he circled the dais, the NanoCube felt alive. When it unlocked, a miracle occurred.

"Father!" Lily screamed.

"Oh, my..."

In the cosmology world, Darren Parsons was known as a showman. Even in death, he did not disappoint. Before their eyes, a collection of pixels was coalescing into an ever-more-perfect 3D replica of the man they knew and loved. Neither had ever seen this level of tactile resolution.

Once the avatar was completely manifested, it... yawned.

Looking directly at Bernard, it said, "Dear friend, if you're seeing this, I am dead. I assume Lily is with you. My dear, I am so, so sorry I'm not there to guide you. Don't ever forget, you're far more brilliant than I ever could be. I am better looking, though. Joking, just joking... I'm sure you're wondering why I'm here, better yet, how I'm here."

"Yup," they both said, as if he could hear.

Apparently, he could. "I used experimental neurodigital interface tech of which our scientific friends Medina Karimov & Ava Auburn had started toying with to link my brain to the cube. The process was... oh, let's call it... messy. I am in fact, the preserved consciousness of Darren Parsons, more specifically, his memory cortex drive, an **MCD** as I like to call them, a living copy of a human mind. Think Jor-El at the Fortress of Solitude in those 20th century Superman movies. I continue to exist, within this hologram, in a stable digital form. Bernard, sorry for not sharing the tech with you. If memory serves -heh- I planned to once we finished Project Phoenix Fires."

Lily burst into tears. Though trembling, Bernard held himself together so he wouldn't miss a word.

"The bigger issue is what I was last working on when I made this self-backup—a way for neurons and synapses to communicate on the quantum level. In short, telepathy. Once I fully awaken, I can be more help to you, but it'll take several days to decompartmentalize. In the meantime, you'll have to rebuild the interface. I destroyed the prototype after I used it to upload. My designs were too close to completion to be in anyone's hands but yours. You need to promise me, Bernard, promise on Lily, that it will stay safe, and you'll work together to finish it."

Without hesitation, Bernard said, "I promise."

Digital Darren smiled.

The fact that Darren kept this from him was almost as astonishing as the tech itself. Telepathy had been a science fiction dream from the beginning. It would not only prove incredibly useful to the Nomad, the long voyage would give them time to field test it properly.

Seeing her father again, coupled with the revelation, apparently softened Lily. "Do you realize what this could mean for communication in space?"

"I do, Lily." Instead of embracing the possibilities, he frowned.

"What are you afraid of now?"

"I'm not sure, but the timing is too perfect."

"Ugh, shut it, Bernie. Timing my ass. If you'd come around sooner, we'd have had it years ago. And what in heaven's sake is Project Phoenix Fires?"

Avoiding the question, he replayed the message over and over delving deeper into the concepts and schematics of neural communication at a quantum level. Six hours later, he broke his silence.

MCD

Memory Cortex Drive, is a living, digital copy of a human mind. It exists within a HoloCube in stable form. It retains all of the personality, memory, and characteristics of the original person. This technology was created by Darren Parsons, who before his death, surgically implanted a series of neurodigital interfaces between his brain and the HoloCube in secret. This provided a hardlink for the software that could map and duplicate a human mind. The failsafe MCD was activated by Bernard Hubert. The construct gives a person the ability to contemplate and analyze problems, equations, strategies, realities, and their own thoughts at quantum computing levels.

"It's astounding."

"Do you think we can complete it?" Lily asked.

He thought awhile before answering, "I think so... yes. We'd have to bring William, Angelika, and Isaac in on it. I don't even understand a third of Darren's math."

"Go, make it happen. I'll start deciphering the blueprints." Before he exited, she gave him a look. "Don't think I'm letting you off the hook. You will tell me what you and my father were working on." With an indignant snort, she muttered, "Project Phoenix Fires. Peh. The way the two of you name things..."

Bernard left the office and nearly blacked out. The curveball was utterly unexpected and equally electrifying. Darren's last act may have saved Bernard and Lily's relationship. Perfect timing, indeed.

Back at the hangar, William and Isaac were studying a life-size hologram of the Nomad when he rushed in and stopped them. "You won't believe who I just talked to for hours."

"Um... Lily?"

"Well, yes, but also... Darren..."

"WHAT!?"

Once Bernard recapped it all, they raced to Angelika's to bring her up to speed, and then headed back to the nanolabs as quickly as possible.

As they ran, Bernard looked at William. "I don't know exactly what we'll make of Darren's work or even if the functionality will be solid enough for our journey. What I can tell you, old friend, is that the adventures of the Nomad have truly begun."

William provided a bemused laugh. "Oh, Bernie... the adventures of the Nomad truly began months ago."

William grinned and moved past him reaching the doorway to Angelika's office first. The two of them moved to their respective seats: Bernard left, William right, as it always was. Angelika looked at them and ushered a movement employing an explanation.

"Angie, Darren is back; he'll be coming on the ship with us." Bernard spoke in boyish joy.

"That bastard, he actually did it. A functional M.C.D..."

CHAPTER 16 M.C.D.

CHAPTER 17
CREATORS OF SPACE

All who live in the underbelly of the galaxy know the tale. Some use it to induce fear, some as a bedtime story. Every Creator, though, knows it to be true.

Deep in the void between stars, through nebula alleyways consumed by blackness, a dead planet drifts. Now home to a legendary band of rebels, its broken mass silently orbiting a rogue black hole... moves invisibly through the cosmos. Unbound by the usual galactic flow, free from the galaxy's rules, it is impossible to find.

Its strange journey began when the black hole passed through its native system killing the sun and shattering its worlds. Fifteen billion died as the planet *Xaraka* cracked in two. One half was dragged into the dark—gone—but the rest locked into an orbit so close to the black hole, time slowed down.

At the *Threshold*, one can see the galaxy change.

General Odian Spek, the Valkon who learned the secrets of phasing, who led with an iron fist and an immovable will, had become an aimless fugitive in the aftermath of the Saaryki Incident: his family murdered and his Creators too scattered and weak to fulfill their mission. He fled beyond the protected quadrants hoping only to be reunited with the fallen House of Spek.

Xaraka
The former name of planet XXX. It was a planet in the Warpgate system with an advanced, sentient, subterranean species. Harnessing the planet's heat, they sculpted giant tunnels and cities that spanned across the core. Sadly, a rogue black hole passed through the planet's system, cracked the planet in half with tidal forces, and swept it along on it's dark journey. It wasn't until 25 million turns later that XXX was discovered by Odian Spek and became the Creators of Space's base of operation and home to the fierce warrior.

Threshold
The space around XXX's parent black hole where time is distorted. At XXX's orbit, time moves 10x slower than the rest of the galaxy.

Instead, a gravitational anomaly caused his ship to patch-out unexpectedly. As the growing blackness swallowed the stars in his path, an onyx shimmer illuminated his viewport. A vantablack sphere christened only by the cracks of molten lava protruding from its every crevasse devoured the opaque space. But in its shadow he found the will to live as he transversed from reaper to explorer. Fifteen prikes later, he found the remains of a once subterranean city forever left facing the cosmic sea when the land above it shattered.

The moment he opened its doors, he decided he hadn't found this place by happenstance. No, it was a sign from his wife and child that he still had a job to do. The fractured world would become a home and fortress for a rebuilt army: a base from which to find and strike at lower species unworthy of equality or mercy.

He dubbed it XXX.

For his followers, knowing his obsession with duality and with balance, his words became a rallying cry. "Only those who've failed in every possible way can learn how to lead in every successful way."

It wasn't difficult to find those who shared his vision; Soldiers, doctors, engineers, artists, politicians, parents, pariahs, deserters, dissidents, anarchists, heroes, villains, people of science, and more. Recruited over hundreds of turns, they sacrificed their ties for the cause leaving loved ones to grow old in the faster time beyond the Threshold.

The Creators were a small but clever group. Their advanced custom stealth ships were designed from the original Voidwhisperer fighters. Numbering no more than 16,000, with over half deployed at any given time, they leveraged bleeding-edge technology to enhance their troops ten-fold with drones and artificial life such as *VIRGL*. Odian's voice united more than the GSA would ever publicly admit.

Once they began to journey out again, before each mission Spek would say, *"Those who allow conquerors to exist allow themselves to be conquered."* To him, the GSA's inability to do what they must posed risk to the galactic civilization as a whole. Species with violent tendencies should be eliminated—not quarantined

---

VIRGL
Short for Virtual Intuitive Relationship Growth Lifeform, it is the 8th Generation AI companion of Odian Spek. It was developed by the Toridians and perfected by the Valkons. It is a passive, inquisitive, sentient digital being with limitless learning capability. They grow slowly from infant digital consciousnesses that are reared with compassion and respect. They can compute vast quantities of information and usually aid the logistics of special groups.

and not put under some review board. Extirpate their infestation before they erode the fabric of the Alliance.

- - -

The Valpax, the only remaining ship from the Nova System attack, had returned. It slipped gracefully around the asteroids barricading the dark planet's surface. As a chime echoed through the fissures signaling its arrival, the ship skimmed sundered mountains and onto a scarred, fossilized ocean bed that appeared to stretch forever.

A balanced view of faint stars and pale sand shifted until the stars threatened to consume all. But they, too, dropped away completely as the ship dove over the massive cliffs marking where a quarter of the planet used to be. It drifted into the chasm to their fortress. No signals were transmitted, no security codes requested, yet the railguns and plasma nets stood down. The starlight, diminishing the already dark rock, faded to a void-like blur.

Bearing its hard-won cargo, the ship slowed. Threading between three mountain-sized slabs, it curved in and around to avoid being hit. Emerging into open space, it was met with a strange vista. Near the chasm base, the broken rock revealed a perpendicular cave a full rudon tall. In it, pyramids hewn by ancient Xarakan workers reached floor to ceiling overlapping in a huge hexagonal network. The first Creators had found others like it still sealed deeper within.

The Valpax passed among these columns, moving on and on, guided only by radar until a beam of light made the high walls glimmer. The hangar bay blast doors slowly opened. Entering, the starship passed through the forcefield holding the atmosphere and was briefly surrounded by a purple nimbus.

As its thrusters adjusted to the artificial gravity, technicians vaulted from slip-tubes and flew down from balconies. The landing gear hissed; the primary cargo hold creaked open.

Three figures stepped out, each wearing sleek, black vacuum jumpsuits adapted to their physiologies. They removed their helmets revealing a rocky, broad-backed

---

Valpax
A modified Pandula Class Drop Ship, under the command of RuCreator Velora Tunami. It was originally designed for shuttling 40-60 ground troops to and from a planet's surface. This craft has Beacblocks, missiles, a sensor defeating hull, and upgraded engines for running in deep space. The Pandula Class Drop Ship was imagined by Sector Prime Niro Hadriianna during his time at Havlanager. After becoming increasingly bored of retirement, he designed a ship that would be capable of making his escape, then gave the plans to the GSA so they would know their flaws. The Pandula Class was built by Sector 7 Enterprises on Mijorn.

Tragdor, a humanoid Dragsan male, and a beautiful, orange-scaled Fandaxian *traa-female* who deftly balanced on two legs with a long, powerful tail.

The crowd pushed in eager to set eyes on their prize.

A repair jockey cried. "Come on, let's see it! I bet it's funnier-looking than that pathetic ship from *Nulusoorg III*."

A gleeful technician nudged a Kitta medic beside her. "Took eighty prikes to decode the last one. Bets on over-under?"

A Baleen pilot turned to his gunner. "Remember how polluted the oceans were on the last mission out there? Those creatures were savages."

The loud agreement grew louder until a tall Zundrillian in a modest, green uniform shouted, "Creators, enough!"

Despite her unassuming appearance, the crowd quieted separating to allow her easy passage. The crew snapped to attention at her approach. The Zundrillian gruffly directed a question at the Fandaxian.

"Creator Velora, was your mission a success?"

After a tail-salute, Velora addressed her reply properly. "Affirmative, RuCreator Maroona. Primary objective completed. Our intel was solid. The native probe was retrieved unharmed."

Maroona peered over her eye shaders. "Twenty-six ships were sent, yet you return alone. What are our losses?"

Velora stiffened. "Heavy, RuCreator. Twenty-four ships destroyed, one captured."

There was a sharp, collective intake of breath and many looks of disappointment and anger. Maroona, at least, appeared to be withholding judgement. "Why?"

"They had Voidwhisperers, as NüCreator Spek anticipated, and the Quarantine forces were unexpectedly aggressive sacrificing their own fighters to block our field breakers."

Maroona's voice flared. "The GSA is willing to send its own to their deaths to

---

Tragdor
A large, sentient species standing over 8 tradons tall that are composed partially of rock, including their granite-like scales. They are extremely durable and are even able to absorb low energy plasma blasts. They have a high tolerance to heat and cold, can survive short durations in vacuum, and can hold their breath for up to three trikes. Their neural physiology is incompatible with Voidwhisperer implants.

Traa-female
The birthing gender of Fandaxians. Fandaxians have four genders; Saa-male, Traa-male, Saa-female, and Traa-female. All four genders are required to breed. A Saa-male fertilizes a Traa-male who in turn fertilizes the egg cell in a Saa-female who then impregnates a Traa-female who then carries and gives birth to a Fandaxian.

protect these savages?" She shouted so all could hear. "It was a steep cost for a victory that could not have been achieved without our machine friends. They shall be remembered in the stories; their code copies shall live forever in the *Halls of the Created*!"

Cheers erupted.

A levitated stasis field generator floated from the cargo bay to the brightly-lit hangar floor. Its burden looked primitive, as old as the dead city but far cruder. Maroon's hand gently skimmed the field holding the Voyager 2. Pale, blue ribbons flowed where she touched the invisible barrier.

"Fascinating," she crooned.

Velora interjected. "Unfortunately, RuCreator, its power source is a primitive radio decay generator. Largely depleted, but still harmful. We'll have to contain and remove it before analysis."

Maroona retracted her hand. "Then the humans are nuclear-capable. There's less time than we thought. Interpreter Roliath, take this to the labs."

A Metawing wearing an academy faculty uniform saluted and retreated with the probe.

Maroona turned to the crew. "*NüCreator* Spek is expected back soon from a recon mission. Once he arrives, you will provide him with a full mission debrief. I suggest you grab some food and make your way to the Matüridan."

They saluted, each according to their custom. Maroona returned the salutes, then departed. The throng dispersed, many heading for the inner blast doors as the trio made its way into the fortress proper.

In the hexagonal hallways, combat troops marched, flew, or crawled past them. Sliptube occupants, a luxury in remote space, periodically zipped overhead. Luckily, once the Creators patched the ancient power relays and installed their own fusion generators, the original luminary system functioned. An approximation of warm daylight emanated from two upper angled walls leaving the ceiling a detached

---

Nulusoorg III
A Distant Zones' world previously visited by the Creators of Space. The planet's ecosystem was completely destroyed; the atmosphere and oceans were poisoned. The COS intercepted the inhabitant's arkship on its way to a new planet. Deeming them unworthy, the COS killed all the inhabitants.

NüCreator
The highest rank of the Creators of Space. There is and has only ever been one, Odian Spek. They may be challenged by a RuCreator for leadership of the COS, though they must possess the ability to harness the thought stream that links the Creators. No RuCreator has ever attempted a challenge to date.

Halls of the Created
A digital afterlife and tomb for machine and biological life who die in the service of the Creators. A machine's code copy is downloaded when they "die" with their memories wiped. They are reborn in a new world to start fresh. The Halls of the Created are both functional and spiritual for the Creators of Space.

strip. The other walls were more smooth stonework, like the entrance cave. Now illuminated, they were revealed to be stunning, pale, green granite swirling with veins of gold and purple amethyst.

"What now?" Bluuimpus said.

Velora shrugged. "Beats me. That was sorta anticlimactic after all we've been through."

Marriko's usual optimism was unaffected. "I can't wait to see those new episodes of the Epiko Entertainment shows. It's crazy, each time I return to XXX, there are so many new seasons available. What about you two?"

"I'm going for a quick scale-scrub," Bluuimpis replied. "Then I'll meet you at the dining area. Velora?"

Her rhythmic tail flicks made it clear she was distracted. A faint sensation seeming to touch her shoulder pulled her mind ever further away. Her consciousness wandered trying to find the source of the feeling. Memories of warmth and power of soaring through Valkürin flickered before her.

But those memories of soaring through the clouds, of dancing with a Valkon woman and child, of happiness—were not her own.

"Your shower is going to have to wait, Bluuimpus," she said. "He's here."

Even her own words sounded distant.

Marriko was skeptical. "How do you know?"

Another chime sounded proving her right.

Marriko stared at her. "Wow, you're really starting to connect with the implants, huh?"

She rubbed the metal plates and ports poking from the scar tissue on the back of her neck unable to tell whether or not she liked the look her crewmates were giving her.

"Barely, I think he was just shouting really loudly."

Bluuimpus was crestfallen. "It's really cool for you, but I'm so bummed that they don't work on my kind."

"Yeah, well, you can turn parts of your body to stone and hold your breath about thirty times longer than I can."

The three chuckled. Marriko said, "Well, guess we'll shower and eat later. Best head to the *Matüridan*."

They hopped the nearest sliptube access, jumped in, and flew down the hall. The vector quickly filled with fellow Creators all heading for the Rallying Fields. The hallway beneath them went into a gentle curve then rapidly approached another doorway.

A dazzling light beyond it blinded them to what lay beyond.

"This never gets old!"

Marriko's shout made Velora smile. Speeding up, they were shot into another vast chamber with more carved, vaulting honeycombs; golden light was emanating from the pyramidal columns.

Velora, Bluuimpus, and Marriko glided over a high plateau before the ground suddenly dropped 300 tradons to a giant, flat surface. The sliptube brought them swiftly down rapidly altering their viewpoint.

The Matüridan was nearly four rudons away. The half-planet's sole disconnected pyramid, the Creators thought it may have been the center of some ancient, monstrous engine. It was flattened at the top with a corresponding column descending from the ceiling.

That was where the Creators would gather not only to hear their Odian but to connect mind-to-mind, soul-to-soul, and push forward to build the bridge between them stronger bit by bit. The Voidwhisperer implant, once used to fight technological and psychic warfare, was now used to create an equal and cooperative world the GSA never could.

Across the plain, small ships flew in from the edges. Dozens of sliptubes parallel

---

Matüridan
The central engine of a vast, ancient machine built by the extinct Xarakans within what is now XXX. It is used as the primary gathering location for the Creators of Space.

to their own carried scores. Others jet-packed, impulsed, drove, hopped, crawled, ran, or flew to their common destination. The gathering felt primeval to Velora as if they were one of the primitive tribes of her home world, *Azoeleo*, congregating by a village fire.

At the base of the pyramid, what had appeared smooth cut stone clarified as the interior of a vast machine. Staired ramps ran along the slabs of unknown alloys that interlaced with conduits to form the whole of the structure.

Though it looked like the sliptube occupants would slam the strange surface, they angled upward. Passing their slower but perhaps more determined fellows on the stairs, Velora flipped onto her back to better admire the incoming vessels. Near the top, the tube slowed signaling the imminent terminus. Ahead, a disembarkment ring was set up where travelers were propelled from the magnetic stream.

Before Velora got there, she pulled herself from the rivulet with a rolling tail flick perfected by years of quazmat stunts. Gracefully passing over the top edge, she landed deftly on her feet and gave a hearty salute to the passing soldiers. Then, she ran to the disembarkment ring to meet an unimpressed, Marriko and Bluuimpus.

"Showoff!" Bluuimpus said, "What is the point of a stunt like that?"

"You've obviously never gotten a concussion from someone behind you jumping out of the sliptube hooves first. "

"Fair point."

Another, stronger mental wave washed along Velora's thoughts. She was faintly aware of others nearby responding in sync. Those on the steps and in their ships picked up speed. Those in the sliptubes flipped and rolled for better views.

At the front of the chamber, on a cliff edge between ramps, a solitary figure stood. Even from this distance, his swagger and cool demeanor were unmistakable. All eyes on him, he leapt from the precipice plummeting countless tradons before unfurling his magnificent wings and soaring majestically.

As he approached the Matüridan, he sailed over ships and dove between carriers:

Azoeleo
The homeworld of the Fandaxians and capital world of Sector 4. It is the middle of five rocky planets that orbit a red dwarf star. The Endon came from the planet's mean radii of its orbital distance with an eccentricity of only .000007. The perfect gravitational resonance between the planets maintains Azoeleo's rotation despite it being well within the tidal locked zone of its parent star.

Paraluar Horns
Horns that grow in the same direction. A sign of evolutionary superiority amongst the Valkon. Those of lesser blood have horns that grow sideways called Paxaluar.

Boon Bonx
Was a sentient interplanetary species in the Distant Zones that attempted to conquer their neighboring species, the Tipaaroo. They were defeated and eradicated by the interceding Creators of Space.

his speed seemingly at odds with the distance he covered.

He rose high above the pyramid, so close to the vaulted roof he flipped and ran upside down on its surface. Detaching, he dropped trading elevation for speed as he circled the upper monolith. As he passed lower and lower, cheers erupted reaching a crescendo when, with a final magnificent swoop, he landed gracefully on the flowing mosaic-like floor. NüCreator Odian Spek was home.

The powerful wind from his beating wings pushed back the lighter creatures. Once they folded, razor feathers still protruding mid-spine, he stood in the center of the machine posing like a hero of old. Twin *laser blades* were strapped to his back. A holster on his left hip carried a telescoping *stunstaff*: the one on his right, a *plasma repeater*.

Hexapedal but bipedal, he was similar to a Dragsan replacing blue and silver feathers for jet black across the back, shoulders, and thighs: roughly humanoid, save for the large *paraluar* horns jutting from his skull. His stripped-down Void-whisperer armor revealed that his right arm, shoulder, and a portion of his torso weren't flesh, but woven Kalean steel neurofiber shaped into muscles and sinews that moved naturally.

He'd made his powerful body a history of success and failure and a remembrance for the fallen. The flex armor covering his left side was covered with words, pictograms, and symbols from each species they'd cleansed. His right, held the iconography of those the Creators saved. His chest bore the symbol of his home world, Valkürin. Around his neck he wore an amulet with his family's emblem formerly carried by his daughter.

As he raised his fist, the cheering horde hushed. "Creators! Another world has been saved from the aggression of a T-Class planet. When we found Rivaawool far in the Distant Zones, its people were under attack from the neighboring planets species, the **Boon Bonx**. Not content with their own space, they tried to take what belonged to others. But we are not the GSA. We do not allow conquest to proceed with impunity. No, we are the arbiters of justice with the courage to ensure balance

---

Laser Blade
A handheld weapon shaped like a sword or dagger that generates a flow of superheated plasma through a magnetic field along the blade. When activated, it can cut through most materials without resistance. The origin of handheld weapons like this was lost during the Second Dark Era. Its existence has been recorded back at least 15 million turns.

Stunstaff
A two hand weapon shaped like a long pole, about a tradon long, that when activated, emits a concussive shockwave on contact that usually incapacitates the target. They are commonly used for crowd control.

Plasma Repeater
A common galactic firearm. A fusion battery superheats pellets of compressed air into plasma that is accelerated in incinerating bursts at a target.

across the known and unknown worlds! The Boon Bonx have been cleansed by our weapons and the *Neper*. Their planet is quiet now—ready for Rivaawool to enjoy should they choose. So, raise a shout for our fallen comrades. The Halls of the Created received new heroes today. Moon Mooka, Durest Ka, Coomraya, and Negaan, we thank you for your sacrifice."

The congregation roared in unison, *Creators of Peace, Creators of Space, we salute you in your bravery, for your sacrifice. You have made the galaxy we live in more peaceful, allowing peaceful life to flourish!*

Velora felt a pull in the back of her mind. Others connected to the collective began transmitting sending their memories of their own fallen comrades. From their fragmented memories and emotion, they wove a narrative felt by all.

Odian raised his other hand. In it, he contained a hologram projector. As the narrative channeled through him and he added his own, all could see and hear the stories of Moon Mooka and the others play out in towering images; their childhoods, loves, battles, losses, and friendships. Some of the worlds on display were familiar to Velora, others not, but whenever a word or context was indecipherable, another mind somewhere in the crowd translated for her.

Acidic tears trickled harmlessly down her arm glistening against her bright amber and scarlet scales. Looking around, she saw many similarly affected. Ultimately, the pull of the collective waned, its emotional storm ebbed, leaving her with a wordless longing.

The projector stored in his inorganic arm, Odian unfurled his wings with a loud snap that cracked the air. His words echoed off the distant walls.

"So many turns have passed out there that few on Valkürin even remember the Saaryki. But here at the Threshold, memories need not be long to know why we do what we must. Combing the Distant Zones has again shown us the aggression inherent in so many. Where glorious species once thrived, we found dead worlds ruined by nuclear weapons or invading armies seeking territory and slaves. It is time to return to GSA territory and prove the worlds they try to protect are not

---

Neper

N39 is the preferred bioweapon of the Creators of Space. It is a neural interruptor pathogen with each batch tailored to infect a single species. Spreading like a virus, once injected into a planet's atmosphere it can wipe out 99.9% of a species within three frikes. It derives from an old GSA chemical used to wipe out failed First Contacts in the early Alliance. It was later developed by a group of geneticists who were angry and joined the COS during the Saaryki War adding components of the Saaryki Plague itself to finish the compound.

only unworthy, they are lethal. We will not let them make the same mistakes again. The Nova System is just the beginning."

Odian let a sweep of doubt and hesitation bury itself before continuing. "There will be no repeat of the Loronzon Incident. For 200 turns, we've inspired countless civilizations, not through fear, but hope and action. They know we are not criminals; they know we are not terrorists, and they will cheer us on because we are CREATORS!"

A great roar erupted. Odian stood, arms and wings outstretched, to better draw the collective energy. He spoke again, but his words were muted by a powerful pull in Velora's psyche. She could still hear him, louder now in fact, since he spoke directly to her through the implant.

"Come Velora, I wish to hear of your exploits at Nova."

Suddenly she was standing next to Odian atop the Matüridan. She realized she was fully in the collective now, and that Odian had the ability to tune out all the others.

"Take my hand."

Resistance futile, she placed her orange claws into his big, blue palm—and fell. Her collapsing mind flowed into his. She was in the Valpax with Marriko and Bluuimpus watching the scopes as their fighters drew off the Peacekeeper forces, then made a diversion run for Nova.

It was all there, everything from the pale starlight to Bluuimpus' chalky smell. Then, events became faster scattering as Odian flipped through her memories. They were flying toward the probe, then she was in her suit guiding it into the cargo bay. They were back on the bridge preparing to patch into flowspace.

As she looked at the sensors, the memory froze. Velora couldn't tell if she still had a body or had become an observing spirit.

"I sense your skepticism. I know you wondered why I ordered the MFs to Earth. After all, the distraction could have worked all the same without such a sacrifice. But they

do not have the same aversion to death we do. We needed them to prove something, and they did."

Odian released her mind and everything dissolved bringing the present back in full volume. All the while, he'd been speaking to the crowd, finishing only now.

"Go! Prepare your groups for our next phase!"

For a moment, his gaze singled hers out from the massive audience. With a mighty flap of his wings, he soared upward, again creating a strong wind that nearly toppled those closest. He climbed toward the base of the monolith, then wheeled and dove, gathering speed before rocketing over the Matüridan's top and back towards the fortress.

The crowd headed back the same way they came; ships, stairs, and sliptubes... renewed purpose speeding them on their way.

Velora let them pass her, preferring to gaze at Odian's receding figure. Innumerable turns as a Creator had shown her incredible things, but none so incredible as him: the legend that unified these species, the Valkon with the vision who would do what was needed.

But, the Fandaxian knew that peace never came peacefully.

MF's
Is a Creators of Space acronym for "Machine Friends."

CHAPTER 18

THE NEXUS

At the heart of XXX lay the Nexus, where the broken world's oddly distributed mass created a weightless cave. Here, Odian Spek, along with the Nova probe and those attempting to decode the language written on its panels and examining its innards with robotic eyes—floated. His vacuum armor was safely stowed in his chambers. As Odian moved to the pivot of the Nexus his mind wondered...

"We Creators are not warmongers; we wished for an expanded universe without need for conflict, where there would be plenty for all—always."

Everything had gone as planned. The information from their agent had proven fruitful. While some might wince at the loss of twenty-four ships, it wasn't mere spectacle. If he'd wanted the humans eliminated, they'd be gone. Instead, gunning for Earth forced the failsafe and proved how dangerous they could be.

But humans remained to be judged.

Linked with many others in the space through their Voidwhisperer implants, Odian let himself drift into the river of voices.

RuCreator *Daminus peered from behind a spectral display thinking. "If this scrawl was their primary form of communication, they did a poor job using it."*

RuCreator
The second rank of the Creators of Space. There are approximately 1000, all chosen by Odian himself for their deeds to the cause. They are leaders to all the groups within the COS; including battle command, research labs, spy networks, recruitment, and more.

RuCreator Diiusk used a combination of tail-finger and eye movements to manipulate the datachip's holofield. *"It's command driven, so they must have a digital-type storage."*

This whispering in the dark was part of what kept the true believers from being caught. Their collective debating had begun with the core dissenters led by Odian so long ago. But the tech was granted to the true believers in the cause, so they could join the ranks of the enlightened. Absorbing their analyses, Odian took pieces from each to build his own. Once complete, he pulsed the word enough through the ether.

The others quieting, he said aloud, "Disassemble!"

At once the Voyager separated into its myriad components; nuts, bolts, washers, wires, brackets, bushings, batteries, lens, struts, microchips, thrusters, panels. Odian reached forward—the pieces sorted into junk piles dispersed around the space.

From this chaos, Odian was able to gently pluck what he was looking for: a golden disc. Untarnished since it was installed, its burnished faces glowed in the hololight.

He balanced it between his hands, keenly studying its deliberate etchings. *"This is it. No more hiding. All your sins revealed."*

Releasing the disc, it floated. Lasers swept its surface, scattering neon beams as they produced a massive, perfect holographic copy. The eleven-point Carl Sagan map with 2D vectors moved away from the rest and was overlaid with a hologram of the galaxy. The central node stopped over the Nova System, rotating and scaling until each vector aligned with a blinking dot.

Words, the same words, came rushing through the river. "A pulsar map!"

"Indeed," Odian said. "Any race naïve enough to hand over a map of their home world is sorely lacking in basic self-preservation skills. VIRGL, please begin a cross-check of its spectral analysis and vector language to find a constant."

In a moment, VIRGL answered. "Language period of pulsars determined.

Analysis indicates rotational period for data reveal."

The 8th Generation AI had first been developed by the Toridians, then perfected by the Valkons before their home-world was exterminated by the Saarkyi.

"VIRGL, please show me how it can be read."

His consistent courtesy was as pragmatic as it was polite. He'd seen many organics trod over their creations, ultimately creating a backlash that turned their servants into nearly unstoppable threats. VIRGL was alive, as much a companion as his biological allies, and would be treated with the same respect.

"Visual records show a device that can read the disc... here."

On the hologram, a diamond-shaped glyph glowed. The matching stylus, invisibly drawn from the debris, flew over the disc and stopped perpendicular to its surface. Cords of light from Nexus hardware created a connection to it.

"VIRGL, please compensate for Nova's atmospheric content, link electrical feed, begin playback, and sweep data-absorption until you get a hit."

The disc spun. The stylus produced groans and gibberish. It was likely language, but to Odian it sounded like the hooting of animals.

"Stabilize feed. Repeat on various inputs, please."

The disc continued playing harsh sounds, some barely perceptible. And then... a burst of what a human might recognize as whale-song made one of the Creators howl. Her mental pain bled through the river, inciting anger from Odian before he could close himself off from it.

The cry came from Diiusk, a Baleen of the water world *Yallaweh*. One of his earliest recruits, she twitched as she floated. Two of her compatriots held her steady. Salty tears drifted from her eyes in tiny beaded drops.

Using the tiny thrusters strapped to his wrists and ankles, Odian propelled himself the three tradons between them. The rest moved closer as well, unaccustomed to seeing a Creator weep so unabashedly, let alone one with battle scars on her outer claws and a half fin missing.

Yallaweh
"Home" in the ancient tongue of Baleen, is a waterworld with 100% of its surface covered in ocean with a max depth of 70 rudons; it is the Capital planet of GSA Sector 5. Yallaweh was originally inhabited by the Builders who connected its system with the Warpgate network before the Dark Era. It was seeded with other ocean species and seeded other worlds in turn. One such example were the Murakoor (humpback whales) to the planet Earth (Nova). Builder installations on or in orbit around the planet fell and sank into the oceans during the Builder Era far before the Baleen evolved. The Baleen rose to sentience during the First Dark Era and became a highly evolved and technologically advanced species. Due to their anatomy and the tremendous weight a water pressurized spacecraft would require, they did not leave Yallaweh. The planet was connected to the rest of the galaxy when explorers arrived via the surviving Warpgate during the Classical Era.

He put a hand to her claw. "We've chased the stars for many a turn. I've never seen anything rattle you. What is it?"

Her voice echoed an inconsolable pain. "That sound, it was a *Murakoor*—one of the Peace Whales—a peaceful species of music, song, and memory. They came on the Agnessil ships from Eladium, and they made my world their home ages before my people could build sky-platforms. We have long lived in harmony. That piteous cry was a scream for help. Its people are being slaughtered... almost extinct. I've heard more than enough to judge these barbarians."

Odian's wingtip tapped her carapace. "Channel the anger, Diiusk, we'll need it. But we're not one of them. We must know their history and intent before any hammer is swung."

Though the Baleen calmed herself, her fury still echoed through the river.

"Continue the playback, please." There was more and more gibberish until the plane projection became scrambled bars of light and static.

"VIRGL, take over translation, please, and use your intuition."

VIRGL voiced each step, somehow making the process sound both soothing and important.

"Assume pixelation style data output."

"Assume 4:3 grid ratio."

"Assume output is circular in shape."

"Attenuate... I'm now running the closest five billion iterations within the mean differential. Looking for image match for a hieroglyph of a circle within a rectangle."

The crude symbology on the hologram overlaid the projection. Once it stabilized to grey, a blurry, warped line formed into a curve.

"Enhance," Odian said.

When the edges sharpened, the eager collective mirrored his thoughts.

"Enhance! Enhance!"

Murakoor
Also called "peace whales," as they are known to the Baleen, are a sentient, non technological species who inhabit oceans of waterworlds across the galaxy. It is believed they originated from Eladium, and were transported by the Builders to Yallaweh and Nova (Earth). Their descendants are humpback whales. The Baleen and Murakoor have a mutual language they speak to one another called "Omm Drooma."

The curve became a circle.

"Decryption complete. Readout is nominal. Would you like to see, Odian?"

"Yes, VIRGL. Thank you."

Wheeling lines clicked into crude pictures of humans and their solar system. The additional images depicted the benign existence of bland creatures. Odian had no doubt the way the humans presented themselves was highly sanitized. He'd seen it all before.

As every child in the galaxy knew, never trust a Saaryki.

They were just another T-Class Planet until an evaluation cycle indicated there'd been a quantum leap in their progress. No nuclear wars, no civilization-induced ecosystem collapse... there was nothing that might be cause for worry. Many felt the near extinction-level asteroid impact prior to their modern era had made them wise.

First contact was a resounding success: their diplomats invited to GSA worlds, trade routes opened. Their language was adapted into the Galactic Star Alliance translation nanobots with little resistance.

Unknown to any, the Saaryki knew the GSA had been monitoring them during the asteroid collision and stood by rather than prevent the near-extinction of their species. Their affability a farce, they were bent on vengeance. In short order, they bioengineered pathogens based on the DNA acquired in their travels through the Alliance.

Valkürin was one of their first targets, losing a quarter of its population to the artificial plague. By the time they realized the Saaryki relief ships were actually troop-carriers, the invaders had gained control of their FTL ships, industrial areas, weapons platforms, and extensive natural resources.

Then, they proceeded to do the same to three more systems.

General Odian was three sectors distant on a mission whose objectives were murky at best. Many of the Vdubs with him were his own species, so when news reached them that their world had been conquered, Odian abandoned the mission and led his fleet home.

Jumping three sectors in under 12 *fikes* was unheard of. Odian did it in two. As the *Valnur* dropped from Patch 5 flowspace, hull groaning from quantum instability, he was greeted by a surface glassed by nuclear weapons—from the Saaryki's attempts to hold the planet.

Though the nearby capital, Radan, was ash, Odian found his humble skytower home unharmed. Still, his relief melted into despair; his family and friends had the plague. As he held his dead daughter in one arm, his dying wife in the other, cheers of victory came over the comms. The Saaryki were no match for his enraged VW fleet.

Kissing his beloved's brow, he promised her vengeance. With her last breath, she whispered, "From your pain, create a better world."

Those words were now etched in every hall of XXX, but back in that moment, he was broken. Having disobeyed orders, the Vdubs were forbidden to take part as the GSA drove the Saaryki further back. They did so anyway, utterly ignoring orders, widening the gap between the great government and its greatest warriors.

Once the fighting was complete, General Spek contacted Mijorn honestly expecting an order to eliminate the species. Instead, he and his crew received a command to cease any further engagement and turn themselves in for dereliction of duty.

Their stealth ships untraceable and near impossible to capture, Odian and his fleet did not oblige. Meanwhile, the GSA destroyed any remaining Saaryki ships, stripped the planet of space technology, and condemned them to three-hundred turns without aid.

Odian reviled the pathetic half-measure. His family was only one among billions of GSA killed by a species that was being coddled rather than neutered.

Broadcasting to the full Council, he screamed. "WHAT MESSAGE DOES THIS SEND TO FUTURE WORLDS!? Saaryki should be cleansed of its

---

Fike
Conversion: 1 Fike = 1 Week

Valnur
Odian Spek's personal warcraft. She is a Vitidor Class Stealth Fighter, extremely fast and maneuverable which can carry four crew but are usually solo operated. It can be piloted via neural interface, is equipped with a reinforced hull with kinetic absorption weave inner layers, cloaking, sensor jammers, is Patch 5 capable, and has a negligible flowspace signature even at Patch 3. It is also equipped with railguns, laser cannons, and rainstar missiles.

inhabitants and divided among the survivors of their crimes!"

The broad-channel plea advocating genocide was officially dismissed as the ravings of a madman. Discredited, he was again ordered to surrender. Nevertheless, many felt, secretly, as he did. It was easy to find those capable of building a bioweapon of their own. The timing was perfect. Odian ordered the strike as the Saaryki government agreed to the GSA sanctions. Within ten rotations, all eleven billion were dead.

As news of his bold action spread, it earned accolades in some corners, while the Council condemned him to death. Denying them the option of dealing with him quietly, he turned himself in for a public trial.

His presence on all media, coupled with an implanted failsafe, provided for his safety during the trial. Should the Investigation Department "tamper" with him while he was in custody, hundreds of highly classified Vdub mission files would appear on every comm channel throughout the worlds.

Odian was confident his very presence as head of the Vdubs would prove the GSA's darker tactics and create a massive disruption that would force change. Disappointingly, the trial quickly shifted focus from the Saaryki to the Voidwhisperers. He refused to name allies or explain how he'd mastered the supposedly impossible art of *phasing*.

When he was legally sentenced to death, he rebuked the decision and instead proclaimed his intention to fulfill his vision. In truth, he felt a failure. His family was avenged, yes, but he'd made the world no better.

GSA Security was sure even the Voidwhisperers couldn't reach him in the maximum security prison a full rudon beneath Mijorn. They were wrong. When the **Darkness Matters** came for their leader, pandemonium ensued. Shadows moving with purpose eluded all, and after the surveillance systems rebooted post EMP, there were 191 dead guards, 3 destroyed ships, 4 decoy detonations, and 1 empty cell.

Phasing
When a Voidwhisperer moves between the control of their GSA hardware and their own will, allowing them to use the neural implants to secretly communicate their thoughts and needs. Odian Spek had the mental will to overcome his control and stubbornly resisted revealing it to the GSA. This is how the Darkness Matters were able to defect. The GSA Dept. of Military has yet to reverse engineer how Odian and the Darkness Matters were able to do this.

Darkness Matters
Was the most decorated Voidwhisperers squad that served the GSA under the direct command of General Odian Spek. They were the top elite killsquad for the Security Council until they defected to fight in the Saaryki War. They fought to reclaim Valkürin, then continued to attack the Saaryki against orders. Eventually, they unleashed a genocidal bioweapon on the Saaryki when the GSA would not kill them. They sprung Odian from GSA custody, disappeared, and later became the first Creators of Space.

Odian ordered his Voidwhisperers to go dark, disperse, and avoid the central Sectors. Satisfied as he was to be free, Odian felt lost until he found XXX.

It was all over two-hundred turns since he left the GSA, but the pain of losing his family was still a fresh wound—partly because only twenty turns had passed for him on the Threshold, mostly because the pain defined Odian and his cause.

"VIRGL, please decrypt all stored electromagnetic signals collected from the Nova System and sort them by your usual hierarchy protocols. Begin linguistic and mathematical translations and bring up pertinent planetary ecological information."

Odian's words sounded like fate's hand.

The Nexus brightened the disc hologram replaced by swirling code. A giant replica of Nova was built before their eyes: wind currents, magnetic fields, and mapping patterns swirling across its surface. Descriptions and demographics appeared beside population centers. Temperature readings, ozone damage, and pollution maps overlaid the oblate spheroid. All of Nova's data laid bare.

Diiusk spoke first. "VIRGL, ecological status?"

"Planet is experiencing a severe artificial temperature rise due to a feedback loop that has progressed beyond the native species' ability to reverse it. Atmospheric pollution is significant. Unacceptable toxin levels pervade all known regional ecosystems."

"They're killing Nova and themselves." Maroona's words echoed in Odian's head. *"Our informant indicated nuclear exchanges had occurred. VIRGL, please confirm."*

The planet's surface shifted—clouds and pollution replaced by the trajectories of atomic missiles and the resulting contamination zones.

Saruk, one of the few members left from Odian's first Vdub squad, spoke up. "Nuclear weapons used in two wars and they survived both occasions. Perhaps this indicates more a propensity for survival and change than we thought?"

Maroona tsked. "Doubt it, brother. VIRGL, sort and play planetary history condensed for reasonable observation."

"I assure you, this civilization is easily brief enough for full observation."

Images came and went; pictograms and photographs of empires, cities, people, armies, wars, triumphs, sports, countries, families, scientific achievements, animals, plants, and art... All of humanity's proudest moments and its most regrettable failures.

Still, the beauty, joy, justice, peace, and love swelled their river with emotion. But there was also so much suffering inflicted so often, so long, in ages when clearly the species should have known better. They had to stop.

Odian winced. "VIRGL, enough, please."

The history froze on a final two images; a woman shielding her child from a nuclear blast at Jerusalem's obliteration and a humpback whale being butchered on a ship deck.

Diiusk's renewed rage forced Odian to dampen their bond. "Creators, I do believe we've now seen enough to vote. Who agrees we should bring the justice of the Creators to the humans?"

"Aye!"

And then silence—only VIRGL's processors hummed in the background.

There were many, enough to seal Earth's fate, but there was also hesitation. *Through the river*, he asked, *"Saruk, what gives you pause?"*

"Since this second nuclear exchange, they've expressed an increased understanding of their ecological impact, while their spacefaring technology is still far too primitive to be any threat for hundreds of turns."

"That's where you're wrong, RuCreator Saruk." He took their conversation to the spoken word. "Creators, we lost twenty-four Machines. A steep price, but thanks to that sacrifice, we now know that the humans possess antimatter. Valera's debrief, confirmed by her ship's data recorders, indicate the heist at Nova forced the GSA to activate a planetary failsafe."

A soft "lunatics" could be heard under his breath. Newcomers didn't know if he was talking about the humans or the GSA. Any Creator who lived through the Loronzon Incident, though, knew he meant the GSA.

"If I may," VIRGL said, "All organics require self-sustaining ecosystems. Without terraforming capabilities, allowing the humans to destroy this world would be unethical."

Odian grimly smiled. "Satisfied, Saruk?"

Saruk folded his wings and nodded. "Yes, NüCreator Spek. Clearly, the humans must be ended for the sake of Nova and the galaxy."

Surprisingly, VIRGL interrupted again. "I have just received a mission update from a deep asset. It states: *We have their attention.*"

Thoughts flowed through the stream. Old questions, thought answered, resurfaced: What if Nova was fortified? Or a trap? How many resources were being deployed? What were the dangers to their spy networks, research facilities, outposts, drop points, weapons caches, and hidden fleets? Would T-Class quarantine protocols change?

It was terrifying and wonderful. Living inside the Threshold, they could watch the consequences unfold in prikes instead of fikes.

Carefully floating closer, balancing thrusters on four of six limbs, RuCreator Arakron, an **Osanii**, vocalized a concern. He noticed Odian's continuing silence. "NüCreator...?"

He thought rather than spoke his response. "Time to ask our new allies for assistance." Switching again to speech, he said, "We'll finish what we started on our terms. For now, let's get a few operatives down to Nova while the rest of us prepare. Arakron, setup bioweapon creation. Cross-check the results with VIRGL to ensure we don't take out any other species by accident. Diiusk, draft an eco-recovery plan. Saruk, head up secondary research. If you think they have a worthy reason to live, I want it up for review. And Maroona? Find out what our newfound fame in the GSA affords us."

Osanii
Which translates as "of one tree" from Osanii to Drotean, is a sentient, plantlike species from the planet Osanix. They grow from buds on giant trees, breathe carbon dioxide, use photosynthesis, have a 0.1 tradon diameter body, and 7 stiff, leaflike appendages shaped like fronds with serrated edges, that are .4 to .55 tradons long, and .17 tradons wide. They are naturally telepathic and require tech to convert their thoughts to auditory responses and vice versa. They are peaceful to their own kind but are usually reclusive due to their significant communication barrier with other species. Many are unsettled by Osanii. They have no head, ears, mouth, or eyes. They use their leaves to create light-maps so they can "see." They do not antagonize but are quick to show strength if provoked. They walk and run on 4 leaves, stand on three, can glide by spinning, and are deadly warriors in zero g. These damaged leaves can be dropped and regrown. They were aware of alien life from early on because their leaves picked up signals, thus they are one of the few species offered First Contact despite being non-spacefaring.

Affirmation pulsed through the Nexus. "Then, we are in agreement."

He plucked the golden disc from the air. It would remain in his quarters until the Humans were a memory.

Raising his other hand, he clenched it into a fist. Voyager 2's journey between stars ended with a horrible, metallic squelch that left only a pile of scrap.

A sinister grin consumed Odian's stoic face. "Let us proceed."

CHAPTER 19

IN THE SHADOWS

A cold wind blew down the western slopes, funnelling along jagged mountain ridges, swaying the tall pine boughs, and whipping between the buildings of the Kepler Institute. The campus green, so vibrant and noisy the rest of the year, was barren, save for a shivering Isaac.

Pulling down the flaps of his winter hat, Isaac hurried across the brown grass closing his eyes as he moved. He was tired—still jet-lagged despite having returned from O.L two days ago. The weather was a blessing, though, enough to quell the hurricane of thoughts battering his mind. Unlike the fevered dreams of distant places, this made him feel fragmented, anxious, distant, as bleak as his surroundings.

His stomach rumbled over the wind. He'd left the library to pick up the nutrition pack in his room. He found the need to eat such a thing absurd. Given the fantastic dining hall a stone's-throw away, retrieving a meal replacement half the campus away was blasphemous. He only opted for the trek because everyone from enemies to friends had gone passive aggressive.

The fifteen months since the meeting in Professor Hunt's office felt like an eternity. Much as he knew hiding something of the Nomad's magnitude wouldn't be easy, he didn't think it would be like this.

At first, he'd overhear things like, "There goes Hubert, jetting off to O.L. and who knows where else, helping save the world."

Then, after Madeline Good's campaign against his father began, and he was allowed to miss some key exams, and he won the Explorer's Cup, the narrative changed. His fellow students grew more annoyed than envious, unaware his work really could save humanity.

The moved from cold earth to paved stone jostled his pocketed cryptocube. It contained all his Nomad, work and he kept it with him at all times. Having gone to bat against Angelika on his behalf, Professor Hunt made the need for extreme security crystal clear. He couldn't leave it in a dorm room safe or even the deepest depths of his lab's protective rooms.

In fact, it had been taken once. Shortly after he won the Explorer's Cup, someone piggybacked a touch-download virus onto Chelsea's tablet. It auto-uploaded, disabling their house's security measures. When he and his housemates returned, several projects were gone as well as the cube.

Breaking decades of precedent, Professor Hunt called a full-school meeting and suggested, with deadly calm, that unless the removed items were returned within one day, he might take a personal interest. No one knew what that meant, but no one wanted to find out. Unless there was physical injury or the loss of homework, faculty never intervened in student espionage and sabotage.

Looking back, that was the last straw... the moment attitudes toward Isaac dove off a cliff. Overnight he became a pariah. Even Marcus and Chelsea stayed away. Given the choice, he'd have preferred to stay at O.L. far from the treacherous swamp Kepler had become. But his mother, his father, and even Professor Hunt were adamant his schooling continue.

His father in particular felt that maintaining human connections was crucial, even for an engineer as gifted as Isaac. All well and good for the K.I.N.G. but Isaac thought the viewpoint naive or, perhaps forgetful of youth's brutality. There were students, boys and girls, more than willing to steal his cube for the simple pleasure of inconveniencing him.

Lydia became his sole peer support. Now waiting in the library to study with him for their upcoming vibrations midterm, she even offered to walk with him, but he didn't want her to suffer for being seen together.

Gut rumbling, he plodded past the mobius strip-inspired group dormitory and into the trees. It was incredible how the beehive shaped building he'd called home for almost two full cycles had become so foreboding.

He practically ran in. Marcus and Chelsea sat on the couch working on heat-transfer homework. Nothra, Chelsea's drone, swooped about menacingly. Without acknowledging them, he activated the maglev rings and jumped to his room.

The tension was palpable, bleeding into uncomfortable, for eight months now. He was so aggravated, he input the wrong door code three times forcing him to wait for the reset. The pack finally in hand, he leapt back down, this time delaying activating the rings. He plummeted alarmingly before slowing at the last second and landing on his hands and knees.

He was two steps from the door before remembering he had the same heat transfer assignment due tomorrow. On top of his makeup work, that would make sleeping at all tonight highly unlikely. Maybe he'd finally crack and barter for a stim pack. Then again, he doubted anyone would trade with him.

Desperate for an alternative, he spoke to his suitemates. "Marcus, Chelsea? Could you spot me the Heat Transfer assignment? I'll trade you the next two weeks of vibration proofs."

Marcus looked to Chelsea. "Chelsea, did you hear something?"

She joined in the juvenile taunt. "Why, yes. It sounded like Isaac asking for help."

Marcus tsked. "That can't be right. Someone who can balance school, winning the Explorer's Cup, and working at Outer Limits couldn't possibly need our help."

"What a shock," Isaac said. "I knew trying again would be a waste of time."

Disgusted, he headed to the door.

Marcus called after him. "Hey, Hubert! Remember all those times we defended you against Naomi and the others? And I was so sure they were the privileged assholes."

Isaac quickened his pace. Marcus continued. "But now, I realize they were right. You do hog all the glory, just like your father."

Tired, sad, overworked, and most of all, lonely, Isaac stopped dead. He weighed how much taking the bait would be worth. Maybe if he was rested, or older or wiser, he would have kept walking, but he was none of that.

Smiling grimly, he motioned open the door with his nano palmer. The instant it did, a shiny, orange blur burst through. It whisked over his shoulder and, snarling, slammed into Nothra.

Before Chelsea or Marcus could react, Isaac grabbed his discblade so hard he cut his own palm with it and furiously threw it across the room. He imparted his weapon with all of his anger and frustration, slamming the blade's edge deep into the table between his two roommates, shattering Chelsea's tablet, and splitting the table on which it sat. Both yelped and pulled away, shielding their faces from the shower of splintered wood.

Chelsea screamed. "ARE YOU OUT OF YOUR FRIGGIN MIND!? MY TABLET..."

Isaac reached them in three bounds and thrust his cryptocube in their faces. "OH, YOU MEAN THE STUPID, GOD DAMN TABLET THEY USED TO STEAL THIS?!"

Both wincing from the sound, he lowered his voice slightly. "Do you think I wanted to ask help from a teacher, for anything? That I had no clue it would make everyone despise me? But, I did it anyway because this cube holds my share of humanity's most important endeavor. I am so, so very sorry my special treatment made my friendship inconvenient. I'm also sorry you can't see past this pubescent idiocy, but I've been working nonstop for fifteen months with zero margin for error, barely sleeping, while trying to get a week's worth of schoolwork done on a two-hour plane ride. And when I'm here? All I can look forward to is everyone trying to take a piss at me. A glory-hog, am I? Jeez... wow, doesn't that all sound so magnificently glorious?"

Pinned to the wall by Isaac's drone, Albus, Nothra trilled painfully.

Marcus and Chelsea glared back with fury and fear. Their discblades were in easy reach. With Isaac's buried deep into the quartzite flagstone floor, he couldn't fight back—yet neither made a move to retaliate.

Had he given them pause? Maybe there's hope?

The room his stage, there was so much he wanted to vent about it clogged his brain and made him hyperventilate. "All I was asking was a little help from my friends. For one assignment, I offered to trade the next two weeks of homework. But no, you had to spit in my face and make it about my dad. Right now, he's doing more for everyone on this planet than all of your family members ever did, combined."

There was not a shred of regret in his words.

Chelsea found her voice. "Oh, there it is, Tycho. You and your father are God's gift to Kepler, to engineering, to the scientific community, and the whole world. You get whisked away on a project that's sooo important, you can't possibly tell your friends, so important that when your stuff gets stolen, we pay the price."

Isaac threw his hands up. "Jesus Christ, why do I keep having to explain this? It's top secret! If I told you, they'd throw all of us in prison! Two more months, that's all, and the project goes public. It'll all be over."

Marcus still seethed. "If you're so damn busy, why couldn't you stay out and let someone else win the Explorer's Cup! One of US, for instance. Don't tell me that's not about arrogance."

Winning the cup had accelerated Isaac's social demise, but the idea, that with the grant money his space elevator could be realized hundreds of years sooner, blinded him to the inevitable backlash. Already an "intern" at O.L., already receiving special treatment, he could finally see how trying for the cup could be considered redundant, offensive, and greedy.

Marcus, in particular, felt blindsided, especially since Isaac encouraged him to submit his nano skeleton key prototype. It was pragmatic but no space elevator. Still, Isaac figured W.C. espionage reps would take interest. Marcus must have thought he was only going through the motions. When Isaac won, his friends felt deceived. Even so, and there was no way to say it without seeming arrogant. Out of all Kepler's students, he was best suited to maximize the resources.

"What do you want from me? I won, fair and square. You want me to apologize for trying? Has there been anything I've done the last six years that would make you think I'd ever hold back? We didn't become friends because we parse words."

Chelsea replied coldly. "We were friends because we had each other's backs." Her use of the past tense felt like a trapdoor opening at his feet.

Lydia has my back. She understands. Why can't they?

"It was just the dumb Cup... it's done. At Kepler, it's life itself, but in five years? It'll be inconsequential compared to what job you get or company you create. Can't we move on?"

Marcus echoed Chelsea's finality. "No, Tycho. It's not just the Cup. It's everything."

The argument was as pointless as it was redundant. They'd had the same talk countless times: spinning the same wheels, getting to same nowhere. They couldn't see past their perceived betrayal. Or maybe Isaac couldn't see past his own pride. Either way, for the first time, he wished school was over.

"Get out before we report this," Chelsea demanded.

Albus screeched and released Nothra, unharmed. The tiny regal monster flew back to his master's shoulder, ready to protect him.

Isaac gave them a burning stare and departed. When the doors opened again, the cold wind brought flakes of snow inside. A storm was coming. He stood there, letting the thickening whiteness howl around him, then walked out into the night.

As the day drew on, the vast grounds remained peaceful; their purpose as a haven for gifted students belied by a natural, almost wild, appearance.

But there were always those ready to disrupt the status quo. A shadow had crept closer to the dorms, icy voices apparently speaking to the deep, deserted forests.

"They're fighting again, sir."

"Excellent. Ready *Ghost Squad Alpha*."

Squad leader Captain Kudimo complied. He had his orders: single target termination, no trace of the body—the sort of mission they'd completed dozens of times. Gone were the days of nocturnal stealth choppers. In the aftermath of an irradiated ionosphere, RT satellite surveillance was a shadow of its former glory.

Ghost Squad Alpha consisted of five brutal assassins, more myth than mortal, who could destabilize any regime on the planet.

Intel indicated the children at this school could create all manner of surveillance devices, so they arrived at five separate locations, hundreds of miles away. From there they'd continued on foot, rendezvousing at a waterfall, four klicks north of Paonia before taking position here. They'd all spent the three hours since dusk up in these trees prepared to pounce. Fortuitously, the incoming blizzard further masked their already wraithlike presence.

Kudimo could feel his fellow Ghosts waiting for their target to move again. He knew the target but not the crime. From the photo, he was less than eighteen. He couldn't imagine what harm a child could cause, but it wasn't his place or his way to challenge orders. If the *Peacekeeper Division* marked him for elimination, he was a threat.

Apparently, a very high-level threat. The mission was AAC (At All Costs), extremely rare, except in the case of insurrection leaders. They'd even given Kudimo

---

Ghost Squad Alpha
An unofficially recognized five person assassination squad for the World Council Peacekeeper Division. They can destabilize a regime on their own and are supposedly used to eliminate threats to the cohesion of the world nation.

Peacekeeper Division
The military branch of the World Council. They are responsible for maintaining order across Earth and are composed of military volunteers from every former nation.

access to a reestablished GPS uplink from the fifth-generation constellation. Given the breadth of data they'd received, it didn't require a deep analysis to surmise that someone was helping them from inside the school.

He remembered his time as a reformed cadet in the First Division of Triumphant Resolution. There were two universal rules; don't mess with someone else's stuff, and stay in your lane. Plain and simple. If this dragon drone was a protector, like the BoDyn Wolves in the Third War, the target would not let those he did not trust handle it.

Then again, he shouldn't have trusted anyone.

A woman with Australian Aboriginal features dropped silently from a ponderosa branch above him. She flashed some complex *Milspeak*—a combination of English, Arabic, and Chinese—military sign language. Since it involved the entire body, those with decent visual acuity were capable of signaling from over two klicks away.

As her body contorted into patterns, Kudimo read the message. *"Yes, well, that was his undoing."*

Kudimo flashed a response. *"You are creeping me out with your intuition training, Maria."*

They'd spent eight years on missions across the globe eliminating threats to the glorious world peace achieved by the W.C. Without having to look, he knew she was grinning. He was staring into the dark, looking at the horizon, thinking ten times as far when an onslaught of Milspeak commenced.

"What is bothering you?" Maria shot to Kudimo.

"I've had a lot of time to think up here." He replied.

"You're doing that, now? She looked amused."

He shrugged her off. *"It seems too easy. Just kill the kid and take the body? When was the last time we got an assignment this straightforward?"*

She shook her head. *"You actually think killing a boy is straightforward?"*

Milspeak
The universal W.C. Peacekeeper communication, merged from the sign language of Morse code, English, Mandarin, and Arabic. The World Council needed to overcome initial language barriers between the merging armies of the world. Leveraging the newly-discovered farsights, deaf at birth humans with mind-boggling visual acuity, the Peacekeepers developed a new, silent communication system.

"Comparatively, yes. The only complicated part is waiting until he's alone. God damn kids band together, and we have strict orders: no collateral."

The wind carried the chuckling of girls. The squad froze. The sources were walking the path below blithely unaware of the danger perched above their heads.

Kudimo looked to Parker, their tech expert, who signaled. *"No drones. All clear."*

Their jamming tech could easily handle the toys these kids built, but that didn't preclude their accidental discovery by a drone pet innocuously flying about. Each team member had a small EMP grenade just in case, but that would almost certainly blow their cover.

They held their breaths until the students passed, and the silence resumed.

Maria jabbed more Milspeak. *"The target's probably pretty lonely. After all, we all know how shitty it is to be at the top always threatened by challengers."*

"If you are referring to me winning the sharpshooting triathlon every year at the academy, you can shove it." Kudimo responded.

Maria's torso was forming a response when their transponders vibrated. The target was on the move heading their way. Her head snapped up looking over Kudimo's shoulder. Following her gaze, he peered beyond hundreds of crisscrossing branches to a dim lamppost that illuminated an otherwise dark pathway through the enshrouding trees.

Noiselessly, he adjusted his shouldered rifle and activated the infrared overlay on his HUD. The pines became dreamlike silhouettes allowing him to occasionally make-out the warm glow of movement. It was their target, but they couldn't yet tell if he was alone.

Maria withdrew a spotter's scope and set it up. A strong gust had them both swaying. *"Damn this wind is high."* he gestured.

Maria gave him a playful smack on the shoulder. *"Oh please, is that an excuse? It's not even four-hundred meters. You hit that Saudi prince between the eyes at a full klick."*

Kudimo held up his hand for silence. Maria's demeanor shifted into kill mode.

Looking back through her scope, she froze a moment before signaling.

"Target is all alone."

Through his sniper scope, Kudimo watched a lone figure walking along the path. A tiny shimmering something was perched on its shoulder. Briefly illuminated as it passed the lamppost, it was revealed as a shiny, miniature dragon.

Kudimo signaled the team. *"Tracker confirmed. Target confirmed."*

Smith, Parker, and Valdok dropped to the forest floor, ready to retrieve the body and remove any evidence. The boy moved into a clearing away from the light.

"Almost there."

To ready himself, Kudimo sought to void his mind—clearing his thoughts, dropping his heart rate. Then he rested the crosshairs on the target's center-mass.

"Four-hundred eight meters and closing." Maria murmured.

Kudimo whispered into his comm. *"Confirm position."*

Three voices quietly answered in near unison. *"Confirmed. Standing by."*

"Take the shot." Maria said.

Kudimo placed his finger on the trigger.

Far below, hidden behind a fallen ponderosa trunk, Parker was facing the trail—the boy ten meters away, and closing fast. He heard Kudimo through his earpiece.

"Taking the shot."

Across the open space, he could make out Smith's shadow molding almost seamlessly with a twisted tree root. A voyeur of the moment where life so swiftly, yet gracefully departs, Parker waited for the bullet's zip and the boy to fall.

But nothing happened.

Oblivious, the target passed within arm's reach. Parker glanced to Smith who shifted enough to Milspeak, *"WTF?"*

Parker had no answer.

The wind sufficiently muffling, he whispered into his comm. *"Maria? Do you copy?"* Silence. Something's wrong.

Normally they'd abort, but this was AAC. So, he gave the sniper duo the time it took a snowflake to fall from eye level to the ground, then unpinned his EMP grenade to take care of the dragon. For the boy, he drew a long blade dulled with charcoal.

He glanced once more to Smith, just in time to see him tumble into shadow. Before he could process what he just saw, something punched through his lung, shattered a rib, and burst out the other side. The bullet having travelled faster than sound, it was only then he heard the familiar:

Zip.

Though he couldn't scream anyway, a cold gloved hand descended to cover his mouth as he, too, fell backwards, falling, seemingly forever into cradling arms. His final synaptic connections were spent pondering what had happened before the darkness took him forever.

Isaac thought he heard a twig snap, but chalked it up to his weary mind. He walked on taking large chunks from the nutrition bar. At the end of the trail, he was surprised to see Professor Hunt. He was in a dark overcoat, facing the wind, peering skyward at the billowing, flowing clouds.

Swirling flakes surrounded him, seeming to merge him with the atmosphere's violence. "Lovely night, isn't it, Isaac?"

"Invigorating, Professor, but a storm is coming."

William smiled knowingly. "No. I think this one is going to stay away." He gestured to the pyramidal library behind him. "Let me walk you."

Side by side, they moved on. "Isaac, I know it's been hard that you've felt alone at Kepler these past months."

The directness caught Isaac off guard. He was used to the professor's seeming omniscience but uncomfortable admitting to the feelings.

Professor Hunt put a hand on his shoulder and gave him a paternal look, not unlike his father's. "There will always be those who misinterpret our intent or can't accept the success of others, but remember, this trying beginning can lead to a boundless future. Isaac, we're close to launch, and you have been crucial."

As Isaac stood there stunned; his teacher blithely returned to his cheery self. "Better get in there. Lydia's been waiting a while."

- - -

Despite the biting cold, William Hunt strolled casually all the way to the mathematics building then slowly up each student-cursed step. He opened the door to his magnificent office and shook the tiny snowflakes from his dark overcoat before placing it on the rack.

Taking his NanoCube from his pocket, he touched it to a tablet. It glowed to life, its screen reading, MALWARE SCAN COMPLETE, SYSTEM CLEAN.

"Open a secure channel," William commanded.

FaceTime screens popped up, one for Angelika, another for Marcus Medneon.

"Is it done?" Angelika asked.

William poured himself a glass of brandy. "It is. Isaac's fine and unaware. I assume your shadow team eliminated the ghost squad, Marcus?"

"Yes, we have confirmation that the entire team is dead. Thanks for the call."

"Glad we're all on the same page again." William said.

"In times like these, petty differences are beneath us," Angelika said. "Thank you."

"No, thank you for keeping those shadow forces here just in case Isaac was targeted. Madeline Good was behind the attack, I assume?"

Her face soured. "Undoubtedly, but she's too good to leave a trail. Pursuing her now would only derail Bernard. He doesn't need the distraction of his child nearly being killed. If it is her, she's gotten too bold. We have to make sure she doesn't try again."

Marcus calmly agreed.

William looked at their feeds. "And I'll do my part watching over him here. They'll both be protected at all costs, as they say."

The screens flashed off. William sat clutching his brandy, gazing at his NanoCube, admiring the circuit pathways across its surface. It was astounding, he thought, how much effort it took to keep humanity from sabotaging its own dreams.

--- - ---

After picking all the splinters from the couch, Marcus and Chelsea decided to give up on schoolwork for the night and collapsed on the cushions.

"What do you want to watch?" Marcus asked.

"Anything," Chelsea replied.

He sent his streaming service collection to their big screen. They'd barely settled on an old episode of David Attenborough's Planet Earth III, when a notification popped up.

Chelsea groaned. "Jeez, Marcus, update your notification blocker."

"It's updated, girl, I assure you. My system detects any rapidly accelerating web trends, particularly space news. Looks like there's a higher-than-usual level of campus network activity. Must be something important."

Chelsea opened a news website and was instantly drawn to the words "Hubert" and "Live." Clicking the link, they were greeted with a view of a W.C. podium, where Angelika On, CEO of Outer Limits, stood side by side with Bernard Hubert.

A massive covered structure stood behind them. Angelika, a fierce looking predator, stood with a man that looked less like a dad of their renounced friend and more like a lion looking for its prey.

"Outer Limits," she said, "is excited to reveal the details of its previously unspecified partnership with CORE."

With that, the structure was unveiled. It was surreal, something out of *Star Wars*.

"A five-year, interplanetary mission to explore the Kuiper Belt will launch in the coming months. Ph.D. Bernard Hubert, founder of CORE, and a dear, lifelong friend, will captain the mission along with the following crew:

William Hunt, Mathematics

Godric Adams, Interplanetary Relations

Aubree Gates, History

Odin Tiberius King, Botany

Ilya O'Connell, Mechanical Engineering

Galena Hunter, Medical

Ava Auburn, Biology

Lily Parsons, Particle Physics

Conrad Roy, Tactical

Medina Karimov, Chemistry

Nawal Hawass, Linguistics

Marcus and Chelsea stared at the screen, then at each other. Neither would remember who said it before the shame came rushing through their veins. "Isaac built that."

"At Outer Limits and throughout the W.C.," Angelika On said, "we look forward to a bright future of exploration and advancement."

She ended with a wildly uncharacteristic, wildly bright grin. She was still wearing it when she turned to Bernard and nearly collided with his. Six years of pain and doubt had been washed away by the pursuit of science, renewed trust, and the memory of a dear friend.

Bernard looked out across the ocean of faces, the abyss of rising arms and shouts, and said, "We'll be happy to take your questions, now."

THE VOYAGE OF THE NOMAD

MEET THE 9 SECTOR HOME WORLDS OF THE

GALACTIC STAR ALLIANCE

MIJORN

RADIUS = 1.3X EARTH RADIUS
MASS = 2.10X EARTH MASS
SURFACE GRAVITY = 1.25G
MOONS: 3 SMALL (METALLIC)

A verdant world covered in 50% water oceans and 50% land, dominated by very high mountains, fjords, and plateaus. Its plants are mostly green, it has a purple tinged atmosphere, and it orbits a yellow G class star. There is a massive alien built ring that encircles the planet, containing its own habitable inner surface.

AZOELEO

RADIUS = .99X EARTH RADIUS
MASS = .96X EARTH MASS
SURFACE GRAVITY = .98G
MOONS: 2 SMALL (ROCKY)

The middle of five rocky planets orbiting a M class red dwarf star. It is a very old world, formed at least 10 billions turns ago. The surface oceans evaporated off long ago, and there is little tectonic activity. The perfect gravitational resonance between the five planets maintains Azoeleo's rotation, despite it being well within the tidal locked zone of its star. There are vast, arid deserts circumferencing the equator, giving way to plains and then polar jungles, fed by subterranean lakes.

VALKÜRIN

RADIUS = .90X EARTH RADIUS
MASS = .598X EARTH MASS
SURFACE GRAVITY = .74G
MOONS: 1 LARGE (HIGH ALBEDO)

A lush, temperate planet orbiting a binary star system with a rare F class yellow-white dwarf star and a M class red dwarf star. Due to its relatively young age, the planet's large moon still orbits closely, producing large tides. With green oceans full of phytoplankton like microbes, the planet has a powerful ozone layer that shields it from the high UV radiation emitted by its larger sun. There are five continents covered in rich forests and grasslands, and the poles have small icecaps. The Valkon worked tirelessly to repair the biosphere after it was significantly damaged by nuclear bombardment in the Saaryki War.

 # EPIKO

RADIUS = .7X EARTH RADIUS
MASS = .26X EARTH MASS
SURFACE GRAVITY = .54G
MOONS: 1 LARGE (ROCKY)

A small planet blanketed by a thick,
humid atmosphere. The surface consists
of steep mountain ridges, divided by
planet spanning rivers, and no oceans.
Giant swamps and marshes nestle
between peaks. The Rakilla chose it as
their new homeworld, during the Reclamation Era, because it's low gravity and
dense air support their flight capability.

 # YALLAWEH

RADIUS = .93X EARTH RADIUS
MASS = .726X EARTH MASS
SURFACE GRAVITY = .84G
MOONS: 1 MEDIUM (ICY)

A water world. The entire surface is covered in deep, azure oceans, full of
marine life. Underwater mountains and
volcanoes provide oases, but most creatures exist in or near giant, floating coral
like biomass continents constructed from
millions of turns of skeletons, shells, and
carapaces. Because there are no continents to dissipate them, hypercanes fre-
quently form, feeding on the warm equa-
torial oceans. These storms can cover
over 20% of the planet. Similarly, the
uninhibited tides are enormous, gradually
building over the eons. Its first underwater
civilizations were founded on the sunken
ruins of a Builder space elevator that collapsed before recorded time.

 # ANDUUZ

RADIUS = 1.6X EARTH RADIUS
MASS = 4.59X EARTH MASS
SURFACE GRAVITY = 1.80G
MOONS: 1 SMALL (ICY)

A large, cold planet where life has
adapted to harsh conditions. Due to its
79 degree axis tilt, coupled with its wide
orbit, the planet experiences extreme
seasons that last over an Earth year.
Granite continents continuously support
little life except near the equator, and
much of the surface is rocky tundra.
Giant ice caps form on the poles in the
winter, and give way to searing polar
deserts in the summer. Most species
on this world are migratory, with the notable exception of the Anduuzil.

 # NERUDA 8

RADIUS = 1.10X EARTH RADIUS
MASS = 1.34X EARTH MASS
SURFACE GRAVITY = 1.11G
MOONS: NONE

A nurturing, living world. Originally seeded with life from an impact on nearby Neruda 7, 99% of all Ulron are born here, requiring very specific environmental conditions to sustain their nascent forms. Most of the surface is covered in huge, continent size blue biomes that heal, shelter, provide food and longevity for its native species. These biomes also balance the surface temperature across the entire planet, and build a biodigital network. infrastructure is built high above the surface in raised platforms or floating cities to respect nature.

 # DRAGSA

RADIUS = .80X EARTH RADIUS
MASS = .51X EARTH MASS
SURFACE GRAVITY = .79G
MOONS: 1 MEDIUM (LOW ALBEDO)

A dry, rocky world with pockets of blue seas. It orbits a trinary star system, consisting of 2 orange K class stars and a neutron star. The neutron star went supernova 587 million turns ago, stripping Dragsa of most of its oceans, and seeding the planet with an enormous quantity of rare elements. The neutron star radiation contributed to the evolution of Dragsan Recall.

 # KRAMER DE LA KU

RADIUS = .90X EARTH RADIUS
MASS = .598X EARTH MASS
SURFACE GRAVITY = .74G
MOONS: 1 SMALL (METALLIC)

A terrestrial moon of the gas giant Ku. It possesses a small moon, made almost entirely of iron, which maintains Kramer de la Ku's rotation, and thus its magnetic field, which shields the world from the intense radiation of it's parent planet. It is covered in volcanic activity and lots of jungles and swamps. Kramer has a small, metallic looking moon of its own.

SYMBOLS OF THE ALLIANCE

 ANDUUZ

 GSA NON
BUILDER WORLD

 GSA

 AZOELEO

 EPIKO

 KRAMER DE LA KU

 DRAGSA

 DUMAR TAR'RAIN

 MIJORN

 NERUDA 8

 PRIMIDIOUS

 ULRONDA GATE

 VALKÜRIN

 WARPGATE
BUILDER WORLD

 YALLAWEH

 VIRGL AI

TIMELINE
GALACTIC

91-45 MILLION TURNS AGO
THE BUILDERS

The oldest known sentient race in the Karandu (Milky Way) Galaxy - they created the Warpgate System: An ancient advanced race invented a way to warp spacetime to move faster than light. However, for this warp technology to work it required machinery placed through space, like a railroad for the ship to travel upon. Automated sublight ships were sent throughout the galaxy laying the groundwork over half a million turns. Through this exploration, The Builders discovered many other planets with civilizations. When completed, The ljusgäv (path of light) spanned across the galaxy connecting every planet upon which intelligent life lived. An alliance of alien races ruled in peace. Once, this grand consortium of planets traded with each other, built monuments, created art, and disappeared. Their demise is unknown. There are no signs of war. It is suspected that the entire civilization suddenly decided to leave this galaxy for another.

45-20 MILLION TURNS AGO
THE FIRST DARK ERA

There is no known record of interplanetary communication during this time. The Dragsan, Anduuzil, Valkon, Fandaxians, Baleen, Metra, Rakilla, Ulron, and Droteans all evolve concurrently, all on planets with Warpgates in their star system.

Xaraka is destroyed by a black hole and becomes the remnant planet XXX, travelling through the galaxy.

20-19 MILLION TURNS AGO
THE DISCOVERY ERA

Sentient races expand slowly at sublight to adjacent systems. First Contact occurs occasionally. Civilizations are aware that the Builders came before them but are unable to manipulate their technology. This age abruptly ended when a new group of aliens called the Legkaart rose, invented space travel, and discovered the ljusgäv. Eventually they discover how to use the path of light and begin to explore the galaxy using the Builder Warpgates. Some planets they settle on and others they encounter intelligent races.

19-9 MILLION TURNS AGO
THE CLASSICAL GALACTIC ERA

The galaxy is reconnected via the Builder Warpgates. In time control of the Warppaths was key to control of the galaxy. Many empires rose and fell for the next several hundred thousand turns. Eventually, thousands of worlds join together in The Cooperative which existed peacefully for millions of turns. This included the Dragsan, Anduuzil, Valkon, Fandaxian, Baleen, Metra, Rakilla, Ulron, and Drotean. Technology was mighty, but FTL was dependent on technology that could not be replicated. In time sublight expansion could not keep up with population and The Cooperative rifted over fights for resources. A galaxy spanning war followed in which billions died. This era ended in an endgame device being activated that created a vast self replicating machine army that destroyed many civilizations near the center of the galaxy. Devouring entire planets, and using the Warppaths to move from place to place, it left one option. Sacrificing themselves, entire armies first destroyed some paths, trapping themselves and the robots in a certain portion of space. This bought time for the remaining worlds to band together to build The Wave. It was a pulse weapon that would travel through the galaxy, spread along the Warpgate paths destroying all the robots, and the Warppaths too. It was a pyrrhic victory. Technology across the center of the mapped galaxy was wiped out, frying out robots, ships, and entire planetary infrastructures to ensure no machines escaped. Almost all planets supporting complex life experienced a sudden and total loss of technology which wiped out the resources needed to maintain an operable space program.

TIMELINE
GALACTIC

9-8.6 MILLION TURNS AGO
THE SECOND DARK ERA

All of the major Warpgate hubs are destroyed, so use of the Ijusgäv is extremely limited and only in small jumps. Power drain from systemic system damage eventually takes all remaining gates down. Mass die off of 90% of sentient life: Trillions are stranded and any planets that were not destroyed by the machine army, were caught in The Wave, faced massive starvation, and being flung back to a pre-interstellar age. Planets that did survive with their civilizations intact usually had large agricultural aspects of their infrastructure. A great dying and wars on many worlds reduced countries to rubble, and natives huddled in the ruins of their once grand cities.

Outer sections of the Karandu galaxy survived through this twilight era. The outer rim maintained a loose contact, but that slowly degraded over time. Signals continue to be sent at lightspeed between worlds, and occasionally, subluminal ships do traverse between planetary systems of relatively close distance. One by one, planets retract from trade and consolidate themselves; some lose to infighting. Knowledge of the existence of other worlds is not lost, but the destruction of much of the trade eventually prompts some worlds to invade others. Without an overarching government, there is little that can be done if one group has military superiority. Communication between stellar clusters ceases. The end of this time period fades into a long dark period of each, individual world having to fend for itself.

8.5-8.2 MILLIONS TURNS AGO
THE RECLAMATION ERA

A nearby star to Dramur, a terraformed world, goes supernova. Forced to flee their planet, too far from another world, and with not enough time for generation ships to escape; the Dramurians discover flowspace. They arrive at Zesparana, having sent messages ahead of time, and asked for refuge in exchange for knowledge of the flowspace drive. With FTL, intelligent life spreads throughout the galaxy, finding thousands of old and new worlds and species, most outside of the Warpgate system.

8.2 MILLION TURNS AGO
FORMATION OF THE GSA

Nine planets' civilizations endure from the Classical Era; the Dragsan, Anduuzil, Valkon, Fandaxian, Baleen, Metra, Rakilla, Ulron, and Drotean. The Metra write the TAOTA "The Accords Of The Alliance" and propose a new galactic government. Together, the nine species ratify the TAOTA and form the GSA, the Galactic Star Alliance.

Sometime among the first turns of expansion and recruitment, there are several miscalculations by the Dept of First Contact, and aggressive species are given the tools to break free. These species are eliminated by the GSA, rather than have their credibility tarnished. The events are removed from all records, and any invaded planets are memory wiped by hard chemicals.

8.1-6.8 MILLION TURNS AGO

The GSA rapidly expands its memberships and establishes an interstellar infrastructure.

The Udari, a vastly intelligent silicon-based species, are discovered and quickly die from a disease contracted from GSA members.

4.5 MILLION TURNS AGO

The GSA passes 100,000 planetary members.

2.25 MILLION TURNS AGO

The GSA passes 400,000 planetary members.

.75 MILLION TURNS AGO

The GSA passes 570,000 planetary members.

380,000 TURNS AGO

The GSA meets and discovers the Kaleans.

367-330,000 TURNS AGO

The great Kalean galactic survey transpires.

300,000 TURNS AGO

The GSA amends the TAOTA to include Kalean safeguards.

113,000 TURNS AGO

The GSA reaches 595,000 planetary members and covers about 1/3 of the galaxy.

TIMELINE
EARTH HISTORY

2020
Donald Trump is re-elected.

2023
Iran renegs on the nuclear deal, the United States reinstates sanctions.

2024
The US lands a woman on the south pole of the Moon.

2025
China lands a crew of three on the Moon.

2030
UN Outer Space Resource Treaty is ratified by 135 nations, creating a framework for companies to "purchase" mining rites on celestial bodies. All purchases are evaluated by the UN.

2035
Savannah, GA is destroyed by category 5 Hurricane Tanya.

2038
Grayson Freedman (MIT undergrad), Candice Oliver (Harvard grad), and Aiden Alexander (Cal Tech post doc) found RNA Industries, with a focus on AI and advanced robotics.

2040
First time the term "Overheat Zones" is used, the populations of Phoenix and other southwest US cities begin to decline.

2041
The UN operated lunar base is established.

2042
Year round oil drilling begins in the Arctic Ocean.

2043
The founders of RNA Industries begin philanthropic work and found the first three SETI Schools (Scientific Education Technological Institutes); Kepler, Hubble, and Jefferson.

2044
California passes driverless car tax incentive bill - Introduced by Ron Wolfenstein of Plato's Inc.

2045
Rare earth metal shortages begin.

2047
B.E. yam crop is a carrier for a mutated GMO pathogen that wipes out staple crop harvests. 30 million people starve to death

2050
The first human colony is established on Mars.

2052
Iron Corp is founded.

China, India, US, and Russia begin exploratory lunar mining missions.

Xio Industries by Xio Ping Fu leases the Paracel Islands from China, Vietnam, and Taiwan.

2056
Chinese experimental antimatter drive fails, destroys the Paracel Islands and generates a tsunami that wipes out Hanoi, Manilla, and Hong Kong, 117 million confirmed dead, 93 million missing.

Construction of sea wall around New York City begins.

2057
First time the term "Overheat Zones" is used, the UN commissions World Council Safety Board.

2058
Japan begins human operated automobile phase out over the next five years.

2059
US bans production of new fossil fuel powered automobiles. (sales dropped 90% since 2050)

2060
Iron Corp. begins full scale mining operation on the moon.

2061
RNA AI used in Plato's Inc. recalled due to AI communication anomaly.
(One car told another other to save itself).

2062
Las Vegas suspends government services.

2063
Committee created by Outer Limits, Iron Corp, and RNA, funded by US government with unlimited resources, create first robot to pass a physical Turing Test.

2064
Quincy Adams elected 53rd President of the United States.

2066
Euro crashes, flu pandemic begins with 5% mortality rate, EU borders are closed due to overwhelming refugee crisis.

2067
Quincy Adams calls for World Council Peace Board to create unified Security Council (US, Russia, China, France, and UK) troop alliance to manage refugee crisis.

ABOUT THE ARTISTS

UTKU ÖZDEN
- Illustrator and Graphic Designer

Utku graduated from Bilkent University Department of Graphic Design and began working in the industry in 2006, where he designed logos, brochures, book covers, CD covers, and unique corporate identity, while specializing in character design and conceptual art development. Most recently, Uktu was the creative powerhouse of the wildly successful Kickstarter campaign for the game *Oathsworn: Into the Deepwood*, which surpassed its goal of 50,000 USD and reached 1.95 Million dollars. "Currently working on the *Beyond Kuiper* series with Matt and John has proven to be one of the most challenging and rewarding projects I've ever been a part of. The world isn't prepared for what we have in store for this series."

PETE "VOODOO BOWNZ" RUSSO
- Creative Director, Designer & Visual Artist

Pete, who is known by the artistic pseudonym "Voodoo Bownz," is a brand strategist and multi-disciplinary visual artist in the form of design, illustration, animation, typography, and more. He is Co-Founder and Executive Creative Director of Herø Projects and the Founder and Executive Creative Director of Skeleton Agency. A graduate of New York's School of Visual Arts, Pete quickly built a name for himself within the music industry by launching his business as a freshman and relentlessly attending shows to hand out business cards to the artists that performed. His perserverance has led him to create for prominent entities including IBM, (RED), MTV, Tony Awards, AT&T, NCAA, Bad Bunny, A$AP Ferg, Monster Energy, Deadmau5, Iggy Pop, John Oates of Hall & Oates, Mike Shinoda of Linkin Park, Rivers Cuomo of Weezer, and speak on his experience to audiences at SXSW, Pace University, and NYU.

STEFAN PETRUCHA
- Editor

Stefan Petrucha has written over 20 novels and hundreds of graphic novels for adults, young adults and tweens. His work has sold over a million copies worldwide. He also teaches online classes through the University of Massachusetts and proudly works as a Writer/Editor for Center for Responsive Classrooms in Turner Falls, MA.

Born in the Bronx, he spent his formative years moving between the big city and the suburbs, both of which made him prefer escapism. A fan of comic books, science fiction and horror since learning to read, in high school and college he added a love for all sorts of literary work, eventually learning that the very best fiction always brings you back to reality, so, really, there's no way out. Much more on him and whatever madness he's currently perpetrating can be had at www.petrucha.com.

TIMELINE
EARTH HISTORY

2068
Lt. Conrad Roy deploys on the 8th Mars Colonization Mission.

2069
Russian spies assassinate UK Prime Minister. UK calls upon NATO allies to declare war on Russia, World War Three begins.

2070
US rolls out first AI robot troops to support their own with contained laser capability.

2071
UN International AI Warfare Ban Treaty fails ratification.

China secretly develops a weaponized digital AI to take over US AI troops.

2072
CLM (international AI watchdog terrorist, activist, hactivist, paramilitary group) is able to obtain information about Chinese AI weapon. Terrified of an impending Skynet, they operate a suicide mission to break into a Russian nuclear silo and launch a nuke at China to take out the AI facility with an explosion and EMPs.

Light nuclear exchange occurs between all Atomic Nations, hundreds of missiles are fired. Earth's militaries use every antimissile available to counter the attack with only 17 nukes reaching their target. Others are destroyed or detonate high in the atmosphere. Resulting EMPs disable all electronics on Earth. Satellite constellations are also targeted. The resulting debris field wipes out 60-70% of all satellites over the next year. Low earth satellites are destroyed, the ionosphere is irradiated and significantly impedes signals from space for the next 8-10 years. 10 days before first power stations are restored.

Meltdown of two US nuclear power plants due to infrastructure disabling.

World War Three ends when Lt. Conrad Roy returns to Earth and uses the Mars ship Tyr to drop the US space station onto a three way naval battle occurring between China, Russia, and the US. This stops the fighting and a cease fire is called.

Quincy Adams hands power over to the World Council stating that nations were the problem – makes unilateral decision utilizing Congress being dead after Washington D.C. was destroyed in the nuclear exchange.

Sign of authority granted by US prompts Russia to quickly follow suit, 97% of remaining nations' governments hand over power within 6 months.

Church of Latter Day Saints secede from US, deny legitimacy of W.C., and declare themselves the Kingdom of Deseret.

2073
W.C. rebuilding mission begins, reestablishing contact with areas cut off in the Darkness.

Resources allocated towards cleaning of orbital debris field and rebuilding of satellite constellations when the sky clears.

First W.C. Space Symposium conducted – For Continuity of Technology.

2074
Marcus Medneon applies for W.C. business grant.

2075
Marcus Medneon Founds Space Oasis.
Isaac Hubert born.

2076
New Orleans officially abandoned by the W.C. after Category 5 Hurricane Marla results in a levee breaching storm surge, drowning the city.

2078
Atlantic Ocean ecosystem collapse, fish harvest drop by 95%.

2079
African Tuberculosis Epidemic.

2086
CERN Disaster.

2087
Lisa Hubert recruits for CORE, Lisa and Bernard Hubert found CORE.

JUNE 10 2091
Sagan Test Launch.

AUGUST 2091
Bernard visits Angelika On in Iceland with a proposition.

SEPTEMBER 2091
Bernard, William Hunt, and Isaac meet at Kepler.

OCTOBER 2091
Dinner in Hastings, NY with Angelika, Godric, Bernard, and William.

NOVEMBER 2091
Bernard, Ava, Galena and Lisa have dinner.

JANUARY 2092
Medina recruited from Kazakhstan.